# The World of Premchand

*For Ainslie and Suzanne Embree*

# The World of Premchand
## Selected Short Stories

*Translated and with an Introduction by*
David Rubin

OXFORD
UNIVERSITY PRESS

# OXFORD
UNIVERSITY PRESS

YMCA Library Building, Jai Singh Road, New Delhi 110 001

Oxford University Press is a department of the University of Oxford. It furthers the
University's objective of excellence in research, scholarship, and education
by publishing worldwide in

Oxford    New York

Auckland   Bangkok   Buenos Aires   Cape Town   Chennai
Dar es Salaam   Delhi   Hong Kong   Istanbul   Karachi   Kolkata
Kuala Lumpur   Madrid   Melbourne   Mexico City   Mumbai   Nairobi
São Paulo   Shanghai   Taipei   Tokyo   Toronto

Oxford is a registered trademark of Oxford University Press
in the UK and in certain other countries

Published in India
By Oxford University Press, New Delhi

ISBN  019 565772 1

Printed in India by Pauls Press, New Delhi 110 020
Published by Manzar Khan, Oxford University Press
YMCA Library Building, Jai Singh Road, New Delhi 110 001

# Acknowledgements

I would like to express my appreciation and gratitude to Mrs Bonnie R. Crown, who as Director of the Asian Literature Program of the Asia Society encouraged and assisted in the original publication of this book; to the late Sripat Rai, Premchand's son, for generously giving permission to publish my translations; to Mrs Shaista Rahman of Brooklyn College, Edith Irwin, Neil Gross, and the late Gordon Roadarmel; to Frances Pritchett and Susham Bedi of Columbia University, for many valuable suggestions and comments; to my students who have taught me so much while we studied many of these stories together; to Robert O. Swan, and particularly Ainslie Embree and the late Barbara Miller for their encouragement and support; and finally, to the American Institute of Indian Studies for the fellowship which made this undertaking possible.

# Introduction

The blossoming of Hindi fiction in the second half of the twentieth century, with writers of such psychological subtlety and satirical brilliance as Shrilal Shukla, Mohan Rakesh, Nirmal Verma and Mudrarakshasa, to name only a few, was made possible in large part by the novels and short stories of Premchand. When his works began to be published around 1905, fiction in Hindi and Urdu consisted primarily of romantic chronicles of a historical or fantastic nature, or didactic tales. By the time his last stories and novels appeared in the nineteen thirties the realistic psychological novel had been firmly established in these languages and set the standard as well as the social themes and character studies that typified the accomplished fiction by the younger writers who followed.

Dhanpat Rai, known from 1910 on by the pen-name of 'Premchand,' was born in the village of Lamhi, near Varanasi, in 1880, in humble circumstances but with access to a good education in Persian and Urdu letters, as might be expected in a literate family of the Kayasth community, so well-known for producing men of letters, teachers and lawyers. Some of the difficulties of his early years are described in the autobiographical sketches that conclude this volume.

From the time he began writing, near the beginning of the twentieth century, Premchand's life was extraordinarily active. When he died in 1936 Premchand left fourteen published novels, about three hundred short stories, countless letters, editorials and essays, several plays and screen plays, and a number of translations from English and adaptations of European novels. He also had a busy career as editor and publisher. A passionate advocate of both the Independence movement and Hindu–Muslim harmony, he devoted many editorials to India's political and communal problems and played an active role in the movement for Hindustani as a national language. He was a generous critic as well and championed the work of younger writers such as Jayshankar Prasad and

Jainendra Kumar. His productivity is all the more astonishing when one learns that he suffered from poor health throughout much of his life.

From the early to the late fiction there is a steady and readily perceptible growth in Premchand's mastery of the short story. The first stories, written often with a patriotic or nationalistic bias, tend toward romantic and melodramatic evocations of heroic exploits from legend or Indian history. Turning to the past also provided Premchand, along with some of his contemporaries such as Prasad and Nirala, an opportunity to criticize foreign oppression without naming the British, although this did not save his first collection of stories from being banned and burned in 1909. The plots of most of these early tales, full of chivalric idealism and noble sacrifice, disguises and amazing adventures, show the influence of the Urdu *dastans,* the favourite reading of his youth.

Like most of his work until about 1916, these stories were written originally in Urdu — not so much a language distinct from Hindi as a phase of the same language, with a different alphabet but sharing with Hindi its basic grammatical system and a major proportion of the working vocabulary. Although in the popular imagination Urdu is associated with Muslims and Hindi with Hindus, in fact educated Hindus of Uttar Pradesh — one thinks of Pandit Nehru — were likely to be more at home in Urdu, and the literary Hindi of current fiction draws freely and constantly on Urdu vocabulary. Premchand described his own background as deriving more from Muslim culture (particularly Persian and Urdu literature) and indignantly rejected as a myth the idea that Urdu was for Muslims and Hindi for Hindus. From early in his career he frequently prepared Hindi editions of his Urdu writings and continued to do so, sometimes with collaborators, and later supervised Urdu versions of works originally written in Hindi.

The principal reasons for Premchand's turning from Urdu to Hindi were the dearth of Urdu publishers willing to publish his work, his lack of sympathy for the elaborate Urdu style fashionable at the time, and his belief that writing in Hindi would reach a wider audience. But it should be noted here, since it is often overlooked, that Premchand never gave up writing original works in Urdu — 'Hindi in the morning, Urdu in the afternoon,' as he once put it. Although in the latter part of his life Hindi versions of his work were the first to be published, we often cannot establish, in the case of the short stories, which language they had originally been written in; and where there are considerable variations in the two texts it is difficult to decide when Premchand himself is responsible for particular omissions and additions or changes in the vocabulary.

Premchand very soon turned for his inspiration to the village world, which would become the richest subject for his best work. The villages and small towns of eastern Uttar Pradesh, specifically the rural districts around Allahabad and Varanasi, apparently perfectly ordered according to mechanically exact social regulations that had functioned more or less unchanged and unquestioned for centuries, offered Premchand an endlessly fascinating stage for the interplay of diverse personalities at every stage of evolution, operating within a rigid, efficient, and often cruel social structure. Caste snobbery (though it is much more than snobbery, since caste operates as a religious imperative), crushing poverty and brutal exploitation by landowners, moneylenders and parasitical Brahmins; the overwhelming desire for sons to carry on the family and perform the rituals; the terror at the possibility of disgrace, loss of face and ostracism; the shame of widowhood; the proverbial conservatism and cunning of the peasant — these are recurring strands in the fabric of Premchand's portrayal of village life. From the early stories on, his compassion, humour and psychological understanding of the villagers are apparent. In the earlier stories there is a tendency toward editorializing, as well as hyperbole and occasional redundancy. Maupassant's influence may be seen in Premchand's preoccupation with the structure of his plots and the occasional trick endings. The best stories of the late twenties and thirties are more often than not free of these characteristics, but many of the early stories as well, 'The Power of a Curse,' for example, move past such limitations and achieve a high degree of success when measured by Western standards of that era.

Influenced by Dickens, Tolstoy, Chekhov and Marx, Premchand very early directed his fiction toward social reform. The inhumanity of caste hierarchies and the plight of women stirred his indignation and remained constant themes throughout his work. The romantic heroism of the earliest tales is later supplanted by realistic studies of character and an idealistic view of the agitation against British oppression, with cutting satire on those Indians (as in 'A Little Trick' and 'A Moral Victory') who set their personal interests above the freedom movement. From Gandhi, and perhaps also from George Eliot's *Silas Marner,* which he freely paraphrased in a Hindi version, he derived his idealistic concept of the potential regeneration of character through the experience of the sacrifice and goodness of others. (Gandhi's call in 1921 for noncooperation was at least partly responsible for Premchand's resignation from his government post as a school teacher.) Although with his maturing as a writer Premchand's narration will become increasingly dramatic and (at least on the surface) objective, and the presentation of character immeasurably subtler than in the early works, didactic and reformist impulses remain strong in his writing. The range of his later fiction expands beyond the village to an India changing in what one of his characters calls 'the new light,' where young intellectuals and emancipated women are now faced with problems very different from those of uneducated villagers. Though they are still preoccupied with social problems naturalistically observed, the tone and technique of the stories following the First World War move closer to Chekhov, while melodrama gives way to tragicomedy, and explicit moralizing to moral fable. In 'My Big Brother' a potentially ludicrous situation is developed with pathos, although the touch remains light and the story is genuinely comic; in 'The Shroud,' one of Premchand's last stories and one of his two most famous, the intolerable grimness of the characters' lives becomes the subject of grotesque comedy, with the reader left free to draw his own conclusions. 'The Chess Players' (1924), probably the most famous of all Premchand's short stories, set in Lucknow at the time of the British annexation, portrays in terms of absurdist tragedy the moral vacuity and madness of the city's aristocracy in counterpoint against the background of a historical crisis.

More than half a century after Indian independence one cannot say that Premchand's world no longer exists. Here and there the surface of things has changed but, outside the big towns and cities, it would be premature to conclude that there has been a radical transformation in the conditions of everyday life in most rural districts. What may strike a Western reader as melodramatic or exaggerated in some of these stories is still commonplace in India, as a perusal of today's Indian newspapers will confirm. No matter how much they are officially discouraged, in the countryside caste restrictions remain a grim reality, and the alarming resurgence of religious fundamentalism does not encourage hope for improvement; dowries determine marriages, and the often perilous status of women is still a major concern; farmers are apt to resort to traditional high-interest moneylenders instead of government banks which offer low-interest loans; the break-up of the great landed estates still has the peasantry at the mercy of the former landowners for marketing their produce; and above all, death may come swiftly and unexpectedly but is accepted with resignation — such are still some of the basic elements which constitute life in the Indian villages.

Premchand's indignation and his very choice of subject matter tend somewhat to set him apart from the Hindi fiction writers who came into prominence immediately after him. Though some writers (Ashk, Renu and Nagarjun, for example) continued to treat social problems and village life, for the most part middle-class experience in urban settings becomes the focus for fiction in the middle decades of the century, with an emphasis on psychological and philosophical questions rather than social reform. This is apparent in the novels and short stories of Jainendra Kumar (a close friend of Premchand) and Agyeya (S. H. Vatsyayan). In the next generation, the writers of *nayi kahani*, or 'new story,' who came into prominence in the fifties and sixties — Nirmal Verma, Mohan Rakesh and Gyanranjan, for example — continued the emphasis on psychological themes, injected now with social satire; for instance, the narrative in Rakesh's portraits of *nouveau riche* Delhi society is now tinged with existentialist angst. Even the city is no longer seen naturalistically but rather as a reflection of the restricted, desperate world of the writer's psyche, turned away from the epic horizons of Premchand's multifarious vision. More recently, however, Shrilal Shukla in *Rāg Darbārī*, Mudrarakshasa in *Daṇḍavidhān*, two of the finest novels in Hindi since Premchand's *Godan*, have returned to the villages of northeastern India for the subject of their work; and although Premchand's idealism is missing (as indeed it was in stories like 'The Shroud'), he is recalled in the implicit passionate indignation that informs their work.

In the matter of style, recent Hindi narrative, mostly preoccupied as it is with the lives of city dwellers, has tended inevitably to dispense with Premchand's inexhaustible fund of humble similes and proverbs while gaining in complexity as it has moved toward a more symbolic representation of experience. In one respect, nevertheless, most contemporary fiction writers have continued to follow Premchand's example: they employ a vocabulary strongly influenced by colloquial speech rather than the highly Sanskritized and artificial vocabulary propagated by many officials and academics — a Hindi satirically dubbed 'sarkari,' i.e. governmental. Colloquial speech has retained a great number of words of Arabic or Persian origin, classified by purists as 'Urdu,' and many writers, like Mohan Rakesh, have sensibly claimed that Hindi and Urdu, except in the hands of academics and fanatical politicians, are in truth one language with two alphabets. Premchand himself, like Gandhi, was a proponent of 'Hindustani,' a blend of colloquial Urdu and Hindi. While conceding that Hindustani was not a 'literary language,' he declared (writing in English), 'I believe in our literary expression coming as close as possible to spoken speech.' His own Hindi style draws heavily on Urdu as well as a vocabulary derived from Sanskrit, and depends on the judicious blending of the two linguistic streams for much of its colour and force.

It is characteristic of the great writer that the significance of his work will extend far beyond his own era and its purely local or immediate context (although, as noted above, many of the social problems of Premchand's time continue to persist long after India achieved independence). I believe he continues to interest us today because of the originality and clarity of his vision and his ability to dramatize universal human problems. His validity as a critic of society stems in part from the fact that he himself had his roots in that society and never set himself above it; in confirmation of his integrity, his criticism remains inseparable from his love and is never tinged with spite. In this he is markedly distinct from some of the new breed of Indian nay-sayers — essayists and novelists born away from the subcontinent or electing to live abroad in exile, and who have made the ferocious denunciation of Indian culture and Indian values something of a fashion.

Although to date *The World of Premchand* is the only English translation of the author's stories to be published outside India, since its original publication several more such collections have been published in his homeland. Nevertheless, despite the great fascination he has never ceased to exert over the minds of his countrymen, at this moment there is no critical edition of his work.

Such an edition is badly needed because of the frequent unreliability of the various printings of his writing and the many divergences among them.

In presenting these stories here my division into three groups is, in part, arbitrary. Stories like 'A Day in the Life of a Debt Collector' and 'A Car Splashing' might well be considered scenes from village life, though it seemed to me that there is a certain urban sensibility in both, and in one the very presence of the automobile suggests the larger sphere of the town. The stories in the third division are more involved with problems of individuality and growing awareness, while 'The Shroud' and 'Deliverance,' though very clearly village stories, transcend the limitations of the earlier rural tales and attain to a greater universality of statement. The thirty stories collected here have been culled from the collections titled *Kafan, Solāh Aprāpya Kahāniyān*, the eight volumes of *Mānasarovar* and the two volumes of *Gupta Dhan*.

# A Note on the Translation

There are certain special problems in translating Premchand because of both his style and the nature of Hindi syntax and idiom. Translation from Hindi into English cannot in any case be quite so precise as (ideally at least) from the French or other European languages. Particular elements of the structure of the language are fairly distinctive, as in the matter of subordination, for example, and the tendency of Hindi, especially as spoken by village people, to elliptical, ironic and abbreviated statement. Idioms and proverbs, unlike those in European languages, often lack any corresponding equivalent in English. There is, furthermore, the special problem of allusion to subjects which are immediately clear to Indian readers but which require explanation for anyone from another culture. Because of this, and since this volume is presented for readers not only in India but abroad as well, I have occasionally interpolated a word or phrase to clarify a sentence without resorting to footnotes. Then, particularly in the stories of rural life, Premchand's characters speak in highly metaphorical language, full of allusions, proverbial phrases and elaborate images. Many of these would be unintelligible if simply 'translated'; clearly, a suitable equivalent has to be found (or invented). Whenever possible I have preserved the idiomatic statement when its meaning is obvious. For one example, where the Hindi has 'Neyur went home as happy as if God's hand had touched his head,' it seemed to me a falsification to replace it with 'Neyur went home extremely happy,' so I have retained the original simile. Many colourful idioms, of course, need no interpretation — 'to try to stop a hurricane with a broom' or to work so hard you 'sweat through the teeth' come to mind. In the matter of the regional dialect spoken by some characters I have preferred not to represent it by any English dialect, as some translators choose to do, but have attempted instead to simplify the language while preserving as much of the original idioms as I could.

In comparison with English, there is little use of subordination in Hindi narrative prose and dialogue, and compound sentences are also much less frequent. There is instead a constant idiomatic use of absolutives and a variety of participial constructions which are awkward when translated literally and often meaningless as well; these must of course be rendered by some kind of English equivalent or a judicious linking of simple sentences with a conjunction, not only to clarify the meaning but to avoid monotony or choppiness in the English.

Another characteristic of Hindi is its comparative poverty in adverbial expressions. This is compensated for by the subtlety of compound verb constructions. Here again, to make the meaning of a particular passage clear the translator must rely on his own judgement regarding how far he may go — much more than is commonly required in translating from Western Indo-European languages.

Premchand often set his dialogue like a printed play, with the speaker's name, followed by a dash, repeated each time the speaker changes. In my translation I have omitted this dramatic script format and introduced an occasional 'he said,' 'she asked,' etc. to keep the identity of the speaker clear.

There are, to be sure, no single definitive translations of any work of literature, just as there is never a single definitive interpretation. A good poem, a good drama, a good story, all will continually provoke new translations and new interpretations in confirmation of their relevance and vitality. It is my hope that the translations offered here will not only give a fair sampling of the range and pleasures of Premchand's short fiction but also stimulate more translations, both of these and many other works from the great treasury of his still untapped novels and short stories.

# Contents

## The Village

## The Town

## The World

# THE VILLAGE

## The Road to Salvation

The pride the peasant takes in seeing his field flourishing is like
the soldier's in his red turban, the coquette's in her jewels or the
doctor's in the patients seated before him. Whenever Jhingur
looked at his cane fields a sort of intoxication came over him. He
had three *bighas* of land which would earn him an easy 600 rupees.
And if God saw to it that the rates went up, then who could complain? Both his bullocks were old so he'd buy a new pair at the
Batesar fair. If he could hook on to another two *bighas*, so much
the better. Why should he worry about money? The merchants
were already beginning to fawn on him. He was convinced that
nobody was as good as himself — and so there was scarcely
anyone in the village he hadn't quarrelled with.

One evening when he was sitting with his son in his lap, shel-
ling peas, he saw a flock of sheep coming towards him. He said to
himself, 'The sheep path doesn't come that way. Can't those sheep
go along the bank? What's the idea, coming over here? They'll
trample and gobble up the crop and who'll make good for it? I bet
it's Buddhu the shepherd — just look at his nerve! He can see me
here but he won't drive his sheep back. What good will it do me to
put up with *this*? If I try to buy a ram from him he actually asks for
five rupees, and everybody sells blankets for four rupees but he
won't settle for less than five.'

By now the sheep were close to the cane-field. Jhingur yelled,
'*Arrey*, where do you think you're taking those sheep, you?'

Buddhu said meekly, 'Chief, they're coming by way of the boundary embankment. If I take them back around it will mean a couple of miles extra.'

'And I'm supposed to let you trample my field to save you a
detour? Why didn't you take them by way of some other boundary
path? Do you think I'm some bull-skinning nobody or has your
money turned your head? Turn 'em back!'

'Chief, just let them through today. If I ever come back this way
again you can punish me any way you want.'

19

'I told you to get them out. If just one of them crosses the line you're going to be in a pack of trouble.'

'Chief,' Buddhu said, 'if even one blade of grass gets under my sheeps' feet you can call me anything you want.'

Although Buddhu was still speaking meekly he had decided that it would be a loss of face to turn back. 'If I drive the flock back for a few little threats,' he thought, 'how will I graze my sheep? Turn back today and tomorrow I won't find anybody willing to let me through, they'll all start bullying me.'

And Buddhu was a tough man too. He owned 240 sheep and he was able to get eight *annas* per night to leave them in people's fields to manure them, and he sold their milk as well and made blankets from their wool. He thought, 'Why's he getting so angry? What can he do to me? I'm not his servant.'

When the sheep got a whiff of the green leaves they became restless and they broke into the field. Beating them with his stick Buddhu tried to push them back across the boundary line but they just broke in somewhere else. In a fury Jhingur said, 'You're trying to force your way through here but I'll teach you a lesson!'

Buddhu said, 'It's seeing you that's scared them. If you just get out of the way I'll clear them all out of the field.'

But Jhingur put down his son and grabbing up his cudgel he began to whack the sheep. Not even a washerman would have beaten his donkey so cruelly. He smashed legs and backs and while they bleated Buddhu stood silent watching the destruction of his army. He didn't yell at the sheep and he didn't say anything to Jhingur, no, he just watched the show. In just about two minutes, with the prowess of an epic hero, Jhingur had routed the enemy forces. After this carnage among the host of sheep Jhingur said with the pride of victory, 'Now move on straight! And don't ever think about coming this way again.'

Looking at his wounded sheep, Buddhu said, 'Jhingur, you've done a dirty job. You're going to regret it.'

*

To take vengeance on a farmer is easier than slicing a banana. Whatever wealth he has is in his fields or barns. The produce get into the house only after innumerable afflictions of nature and the gods. And if it happens that a human enemy joins in alliance with

20

those afflictions the poor farmer is apt to be left nowhere. When Jhingur came home and told his family about the battle, they started to give him advice.

'Jhingur, you've got yourself into real trouble! You knew what to do but you acted as though you didn't. Don't you realize what a tough customer Buddhu is? Even now it's not too late — go and make peace, otherwise the whole village will come to grief along with you.'

Jhingur thought it over. He began to regret that he'd stopped Buddhu at all. If the sheep had eaten up a little of his crop it wouldn't have ruined him. The fact is, a farmer's prosperity comes precisely from being humble — God doesn't like it when a peasant walks with his head high. Jhingur didn't enjoy the idea of going to Buddhu's house but urged on by the others he set out. It was the dead of winter, foggy, with the darkness settling in everywhere. He had just come out of the village when suddenly he was astonished to see a fire blazing over in the direction of his cane-field. His heart started to hammer. A field had caught fire! He ran wildly, hoping it wasn't his own field, but as he got closer this deluded hope died. He'd been struck by the very misfortune he'd set out to avert. The bastard had started the fire and was ruining the whole village because of him. As he ran it seemed to him that today his field was a lot nearer than it used to be, as though the fallow land between had ceased to exist.

When he finally reached his field the fire had assumed dreadful proportions. Jhingur began to wail. The villagers were running and ripping up stalks of millet to beat the fire. A terrible battle between man and nature went on for several hours, each side winning in turn. The flames would subside and almost vanish only to strike back again with redoubled vigour like battle-crazed warriors. Among the men Buddhu was the most valiant fighter; with his *dhoti* tucked up around his waist he leapt into the fiery gulfs as though ready to subdue the enemy or die, and he'd emerge after many a narrow escape. In the end it was the men who triumphed, but the triumph amounted to defeat. The whole village's sugar-cane crop was burned to ashes and with the cane all their hopes as well.

*

It was no secret who had started the fire. But no one dared say anything about it. There was no proof and what was the point of a case without any evidence? As for Jhingur, it had become difficult for him to show himself out of his house. Wherever he went he had to listen to abuse. People said right to his face, 'You were the cause of the fire! You ruined us. You were so stuck up your feet didn't touch the dirt! You yourself were ruined and you dragged the whole village down with you. If you hadn't fought with Buddhu would all this have happened?'

Jhingur was even more grieved by these taunts than by the destruction of his crop, and he would stay in his house the whole day.

Winter drew on. Where before the cane-press had turned all night and the fragrance of the crushed sugar filled the air and fires were lit with people sitting around them smoking their *hookas*, all was desolation now. Because of the cold people cursed Jhingur and, drawing their doors shut, went to bed as soon as it was dark. Sugarcane isn't only the farmers' wealth; their whole way of life depends on it. With the help of the cane they get through the winter. They drink the cane juice, warm themselves from fires made of its leaves and feed their livestock on the cuttings. All the village dogs that used to sleep in the warm ash of the fires died from the cold and many of the livestock too from lack of fodder. The cold was excessive and everybody in the village was seized with coughs and fevers. And it was Jhingur who'd brought about the whole catastrophe, that cursed, murdering Jhingur.

Jhingur thought and thought and decided that Buddhu had to be put in a situation exactly like his own. Buddhu had ruined him and he was wallowing in comfort, so Jhingur would ruin Buddhu too.

Since the day of their terrible quarrel Buddhu had ceased to come by Jhingur's. Jhingur decided to cultivate an intimacy with him; he wanted to show him he had no suspicion at all that Buddhu started the fire. One day, on the pretext of getting a blanket, he went to Buddhu, who greeted him with every courtesy and honour — for a man offers the *hooka* even to an enemy and won't let him depart without making him drink milk and syrup.

These days Jhingur was earning a living by working in a jute-wrapping mill. Usually he got several days' wages at once. Only by means of Buddhu's help could he meet his daily expenses between times. So it was that Jhingur re-established a friendly footing between them.

22

One day Buddhu asked, 'Say Jhingur, what would you do if you caught the man who burned your cane-field? Tell me the truth.'

Solemnly Jhingur said, 'I'd tell him, "Brother, what you did was good. You put an end to my pride, you made me into a decent man."'

'If I were in your place,' Buddhu said,'I wouldn't settle for any-thing less than burning down his house.'

'But what's the good of stirring up hatred in a life that lasts such a little while in all? I've been ruined already, what could I get out of ruining him?'

'Right, that's the way of a decent,religious man,' Buddhu said, 'but when a fellow's in the grip of anger all his sense gets jumbled up.'

*

Spring came and the peasants were getting the fields ready for planting cane. Buddhu was doing a fine business. Everybody wanted his sheep. There were always a half dozen men at his door fawning on him, and he lorded it over everybody. He doubled the price of hiring out his sheep to manure the field; if anybody objected he'd say bluntly, 'Look, brother, I'm not shoving my sheep on you. If you don't want them, don't take them. But I can't let you have them for a pice less then I said.' The result was that everybody swarmed around him, despite his rudeness, just like priests after some pilgrim.

Lakshmi, goddess of wealth, is of no great size; she can, accord-ing to the occasion, shrink or expand, to such a degree that some-times she can contract her most magnificent manifestation into the form of a few small figures printed on paper. There are times when she makes some man's tongue her throne and her size is reduced to nothing. But just the same she needs a lot of elbowroom for her permanent living quarters. If she comes into somebody's house, the house should grow accordingly, she can't put up with a small one. Buddhu's house also began to grow. A veranda was built in front of the door, six rooms replaced the former two. In short, the house was done over from top to bottom. Buddhu got the wood from a peasant, from another the cowdung cakes for the kiln fuel to make the tiles; somebody else gave him the bamboo and reeds for the mats. He had to pay for having the walls put up but he

23

didn't give any cash even for this, he gave some lambs. Such is the power of Lakshmi: the whole job — and it was quite a good house, all in all — was put up for nothing. They began to prepare for a house-warming.

Jhingur was still labouring all day without getting enough to half fill his belly, while gold was raining on Buddhu's house. If Jhingur was angry, who could blame him? Nobody could put up with such injustice.

One day Jhingur went out walking in the direction of the untouchable tanners' settlement. He called for Harihar, who came out, greeting him with 'Ram Ram!' and filled the hooka. They began to smoke. Harihar, the leader of the tanners, was a mean fellow and there wasn't a peasant who didn't tremble at the sight of him.

After smoking a bit, Jhingur said, 'No singing for the spring festival these days? We haven't heard you.'

'What festival? The belly can't take a holiday. Tell me, how are you getting on lately?'

'Getting by,' Jhingur said. 'Hard times mean a hard life. If I work all day in the mill there's a fire in my stove. But these days only Buddhu's making money. He doesn't have room to store it! He's built a new house, bought more sheep. Now there's a big fuss about his house-warming. He's sent paan to the headmen of all the seven villages around to invite everybody to it.'

'When Mother Lakshmi comes men don't see so clearly,' Harihar said. 'And if you see him, he's not walking on the same ground as you or me. If he talks, it's only to brag.'

'Why shouldn't he brag? Who in the village can equal him? But friend, I'm not going to put up with injustice. When God gives I bow my head and accept it. It's not that I think nobody's equal to me but when I hear him bragging it's as though my body starts to burn. "A cheat yesterday, a banker today." He's stepped on us to get ahead. Only yesterday he was hiring himself out in the fields with just a loincloth on to chase crows and today his lamp's burning in the skies.'

'Speak,' Harihar said, 'Is there something I can do?'

'What can you do? He doesn't keep any cows or buffaloes just because he's afraid somebody will do something to them to get at him.'

'But he keeps sheep, doesn't he?'

24

'You mean, "hunt a heron and get a grouse?"'

'Think about it again.'

'It's got to be a plan that will keep him from ever getting rich again.'

Then they began to whisper. It's a mystery why there's just as much love among the wicked as malice among the good. Scholars, holy men and poets sizzle with jealousy when they see other scholars, holy men and poets. But a gambler sympathizes with another gambler and helps him, and it's the same with drunkards and thieves. Now, if a Brahman Pandit stumbles in the dark and falls then another Pandit, instead of giving him a hand, will give him a couple of kicks so he won't be able to get up. But when a thief finds another thief in distress he helps him. Everybody's united in hating evil so the wicked have to love one another; while every body praises virtue so the virtuous are jealous of each other. What does a thief get by killing another thief? Contempt. A scholar who slanders another scholar attains to glory.

Jhingur and Harihar consulted, plotting their course of action — the method, the time and all the steps. When Jhingur left he was strutting — he'd already overcome his enemy, there was no way for Buddhu to escape now.

On his way to work the next day he stopped by Buddhu's house. Buddhu asked him, 'Aren't you working today?'

'I'm on my way, but I came by to ask you if you wouldn't let my calf graze with your sheep. The poor thing's dying tied up to the post while I'm away all day, she doesn't get enough grass and fodder to eat.'

'Brother, I don't keep cows and buffaloes. You know the tanners, they're all killers. That Harihar killed my two cows, I don't know what he fed them. Since then I've vowed never again to keep cattle. But your's is just a calf, there'd be no profit to anyone in harming her. Bring her over whenever you want.'

Then he began to show Jhingur the arrangements for the house-warming. *Ghee*, sugar, flour and vegetables were all on hand. All they were waiting for was the Satyanarayan ceremony. Jhingur's eyes were popping.

When he came home after work the first thing he did was bring his calf to Buddhu's house. That night the ceremony was performed and a feast offered to the Brahmans. The whole night passed in lavishing hospitality on the priests. Buddhu had no opportunity to go to look after his flock of sheep.

The feasting went on until morning. Buddhu had just got up and had his breakfast when a man came and said, 'Buddhu, while you've been sitting around here, out there in your flock the calf has died. You're a fine one! The rope was still around its neck.'

When Buddhu heard this it was as though he'd been punched. Jhingur, who was there having some breakfast too, said, 'Oh God, my calf! Come on, I want to see her! But listen, I never tied her with a rope. I brought her to the flock of sheep and went back home. When did you have her tied with a rope, Buddhu?'

'God's my witness, I never touched any rope! I haven't been back to my sheep since then.'

'If you didn't, then who put the rope on her?' Jhingur said. 'You must have done it and forgotten it.'

'And it was in your flock,' one of the Brahmans said. 'People are going to say that whoever tied the rope, that heifer died because of Buddhu's negligence.'

Harihar came along just then and said, 'I saw him tying the rope around the calf's neck last night.'

'Me?' Buddhu said.

'Wasn't that you with your stick over your shoulder tying up the heifer?'

'And you're an honest fellow, I suppose!' Buddhu said. 'You saw me tying her up?'

'Why get angry with me, brother? Let's just say you didn't tie her up, if that's what you want.'

'We will have to decide about it,' one of the Brahmans said. 'A cow slaughterer should be stoned — it's no laughing matter.'

'Maharaj,' Jhingur said, 'the killing was accidental.'

'What's that got to do with it?' the Brahman said. 'It's set down that no cow is ever to be done to death in any way.'

'That's right,' Jhingur said. 'Just to tie a cow up is a fiendish act.'

'In the Scriptures it's called the greatest sin,' the Brahman said. 'Killing a cow is no less than killing a Brahman.'

'That's right,' Jhingur said. 'The cow's got a high place, that's why we respect her, isn't it? The cow is like a mother. But Maharaj, it was an accident — figure out something to get the poor fellow off.'

Buddhu stood listening while the charge of murder was brought against him like the simplest thing in the world. He had no doubt it was Jhingur's plotting, but if he said a thousand times that he

26

hadn't put the rope on the calf nobody would pay any attention to it. They'd say he was trying to escape the penance.

The Brahman, that divinity, also stood to profit from the imposition of a penance. Naturally, he was not one to neglect an opportunity like this. The outcome was that Buddhu was charged with the death of a cow; the Brahman had got very incensed about it too and he determined the manner of compensation. The punishment consisted of three months of begging in the streets, then a pilgrimage to the seven holy places, and in addition the price for five cows and feeding 500 Brahmans. Stunned, Buddhu listened to it. He began to weep, and after that the period of begging was reduced by one month. Apart from this he received no favour. There was no one to appeal to, no one to complain to. He had to accept the punishment.

He gave up his sheep to God's care. His children were young and all by herself what could his wife do? The poor fellow would stand in one door after another hiding his face and saying, 'Even the gods are banished for cow-slaughter!' He received alms but along with them he had to listen to bitter insults. Whatever he picked up during the day he'd cook in the evening under some tree and then go to sleep right there. He did not mind the hardship, for he was used to wandering all day with his sheep and sleeping beneath trees, and his food at home hadn't been much better than this, but he was ashamed of having to beg, especially when some harridan would taunt him with, 'You've found a fine way to earn your bread!' That sort of thing hurt him profoundly, but what could he do?

He came home after two months. His hair was long, and he was as weak as though he were sixty years old. He had to arrange for the money for his pilgrimage, and where's the money-lender who loans to shepherds? You couldn't depend on sheep. Sometimes there are epidemics and you're cleaned out of the whole flock in one night. Furthermore, it was the middle of the hot weather when there was no hope of profit from the sheep. There was an oil-dealer who was willing to loan him money at an interest of two *annas* per rupee — in eight months the interest would equal the principal. Buddhu didn't dare borrow on such terms. During the two months many of his sheep had been stolen. When the children took them to graze the other villagers would hide one or two sheep away in a field or hut and afterwards slaughter them and eat

27

them. The boys, poor lads, couldn't catch a single one of them, and even when they saw, how could they fight? The whole village was banded together. It was an awful dilemma. Helpless, Buddhu sent for a butcher and sold the whole flock to him for 500 rupees. He took 200 rupees and started out on his pilgrimage. The rest of the money he set aside for feeding the Brahmans.

When Buddhu left, his house was burgled twice, but by good fortune the family woke up and the money was saved.

It was *Savan*, the month of rains, with everything green. Jhingur, who had no bullocks now, had rented out his field to share-croppers. Buddhu had been freed from his penitential obligations and along with them his delusions about wealth. Neither one of them had anything left; neither could be angry with the other — there was nothing left to be angry about.

Because the jute mill had closed down Jhingur went to work with pick and shovel in town where a very large rest house for pilgrims was being built. There were a thousand labourers on the job. Every seventh day Jhingur would take his pay home and after spending the night there go back the next morning.

Buddhu came to the same place looking for work. The foreman saw that he was a skinny little fellow who wouldn't be able to do any heavy work so he had him take mortar to the labourers. Once when Buddhu was going with a shallow pan on his head to get mortar Jhingur saw him. '*Ram Ram*' they said to one another and Jhingur filled the pan. Buddhu picked it up. For the rest of the day they went about their work in silence.

At the end of the day Jhingur asked, 'Are you going to cook sómething?'

'How can I eat if I don't?' Buddhu said.

'I eat solid food only once a day,' Jhingur said. 'I get by just drinking water with ground meal in it in the evenings. Why fuss?'

'Pick up some of those sticks lying around,' Buddhu said. 'I brought some flour from home. I had it ground there — it costs a lot here in town. I'll knead it on the flat side of this rock. Since you won't eat food I cook I'll get it ready and you cook it.'

'But there's no frying pan.'

'There are lots of frying pans,' Buddhu said. 'I'll scour out one of these mortar trays.'

The fire was lit, the flour kneaded. Jhingur cooked the *chapatties*, Buddhu brought the water. They both ate the bread with salt and red pepper. Then they filled the bowl of the *hooka*. They both lay down on the stony ground and smoked.

Buddhu said, 'I was the one who set fire to your cane field.'

Jhingur said light-heartedly, 'I know.'

After a little while he said, 'I tied up the heifer and Harihar fed it something.'

In the same light-hearted tone Buddhu said, 'I know.'

Then the two of them went to sleep.

## A Feast for the Holy Man

A wandering holy man appeared in the doorway of Ramdhan the farmer and said: 'May you prosper, child — and show your reverence for a holy man.'

Ramdhan went to his wife and said, 'A *sadhu's* at the door, we have to give him something.'

His wife had been scouring pots, all the while worrying about what they were going to eat that day, for there wasn't even a speck of grain in the house. It was the first month of spring but even at noon the skies were clouded over. The crops had been cleaned out of the barn; the money-lender had taken half, the landowner's agents had collected the other half, and the chaff had been sold to get the ox-trader off their backs — and that was all. For themselves they had saved one small sack. By threshing it over and over again they had managed to get scarcely one maund of grain out of it. Somehow or other they had got into spring, but God knew how they would go on or what the oxen would eat or even the people in the house. But a holy man had come to their door — how could they send him away disappointed, what would he think in his heart? She said: 'What can I give him when there's nothing at all left?'

Ramdhan said, 'Go look in the clay jug, if there's any flour left bring it.'

'Yesterday I used whatever I could scrape out of it — do you expect a miracle?'

'I'm not going to be heard telling the *baba* there's nothing in the house. Borrow something from one of the neighbours.'

'Look what I've already borrowed without ever being able to pay anything back! What kind of a face can I show them now?'

'Isn't there something set aside for an offering to the gods?' Ramdhan said. 'Get it and I'll give it to him.'

'Then where will we get anything to offer the gods?'

'Hasn't a god come a-begging? If you've got something to give, you give. If you haven't, you don't.'

'And I suppose you think we've got ten or twenty pounds of meal set aside for them! With luck there's about a pound. After that's gone what if another *sadhu* comes? You'll have to send him about his business.'

'We'll take care of this problem first, and then we'll see.'

Grumbling, she got up and picked up a small clay pot in which there was scarcely a pound. With the greatest difficulty it had been kept aside as an offering to the gods. Ramdhan stood reflecting a moment. Then he put the flour in a bowl, went outside and poured it into the *sadhu's* sack.

*

When he had taken the flour the *mahatma* said, 'My child, for today we intend to rest here. Give me just a little *dal* and then the *sadhu's* offering will be complete.'

Ramdhan went in again and told his wife. By chance there was some *dal* left in the house. Ramdhan took it, along with some salt and some cowdung cakes for fuel. Then he fetched water from the well. Methodically the holy man shaped the flour into cakes, cooked the *dal*, and took some potatoes from his sack and mashed them. When all the food was ready he said to Ramdhan, 'Child, for a proper offering to the Lord we need just a spoonful of *ghee*. If the food is not prepared according to the ritual, then what kind of an offering will it be?'

'*Babaji,*' Ramdhan said, 'there's no *ghee* in the house.'

'Child, don't say such things. God has given you much!'

'Maharaj, I have no cows or buffaloes, so how should I have *ghee?*'

'Child, in God's storerooms there's a little of everything — so just go and ask the mistress of the house.'

Ramdhan went back in and said to his wife, 'He's asking for *ghee* — he's a beggar who begs his way but he can't get one bite down without *ghee!*'

'Then take some of this *dal* and take it to the banya. After everything else, why make him angry with us just for this?'

They got the *ghee*. The holy man took out a handful of food as an offering to the Lord, rang a little bell and sat down to enjoy the meal offered to himself.

He ate his fill, then rubbing his belly lay down on the threshold.

Ramdhan brought the *sadhu's* plate, pot and ladle into the house to scour them.

That night nothing was cooked in Ramdhan's house. They just warmed up plain *dal* and drank it.

When he lay down to sleep, Ramdhan said to himself, 'Well, he's a better man than I am!'

## The Power of a Curse

Munshi Ramsevak came out of his house frowning and said, 'Death would be better than living like this.' Death gets quite a few invitations of this sort: if she accepted them all the whole world would be depopulated by now.

In the village of Chandpur Munshi Ramsevak was a very rich man and he was full of all the special qualities of very rich men. The foibles of human nature provided the foundation of his living. He could be seen every day seated on a broken bench under a *neem* tree within the precincts of the open-air small-pleas court, his satchel crammed with papers opened up in front of him. Nobody had ever seen him presenting a brief before the tribunal or arguing a case; but everyone called him 'attorney'. It might blow up a storm, rain or hail, but the attorney could not be budged from his bench. Whenever he made his way to the open court the villagers crowded after him. He was regarded by everyone with respect and trust, and he was renowned for possessing the eloquence of the divine Saraswati herself. Call it an attorneyship or a legal practice, but it was only maintaining a family tradition. He had no very great income; people might talk about silver coins but even copper coins rarely came his way. Though there was no doubt about Ramsevak's legal knowledge, he was compelled by complications to forego a real lawyer's job. Anyway, whatever it was, his profession was kept up only for the sake of continuing the family tradition. In actual fact his real means of livelihood was provided by widows without family but rich in the good things of life and by old men with lots of money and little sense. The widows handed over their money to him for safe-keeping and old men who feared their wastrel sons entrusted their wealth to him. But once any money went into his fist it forgot the way to come out again. When the need arose he himself would borrow — after all, without borrowing whose work would make any headway? He borrowed in the morning to give back by evening, but the evening never came. In brief, Munshi Ramsevak knew how to borrow but not to give. This too was the family tradition.

All these matters frequently presented obstacles to Ramsevak's peace and quiet, but he had not the least fear of law and justice. To oppose him in this sort of business was like tackling a crocodile in the water. And still whenever any wretch did tangle with him, cast aspersions on his honesty or insulted him, Ramsevak was deeply hurt. And this sort of unfortunate incident kept on happening; there were shallow creatures everywhere who took delight in demeaning others. Egged on by such people, petty fellows would sometimes slander him. Otherwise, to take one example, how would an insignificant green-grocer's widow have the audacity to march right into his courtyard and curse him? He'd been an old customer of hers, for years he'd got vegetables from her. If he didn't pay, the woman ought to have been content —sooner or later she would have received it. But the foul-mouthed bean-monger went to pieces about it after only a couple of years and for a matter of a few pice tried to disgrace an established gentleman. Munshi Ramsevak got so irritated he was ready to do away with himself — he was not to blame for any of it.

*

In the same village lived a Brahman widow named Munga. Her husband had been a sergeant in the native Indian battalion in Burma and had died in battle there. In view of his fine service, the government had bestowed a sum of rupees 500 on her. Being a widow and times being hard, the poor creature entrusted all her money to Ramsevak, and begging back tiny sums every month she managed to eke out a living.

Munshiji had carried out his duty for several years now with full honesty. But when Munga had grown old without any sign of dying and he realized that perhaps from the whole amount she did not intend to leave even half to pay for her funeral expenses, he said to her one day, 'Munga, are you going to die or aren't you? Or just say straight out that you'll look after your own funeral fees.' That day Munga's eyes were opened, her dream dispelled, and she said, 'Give me back the full amount!' The account book was ready: not a pice of it remained according to the book. She violently grabbed his hand and said, 'You've made off with 250 rupees of mine but I won't let you keep a pice of it!'

But a poor widow's anger is just the sound of a blank bullet that may scare a child but has no real effect at all. She didn't have any influence in the courts, she couldn't read or write or keep accounts. To be sure, there was some hope in the panchayat, the village council. The panchayat met, people gathered from several villages. Munshi Ramsevak was ready and agreeable; he stood up in the council and addressed the members: 'Friends! You are all noble and devoted to the truth. I bow to you all. I am grateful to the core to you for your generosity and mercy, your charity and love. Do you people think I really made off with the money of this unfortunate widow?'

With one voice the councillors said, 'No, no! You couldn't do such a thing!'

Munshiji said, 'If you all agree that I've stolen her money, then there'll be nothing left for me except to drown myself. I'm not a rich man, nor can I take pride in being munificent. But thanks to my pen and to your kindness I cannot call myself needy. Am I so petty as to embezzle a widow's money?'

The councillors were unanimous. 'No, no, you couldn't do such a thing!'

They had had a taste of his money and that was that. The council acquitted him and adjourned.

Munga heaved a sigh and, making the most of it, said to herself, 'If I'm not to get it here, then all right, I won't, but I'll get it back in heaven.'

*

There was nobody now to help Munga or listen to her grieving. Whatever woes poverty bestowed she had to bear them all. She was strong of body and if she had wanted she could have worked hard. But from the day the panchayat gave its judgment she swore she wouldn't work. Now she was obsessed with the thought of her money. All day and all night, walking or sitting, she had only one idea: to inveigh against Munshi Ramsevak. Seated day and night at the door of her hut she fervently cursed him. For the most part in her pronouncements she employed poetic speech and metaphors so that people who heard her were astonished.

Gradually her mind gave way. Bare-headed, bare-bodied, with a little hatchet in her hand, she would sit in desolate places. She

35

abandoned her hut and was seen wandering around the ruins in a cremation *ghat* along the river — dishevelled, red-eyed, grimacing crazily, her arms and legs emaciated. When they saw her like this people were frightened. Now no one teased her even for fun. Whenever she came out in the village, women shut the doors of their houses, men slunk away and children ran off screeching. But there was one child who didn't run away and that was Munshiji's son Ramgulam. Whatever defect had been omitted in the father was to be found in the son, and he was always getting the other boys into trouble too. The village one-eyed and lame men hated the sight of him. And he enjoyed insults as much as though they were compliments. He would keep after Munga, clapping his hands and taking the village dogs with him, until the poor woman, utterly bewildered, would flee the hamlet. Having lost her mind along with her money she had earned the title of the local madwoman. She would sit alone, talking to herself for hours, expressing her intense desire to eat, smash, pinch and tear Ramsevak's flesh, bones, eyes, liver and the like, and when her hatred reached its climax she would turn her face toward Ramsevak's house and shriek the terrible words, 'I'll drink your blood!'

Women were frightened when they heard her howling voice in the stillness of the night. But more terrible than her words was her wild laughter. In the imagined pleasure of drinking Munshiji's blood she would burst into laughter that resounded with such demoniacal violence, such bestial ferocity that when people heard it in the night their blood was chilled. It seemed as though hundreds of owls were hooting together. Munshiji was a man of great courage and tenacity, not one to be afraid of a madwoman any more than of the courts, but when he heard Munga's awful words he was scared. We may not be afraid of human justice but the fear of God's justice resides by nature in every man's heart — Munga's dreadful night-wanderings sometimes inspired such reflections in Ramsevak's mind, and even more in his wife's.

Nagin, who was pregnant now, was a very shrewd woman. She advised her husband about all his business dealings. The people who said Munshiji possessed the eloquence of Goddess Saraswati were mistaken: this virtue really belonged to his wife. She was as brilliant in speech as he in writing. And these two, husband and wife, would now consult together on what to do about this situation in which they found themselves powerless.

36

One midnight when Munshiji, according to his regular custom, had banished his troubles with a few swallows of liquor and gone to sleep, suddenly Munga let out a shriek right on his door-step and howled, 'I'll drink your blood!'

Munshiji was electrified by her horrible peals of laughter. His legs shook with fear, his heart thumped. Gathering up his courage with a great effort he opened the door and woke Nagin. Peevishly she said, 'What's the matter?' Munshiji whispered, 'She's standing on the door-step.'

Nagin sat up. 'What's she saying?'

'Don't be stupid, what do you think she's saying?'

'You mean she's right at the door?'

'Yes, can't you hear her?'

Nagin was not afraid of Munga but she was very much afraid of the misdeed she symbolized; still, she believed she could get the best of her by talking. 'Just let me talk to her,' she said but Munshiji forbade her.

The two of them tiptoed to the threshold and peeking from the door they saw Munga's dim figure lying on the ground, they heard her panting. In her hungering for Munshiji's flesh and blood she had completely used up her own: even a child could have knocked her down — and yet she could make the whole town tremble.

The night passed. The door was shut but Ramsevak and Nagin spent the hours sitting up. Munga could not get inside but who could stop her voice? Her voice was the most terrible thing about her.

At dawn, Munshiji went outside and said to her, 'Why are you lying there?'

'I'll drink your blood,' Munga said.

Rearing up, Nagin said, 'I'll knock your head right off!'

But Nagin's venomous tone had no effect on Munga, who shrieked with laughter.

Disconcerted, Nagin fell silent before that laughter. Then Munshiji spoke again: 'Get up!'

'I won't!'

'Just how long do you think you're going to lie here?'

'I'll go when I've drunk you blood!'

In these straits Munshiji's pungent pen was of no use and Nagin's fiery eloquence grew cold. They went inside to consult on how to put an end to this calamitous situation.

37

When the Goddess comes she has a drink of goat's blood and goes on her way, but this witch came to drink human blood, the very blood which, if even a drop of it was spilled while Munshiji was sharpening a pen nib, was lamented throughout the household for weeks and months while the event was related from house to house in the village. Would Munga's shrivelled body become young again from drinking that blood?

The news got around the village that Munga was squatting on Munshiji's doorstep. The villagers took great delight in his embarrassment and loss of face. Whole flocks of people gathered around at once. Little Ramgulam didn't like this crowd and he got so angry with Munga that if he had had the power he would have flung her into a well. As soon as an idea like this struck him he would be so tickled that he could hardly control his laughter. Oh, what fun it would be to dump her into a well! But the bitch wouldn't get away from the door, what could you do? Munshiji kept a cow, which was very well fed with oilseed cake, grain and straw; but all of it went to her bones and her frame became ever more robust. Ramgulam collected the dung of this cow in a pot and flung it at the poor woman. Some of it splashed on the onlookers too. Munga was completely covered and the people hastily retreated, saying, 'This is Munshi Ramgulam's door where you can expect such fine manners! Get away quickly or there'll be some even greater show of courtesy.' While the crowd dispersed Ramgulam went into the house and had a good laugh and clapped his hands. Munshiji congratulated his son on this ingenious and appealing way of getting rid of that good-for-nothing crowd. The whole mob finally disappeared, but Munga went on lying there exactly as before.

Noontime came. Munga ate nothing. Then it was evening. Even after a barrage of threats and abuse she refused to eat. The village headman came and coaxed her, and Munshiji even begged her with folded hands, but she would not agree. Finally he got up and went inside. He said that hunger alone could overcome so fierce a hatred.

That night Munga neither ate nor drank anything and once again Munshiji and Nagin lay awake until morning. By now Munga's howling and laughing were heard much less frequently. The people of the household assumed that the worst was over. As soon as it was daylight Munshiji opened the door and saw Munga lying motionless. Flies were already buzzing around her mouth; her breathing had stopped. She had come just to die at his door. To the man who'd taken her life savings she had entrusted her corpse as well, she was making him a gift of the very clay of her body.

It is impossible to describe the sensation this event produced in the village and the extent of Ramsevak's disgrace. As much of a commotion as there can be in such a tiny village over such an extraordinary event, well, it was even greater than that, and Munshiji's dishonour was not a whit less than it ought to have been. Whatever prestige he'd been able to maintain vanished. Now not even the leather-tanners would have accepted water from him or touched him. If a cow in somebody's household dies while tied to a peg, then that man goes around for months begging from door to door; no barber will shave him, no water-carrier bring him water, nor anyone touch him; such is the penance for cow-slaughter. The punishment for the murder of a Brahman is even stiffer and the disgrace immeasurable. Knowing this, Munga had come to die on his doorstep. She knew she could not accomplish much alive but dead she could do a great deal.

*

Munshi Ramsevak was versed in law: according to the law he was innocent. Munga had not died according to any legal instance, no example of it could be found in the Indian Penal Code. Therefore those people who wished to impose a penance on him were entirely mistaken. There was no great harm so far as he was concerned: if the water-carrier did not want to draw his water, Munshiji would draw it himself — anyway, what was wrong with doing such little chores for yourself? And what if the barber wouldn't shave him? — what's the use of getting shaved? The beard's a lovely thing, the very glory and embellishment of man. And then if later you get fed up with the beard, you can always buy a razor for a paltry sum. He wasn't worried when the *dhobi* refused to wash his clothes. In any street in town there was nothing cheaper than soap. With just one cake a whole pile of clothes could be made clean as a duck's feathers. How could the *dhobi* make clothes that clean? He whips them on the stones until they're in tatters. He wears your clothes, rents them out to others, throws them into his boiling cauldron and steeps them in fuller's earth. And of course they're ruined. That's why shirts don't last more than two or three years. If that hadn't been the case grandfather would have got along with having only two jackets and two shirts made every fifth year. Throughout the day Munshiji and his wife consoled themselves with such reasoning. But as soon as it was evening their rationalizing petered out.

Fear took hold of them when darkness fell. As the hour turned late this fear grew all the stronger. They'd left the front door open by mistake and not one of them was daring enough to get up and shut it. Finally Nagin took a lamp, Munshiji his axe and Ramgulam the sickle, and the three of them, quaking and shrinking, went to the door. There Munshiji boldly tackled the problem: he made a valiant attempt to go outside. Trembling but with a loud voice he said to Nagin, 'You're frightened for nothing. Do you think she's sitting out there?' But his loving Nagin pulled him back inside and said angrily, 'You're wicked to joke about it.' Having won this tilt the three of them went into the kitchen and began to cook something.

But Munga had got under their skins. Seeing their own shadow they'd jump, sure it was Munga. It seemed to them that she was sitting in every dark corner. That emaciated body and scattered hair, the mad look, the horrible eyes — it was Munga to a tee!

In the kitchen they had set several large clay pots for flour and pulse and there were some old rags lying around too. Driven by hunger a mouse came out looking for the grain which those pots in fact had never had a taste of — but it was well-known in the village that in this house the mice had to be resourceful thieves.

The mouse crept under the rags with a rustling sound. The way those rags were spread out they looked exactly like Munga's skinny legs. When she saw them Nagin jumped and let out a shriek. Losing his head completely Munshiji sprang for the door and Ramgulam started running and got entangled in his father's legs. Just then the mouse emerged and when they saw it they recovered their wits. Ramsevak walked boldly toward the pot. 'Leave it alone,' Nagin said. 'We've seen how brave you are.'

Her contempt made Munshiji very angry. 'Do you think I was afraid?' he said. 'What was there to be afraid of? Munga's dead, so how could she be there? Didn't I go outside yesterday? You tried to stop me but I didn't pay any attention.'

This argument silenced Nagin. Yesterday it had been no ordinary deed to go outside the door or even to try to. Whoever had shown such evidence of bravery could not be called a coward by anybody. Nagin was just being perverse.

After they'd eaten the three of them came into the bedroom. But even there Munga did not leave them alone. They were talking, enjoying themselves. Nagin told the tale of Raja Hardaul and Rani Sarandha, Munshiji recounted the circumstances of several criminal cases. But even in these diversions Munga's image refused to leave their minds. The very slightest tap would startle them. If there was a rustling of leaves the hair would stand up on all three of them. Several times a low voice reached them from within the earth: 'I'll drink your blood . . .'

At midnight Nagin was startled from her sleep. It seemed to her that Munga, with her red eyes and sharp pointed teeth, was sitting on her chest. Nagin screamed. She started running toward the courtyard like a madwoman, and suddenly she fell senseless to the ground, sweating all over. Munshiji had been awakened by her yell but he was so frightened he didn't open his eyes. Like a blind man he felt his way to the door. After a long while he found it and came into the courtyard. Nagin was lying on the ground writhing. He lifted her up and brought her inside, but she didn't open her eyes the whole night. Toward dawn she began to rave incoherently. In a little while her fever rose, her body turned hot as a griddle. By evening she was in a delirium and at midnight when all the world was plunged in silence she took her leave of it forever. Fear of Munga had killed her. While Munga lived she had always feared Nagin's hissing. But sacrificing her own life, she could now take Nagin's.

The night passed, day drew on, but not one person in the village showed up to bear Nagin's corpse away. Munshiji went from house to house, but no one answered the door. After all, who will go to a murderer's house? Who will do honour to the corpse of an assassin? This time Munshiji's prestige, his genius at law and the fear of his mighty pen were of no use to him at all. Rejected everywhere, he turned back to his house. Here everything appeared to him as gloomy as possible. He came as far as his door but he didn't set foot inside. Outside was Munga, inside Nagin. Mustering his courage, he finally entered the house reciting passages from the 'Holy Acts of God Hanuman'. Only he knew what was passing in his mind. There was the corpse: no one of the earlier generation was

41

left, no one from the coming except his son. To be sure, he might marry again. This last spring he'd only reached fifty. But where could he find a worthy and sweet-tongued wife? What a loss! Who was there now to cope with dunning creditors, who could silence them? Who could keep the accounts of all his transactions so well? Whose sharp voice could shoot out like an arrow to pierce the hearts of his creditors? There was no compensation for such a loss. The next day Munshiji loaded the body on to a wheel-barrow and went toward holy Ganges.

*

The number of people attending the cremation was not large. There was Munshiji himself and one other, his dear son Ramgulam. Even Munga's corpse had not had to suffer such humiliation.

Having done away with Nagin, Munga was not going to leave Munshiji alone. At every moment her image remained before his eyes. Wherever he might be his mind always harked back to her. If he could have devised any little diversion perhaps he might not have been so nervous, but not even the village scarecrows would give him a nod. The poor man had to draw his own water and even wash the pots. No mind can remain stable with only worry, anger, anxiety and fear before it, especially this mind that had been preoccupied every day with the disputes of law.

Like a prisoner in solitary confinement, somehow or other he managed to get through the next ten or twelve days. At the end of two weeks, his mourning over, Munshiji changed his clothes and with his mat and satchel went to the open court. Today his expression was a little brighter. Today, he thought, his clients would flock around him, they'd condole with him and he'd shed a few tears. Then there would be an abundance of foreclosures, settlements and mortgages and he'd be rolling in money. In the evening he would celebrate a little with some liquor — giving *that* up had increased his depression. Full of these thoughts he reached the court.

But there, instead of the abundance of mortgages and the flood of foreclosures and the merry greetings of clients, he encountered the sandy wastes of disappointment. He sat for hours with his satchel open but nobody came near him, or even inquired about how he was. Not only were there no new clients but very old ones, whose business Munshiji's family had handled for generations, today hid their faces from him. That incompetent and loutish Ramzan, whom Munshiji used to laugh at and who could not even write properly, today he was as mobbed as Krishna among the milkmaids. It was all a matter of fate. The clients walked around with their faces averted as though they didn't know him. After wasting his whole day at the court Munshiji went home, sunk in worry and disappointment. As soon as he came close to the house Munga's image rose before him. He was so nervous that when on opening the door two dogs, shut in by Ramgulam, came rushing out he completely lost his wits, let out a shriek and fell senseless to the ground.

What happened to Munshiji after this is not known. For several days people saw him go to the court and come back drooping. It was his duty to go to the court and although there was a dearth of clients there this was now the only trick left to keep the creditors off his back and inspire confidence in them. After that he went off to the shrine of Badrinath and was not seen for several months.

One day a *sadhu* came to the village — on his forehead ashes, locks long and matted, a clay waterpot in his hand. His countenance closely resembled Ramsevak's and his speech also was not much different. He sat in meditation beneath a tree. That night smoke rose from Ramsevak's house, the glow of a fire was visible and then a burst of flame. All the villagers came running — not to put the fire out but to see the fun.

As for Ramgulam, when Munshiji disappeared he went off to live with an uncle and stayed there a while, but no one there could put up with his ways.

One day he was digging up radishes in somebody's field. The owner gave him a few slaps. This made him so angry that he went into the man's granary and set it on fire. It burned down completely and thousands of rupees went up in smoke. The police investigated and Ramgulam was arrested. For this offence he is at present in the reformatory at Chunar.

# A Catastrophe

In Banaras district there is a village called Bira in which an old, childless widow used to live. She was a *Gond* woman named Bhungi and she didn't own either a scrap of land or a house to live in. The only source of her livelihood was a parching oven. The village folk customarily have one meal a day of parched grains, so there was always a crowd around Bhungi's oven. Whatever grain she was paid for parching she would grind or fry and eat it. She slept in a corner of the same little shack that sheltered the oven. As soon as it was light she'd get up and go out to gather dry leaves from all around to make her fire. She would stack the leaves right next to the oven and, after twelve o'clock, light the fire. But when, according to custom, she did not start her fire on such fast days as the eleventh of the month and the day of the full moon, or on the days when she had to parch grain for Pandit Udaybhan Pandey, the owner of the village, on those days she went to bed hungry. She was not only obliged to work without pay for Pandit Udaybhan but she also had to fetch the water for his house. And, for this reason, from time to time the oven was not lit. She lived in the Pandit's village, therefore he had full authority to make her do any sort of odd job. It couldn't be called an injustice; it would have been an injustice only if he'd paid her for it. In his opinion if she received food for working for him, how could it be considered as work done without pay? The peasant has a full right to tether his bulls without feeding them after they've worked a full day in the fields. If he doesn't do this, it's not from any kindness of his but only concern for his profit. Panditji did not have this worry because Bhungi wasn't going to drop dead after staying hungry for a couple of days. And if by chance she should die, then some other *Gond* could very easily be found to fill her place. He was doing her a favour, as a matter of fact, by letting her live in the village at all.

*

It was spring, the sun was moving into a new sign of the zodiac, a day on which the fresh grain was fried and eaten and given as a gift. No fire was lit in the houses. Bhungi's oven was being put to good use today. There was a crowd worthy of a village fair around her. She had scarcely opportunity to draw a breath. Because of the customers' impatience squabbles kept breaking out. Then two servants arrived, each carrying a heaped basket of grain from Pandit Udaybhan with the order to parch it right away. When Bhungi saw the two baskets she was very alarmed. It was already after twelve and even by sunset she would not have time to parch so much grain. With one or two hours more she could have earned enough food for a whole week. But God had not seen fit to allow it, instead he had sent these two messengers from Hell. Now she would have to stay at the oven parching until after dark for no payment. In despair she took the two baskets.

One of the flunkeys said menacingly, 'Don't waste any time or you'll be sorry.'

'Sit here and wait,' she said, 'and when it's parched take it and go. Cut off my hand if I touch anybody else's grain.'

'Who's got time to sit around and wait? Just have it done by sundown.'

With this command the servants went away and Bhungi began to parch the grain. It's no laughing matter to parch a whole *maund* of grain. She had to keep stopping from the parching in order to keep the oven fire going. So by sundown not even half the work was done. She was afraid Panditji's men would be coming and as soon as they'd arrived insult and beat her. She began to move her hands all the more frantically. She would look toward the road and go on throwing sand into the trough until the sand got cold and the grain began to come out only half-roasted. She couldn't figure out what to do — she couldn't parch and she couldn't stop, and she began to realize what a catastrophe it was. What sort of bread did Panditji give her for her work? He wasn't one to wipe her tears! If she worked herself to the bone it was to earn some kind of food, but as soon as Panditji caught sight of her he'd threaten her, and just because she occupied four inches of his land. So high a price for so little land? And so many plots in the village lying fallow, so many cottages deserted. Saffron didn't grow in those empty fields, why should he be after her every hour of the day? When anything happened he'd threaten to dig up her oven and ruin it. If only she

45

had a man to protect her she wouldn't have to put up with this.

While she was caught up in these gloomy thoughts the servants returned and said, 'Well, is the grain parched?'

Feeling bold, Bhungi said, 'Can't you see? I'm parching it now.'

'The whole day's gone and you haven't finished any more grain than this? Have you been roasting it or spoiling it? This is completely uncooked! How's it going to be used for food? It's the ruin of us! You'll see what Panditji does to you for this.'

The result was that that night the oven was dug up and Bhungi was left without a means of livelihood.

\*

Bhungi now had no means of support. The villagers suffered a good deal too from the destruction of the oven. In many houses even at noon cooked cereal was no longer available. People went to Panditji and asked him to give the order for the old woman's oven to be rebuilt and the fire once more lighted, but he paid no attention to them. He could not suffer a loss of face. A few people who wished her well urged her to move to another village. But her heart would not accept this suggestion. She had spent her fifty miserable years in this village and she loved every leaf on every tree. Here she had known the sorrows and pleasures of life; she could not give it up now in the last days. The very idea of moving distressed her. Sorrow in this village was preferable to happiness in another.

A month went by. Very early one morning Pandit Udaybhan, taking his little band of servants with him, went out to collect his rents — he didn't have any confidence in estate agents. He wouldn't allow any other person to share in his dues, his fines and his fees for religious services. Now when he looked toward the old woman's oven he fell into a violent rage: it was being resurrected. Bhungi was energetically rebuilding it with balls of clay. Most likely she'd spent the night at this work and wanted to finish it before the sun was high. She did not in the least doubt that she was going against the Pandit's wishes, but she had no conception of how long-lasting anger can be, she could not realize that such a great person could have so much hatred for a pathetic old woman. She naturally assumed that human character had somehow to be loftier than that. But alas, the poor creature had grown old without

46

growing wise.

Suddenly Panditji shouted, 'By whose order?'

Bewildered, Bhungi saw that he was standing before her.

He demanded once again, 'By whose order are you building it?'

In a fright she said, 'Everybody said I should build it and so I'm building it.'

'I'll have it smashed again.' With this he kicked the oven. The wet clay collapsed in a heap. He kicked at the trough again but she ran in front of it and took the kick in her side. Rubbing her ribs she said, 'Maharaj, you're not afraid of anybody but you ought to fear God. What good does it do you to ruin me like this? Do you think gold is going to grow out of this foot of ground? For your own good, I'm telling you, don't torment poor people, don't be the death of me.'

'You're not going to build any oven here again.'

'If I don't how am I going to be able to eat?'

'I'm not responsible for your belly.'

'But if I do nothing except chores for you where will I go for food?'

'If you're going to stay in the village you'll have to do my chores.'

'I'll do them when I've built my oven. I can't do your work just for the sake of staying in the village.'

'Then don't, just get out of the village.'

'How can I? After twelve years of working a field the tenant earns a share in it. I've grown old in this hut. My in-laws and their grandparents lived in this same hut. Except for Yama, king of death, nobody's going to force me out of it now.'

'Excellent, now you're quoting Scripture!' Pandit Udaybhan said. 'If you'd worked hard I might have let you stay, but after this I won't rest until I've had you thrown out.' To his attendants he said, 'Go get a pile of leaves right away and set fire to the whole thing; we'll show her how to make an oven.'

*

In a moment there was a tremendous racket. The flames leapt toward the sky, the blaze spread wildly in all directions. The people of the whole village came clustering around this mountain of fire. Hopelessly, Bhungi stood by her oven watching the conflagration. Suddenly, with a violent dash, she hurled herself into the flames. They came running from everywhere but no one had the courage to go into the mouth of the blaze. In a matter of seconds her withered body was completely consumed.

At that moment the wind rose with a gust. The liberated flames began to race toward the east. There were some peasants' huts near the oven which were engulfed by the fierce flames. Fed in this way, the blaze spread even further. Panditji's barn was in its path and it pounced upon it. By now the whole village was in a panic. They began to band together to put out the fire but the sprinkle of water acted like oil on it and the flames kept mounting higher. Pandit Udaybhan's splendid mansion was swallowed up; while he watched, it tossed like a ship amid wild waves and disappeared in the sea of fire. The sound of lamentation that broke out amidst the ashes was even more pitiful than Bhungi's grievous cries.

# January Night

Halku came in and said to his wife, 'The landlord's come! Get the rupees you set aside, I'll give him the money and somehow or other we'll get along without it.'

Munni had been sweeping. She turned around and said, 'But there's only three rupees. If you give them to him where's the blanket going to come from? How are you going to get through these January nights in the fields? Tell him we'll pay him after the harvest, not right now.'

For a moment Halku stood hesitating. January was on top of them. Without a blanket he couldn't possibly sleep in the fields at night. But the landlord wouldn't be put off, he'd threaten and insult him,so what did it matter if they died in the cold weather as long as they could just take care of this calamity right now? As he thought this he moved his heavy body (that gave the lie to his name)*and came close to his wife. Trying to coax her he said, 'Come on, give it to me. I'll figure out some other plan.'

Munni drew away from him. Her eyes angry, she said, 'You've already tried "Some other plan" You just tell me what other plan can be found. Is somebody going to give you a blanket? God knows how many debts are always left over that we can't pay off. What I say is, give up this tenant farming! The work's killing you, whatever you harvest goes to pay up the arrears, so why not finish with it? Were we born just to keep paying off debts? Earn some money for your own belly, give up that kind of farming. I won't give you the money, I won't!'

Sadly Halku said, 'Then I'll have to put up with his abuse.' Losing her temper, Munni said, 'Why should he abuse you — is this his kingdom?'

But as she said it her brows relaxed from the frown. The bitter truth in Halku's words came charging at her like a wild beast.

---

* Halku is derived from *halka*; meaning 'light'.

She went to the niche in the wall, took out the rupees and handed them over to Halku. Then she said, 'Give up farming this time. If you work as a hired labourer you'll at least get enough food to eat from it. No one will be yelling insults at you. Fine work, farming someone else's land! Whatever you earn you throw back into it and get insulted in the bargain.'

Halku took the money and went outside looking as though he were tearing his heart out and giving it away. He'd saved the rupees from his work, pice by pice, for his blanket. Today he was going to throw it away. With every step his head sank lower under the burden of his poverty.

*

A dark January night. In the sky even the stars seemed to be shivering. At the edge of his field, underneath a shelter of cane leaves, Halku lay on a bamboo cot wrapped up in his old burlap shawl, shivering. Underneath the cot his friend, Jabra the dog, was whimpering with his muzzle pressed into his belly. Neither one of them was able to sleep.

Halku curled up drawing his knees close against his chin and said, 'Cold, Jabra? Didn't I tell you, in the house you could lie in the paddy straw? So why did you come out here? Now you'll have to bear the cold, there's nothing I can do. You thought I was coming out here to eat *puris* and sweets and you came running on ahead of me. Now you can moan all you want.'

Jabra wagged his tail without getting up, protracted his whimpering into a long yawn, and was silent. Perhaps in his canine wisdom he guessed that his whimpering was keeping his master awake.

Halku reached out his hand and patted Jabra's cold back. 'From tomorrow on stop coming with me or the cold will get you. This bitch of a west wind comes from nobody knows where bringing the icy cold with it. Let me get up and fill my pipe. I've smoked eight pipefuls already but we'll get through the night somehow. This is the reward you get for farming. Some lucky fellows are lying in houses where if the cold comes after them the heat just drives it away. A good thick quilt, warm covers, a blanket! Just let the winter cold try to get them! Fortune's arranged everything very well. While we do the hard work somebody else gets the joy of it.'

50

He got up, took some embers from the pit and filled his pipe. Jabra got up too.

Smoking, Halku said. 'If you smoke the cold's just as bad, but at least you feel a little better.'

Jabra looked at him with eyes overflowing with love.

'You have to put up with just one more cold night. Tomorrow I'll spread some straw. When you bed down in that you won't feel the cold.'

Jabra put his paws on Halku's knees and brought his muzzle close. Halku felt his warm breath.

After he finished smoking Halku lay down and made up his mind that however things were he would sleep now. But in only one minute his heart began to pound. He turned from side to side, but like some kind of witch the cold weather continued to torment him.

When he could no longer bear it he gently picked Jabra up and, patting his head, got him to fall asleep in his lap. The dog's body gave off some kind of stink but Halku, hugging him tight, experienced a happiness he hadn't felt for months. Jabra probably thought he was in heaven, and in Halku's innocent heart there was no resentment of his smell. He embraced him with the very same affection he would have felt for a brother or a friend. He was not crippled by the poverty which had reduced him to these straits at present. Rather it was as though this singular friendship had opened all the doors to his heart and brilliantly illuminated every atom of it.

Suddenly Jabra picked up the noise of some animal. This special intimacy had produced a new alertness in him that disdained the onslaught of the wind. Springing up, he ran out of the shelter and began to bark. Halku whistled and called him several times. But Jabra would not come back to him. He went on barking while he ran around through the furrows of the field. He would come back for a moment, then dash off again at once. The sense of duty had taken possession of him as though it were desire.

*

Another hour passed. The night fanned up the cold with the wind. Halku sat up and bringing both knees tight against his chest hid his face between them, but the cold was just as biting. It seemed as

51

though all his blood had frozen, that ice rather than blood filled his veins. He leaned back to look at the skies. How much of the night was still left! The Dipper had not yet climbed half the sky. By the time it was overhead it would probably be morning. Night was not even three hours gone.

Only a stone's throw from Halku's field there was a mango grove. The leaves had begun to fall and they were heaped in the grove. Halku thought, 'If I go and get a pile of leaves I can make a fire of them and keep warm. If anybody sees me gathering the leaves in the dead of night they'll think it's a ghost. Of course there's a chance some animal's hidden in my field waiting, but I can't stand sitting here any longer.'

He ripped up some stalks from a nearby field, made a broom out of them and picking up a lighted cowdung cake went toward the grove. Jabra watched him coming and ran to him wagging his tail.

Halku said, 'I couldn't stand it any more, Jabra. Come along, let's go into the orchard and gather leaves to warm up with. When we're toasted we'll come back and sleep. The night's still far from over.'

Jabra barked his agreement and trotted on toward the orchard. Under the trees it was pitch dark and in the darkness the bitter wind blew, buffeting the leaves, and drops of dew dripped from the branches.

Suddenly a gust carried the scent of henna blossoms to him. 'Where's that sweet smell coming from, Jabra? Or can't your nose make out anything as fragrant as this?'

Jabra had found a bone lying somewhere and he was chewing on it. Halku set his fire down on the ground and began to gather the leaves. In a little while he had a great heap. His hands were frozen, his bare feet numb. But he'd piled up a regular mountain of the leaves and by making a fire out of them he'd burn away the cold.

In a little while the fire was burning merrily. The flames leapt upward licking at the overhanging branches. In the flickering light the immense trees of the grove looked as though they were carrying the vast darkness on their heads. In the blissful sea of darkness the firelight seemed to pitch and toss like a boat.

Halku sat before the fire and let it warm him. After a while he took off his shawl and tucked it behind him, then he spread out both feet as though challenging the cold to do its worst. Victorious over the immense power of the winter, he could not repress his pride in his triumph.

He said to Jabra, 'Well, Jabra, you're not cold now, are you?'

Jabra barked as though to say, 'How could I feel cold now?'

'We should have thought of this plan before, then we'd never have become so chilled.' Jabra wagged his tail. 'Fine, now what do you say we jump over the fire? Let's see how we manage it. But if you get scorched I've got no medicine for you.'

Jabra looked fearfully at the fire.

'We mustn't tell Munni tomorrow or there'll be a row.'

With that he jumped up and cleared the fire in one leap. He got his legs singed but he didn't care. Jabra ran around the fire and came up to him. Halku said, 'Go on, no more of this, jump over the fire!' He leaped again and came back to the other side.

*

The leaves were all burned up. Darkness covered the orchard again. Under the ashes a few embers smouldered and when a gust of wind blew over them they stirred up briefly, then flickered out again.

Halku wrapped himself up in his shawl again and sat by the warm ashes humming a tune. The fire had warmed him through but as the cold began to spread he felt drowsy.

Jabra gave a loud bark and ran toward the field. Halku realized that this meant a pack of wild animals had probably broken into the field. They might be nilgai. He distinctly heard the noise of their moving around. Then it seemed to him they must be grazing; he began to hear the sound of nibbling.

He thought, 'No, with Jabra around no animal can get into the field, he'd rip it to shreds. I must have been mistaken. Now there's no sound at all. How could I have been mistaken?'

He shouted, 'Jabra! Jabra!'

Jabra went on barking and did not come to him.

Then again there was the sound of munching and crunching in the field. He could not have been mistaken this time. It really hurt to think about getting up from where he was. It was so comfortable there that it seemed intolerable to go to the field in this cold and chase after animals. He didn't stir.

He shouted at the top of his lungs, 'Hillo! Hillo! Hillo!'

Jabra started barking again. There were animals eating his field just when the crop was ready. What a fine crop it was! And these cursed animals were destroying it. With a firm resolve he got up and took a few steps. But suddenly a blast of wind pierced him with a sting like a scorpion's so that he went back and sat again by the extinguished fire and stirred up the ashes to warm his chilled body. Jabra was barking his lungs out, the nilgai were devastating his field and Halku went on sitting peacefully near the warm ashes. His drowsiness held him motionless as though with ropes. Wrapped in his shawl he fell asleep on the warmed ground near the ashes.

When he woke in the morning the sun was high and Munni was saying, 'Do you think you're going to sleep all day? You came out here and had a fine time while the whole field was being flattened!'

Halku got up and said, 'Then you've just come from the field?'

'Yes, it's all ruined. And you could sleep like that! Why did you bother to put up the shelter anyway?'

Halku sought an excuse. 'I nearly died and just managed to get through the night and you worry about your crop. I had such a pain in my belly I can't describe it.'

Then the two of them walked to the edge of their land. He looked: the whole field had been trampled and Jabra was stretched out underneath the shelter as though he were dead.

They continued to stare at the ruined field. Munni's face was shadowed with grief but Halku was content.

Munni said, 'Now you'll have to hire yourself out to earn some money to pay off the rent and taxes.'

With a contented smile Halku said, 'But I won't have to sleep nights out here in the cold.'

# Neyur

In the sky silver mountains raced along and bumped together. As though the sun and clouds were battling sometimes it was overcast, then again there was the glitter of dazzling sunshine. These were monsoon days that had turned sultry, the wind had died.

Outside the village several workmen were setting up a dike between two fields. Bare-bodied, drenched in sweat, *dhotis* tucked up tight around their hips, they were all busy shovelling the rain-softened earth into line.

Gobar rolled his blind eye and said, 'Brother, my hands won't move. By now they must have fired the signal gun. Let's have something to eat.'

'Finish the dike,' Neyur said, laughing, 'and then have your food. I started work even before you.'

Deena said, putting the basket on his head, 'The amount of *ghee* you ate up in your youth, Brother Neyur, why you don't even get that much water these days.'

Neyur was a short, husky, dark, nimble fellow of about fifty. But the strongest young fellows could not match him in working. Two or three years ago he was still wrestling; he'd given it up when his cow died.

'How can you go on without smoking a pipe, Brother Neyur?' Gobar asked. 'I can manage if I don't get any bread but I can't stand to be without tobacco.'

'And when you go home,' Deena said, 'will you have to cook your own supper? Doesn't your old woman do anything? I wouldn't put up for a day with a little wife like that.'

Neyur's wrinkled face with its tangled moustaches flashed a smiling line of laughter that lent a certain beauty to his ugliness. He said, 'Her young days have gone, son, she can't do any work these days — what can I do?'

'You've spoiled her,' Gobar said, 'otherwise why wouldn't she work? She has a fine time lying on her cot smoking her pipe and fighting with the whole village. You've grown old but she's stayed

55

young right up to now.'

Deena said, 'She tries to give young women a run for their money. All she thinks about is cinnabar, make-up and jasmine for her hair. You never see her without a fancy coloured *sari* and what's more she can't live without jewels. You're a donkey and go on taking care of her. Otherwise why should you put up with scolding and slaps all the time?'

Gobar said, 'It makes me mad the way she fusses about dressing up. She won't do any work. But she has to dress up and eat the best.'

'What do you know about it, son?' said Neyur. 'When she came I had enough land under cultivation for seven plows. She would lie around like a queen. The times have changed now but what's happened to her? Her heart is still the same. If she sits for half-an-hour in front of the hearth her eyes get red and her head starts to pound. I can't stand looking at that. A man gets married for times like these, otherwise why should he get involved at all in the worries of running a household? When I go home I make some bread, bring the water and she'll eat a couple of bites — if it weren't for that, well, I'd do the way you do and gobble down some scraps and a jug of water. Ever since the daughter died she's been a lot sadder, it was a very great blow to her. What do you and I know about the way a mother feels, son? Before, I used to scold her once in a while but how could I scold her now?'

Deena said, 'Why did you climb up the tree yesterday — are the figs ripe already?'

Neyur said, 'I was breaking off some leaves for the goat — we got her to have milk for our daughter. She's old now but she gives a little milk. My old woman lives just on bread and that goat's milk.'

After he got home Neyur had just taken a pot and the well cord to go and wash when his wife, lying on her cot, said, 'Why do you always come home so late? A man shouldn't sacrifice all his life for work. When everybody gets the same pay what's the use of killing yourself working?'

Neyur's heart melted with tenderness — in his wife's devotion to him, he told himself, there wasn't even a hint of selfishness. How much love there was! Who else cared about his comfort, about whether he lived or died? And that was why he would have given his life for her. He said, 'You must have been a goddess in another life, Budhiya, it's true!'

'All right, stop the flattering. Who's sitting here listening to us

56

now that you should talk so fine?'

His heart bursting with pleasure, he went off to bathe. When he came back she was making thick *chapatties* and she'd put potatoes to roast in the fire. He mashed them, then they sat down to eat.

Budhiya said, 'You haven't had any happiness from marrying me. I lie around and eat and I worry and upset you. It would be much better if God took me off your hands.'

'If god comes, I'll tell him, Take me first! If he didn't I'd be left alone in this empty hut.'

'If you're not here what will it be like for me? Just to think about it makes my sight go dim. I must have done something very good to get you. Who else would put up with me?'

For just such sweet satisfaction Neyur was ready to do anything. Lazy, greedy, selfish Budhiya, just by sweetening her tongue the way a sportsman baits the hook, kept on making Neyur dance.

This was not their first conversation on the subject of who would die first. Many times before this the question had come up and been dropped in just the same way. But for some reason or another Neyur had come to the conclusion that he would be the first to go. For so long as Budhiya might survive him she was to live in comfort and not have to hold out her hand to anyone. It was precisely for this that he worked like a dog trying to scrape a few pice together. The hardest work, the work nobody else would do, Neyur would do it. After working the whole day with spade and hoe, during the sugar cane season he would press cane or guard the fields at night. But the days were slipping by and whatever he earned, that too was slipping away. Life for him without Budhiya would — but he couldn't even imagine that.

But this talk with her terrified Neyur today. Like one drop of dye in water the fear began to spread through his mind. In the village there was no shortage of work for Neyur. He got the same wages he'd always got, but in this time of depression those wages didn't go very far.

Unexpectedly a *sadhu* came wandering into the village from somewhere and lit his ceremonial fire in the shade of the *peepul* tree right in front of Neyur's hut. The villagers took it as a stroke of good luck and they all gathered together to do reverence and honour to *Babaji.* They brought wood, spread out blankets, gave him flour and *dal.* Having nothing at home to give him, Neyur took on the job of making his meals. Intoxicating *charas* weed was brought and the holy man began to smoke.

In just two or three days the *sadhu's* fame had spread around. What an enlightened soul he was, he could tell the past and future and everything! And he was entirely without attachment to the world — he would not touch money with his hands, he scarcely ate anything. Throughout a whole day he would eat only a couple of pieces of bread. But his face shone like a lamp and how sweetly he spoke! Simple-hearted Neyur became the holy man's greatest devotee. If by some chance *Babaji* should take pity on him then he would find enlightenment, all his troubles would disappear.

The devotees had all gone home. The night was bitingly cold. Only Neyur was there, rubbing *Babaji's* feet.

*Babaji* said, 'Child, the world is an illusion — why are you caught in its snares?'

'I'm an ignorant man, Maharaj,' Neyur said, bowing his head. 'What shall I do? There's my wife — how could I leave her?'

'You think *you're* taking care of her?'

'Who else is there to help her, *Babaji*?'

'So God is nothing and you're everything?'

It was like a revelation to Neyur. How puffed up you've been, he told himself, how proud! You spend your life labouring and you think you're everything for Budhiya. You think you can meddle in the work of the Lord, who holds the whole world in his keeping. With the full sense of faith springing up in his simple villager's heart he reproached himself. He said, 'I'm an ignorant man, Maharaj.'

He could say no more than this. Tears of remorse fell from his eyes.

The holy man said majestically, 'You are about to learn the wonders of the Lord. If he wanted he could make you a millionaire in a second. In one second he could take away all your worries. I am merely a lowly servant of his like the humble crow of the Puranas, but in me too there's enough power to make you rich. You're a pure-hearted, true and honest man, and I feel compassion for you. I've observed everybody in this village most carefully. There's no strength or faith in any of them. But in you I've found a devoted heart. Do you possess any silver?'

It seemed to Neyur that he stood before the gate of heaven.

' I must have about a half dozen rupees, Maharaj.'

' Haven't you got any old broken silver jewellery?'

58

' My wife has a little jewellery.'

' Tomorrow night bring me as much silver as you can find and see the greatness of God. Right in front of you I'll put the silver in a pot and set it in the fire. Come early in the morning and take the pot out of the fire, but be sure to remember that if you spend any of the gold sovereigns you get in drinking or gambling or any wicked deeds you'll become a leper. Go home to bed now, but just one word more: don't talk about this to anyone, not even your wife.'

Neyur went home as happy as if God's hand had touched his head and he could not sleep all night. In the morning he borrowed two or three rupees from each of various people and got fifty rupees together. People trusted him — he'd never done anybody out of a pice, he was a man of his word, a man of good will. It was not hard for him to get the fifty rupees. But how could he take Budhiya's jewellery? He played a trick. 'Your jewellery's become very dirty,' he told her. 'It ought to be cleaned with lemon juice. If it's left in the lemon juice overnight it'll be just like new.' So Budhiya put the ornaments in a pot and left them to soak. When she had gone to sleep that night Neyur put the money in the same pot and went to *Babaji. Babaji* recited a few spells. He set the pot in the ashes of his fire and after blessing Neyur sent him home.

The whole night Neyur tossed and turned and at the crack of dawn he went to pay a visit to the holy man. But there was no sign of *Babaji.* Alarmed, Neyur searched with his fingers through the burned-out ashes: the pot had disappeared. He beat his chest and desperately started out to look for the saint. Making his way toward the market he reached the edge of the pond. Ten minutes he waited, twenty, a half hour, but not a sign of the saint.

The devotees began to arrive, asking where *Babaji* had gone. Not even his blanket, not even his pots were there.

One man said, 'These wandering saints never stay for long —here today, there tomorrow. If they stayed in one place would they be saints? They might make friends with people and get trapped by worldly attachments.'

'He was enlightened,' another said.

'He had no lust for worldly things.'

'Where's Neyur? The saint was very kind to him — he must have told Neyur.'

They began to look for Neyur, but there wasn't a trace of him. Meanwhile Budhiya came out of the house calling for him. Then what a commotion! — Budhiya weeping and reviling Neyur.

Neyur was running along the boundary dikes between the fields as though he wanted to get clean out of this sinful world.

Somebody said, 'Yesterday Neyur borrowed five rupees from me. He said he'd give them back tonight.'

'He took two from me and promised to bring them back.'

Budhiya wept. 'The good-for-nothing took my jewellery. We'd saved twenty-five rupees and and he took them too.'

People understood that the saint was some kind of fraud and that he'd deceived Neyur. Lord, the cheats there are in the world! Nobody suspected Neyur of anything like that. The poor fellow was honest and he'd been tricked. He was probably hiding somewhere right now because of shame.

*

Three months passed.

In Jhansi district on the banks of the Dhasan there's a quite small village called Kashipur. The river banks are high ridges, and on one of them, for some time now, a *sadhu* had taken up his abode. A short, dark, well-knit fellow — Neyur, dressed up as a *sadhu* to deceive people, the same simple ingenuous Neyur who never looked at what belonged to somebody else, who was happy to earn his bread by his own hard labouring. He hadn't for a second ever forgotten his house, his village and Budhiya. After a few more days of this life he intended to go back and then he'd live happily with his little worries and his little hopes, laughing and playing in the village world. When he came home after the day's work bringing a bit of grain or a few pice, then with what tender affection Budhiya would welcome him. It was as though all his toil and fatigue were sweetened in that sweetness of hers. Alas, when would those days come again? He had no idea of how Budhiya was getting along. Who would treat her kindly? Who would cook for her and feed her? He'd left no money in the house, he'd lost even her jewellery. Then his rage rekindled and he wished he could get his hands on that saint. Alas, greed, greed!

Among Neyur's unquestioning devotees there was a beautiful young woman whose husband had abandoned her. Her father, who lived from an army pension, had married her to an educated man, but the fellow was under his mother's thumb and the girl could not

60

get along with her mother-in-law..The girl wanted to live with her husband apart from his mother, but he would not agree to this. In a huff she'd walked out of the house. In the three years since this had happened the father-in-law's house had not once sent for her, nor had the husband even come to see her. The girl wanted to win control over her husband by any means — surely it could not be difficult for holy men to work a change in someone's heart if only they were compassionate!

One day she was alone with the saint describing her misfortune. It seemed to Neyur that he had found the prey he'd been stalking. He said solemnly, 'Daughter, I am not an enlightened man nor a mahatma, nor do I get involved in worldly problems, but when I see your faith and love I feel compassion for you. If God wishes, then your wish will be fulfilled.'

'You can bring it about, I have faith in you.'

'Whatever God wishes will come to pass.'

'Only you can bring the little boat of an unhappy woman like me safe across to the other shore.'

'Trust in the Lord.'

'You alone are my Lord.'

As though moved by religious scruple Neyur said, 'But daughter, to accomplish what you want a big ritual must be performed and the ceremony costs hundreds, thousands. I can't say if it will succeed in fulfilling your wish. I'll do what I can. But everything's in the Lord's keeping. I don't touch money with my hands, but I can't bear to watch your suffering.'

That night she brought her gold jewellery in a basket and set it down at the saint's feet. With trembling hands he opened the basket and looked at the jewellery gleaming in the moonlight. He blinked. All this wealth was his! The girl was standing in front of him with folded hands. 'Accept it,' she said. There was nothing else for him to do, just take the basket and put it on the ground where he slept and send the girl off with a blessing. She would come early in the morning and he would be as far away as his legs could carry him. This was the luck he'd longed for! To go back to his village with bags full of rupees and to set them down before Budhiya. Oh! He couldn't have imagined a greater happiness than this.

But for some reason or other he could not bring himself to do the little he had to. He couldn't pick up the basket to stow it beneath his blanket. It was a trifle but he couldn't see how to do it, he could not even stretch out his hand toward the basket, he had no control over his hands. But if his hands were useless he still had a tongue, there would have been nothing world-shaking in saying, 'Daughter, pick it up and put it under my blanket,' his tongue would not be cut off for that. But it seemed to him now that he had no control even over his tongue. He could get what he wanted done with just a look, but now even his eyes refused to obey him. The master of his spirit, despite all its allies and ministers, was without power and without will. A hundred thousand rupees might be set before him, the naked sword might be in his hand and the cow tied with a strong rope but he could never bring that sword down on her neck. Even if someone were to kill him for it he could never do it. This abandoned woman was like such a cow to him. Finding the opportunity he'd been seeking for three months his soul was shaken. Greed, like some jungle beast eager for its prey, was chained, its claws drooped, its teeth lost their power.

With tears in his eyes he said, 'Daughter, pick up the basket and go. I was only testing you. Your wish will be fulfilled.'

On the far side of the river the moon had set in the bosom of the trees. Neyur got up slowly and after bathing in the Dhasan started on his way. He had come to loathe the cowdung ashes and sandalwood smeared on his forehead for his masquerade. He was astonished that he had ever gone out of his village. Just the fear of a little derision! He began to experience a strange elation, as though he had freed himself from his chains and won a great victory.

*

Neyur reached his village on the eighth day. Children came running, springing and jumping, to welcome him and took the stick out of his hand.

One boy said, 'Auntie's died, uncle.'

It was as though Neyur had been paralyzed. The corners of his mouth fell, his eyes were stricken. He couldn't ask anything, he couldn't even speak. He stood for a second spellbound, then he ran furiously toward his hut. The swarm of children ran after him, but their meanness and mischief had left them. The hut lay open. Budhiya's cot was right where it had always been. Her pipe was set where it always was. In one corner were a few clay and brass pots. The children stood outside, not daring to go in, for Budhiya's ghost was there.

There was a great commotion in the village. Uncle Neyur had come back! A crowd collected at the door of the hut, everyone was asking questions. 'Where have you been all these days? She died on the third day after you went away. Night and day she cursed you. Even while she was dying she kept up abusing you. When we came on the third day, she was lying dead. Where have you been all this time?'

Neyur did not answer. He just looked at them with pitiable, desperate eyes, as though he had lost the power of speech. From that day on no one ever knew him to speak or cry or laugh.

A half mile from town there is a surfaced road, and a lot of people travel along it. Very early mornings Neyur goes and sits beneath a tree at the edge of the road. He asks for nothing from anybody. But travellers give him a little something — parched grain or wheat or small change. At evening he comes back to the hut, lights a lamp, makes supper, eats, and lies down on the same cot. The moving force of his life has vanished, he merely exists.

How profound humanity is! The plague came to the village; people abandoned their homes and fled. No one bothered about Neyur now; nobody feared him and nobody loved him. When the whole town ran away, Neyur did not leave his hut. Then Holi came, everyone made merry, but Neyur did not come out of his hut. And even today he can still be seen sitting silent, still, lifeless, beneath the tree at the edge of the road.

# The Story of Two Bullocks

The jackass is held to be the most stupid of animals. Whenever we want to call somebody a first-class fool we call him a jackass. Whether the jackass really is a fool, or his meek submissiveness has earned him this title, is something not easy to determine. Cows strike with their horns, and one who's just calved will spontaneously take on the aspect of a lioness. The dog, too, is a fairly pitiable creature, but sometimes even he will go into a rage. But an angry jackass has never been seen or heard. No matter how much you may beat the poor fellow, no matter what sort of rotten straw you fling down in front of him, not even a flicker of discontent will pass over his features. He may possibly prance around once or twice in spring, but we've never seen him happy. He's never been known to change whether in joy or sorrow, winning or losing, or in any condition whatsoever. Whatever virtues the sages and holy men may possess, all have reached their culmination in the jackass; yet people call him a fool. Such disrespect for virtue has never been seen before. Perhaps simplicity is not suitable for this world. Just look now, why are the Indians living in Africa in such a wretched state? Why aren't they allowed to slip into America? The poor fellows don't drink liquor, they put aside a little money for a rainy day, break their backs working, don't quarrel with anybody, suffer insults in silence. All the same, they have a bad reputation. It's said they lower the standard of living. If they learned to fight back, well, maybe people would begin to call them civilized. The example of Japan is before us — a single victory has caused them to be ranked among the civilized peoples of the world.

But the jackass has a younger brother who is scarcely less asinine, and that's the bullock. We use the expression 'the calf's uncle' in more or less the same way we say 'jackass.' There are some people who would probably call the bullock supreme among fools, but we have a rather different opinion. The bullock from time to time *will* strike back, and even a rebellious bullock has been observed occasionally. And it also has several other ways of expressing its discontent, so it cannot be ranked with the jackass.

Jhuri the vegetable farmer had two bullocks named Hira and Moti. Both were of fine Pachai stock, of great stature, beautiful to behold, and diligent at their labours. The two had lived together for a very long time and become sworn brothers. Face to face or side by side they would hold discussions in their silent language. How each understood the other's thoughts we cannot say, but they certainly possessed some mysterious power (denied to man who claims to be supreme among living creatures). They would express their love by licking and sniffing one another, and sometimes they would even lock horns — not from hostility but rather out of friendship and a sense of fun, the way friends as soon as they become intimate slap and pummel one another; any friendship lacking such displays seems rather superficial and insipid and not to be trusted. Whenever they were yoked together for plowing or pulling the wagon and stepped along swinging their necks each would attempt to take most of the burden on his own shoulders. When they were released from the yoke after their day's work at noon or in the evening they would lick and nuzzle one another to ease their fatigue. When the oilseed cake and straw was tossed into the manger they would stand up together, thrust their muzzles into the trough together, and sit down side by side. When one withdrew his mouth the other would do so too.

It came about that on one occasion Jhuri sent the pair to his father-in-law's. How could the bullocks know why they were being sent away? They assumed that the master had sold them. Whether it bothered them or not to be sold like this no one can say, but Jhuri's brother-in-law Gaya had to sweat through his teeth to take the two bullocks away. When he drove them from behind they'd run right or left; if he caught up the tether and dragged them forward they'd pull back violently. When he beat them, both would lower their horns and bellow. If God had given them speech, they would have asked Jhuri, 'Why are you throwing us poor wretches out? We've done everything possible to serve you well. If working as hard as we did couldn't get the job done, you could have made us work still harder. We were willing to die labouring for you. We never complained about the food, whatever you gave us to eat we bowed our heads and ate it, so why did you sell us into the hands of this tyrant?'

At evening the two bullocks reached their new place, hungry after a whole day without food, but when they were brought to the manger, neither so much as stuck his mouth in. Their hearts were heavy; they were separated from the home they had thought was their own. New house, new village, new people, all seemed alien to them.

They consulted in their mute language, glancing at one another out of the corners of their eyes, and lay down. When the village was deep in sleep the two of them pulled hard, broke their tether and set out for home. That tether was very tough, no one could have guessed that any bullock could break it; but a redoubled power had entered into them and the ropes snapped with one violent jerk.

When he got up early in the morning Jhuri saw that his two bullocks were standing at the trough, half a tether dangling from each of their necks. Their legs were muddied up to the knees and resentful love gleamed in their eyes.

When Jhuri saw the bullocks he was overwhelmed with affection for them. He ran and threw his arms around their necks, and very pleasant was the spectacle of that loving embrace and kissing.

The children of the household and the village boys gathered, clapping their hands in welcome. Although such an incident was not without precedent in the village it was nevertheless a great event. The gathering of boys decided they ought to present official congratulations. From their houses they brought bread, molasses, bran and chaff.

One boy said, 'Nobody has bullocks like these,' and another agreed, 'They came back from so far all by themselves,' while a third said, 'They're not bullocks, in an earlier life they were men.' And nobody dared disagree with this.

But when Jhuri's wife saw the bullocks at the gate she got angry and said, 'What loafers these oxen are, they didn't work at my father's place for one day before they ran away!'

Jhuri could not listen to his bullocks being slandered like this. 'Loafers, are they? At your father's they must not have fed them so what were they to do?'

In her overbearing way his wife said, 'Oh sure, you're the only one who knows how to feed bullocks while everybody else gives them nothing but water.'

Jhuri railed at her, 'If they'd been fed why would they run off?'

Aggravated, she said, 'They ran away just because those people don't make fools of themselves spoiling them like you. They feed them but they also make them work hard. These two are real lazy-bones and they ran away. Let's see them get oilseed and bran now!

I'll give them nothing but dry straw, they can eat it or drop dead.'

So it came about. The hired hand was given strict orders to feed them nothing but dry straw.

When the bullocks put their faces in the trough they found it insipid. No savour, no juice — how could they eat it? With eyes full of hope they began to stare toward the door.

Jhuri said to the hired hand, 'Why the devil don't you throw in a little oilseed?'

'The mistress would surely kill me.'

'Then do it on the sly.'

'Oh no, boss, afterwards you'll side with her.'

*

The next day Jhuri's brother-in-law came again and took the bullocks away. This time he yoked them to the wagon.

A couple of times Moti wanted to knock the wagon into the ditch but Hira, who was more tolerant, held him back.

When they reached the house, Gaya tied them with thick ropes and paid them back for yesterday's mischief. Again he threw down the same dry straw. To his own bullocks he gave oilseed cake, ground lentils, everything.

The two bullocks had never suffered such an insult. Jhuri wouldn't strike them even with a flower stem. The two of them would rise up at a click of his tongue, while here they were beaten. Along with the pain of injured pride they had to put up with dry straw. They didn't even bother to look in the trough.

The next day Gaya yoked them to the plow, but it was as though the two of them had sworn an oath not to lift a foot — he grew tired beating them but not one foot would they lift. One time when the cruel fellow delivered a sharp blow on Hira's nostrils Moti's anger went out of control and he took to his heels with the plow. Plough-share, rope, yoke, harness, all were smashed to pieces. Had there not been strong ropes around their necks it would have been impossible to catch the two of them.

Hira said in his silent language, 'It's useless to run away.'

Moti answered, 'But he was going to kill you.'

'We'll really get beaten now.'

'So what? We were born bullocks, how can we escape beating?'

'Gaya's coming on the run with a couple of men and they're both carrying sticks.'

Moti said, 'Just say the word and I'll show them a little fun. Here he comes with his stick!'

'No, brother!' Hira cautioned. 'Just stand still.'

'If he beats me I'll knock one or two of them down.'

'No, that's not the *dharma* of our community.'

Moti could only stand, protesting violently in his heart. Gaya arrived, caught them and took them away. Fortunately he didn't beat them this time, for if he had Moti would have struck back. When they saw his fierce look Gaya and his helpers concluded that this time it would be best to put it off.

This day again the same dry straw was brought to them. They stood in silence. In the house the people were eating dinner. Just then a quite young girl came out carrying a couple of pieces of bread. She fed the two of them and went away. How could a piece of bread still their hunger? But in their hearts they felt as though they had been fed a full meal. Here too was the dwelling of some gentle folk. The girl was Bhairo's daughter; her mother was dead and her stepmother beat her often, so that she felt a kind of sympathy for the bullocks.

The two were yoked all day, took a lot of beatings, got stubborn. In the evening they were tied up in their stall, and at night the same little girl would come out and feed some bread to each of them. The happy result of this communion of love was that even though they ate only a few mouthfuls of the dry straw they did not grow weak; still their eyes and every cell of their bodies filled with rebelliousness.

One day Moti said in his silent language, 'I can't stand it any longer, Hira.'

'What do you want to do?'

'Catch a few of them on my horns and toss them.'

'But you know, that sweet girl who feeds us bread is the daughter of the master of this house. Won't the poor girl become an orphan?'

'Then what if I toss the mistress? After all, she beats the girl.'

'But you're forgetting, it's forbidden to use your horns against womankind.'

'You're leaving me no way out! So what do you say, tonight we'll break the ropes and run away?'

'Yes, I'll agree to that, but how can we break such a thick rope?'

'There *is* a way. First gnaw the rope a bit, then it will snap with

68

one jerk.'

At night when the girl had fed them and gone off the two began to gnaw their ropes, but the thick cord wouldn't fit in their mouths. The poor fellows tried hard over and over again without any luck.

Suddenly the door of the house opened and the same girl came out; the bullocks lowered their heads and began to lick her hand. Their tails stood up while she stroked their foreheads, and then she said, 'I'm going to let you go. Be very quiet and run away or these people will kill you. In the house today they were talking about putting rings in your noses.'

She untied the rope, but the two stood silent.

'Well, let's go,' said Hira, 'only tomorrow this orphan's going to be in a lot of trouble. Everybody in the house will suspect her.'

Suddenly the girl yelled, 'Uncle's bullocks are running away! Daddy, daddy, come quick, they're running away!'

Gaya came rushing out of the house to catch the bullocks. They were running now, with Gaya fast behind them. They ran even faster and Gaya set up a shout. Then he turned back to fetch some men of the village. This was the chance for the two friends to make good their escape, and they ran straight ahead, no longer aware by now just where they were. There was no trace of the familiar road they'd come by. They were coming to villages they'd never seen. Then the two of them halted at the edge of a field and began to think about what they ought to do now.

Hira said, 'It appears we've lost our way.'

'You took to your heels without thinking. We should have knocked him down dead right on the spot.'

'If we'd killed him what would the world say? He abandoned his *dharma*, but we stuck to ours.'

They were dizzy with hunger. Peas were growing in the field and they began to browse, stopping occasionally to listen for anyone coming.

When they had eaten their fill the two of them were exhilarated with the experience of freedom and began to spring and leap. First they belched, then locked horns and began to shove one another around. Moti pushed Hira back several steps until he fell into the ditch. Then even Hira finally got angry. He managed to get up and then clashed with Moti. Moti could see that their game was on the verge of getting serious so he drew aside.

*

69

But what's this? A bull is coming along bellowing. Yes, it really is a bull, and he's heading right their way. The two friends look around anxiously for a way out. This bull is a regular elephant, you'll risk your very life if you try to take him on, but even if you don't fight him it looks as though you won't save your life either. And he's coming straight for them. What a terrifying sight!

'We're in for it now,' said Moti. 'Can we get out of it alive? Think up something to do.'

Worried, Hira observed, 'He's gone crazy with pride. He'd never listen to our pleas.'

'Then why don't we run for it?'

'Running away is cowardly.'

'In that case — die here! But your humble servant just wants to get away.'

'But what if he chases us?'

'Then think up something quick!'

'The plan is this, the two of us must attack at once. I'll strike from in front, you from behind, and when he gets it from both sides he'll take to his heels. When he turns on me gore him sideways in the belly. We may not come out of it alive, but there's no other way.'

Risking everything, the two friends made their attack. The bull had no experience doing battle with a united enemy. He was accustomed to fighting one enemy at a time. As soon as Hira pounced on him Moti charged from behind. When the bull turned to face him Hira attacked. The bull wanted to take them on one at a time and knock them down, but the two were masters of the art and gave him no chance. At one moment when the bull became so enraged that he moved to make an end of Hira once and for all Moti struck from the side and gored his belly. When the bull wheeled around in a fury Hira gored him from the other side. Finally the poor fellow ran off wounded, and the two friends pursued him for some distance until the bull collapsed out of breath. Then they left him.

The two friends went along swaying from side to side in the intoxication of victory.

In his symbolic language Moti said, 'I really felt like killing the bastard.'

Hira scolded, 'One ought not to turn one's horn on a fallen enemy.'

'That's all hypocrisy. You ought to strike the enemy down so he doesn't get up again.'

'But how are we going to get home now? — just think about *that.*'

'First let's eat something, and think afterwards.'

A pea field was right there in front of them. Moti went crashing in; Hira kept on warning him, but to no avail. He had scarcely eaten a couple of mouthfuls when two men with sticks came running and surrounded the two friends. Hira was on the embankment and slipped away, but Moti was down in the soggy field. His hooves were so deep in mud that he couldn't run, and he was caught. When Hira saw his comrade in trouble he dashed back. If they were going to be trapped, then they'd be trapped together. So the watchmen caught him too.

Early in the morning the two friends were shut up in a village pound.

*

The two friends had never in all their life had such an experience — the whole day went by and they weren't given even a single wisp of straw to eat. They couldn't understand what kind of master this could be. Even Gaya was a lot better than this. There were several water buffaloes here, nanny-goats, horses and donkeys. But no food was set before any of them; all were lying on the ground like corpses. Several were so weak that they couldn't even stand up. The whole day the two friends kept their eyes glued to the gate. But nobody appeared with food. Then they began to lick the salty clay of the wall, but what satisfaction could they get from that?

When they got no food in the evening either, the flame of rebellion began to blaze in Hira's heart. He said to Moti, 'I can't stand this any more, Moti.'

With his head hanging down Moti answered, 'I feel as though I'm dying.'

'Don't give up so quickly, brother! We've got to think up some plan to get out of here.'

'All right, let's smash the wall down.'

'I'm not up to that now.'

'What do you mean, weren't you just bragging about your strength?'

'All the bragging has gone out of me!'

The wall of the enclosure was a crude earthen construction. Hira was very strong indeed; when he thrust his pointed horn against the wall and struck hard a little chunk of clay came loose. With that his spirits rose. Running again and again he crashed against the wall and with every blow he knocked off a little of the clay.

At this very moment the pound watchman came out with his lantern to take count of the animals. When he caught sight of Hira's mischief he paid him back with several blows of his stick and tied him up with a thick rope.

From where he lay Moti said, 'So all you got was a beating after all!'

'At least I used my strength as best I could.'

'What good was it struggling so hard when you just got tied up all the more securely?'

'Nevertheless, I'm going to keep on struggling no matter how much they tie me up.'

'Then you'll end up paying with your life.'

'I don't give a damn. Being like this is the same thing as dying. Just think, if the wall were knocked down how many creatures would be saved. How many of our brothers are shut up here! There's no life left in any of their bodies. If it goes on like this for a few more days they'll all die.'

'That's for sure. All right then, I'll give it a good try.'

Moti struck with his horn at the same place in the wall. A little clay tumbled down and his courage grew. Again he drove his horn against the wall with such violence that he might have been battling with a living enemy. Finally, after a couple of hours of violent probing, the top of the wall gave way, lowering it about a foot. When he struck again with redoubled power half the wall crumbled.

When the wall was about to fall the animals who were lying around half dead revived. Three mares took off at a gallop, then the nanny-goats dashed out, and after that the buffaloes also slipped away. But the donkeys were still lying just as they had been before.

Hira asked them, 'Why aren't you two running away?'

One of the jackasses said, 'What if we get caught again?'

'What does that matter? Now's your chance to escape.'

'But we're scared! We'll just stay put right here.'

It was already past midnight. The two donkeys were standing there, wondering whether to run away or not, while Moti was busy trying to break his friend's rope. When he gave it up Hira said, 'You go, just let me stay here. Maybe somewhere we'll meet again.'

With tears in his eyes Moti said, 'Do you think I'm that selfish,

72

Hira? You and I have been together for such a long time! If you're in trouble today, can I just go off and leave you?'

Hira said, 'You'll get a real beating — they'll realize this is your mischief.'

Moti said proudly, 'If I get beaten for the same offence that got you tied up with a rope around your neck, what do I care? At the very least a dozen or so creatures have been saved from death. All of them will surely bless us.'

After he'd said this, Moti thrust at the two donkeys with his horns and drove them out of the enclosure; then he came up close beside his friend and went to sleep.

It's scarcely necessary to describe the hullaballoo set up by the clerk, the watchman and the other officials as soon as it was light. Sufficient to say that Moti got a terrific drubbing and he too was tied up with a thick rope.

*

The two friends stayed tied up there for a week. No one gave them so much as a bit of hay. True, water *was* given to them once. This was all their nourishment. They got so weak that they could not even stand up, and their ribs were sticking out.

One day someone beat a drum outside the enclosure and towards noon about fifty or sixty people gathered there. Then the two friends were brought out and the inspection began. People came and studied their appearance and went away disappointed. Who would buy bullocks that looked like corpses?

Suddenly there came a bearded man with red eyes and a cruel face; he dug his fingers into the haunches of the bullocks and began to talk with the clerk. When they saw his expression the hearts of the two friends grew weak from what their intuition told them. They had no doubt at all as to who he was and why he felt them with his hands. They looked at one another with frightened eyes and lowered their heads.

Hira said, 'We ran away from Gaya's house in vain. We won't survive this.'

Without much faith Moti answered, 'They say God has mercy on everybody. Why isn't He being merciful to us?'

'To God it's all the same whether we live or die. Don't worry, it's not so bad, for a little while we'll be with Him. Once He saved us in

73

the shape of that little girl, so won't He save us now?'

'This man is going to cut our throats. Just watch.'

'So why worry? Every bit of us, flesh, hide, horns and bones, will be used for something or the other.'

When the auction was over the friends went off with that bearded man. Every bit of their bodies was trembling. They could scarcely lift their feet, but they were so frightened they managed to keep stumbling along — for if they slowed down the least bit they'd get a good whack from the stick.

Along the way they saw a herd of cows and bullocks grazing in a verdant meadow. All the animals were happy, sleek and supple. Some were leaping about, others lying down contentedly chewing their cud What a happy life was theirs! Yet how selfish they all were. Not one of them cared about how their two brothers must be suffering after falling into the hands of the butcher.

Suddenly it seemed to them that the road was familiar. Yes, this was the road by which Gaya had taken them away. They were coming to the same fields and orchards, the same villages. At every instant their pace quickened. All their fatigue and weakness disappeared. Oh, just look, here was their own meadow, here was the same well where they had worked the winch to pull up the bucket, yes, it was the same well.

Moti said, 'Our house is close by!'

'It's God's mercy!' said Hira.

'As for me, I'm making a run for home!'

'Will he let us go?'

'I'll knock him down and kill him.'

'No, no, run and make it to our stalls, and we won't budge from there.'

As though they'd gone crazy, joyfully kicking up their heels like calves, they made off for the house. There was their stall! They ran and stood by it while the bearded man came dashing after them.

Jhuri was sitting in his doorway sunning himself. As soon as he saw the bullocks he ran and embraced them over and over again. Tears of joy flowed from the two friends' eyes, and one of them licked Jhuri's hand.

The bearded man came up and grabbed their tethers.

'These are my bullocks,' said Jhuri.

'How can they be? I just bought them at auction at the cattle pound.'

74

'I'll bet you stole them,' said Jhuri. 'Just shut up and leave. They're *my* bullocks. They'll be sold only when *I* sell them. Who has the right to auction off my bullocks?'

Said the bearded man, 'I'll go to the police station and make a complaint.'

'They're my bullocks, the proof is they came and stood at my door.'

In a rage the bearded man stepped forward to drag the bullocks away. This is when Moti lowered his horns. The bearded man stepped back. Moti charged and the man took to his heels, with Moti after him, and stopped only at the outskirts of the village where he took his stand guarding the road. The butcher stopped at some distance, yelled back threats and insults and threw stones. And Moti stood blocking his path like a victorious hero. The villagers came out to watch the entertainment and had a good laugh.

When the bearded man acknowledged defeat and went away Moti came back strutting.

Hira said, 'I was afraid you'd get so mad you'd go and kill him.'

'If he'd caught me I wouldn't have given up before I'd killed him.'

'Won't he come back now?'

'If he does I'll take care of him long before he gets here. Let's just see him take us away!'

'What if he has us shot?'

'Then I'll be dead, but I'll be of no use to him.'

'Nobody thinks of the life we have as being a life.'

'Only because we're so simple . . .'

In a little while their trough was filled with oilseed cake, hay, bran and grain, and the two friends began to eat. Jhuri stood by and stroked them while a couple of dozen boys watched the show.

Excitement seemed to have spread through the whole village.

At this moment the mistress of the house came out and kissed each of the bullocks on the forehead.

# Ramlila

For some time now I haven't gone to see the Ramlila. I find it absurd to watch men running around with crude monkey masks, short pants and black high-collared shirts, and grunting — I don't enjoy all that. The Ramlila of Banaras, now, is world-famous; they tell me people come from far away to see it. Once I also eagerly went to see it, but I could find no difference between that Lila and one in some remote village. Though I admit that in the Ramnagar performance some of the costumes were good. The demons and monkeys had masks of brass, their maces were of brass too; possibly the crowns worn by the exiled brothers were genuine. But apart from the costumes, in Ramnagar too there was nothing but the same grunting. And still, hundreds of thousands of people crowded to see it.

But there was a time when I too delighted in the Ramlila. Delight, though, is much too mild a word. That delight was nothing less than intoxicating. As it happened, in those days the Ramlila ground was not at all far from my house, and the house that was filled with the costumes and make-up of the Lila characters was also close by. The putting on of the make-up began at two o'clock. I would already be sitting there from twelve on, and the enthusiasm with which I ran about doing little jobs —well, it was more than I feel today when I cash my pension cheque. In one room the princes would be getting their make-up on. Ochre was ground and applied all over their bodies, powder daubed on their faces, and over the powder they put little spots of red, green and blue. Forehead, brows, cheeks, chin, all were covered with these spots. One particular man was an expert at this job and he would make up each of the three chief characters in turn. My job was to bring them water in the pots of dye, grind the ochre, and fan them. When, after these preparations, the chariot came forth and I mounted on it behind Rama, the pleasure, the pride, the thrill was such as now I don't get even from sitting in a chair at the Viceroy's grand durbar. Once when the home-member accepted a proposal of mine in the legislature I experienced something of that pleasure, pride and thrill, and when my eldest son was

76

nominated to the post of deputy tax-collector then too similar emotions stirred in my heart. But there is a great difference between those occasions and the childhood excitement. Then it seemed to me that I was enthroned in the very heavens.

It was the day when Guha the ferryman would take Rama across the Ganges. Falling in with three or four boys I had joined them to play stick-ball; thus led astray on this day, I failed to go to see the costuming. The chariot made its sortie and still I did not give up playing. For me to give up my turn at bat there would have to be a much greater need for self-sacrifice than that. Had I been fielding I would have dashed away long before; but being on the winning side is quite a different matter. Well, I finished off my turn. If I'd wanted, then by cheating I could have had another few minutes at bat, I was quite capable of that. But now was not the occasion, so I ran straight for the little river. The chariot had already reached the bank. From far off I saw the boatman bringing the boat out. I ran, but it was hard to move fast in the crowd. When finally I pushed through the mob at risk of life and limb and got all the way to the river bank, Guha had already pushed off in his boat.

How much faith I had in Rama then! Without worrying about my own studies, I'd been coaching him so he wouldn't fail. Although he was older then me he was studying in a lower grade. But this same Ramchandra now seated in the boat turned his head away as though he didn't even know me. Even in acting some hint or other of the truth can emerge. Why after all should one who always casts a severe look on his devotees bestow any grace on me? Agitated, I began to jump like a calf feeling the yoke on its neck for the first time. First I would leap forward toward the river, then spring back looking for someone to help me, but everybody was completely engrossed in their own excitement. My yells were noticed by nobody. In later times I was to suffer many disastrous moments, but what I suffered in that instant I have never since experienced.

I decided that from now on I would never speak to Ramchandra again, nor ever bring him anything to eat. But as soon as he'd crossed the stream and turned back toward the bridge, I ran and jumped on to his chariot and was as happy as though nothing at all had happened.

*

77

The Ramlila had reached its final act: Rama was to be installed on his throne. But for some reason there was a delay. Perhaps the contributions for the performance had fallen short. At that stage no one was bothering to look after Ramchandra. He neither got leave to go home nor was any arrangement made for his meals. At about three every afternoon a light snack was sent over from the house of Chaudhri Sahib, the village headman. But for the rest of the day not even a sip of water was provided. But my veneration for Ramchandra still remained unchanged. In my eyes he even now was Lord Rama. Whenever I got something to eat at home I would take it and give it to him. I found more happiness in feeding him than I myself ever got from eating. As soon as I got some fruit or sweets I would dash headlong for the village meeting hall. If I didn't find him there I'd hunt high and low for him and have no rest until I'd given it to him.

So — the day of Rama's coronation was here. A big awning, beautifully decorated, was suspended over the Ramlila ground. A crowd of prostitutes also came on to the scene. In the evening Ramchandra's procession would be taken out and at every door the *aarti* — the ritual of the lighted lamps — would be performed. According to his faith each man would give either rupees or more ·pice. My father was in the police force — and that explains why he performed the lamp ceremony without giving anything at all. I can't describe how ashamed I was at this. By chance I had a rupee: before Dassehra my uncle had come to visit and given it to me; that rupee I'd saved and not been able to to spend it even during the Dassehra holiday. I immediately took it out and threw it down on the *aarti* tray. My father could only stare angrily at me, though he never spoke a word. But his expression said clearly enough that by this impudence of mine I had disgraced him.

While ten was still striking the ceremony was completed. The tray was full of rupee notes and coins. I can't say precisely but my guess is there couldn't have been less than four or five hundred rupees. Now, Chaudhri Sahib had already spent quite a bit more than that. He was very concerned that he should somehow or other collect no less than another two hundred rupees, and the best plan for accomplishing this seemed to be to use the prostitutes to take up a collection at a grand party. When people had come and sat and the party really got going, Abadijan, one of the girls, was to catch hold of the wrist of each of those fine gentlemen and use such blandishments that even though they were terribly embarrassed they would throw down something or other. When Abadijan and Chaudhri Sahib began to confer, by chance I could hear what both of them were saying. Chaudhri Sahib must have assumed that a brat like me could understand nothing, but by God's grace I was a sharp kid, and I understood the whole plot.

'Listen, Abadijan,' Chaudhri Sahib was saying 'you're being very high-handed. In the past we've never had any business together, but God willing, you'll be able to keep coming to the village. Now, the contributions this time have fallen short, otherwise I wouldn't be putting the pressure on you.'

'But why are you trying out these big shot's tricks with me?' said Abadijan. 'You won't get anywhere, believe me. Bravo! I'm to collect the cash while you take it easy. A fine way you've figured out to make money! This way you'll become a maharajah in no time at all. Compared to you a zamindar won't amount to anything. Why, you'll be able to open a brothel tomorrow morning! God's oath, you'll be rolling in money.'

'You're making jokes while I'm in a tight spot.'

'And still you're trying to cheat me! Look, I make fools of sharpers like you every day.'

'All right, once and for all, what are you after?'

'Whatever I take in, half is yours, half is mine,' said Abadijan. 'Come on, give me your hand on it.'

'Agreed.'

'Fine, but first count out a hundred rupees for me in case you decide to welsh on the deal afterwards.'

'Wonderful! You'll take this, then you'll pocket the rest!'

'Well, did you expect me to give up my wages? Oh, aren't you clever though ! Okay: what's wrong my way? You're a sensible man but you talk nonsense.'

'So you're resolved to get paid double?'

'Even if you object a hundred times, yes. Or else my hundred rupees might just disappear somewhere. Do you think I've been bitten by a mad dog to go around sticking my own hand in people's pockets?'

Chaudhri got nowhere: he was obliged to give way to Abadijan. And now the party began. Abadijan was a flirt of the highest order. For one thing, she was very young, and in the bargain beautiful. Her charms were so remarkable that even I was overwhelmed. And she was also not lacking in skill in understanding the qualities of men. She got something or other from everyone she sat down in front of. Probably nobody was giving anything less than five rupees. She came and sat down in front of Father too. I could have died of shame, and when she caught hold of his wrist I was close to panic. I'd believed that Father would shove her hand away and maybe even rebuke her, but what happened? Oh God! my eyes didn't deceive me. Father was laughing through his moustache. Never before had I seen such a tender smile on his face. His eyes were alight with passion, he was positively ecstatic. But God would preserve my honour, for just look: gently he freed his wrist from Abadi's tender hands. *Arrey!* What next? Abadi flung her arms around his neck. Surely now Father would strike her. The witch was completely shameless.

One gentleman smiled and said, 'You're wasting your time with him, Abadijan, knock on some other door.'

He'd said just what I was thinking, and said it most properly. But for some reason Father held his head high and looked at him with angry eyes without saying a word. But the expression of his face cried out angrily, 'You merchant you! How can you presume to understand me? At a moment like this I'm ready to lay down my very life. What does mere money mean? If you feel up to it, see what *you* can do. If I don't give at least twice as much as you, let me hide my face forever!' Astonishment all around! What a scandal! Earth, why don't you open, sky why don't you shatter!

Why doesn't death claim me! Father thrusts his hand into his pocket, draws out something and after flourishing it at the merchant hands it over to Abadijan. A gold sovereign! Applause on all sides. I couldn't determine whether Father had come out a loser, I only saw that he had taken out a gold sovereign and given it to Abadijan. At this moment his eyes shone with pride as though he had shown himself the most generous man in the world. This is the same Father who when he saw me give a rupee at the *aarti* stared at me as though he would tear me apart. He had been hurt in his prestige by my decent act while this time he could scarcely control his pleasure in this disgusting business.

*

Abadijan *salaamed* Father with a charming smile and moved on. But I couldn't stand sitting there any longer. My head was bowed with shame; if I had not seen this with my own eyes I wouldn't have believed it. Usually I told my mother about whatever I'd seen or heard away from the house. But I hid this business from her, for I knew how much it would have hurt her to learn about it.

The singing went on all night. I kept hearing the beat of the drums. I was tempted to go and watch but I didn't have the courage, for how could I show my face to anyone? If someone happened to mention my father slightingly, what could I have done?

In the early morning hours Ramchandra was to take his leave. As soon as I got up from my *charpoy*, still rubbing my eyes, I went running off to the village meeting hall. I was afraid Ramchandra might already have left. When I got there I saw that the prostitutes' carriages were ready to leave. A score of men were crowding around them, their expressions full of longing. I scarcely gave them even a glance but made straight for Ramchandra. Lakshman and Sita were sitting there crying and Ramchandra standing by, his jug and string swung over his shoulder, trying to console them. Except for me there was no one else there. My voice choking, I asked him, 'Have you already said your good-byes?'

'Yes, already,' said Ramchandra. 'But can you call it a good-bye? Chaudhri Sahib just said, "Leave now, go away."'

'But didn't you get any going-away money and clothes?'

'Haven't got them yet! Chaudhri Sahib says, "Right now there's no money left over. Come again some time and get it."'

'You didn't get anything?'

'Not a pice. He just says, "There's nothing left over." I'd been thinking if I got a few rupees why then I'd buy myself some books for studying. But I got nothing, not even expenses for the trip. He says, "It's not far, is it? You can make it on shank's mare."'

I was so angry I wanted to go to Chaudhri Sahib and tell him off. Rupees for the whores, carriages, everything. But for poor Ramchandra and his companions nothing at all! The people who squandered ten and twenty rupees apiece on Abadijan didn't have even two or three rupees for the players. Father gave a gold sovereign to Abadijan. Well — let's see what he'll give to them. I went running to him. He was just about to go off somewhere on an investigation. When he saw me he said, 'Where are you wandering off to? Is this your idea to go loafing when it's time to study?'

I said, 'I've just been to the assembly hall. Ramchandra's about to leave but Chaudhri Sahib's given him nothing.'

'And just what business is that of yours?'

'How can they go off like that? They don't even have expenses for the road.'

'What, not even expenses? That *is* very unfair of Chaudhri Sahib.'

'If you'll just give a couple of rupees, I'll pass them on to them. Maybe that will be enough for them to get home.'

Father gave me a sharp look. 'Get along,' he said, 'back to your books. I don't have any money on me.'

With that, he rode off on his horse.

From that day on, my faith in my father was finished. I never again took his scolding seriously. My heart said, 'You have no right to give me advice.' I was angered just by the sight of him. Whatever he told me to do, I'd do the opposite. It may have been to my detriment, but at that time my heart was full of revolutionary ideas.

By luck I had just two *annas* left. I took the coins and, though I was terribly embarrassed, went back to Ramchandra and gave them to him. I was completely unprepared for Ramchandra's joy when he saw those coins. He pounced on them as a thirsty man goes for water.

The three players took the two *anna* pieces and set out on their way. I was the only one who saw them off, as far as the edge of the village.

After I said good-bye to them and came back my eyes were full of tears; but my heart was overflowing with happiness.

# The Thakur's Well

Jokhu brought the *lota* to his mouth but the water smelled foul. He·
said to Gangi, 'What kind of water is this? It stinks so much I can't
drink it! My throat's burning and you give me water that's turned
bad.'

Every evening Gangi filled the water jugs. The well was a long
way off and it was hard for her to make several trips. She'd brought
this water yesterday and there'd been no bad smell at all to it then.
How could it be there now? She lifted the *lota* to her nostrils and it
certainly smelt foul. Surely some animal must have fallen into the
well and died. But she didn't know where else she could get any
water.

No one would let her walk up to the Thakur's well. Even while
she was far off people would start yelling at her. At the other end of
the village the shopkeeper had a well but even there they wouldn't
let her draw any water. For people like herself there wasn't any well
in the village.

Jokhu, who'd been sick for several days, held back his thirst for a
little while. Then he said, 'I'm so thirsty I can't stand it. Bring me the
water, I'll hold my nose and drink a little.'

Gangi did not give it to him. His sickness would get worse from
drinking bad water — that much she knew. But she didn't know that
by boiling the water it would be made safe. She said, 'How can you
drink it? Who knows what kind of beast has died in it? I'll go and get
you some water from the well.'

Surprised, Jokhu stared at her. 'Where can you get more water?'

'The Thakur and the shopkeeper both have wells. Won't they let
me fill just one *lota*?'

'You'll come back with your arms and legs broken, that's all.
You'd better just sit down and keep quiet. The Brahman will give a
curse, the Thakur will beat you with a stick and that money-lending
shopkeeper takes five for every one he gives. Who cares what people
like us go through? Whatever they say about giving some help,
we can just die and nobody will even come to this door to have a

look. Do you think people like that are going to let you draw water from their well.'

The harsh truth was in these words and Gangi could not deny it. But she wouldn't let him drink that stinking water.

*

By nine o'clock at night the dead-tired field hands were fast asleep but a half dozen or so idlers were gathered at the Thakur's door. These were not the times — nor were there any occasions — for valour in the field; valour in the courtroom was the topic of the day. How cleverly the Thakur had bribed the local police chief in a certain case and come off scot-free! With what skill he'd managed to get his hands on a copy of the dossier in an important lawsuit. The clerks and magistrates had all said it was impossible to get a copy. One had demanded fifty for it, another a hundred, but for no money at all a copy had come flying. You had to know the right way to operate in these matters.

At this moment Gangi reached the Thakur's property to get water from his well.

The dim glow of a small oil lamp lit up the well. Gangi sat hidden behind the wall and began to wait for the right moment. Everybody in the village drank the water from this well. It was closed to nobody, only those unlucky ones like herself could not fill their buckets here.

Gangi's resentful heart cried out against the restraints and bars of the custom. Why was she so low and those others so high? Because they wore a thread around their necks? There wasn't one of them in the village who wasn't rotten. They stole, they cheated, they lied in court. That very day the Thakur had stolen a sheep from the poor shepherd, then killed and eaten it. They gambled in the priest's house all twelve months of the year. The shopkeeper mixed oil with the *ghee* before he sold it. They'd get you to do their work but they wouldn't pay wages for it to save their lives. Just how were they so high and mighty? It was only a matter of words. No, Gangi thought, *we* don't go around shouting that we're better. Whenever she came into the village they looked at her with eyes full of lust, they were on fire with lust, every one of them, but they bragged that they were better than people like her.

She heard people coming to the well and her heart began to

84

pound. If anybody saw her there'd be the devil to pay and she'd get an awful kicking out of it. She grabbed her bucket and rope and crept away to hide in the dark shadows of a tree. When had these people ever had pity on anybody? They beat poor Mahngu so hard that he spat blood for months, and the only reason was that he refused to work in the forced labour gang. Was this what made such people consider themselves better than everybody else?

Two women had come to draw water and they were talking. One said: 'There they were eating and they order *us* to get more water. There's no money for a jug.'

'The men folk get jealous if they think they see us sitting around taking it easy.'

'That's right, and you'll never see them pick up the pitcher and fetch it themselves. They just order us to get it as though we were slaves.'

'If you're not a slave, what are you? You work for food and clothes and even to get nothing more than five or six rupees you have to snatch it on the sly. What's that if it isn't being a slave?'

'Don't shame me, sister! All I do is long for just a second's rest. If I did this much work for somebody else's family I'd have an easier time, and they might even be grateful. But here'you could drop dead from overwork and they'd all just frown.'

When the two of them had filled their buckets and gone away Gangi came out from the shadow of the tree and drew close to the well platform. The idlers had left, the Thakur had shut his door and gone inside to the courtyard to sleep. Gangi took a moment to sigh with relief. On every side the field was clear. Even the prince who set out to steal nectar from the gods could not have moved more warily. Gangi tiptoed up on to the well platform. Never before had she felt such a sense of triumph.

She looped the rope around the bucket. Like some soldier steal-ing into the enemy's fortress at night she peered cautiously on every side. If she were caught now there was not the slightest hope of mercy or leniency. Finally, with a prayer to the gods, she mustered her courage and cast the bucket into the well.

Slowly, slowly it sank in the water. There was not the slightest sound. Gangi yanked it back up with all her might to the rim of the well. No strong-armed athlete could have dragged it up more swiftly.

'She had just stooped to catch it and set it on the wall when suddenly the Thakur's door opened. The jaws of a tiger could not have terrified her more.

The rope escaped from her hand. With a crash the bucket fell into the water, the rope after it, and for a few seconds there were sounds of splashing.

Yelling 'Who's there? Who's there?' The Thakur came toward the well and Gangi jumped from the platform and ran away as fast as she could.

When she reached home, Jokhu, with the *lota* at his mouth, was drinking that filthy, stinking water.

# A Desperate Case

Some men are angry with their wives for giving birth to one daughter after another but never a son. They know it's not the wives' fault, or if it is, then no more than their own, but just the same whenever you see them they're vexed with their wives, call them unlucky and continue to torment them. Nirupma was one of these unlucky women and Ghamandi Lal Tripathi one of those cruel husbands. Nirupma had had three daughters in a row and everyone in the household gave her unkind looks. Her mother-in-law's and father-in-law's displeasure did not concern her particularly —they were old-fashioned people who considered daughters an unpleasant responsibility, the result of sins in earlier incarnations. But it was her husband's disaffection that grieved her, especially since even the fact that he was an educated man did not restrain him from speaking nastily to her. Far from loving her, he never spoke to her without getting angry; for days at a time he would not even come into the house and when he did he was so on edge that she trembled with fear lest there be a row. Although there was no lack of money in the family Nirupma never dared express a wish for even the most trivial object. She thought, 'I really am ill-omened — otherwise would God have created only girls in my womb?' She longed for a gentle smile from her husband, a tender word, to the point where she hesitated to show affection to her daughters lest people say, 'She's certainly making a lot of fuss over trifles!' When it was time for her husband to come home she would on one pretext or another keep the girls out of his sight. The greatest calamity was that Tripathi had threatened, if she had another girl next time, to leave the house forever rather than tolerate such hell for another second. Nirupma worried constantly about this too.

She fasted on Tuesdays, on Sundays, on the eleventh of the month of *Jeth* and at countless other times. She was always performing rituals, but no ritual had fulfilled her wish. Continually putting up with disdain, insults, scolding and contempt, she had become disgusted with the world. It was inevitable that she should be disheartened in a house where, longing for a tender word, a friendly glance, a loving embrace, no one so much as bothered with her.

One day, feeling absolutely desperate, she wrote a letter to her elder brother's wife; every word of it cost her an intolerable pain. Her sister-in-law replied: Your brother is coming to fetch you right away. Recently a genuine saint has come to the village and his blessing has never been known to fail. Several childless women have had sons after his blessing. We have every hope that with you as well it will have the desired effect.

Nirupma showed this letter to her husband. Sadly he said, 'Saints have nothing to do with procreation and conception, it's God's business.'

'Yes, but saints can attain to special powers.'

'Maybe so, but visiting them won't do any good.'

'Still, I'll go and visit this one.'

'Go if you want to.'

'If barren women have had sons, am I any less worthy than they?'

'Didn't I tell you to go? When you do you'll find out. But it seems to me that it's not in our fate to see a son's face.'

                                        *

A few days later Nirupma went with her brother to her father's house. She took the three girls with her. Sukeshi, her sister-in-law, embraced her affectionately and said, 'The people of your house are very cruel — to curse fate for having three such darlings! They must be heavy for you, give them to me.'

When, after dinner, with Sukeshi and the younger brother's wife, they were going to bed Nirupma asked, 'Where does this saint live?'

'Why such haste?' Sukeshi said. 'I'll tell you in good time.'

'It's close by, isn't it?'

'Very close. When you want, I'll send for him.'

'He's very fond of you people, is he?'

'He eats here twice a day. He lives right here.'

'Then why suffer when the doctor's already in the house? I want to see him right away.'

'What will you give me?'

'What is there I could give you?' Nirupma said.

'Give me your youngest girl.'

'Go on, you're making fun of me.'

'All right, but you'll have to let him hug you just once.'

'Sister, if you laugh at me I'll go away!'

'This saint's very fond of pretty women.'

'Then he can go to the devil,' Nirupma said. 'He must be a scoundrel.'

'But that's the payment he demands for his blessings. He doesn't accept any other award.'

'The way you talk anybody would think you were working for him.'

'Well, he arranges everything through me. I take the offerings, I also give the blessings, I also make the food for him,' Sukeshi said.

'So you made all this up, admit it, just to get me here!'

'No, not at all, I'm going to tell you of a plan that will allow you to live in peace in your own home.'

Then the two of them began to whisper. When Sukeshi had finished talking, Nirupma said, 'And what if it should be a girl again, after all?'

'So what? You'll have spent a little while in peace and quiet anyway. No one will be able to take those days away from you. If you have a son, then all will be fine; if it's a daughter then some new plan will have to be worked out. With the idiots you've got in your house what else can we do except resort to tricks like this?'

'I feel a little nervous about it.'

'In a couple of days write to Tripathi to tell him you've seen the saint and that he's told you he'll grant your wish. God willing, from that day on you'll be treated with a lot more respect. Tripathi'll come on the run ready to sacrifice his life for you. For at least a year you'll have a pleasant time of it. After that, we'll see.'

'But won't it be a sin to lie to my husband?'

'To pull the wool over the eyes of a selfish fellow like him is a virtue!'

*

After three or four months Nirupma went home. Ghamandi Lal came to get her. Sukeshi was very detailed in her description of the saint. She said, 'It's never been known that a holy man gave a blessing like that without producing results. But of course, some people are so unlucky there's nothing to be done for them.'

Ghamandi Lal openly expressed his contempt for blessings and promises; he seemed ashamed to give credence to such things in this day and age, but there was no doubt that he was impressed.

Nirupma was welcomed back. When she became pregnant everyone's hearts thrilled with new hopes. The mother-in-law, who before had never done anything but revile her, treated her like a guest. 'Daughter, let it be, I'll make the supper, you'll get a headache.' Whenever Nirupma began to take out the water jug to fill it or to move a cot, then the mother-in-law would run to her. 'Daughter, leave it, I'm here, you mustn't lift anything heavy.' If she had been going to have a girl none of this would have had any effect on the child, but boys, even while they're still in the womb, begin to sit up and be proud. Now Nirupma was made to eat quantities of milk pudding so the boy would be robust and fair. Ghamandi Lal made a habit of getting clothes and jewellery for her, every month he would bring something new. Even when she'd been a new bride Nirupma had not led so pleasant an existence.

The months began to slip by. According to signs and omens she recognized Nirupma began to be convinced that it would be a girl this time too. But she kept this heretical opinion to herself. She would think, 'It's like a monsoon sunshine — how can you trust it? Enjoy it while you can, the rain-clouds are going to cover it all.' She was jumpy about every little thing. She had never been particularly temperamental, but no one in the house would make the slightest noise lest she be upset and thus produce an ill effect upon the boy. Sometimes just to torment the family Nirupma would carry out a religious fast, and she found pleasure in tormenting them. She would think, 'The more I torment you selfish ones the better. You honour me, don't you, only because I'm going to give birth to a child who'll carry on your name. I'm nothing, the child alone is everything; I have no importance, everything hinges on your child. And this is my husband: at first how much he loved me, he wasn't worldly and greedy then. Now his love is a little trick to satisfy his selfishness. I'm an animal to be stuffed with fodder and water for the sake of my milk. If that's the way it is, fine, but now I can control you all. I'll make you give me as many jewels as I can, you won't be able to take them back.'

And so the nine months came to an end. Nirupma's two sisters-in-law were sent for from her father's house. Golden ornaments had already been made for the child; a fine milch-cow was purchased for his milk and Ghamandi Lal brought a little pram to take him on

90

walks. On the day the labour pains started the astrologer was summoned to the door to cast the horoscope. A huntsman had been called to fire off the shotgun and women were gathered together to strike up a hymn. Everyone wanted details of what was happening inside the house. The woman doctor had been sent for. The musicians sat waiting for the word; the village singer with his fiddle was ready to sound the strains of 'Let the mother be proud, Lord Krishna.' All the preparations, all the hopes, all the jubilation was hanging on one word only. With every moment of delay the impatience grew. To hide his excitement Ghamandi Lal was reading a newspaper, just as though it were all one whether it was a boy or a girl. But his old father was not so controlled. He could not restrain his exuberance, he talked to everybody and laughed and kept rattling a bag full of coins.

The huntsman said, 'I'll take a turban and scarf from the master.'

Delighted, the old man said, 'Go on, how many turbans will you take? I'll give you such an expensive one every hair on your head will fall out.'

The singer said, 'And I'll accept something to live on from the master.'

'And how much will you eat? We'll feed you till your belly bursts.'

Suddenly a housemaid came out looking flustered. Before she had managed to say anything the huntsman fired off the shotgun and immediately afterwards the pipes struck up a tune and the singer, hitching up his *dhoti*, sprang up to dance.

The maid shouted, 'Are you all drunk on *bhang*, you people?'

'What's happened?' the huntsman said.

'What's happened? It's a girl again, that's what's happened.'

'A girl?' the old man said, and with that he threw up his arms and sat down as though hit by a thunderbolt. Ghamandi Lal came out of his room and said, 'Go and ask the lady doctor — you just came running out here without really seeing anything.'

'Babuji,' the maid said, 'I saw with my own eyes.'

'And it's really a girl?'

'Such is our fate,' his father said. 'Go, everybody, get along. If it's written in your fate that you're not going to have something, then how can you ever get it? Go, run! Hundreds of rupees thrown away, all our preparations ruined!'

Ghamandi Lal said, 'We'll have to talk to this saint. I'll go today to make inquiries about the bastard.'

'He's a fraud, a fraud!' his father said.

'I'll expose all his cheating,' Ghamandi Lal went on. 'If I don't crack his skull then I'll eat my words. He's some kind of swindler. Because of him I've thrown away hundreds of rupees. The pram, the cow, the swing, the golden ornaments — whose head can I throw them at? Think how many he must have cheated like this! If the score is paid off for once, then it will be some satisfaction.'

'Son, it's not his fault, it's the fault of fate.'

'Why did he claim this wouldn't happen? How much money women must have squandered on the cheat! He's got to be made to cough it all up, otherwise I'll report him to the police. The law has punishments for swindling too. From the very first I was afraid it might be a fraud. But my brother-in-law's wife fooled me — if she hadn't I'd never have been caught in such a swindler's trap. He's just a pig.'

'Be patient,' his father said. 'What God has wished he has wrought. Both girls and boys are gifts of God. And where there's three you can be sure there'll be another.'

Father and son went on talking. The singer, the huntsman and the others picked up their staffs and set out on their way. The house seemed to have gone into mourning. The lady doctor had also taken leave, and apart from the mother and the midwife there was no one in the lying-in room. The old mother was so disconsolate that she'd taken to her bed.

When the child's twelfth-day ceremony had been performed Ghamandi Lal went to his wife for the first time and said angrily, 'So it's a girl again!'

'What could I do,' Nirupma said, 'it's not in my control.'

'That wretched swindler really cheated us.'

'What can I say now? If he were a swindler, why would all those women keep going to the saint day and night? It's not in my fate. If he'd taken anything from anybody then I'd say he was a fraud, but I take an oath that I never gave a pice to him.'

'Whether he took anything or not I've spent a fortune. We've learned that it's our destiny not to have a son. If the family line is coming to an end, then what does it matter if it happens now or in ten years? I'll go away somewhere, there's no joy left in this household.'

For a long time he stayed on bemoaning his fate; but Nirupma did not even lift her head.

92

The calamity had fallen on her once again, and again the same reproaches, the same insults and snubs, and no one cared whether she ate or not; whether she was sick, whether she was happy. Ghamandi Lal did not go away but the threat was almost always in Nirupma's mind. In this way several months passed and then once again Nirupma wrote Sukeshi to tell her she had put her in a more wretched situation than before, and now nobody even cared whether she lived or died. If this state of affairs went on, then whether her husband renounced the world and became an ascetic or not, she herself would certainly leave the world in a different way.

When she read this letter Sukeshi understood how things were. This time she did not invite Nirupma, knowing that they would not let her come, so she herself went, taking her husband along. She was a very lively, clever and fun-loving woman. As soon as she arrived she saw the baby girl in Nirupma's lap and said, '*Arrey!* what's that?'

'It's fate — what else?' said Nirupma's mother-in-law.

'What do you mean fate? You must have made some mistake in following the saint's instructions. It's not possible that whatever he's promised should fail to come about. Now tell me, did you fast on Tuesdays?'

'Without fail, I didn't skip one fast,' Nirupma said.

'And did you feed five Brahmans on Tuesdays also?'

'But he didn't tell me to do that.'

'Don't you tell me, I remember perfectly, he said it right in front of me and with a lot of emphasis too. You must have thought, "What's the point of feeding the Brahmans?" You didn't understand that unless you fulfilled every part of the ritual it wouldn't come out the way he said.'

'She never said anything about it,' the mother-in-law said. 'And why five? We would have fed ten Brahmans — we're not lacking in religion, after all.'

'Of course not, she just forgot, that's obvious. There's no possibility of getting a son this way. Great devotion and piety are necessary and you were confused by just one Tuesday fast?'

'She's unlucky, what else?' said the mother-in-law.

Ghamandi Lal said, 'How could anybody not remember what he made such a fuss about saying? She's just trying to upset us all.'

'And I ask you,' his mother said, 'how the saint's words could fail

93

to be fulfilled. For seven years I've lit the lamp and made offerings to the Goddess of the *tulsi* plant to get a grandson.'

'And she thought it was going to be easy as eating rice,' Ghamandi Lal said.

'Well,' Sukeshi said, 'what's happened has happened. Tomorrow's Tuesday, fast again and give a dinner to seven Brahmans. We'll see whether or not the saint's promise will be fulfilled.'

'It's useless,' Ghamandi Lal said, 'nothing will come of doing it.'

'Babuji,' Sukeshi said, 'you're educated, but with your learning how much your heart has shrunk! How old are you right now? How many sons would you like to have? If you don't have so many you're fed up with them I'll eat my words.'

The mother-in-law said, 'Daughter, how can anyone have that many sons?'

'If God wills,' Sukeshi said, 'then you'll get your wish. I got mine.'

'Are you listening, my dear?' Ghamandi Lal said. 'Don't make any mistake this time. Make sure you understand everything sister-in-law tells you.'

'You can be sure,' Sukeshi said, 'I'll remind you. How to prepare the feast, how to go about everything, how to perform the ablutions, I'll write it all down for you and Mother, and no more than eighteen months from today I'll claim a fat reward from you.'

Sukeshi stayed a week and after giving careful instructions to Nirupma she went back home.

*

Nirupma's star shone again; Ghamandi Lal was consoled with the thought that the future would redeem the past. Again Nirupma went from slave to queen, the mother-in-law treated her with the highest consideration, and everybody paid her the greatest attention.

The days passed. Nirupma would sometimes say, 'Mother, last night I dreamed that an old woman came to me and called out and gave me a coconut. She said, "This is what I've given you."' And sometimes she would say, 'Mother, I don't know why but a great joy has sprung up in my heart, I long to hear beautiful singing, to bathe in the river. It's almost like being intoxicated.' When the mother-in-law heard these things she would smile and say, 'Daughter, these are good omens.'

Nirupma had *bhang* brought to her on the sly and ate it, because

red and drunk-looking eyes meant a son, and then looking at Ghamandi Lal with her drowsy eyes she would say, 'Are my eyes red?'

'It seems as though you were actually drunk,' he would observe
contentedly. 'This is a good omen.'

Nirupma had never been especially fond of perfume but now she
was ready to give her life for a fragrant garland.

Before going to bed Ghamandi Lal now made a habit of reading
heroic stories to her out of the *Mahabharata*; sometimes he would
describe the glorious deeds of Guru Govind Singh. Nirupma was
very fond of the story of Abhimanyu. Ghamandi Lal wanted to
ensure that his unborn son would be a hero.

One day Nirupma said to him, 'What name will you give him?'

'I'm sure you've already picked one out. I haven't thought about it
at all. It has to be a name associated with valour and glory. You think
of a name.'

The two of them began to discuss names. They went through
every name from Harishchandra to Zoravar Lal but they couldn't
pick one out for this extraordinary boy. Finally Ghamandi Lal said,
'What do you think of Teg Bahadur?'

'That's fine, I like it.'

'It's a splendid name. You've heard about the great deeds of Teg
Bahadur. The name has a tremendous influence on the person.'

'The name is really everything,' Nirupma said. 'Whether it's
Damri, Chhakauri, Ghurhu, or Katvaru, whenever you look at somebody's name you find, "As the name, so the man." Our child's name
will be Teg Bahadur — the warrior's sword.'

*

The time for the delivery came. Nirupma knew what was about to
happen. But outside everything was ready for the celebration. This
time nobody had the slightest doubt. Everything had been made
ready for the singing and dancing. A canopy had been put up and a
throng of friends sat under it chatting. The sweets-maker took *puris*
and sweets out of his boiling pan. Several sacks had been filled with
grain so that as soon as the good tidings had been received it could
be distributed among the beggars. To avoid all delay the sacks had
already been opened.

But with every second Nirupma's heart sank. What would happen
now? She had got through three years by some sort of deceit, and

95

they'd been happy years, but now disaster was hovering over her head. Alas, she thought, what a victim she was. To be punished this way without guilt! If it was God's wish that no sons should ever be born from her womb, what fault was it of hers? But who listened? She was really an unlucky woman, she ought to be abandoned, she was ill-omened, and that was why she was a victim. What was going to happen? In a second all the joy and jubilation would collapse in lamentation. They would begin to revile her, curse her inside and out. She was not afraid of her mother and father-in-law, but her husband might once again cease to look at her, in his disappointment he might renounce his house and home. There was nothing but evil fortune on every side. 'Why should I live to see the misery of my family?' she said to herself. 'The trick is done with, there's no hope to be had from it any more. There used to be such longings in my heart; to bring up my darling girls, to get them married and see their children would have been happiness. But it's all finished now. Lord, be their father, look after them, but I'm going now.'

The woman doctor said, 'Well, it's a girl again.'

Inside and outside there were sounds of lamentation. Ghamandi Lal said, 'A curse on such a life, I'm ready for death!'

His father said, 'She's ill-omened, damned ill-omened.'

The beggars said, 'Weep your destiny, we're going to look for some other door!'

The noise had not died down when the doctor said, 'There's no hope for the mother, we can't save her — her heart has stopped.'

# THE TOWN

# A Day in the Life of a Debt-Collector

Seth Chetaram bathed, poured water in sacrifice to Shiva, chewed two peppercorns, drank two pots of water and taking his stick went out to dun the people who owed him money.

Sethji was some fifty years old. The hair had fallen from his head and his skull was as clean as a sandy field. His eyes were small but absolutely round. Right under his head was his belly and beneath his belly his legs looking like two pegs stuck in a barrel. This barrel, by the way, wasn't empty. It was chock full of energy and vitality. The way it jiggled and danced when Sethji was putting the pressure on some defaulting debtor would have shamed an acrobat. He would glare so fiercely and roar so loudly that a regular mob would gather to watch him. But you couldn't call him a miser because, when he was in his shop, he threw down a pice to every beggar. Of course, at those times his frown was so severe and his eyes so terrible and his nose so wrinkled that the beggar would never go by his shop again.

He was absolutely dedicated to the theory that persistent dunning was the way to prosper. From right after breakfast until evening he was constantly occupied in dunning. In the course of his visits he would find a lunch set aside in one house, in another he would partake — at his debtor's expense — of milk, *puris*, sweets and other dishes. A free meal is nothing to be sneezed at. Save just one *anna* per meal and then for this one item in his thirty years of money-lending he would have saved some 800 rupees. Then when he came back a second time he could get milk, curds, oil, vegetables, and cowdung cakes or other fuel. Generally he didn't have to get his own dinner in the evening either. So he never failed to go out on his dunning expeditions. The heavens could burst asunder, fire rain down, a tornado strike, but Sethji, as though obeying an immutable law of nature, was sure to go out to collect his debts.

This morning his wife asked, 'Lunch?'

'No!' Sethji thundered.

'Supper?'

'We'll see when I get back.'

There was a farmer who owed Sethji five rupees. For six months the rogue had paid neither principal nor interest, he hadn't even come around with some little offering. His house was at least three miles away and therefore Sethji had put off going. He decided that he would go today and not leave without getting his money from the rascal no matter how much he might squirm and moan. But it was most unpleasant to make such a long journey on foot. People might say, 'A big name but a poor show! He wants to be called a Seth but he hops it on foot.' So he ambled along at a leisurely gait looking here and there and chatting with people he met so it would be understood that he was just out for a stroll.

Suddenly he met an *ekka* coming his way. The *ekka* driver, who was Muslim, asked, 'Where do you have to go, Lala?'

'I don't have to go anywhere,' Sethji said. 'It's just two steps more. However, I suppose I might as well have a seat.'

The *ekka* driver gave Sethji a piercing look, and Sethji stared back with his fierce red eyes. Both of them understood that the other was going to prove a slippery proposition.

The *ekka* started to roll. Sethji made the first move. 'Where is your house, my good man?'

'Excellency, my house is wherever I lie down. When I had a house — well, then I had it. But now I'm houseless, homeless and, worst of all, wingless. Fate has clipped my wings, cut off my tail and abandoned me. My grandfather was a revenue collector for the Nawab, excellency, the master of seven districts. Anybody he wanted shot was shot and if he wanted somebody hanged, he had him hanged. Even before the sun came up thousands and thousands of purses appeared before him. The Nawab treated him like a brother. That was how it was then but now we're forced to work for people like you. Times change.'

Sethji realized that he was up against a tough opponent, a regular champion. It wasn't going to be easy to get the better of him, but since the challenge had been offered he'd have to take it up. He said, 'But surely you belong to the Imperial household? Your very appearance bears witness to that. Times change, brother, not every day turns out the same. At home we say that Lakshmi is fickle, she doesn't always act the same: today she comes to my house, tomorrow to yours. Your father must have left you a regular pile of rupees?'

100

'*Arrey*, Sethji, there was no counting that wealth. I don't know how many cellars it filled. The gold and silver were piled up by the boxful and there were baskets jammed full of jewels. Every single gem was worth half a million. The glitter was so great it put lamps to shame. But fate was still around to be reckoned with. One day Grand-daddy passed away and then we lost our connection with the Nawab. The whole treasure was looted. Peple loaded trucks with the jewels and carted them off. Even then, enough was left in the house for Daddy to live out his days in luxury — the luxury a fool would live in. He used to go out in a palanquin carried by sixteen attendants. There were mace-bearers scurrying both in front and behind. And still he left enough for me to live on. If I'd lived sensibly I'd be well off today. But a rich man's son has got to live like a rich man. I used to get out of bed clutching a bottle of booze. All night long there'd be wild parties with whores dancing. How'd I know I'd have to suffer for it one day?'

Sethji said, 'Brother, thank Almighty God that you can look after your family honestly. Just think of how many of our brothers, on the other hand, tread the paths of wickedness day and night — nevertheless they stay as poor as templemice. You've got to keep to religion, without religion you just live out your days — and what's the difference if you spend them eating fine things or chewing a dry crust? Religion's the big thing. As soon as I saw your face I knew you were a man of principle and integrity. When people are dishonest it's written all over their faces.'

'Sethji, what you say is true. You've got to keep up religion, it's everything. When I get four pice from you people I use it in feeding my children. *Huzoor*, just look at other *ekka* drivers — why, everyone of them is given up to bad habits, every one of them is. But I've taken the pledge. Why should you do something that just brings on misfortune? I have a big family, *huzoor*, my mother, my children, several dependent widows, and all my earnings come from this *ekka*. Still, somehow or other the good Lord looks after us.'

'He's the author of all things, Khan Sahib. May there always be abundance in your earnings.'

'That depends on the generosity of people like you.'

'It depends on the generosity of God. And you've turned out fine. I've had a lot of trouble from *ekka* drivers but now it seems that everywhere there are good and bad alike. I've never before met a man as honest and decent as you. What a fine nature you've got, I congratulate you!'

When the *ekka* man heard this fulsome praise he understood that the gentleman was a champion talker. He wouldn't have praised him, he thought, unless he intended to cheat him. So the *ekka* man decided he'd have to use some other angle to get what he wanted. It was going to be hard to get anything on the basis of generosity, so maybe he'd give if he was scared. The *ekka* driver said, But don't assume, Lalaji, that I'm as nice and honest as I look. I'm honest with the honest but with the bad ones I'm a regular son of a bitch. So just tell me, if you want me to shine your shoes I will. But when it comes to the fee I don't do any favours for anybody. If I did, how would I eat?'

Sethji had been convinced that once he did battle with the *ekka* man he'd finish his journey without so much as a pice in payment. But after this speech his ears pricked up. 'Brother,' he said, 'I don't do anybody any favours either when it's a matter of money. But there are times when it's a matter of friendship and then one's more or less obliged to give in. You too will have to make sacrifices from time to time. There should be no sharp dealings and harsh treatment from friends.'

The *ekka* man observed dourly, 'I'm not kind to anybody. No teacher taught *me* lessons in kindness. I'm about as kind as a rat. Who'd dare hold back a penny from me? I don't let even my wife get away with a penny, so how should I act with others? Other *ekka* drivers flatter their moneylenders, they hang around their doors. But I kick the moneylenders out. Everybody wails when they hear my name. When I get my hands on some money, I gobble it up plain and simple. Just see, friend, what you can get out of me, you can cart off anything I've got in my house —if you can.'

Sethji felt he was coming down with fever. He thought, 'This devil won't let me off without getting his money. If I'd known this calamity was in the offing I wouldn't have got into his *ekka* for anything. Whoever wore his feet out from such a little walk? If I had to fork over money like this every day business would be ruined.'

Sethji was a pious soul. He had sacrificed to Shiva from the time he'd reached the age of reason and never once neglected the ceremony. Surely Shiva the Benevolent Lord would not fail to come to his aid on this occasion. Concentrating on the Lord, he said, 'Khan Sahib, extort from somebody else, but you'll have to cope with the police too, they don't show favouritism to anybody.'

102

The *ekka* driver burst out laughing. 'On the contrary,' he said, 'they pay *me*. Whenever I find a victim I invite him in at once for a low rate and set out for the police station. I get my fare and I get a reward too. Who dares protest? I don't even have a license but I drive my *ekka* merrily right through the market. No bastard can touch me. I do best where there's the biggest crowd. I pick up the finest people and take them to the police station. Who comes out on top at the police station? There are twenty excuses to hold people. If it's a man they say it's suspected that he went chasing after a certain woman or if it's a woman they say that she's run away in a huff from her father-in-law's house. Then who can say anything? The police inspector may want to get out of it but even he can't leave. Don't think I'm honest. I'm a son of a bitch. When passengers don't agree on the fare I take them to the police station and get two for one. If they even make a squeak, I roll up my sleeves and get ready to take care of them — then there's nobody who can stand up to me.'

Sethji was aghast. True, he held his staff in his hand but he felt too weak to use it. He'd really got himself into a mess —there was no telling what evil omens had marked his leaving the house. If he fell foul of this wretch he might be laid up for a week or more. From now on he'd have to use his wits and get down and away as well as he could. Humble as a wet cat he said, 'Very well, Khan Sahib, stop now, we've reached my village. Tell me, how much do I owe you?'

The *ekka* man whipped the horse all the more and said roughly, 'Consider how much I've earned, brother. If you hadn't got on I could have taken three passengers. I would have been paid four *annas* from each one of them, which makes twelve. I'll just ask you for eight.'

Sethji was thunderstruck. In his whole life he'd never paid so much for a ride. Under no circumstances could he pay such a fare for a distance like this. In every man's life there are occasions when he takes no heed of the consequences; for Sethji this was such an occasion. If it had been a matter of one or two *annas* then (though they would have been like drops of his own blood) he would have given them. But for eight *annas* — why, it was half a rupee — he was ready not only for an argument but even a scuffle. Fully resolved, he sat firmly in his place.

At this moment they reached a hut at the edge of the road. The *ekka* stopped, Sethji stepped down, took a two-*anna* coin from the

knot in his *dhoti* and reached to give it to the *ekka* driver, who
scowled back at him, accepting the fact that he'd lost this round.
The savour of the struggle had gone sour, it set his teeth on edge.
Souring it for Sethji as well was the only consolation. Gently he said,
'Take it as a gift from me to buy your kids some candy. Allah keep
you in safety.'

Sethji took out another *anna* and said, 'Enough, now wag your
tongue all you like, I won't give a pice more.'

'No, master, as you yourself would say, how are we poor people
going to feed our children? We people are human too, *huzoor*.'

In the meantime a woman had come from inside the hut. She
wore a pink sari and was chewing on *paan*. She said, 'You took a
long time this morning.' Then she looked at Sethji. 'Fine, today you
got a high-class passenger, so I suppose you're in a mood for some
mischief. You must have hooked on a coin — hand it over this
minute.'

With this she came up to Sethji and said, 'Sit down on our *charpoy*
and rest, Lala. It's great luck that we've got a glimpse of you so early
in the morning.'

A languorous fragrance came from her clothes. Sethji was all
attention and he leered at her. The woman was graceful, saucy,
mettlesome and tempting. The image of his wife rose before his
eyes: lumpish, flabby, clumsy, her clothes musty. Sethji was not in
the least of an amorous disposition but this time his eyes were
overwhelmed. Trying not to·stare at her he took a seat on the
*charpoy*. He was still a mile off from his destination but he didn't so
much as think of that.

The woman picked up a small fan and began to wave it over
Sethji. With every motion of her hand a whiff of fragrance hit him
and intoxicated him. He'd never experienced such bliss. He was
used to looking at everything with disgust, but now his very body
was drunk. He tried to take the fan out of her hand.

'It's too much trouble for you, let me do the fanning.'

'Nonsense, Lalaji, you're in our home. Won't you let me take even
this little trouble over you? What else would be fitting for us to do?
Do you have far to go? It's late now — where are you headed for?'

Sethji turned his old sinner's eyes away and restrained his wicked
thoughts. He said, 'There's a village I have to go to, not far from
here. I'll be coming back right past here this evening.'

Delighted she said, 'So you'll be here again today! And where would you be going in the evening? For once you ought to have a little fun away from your house. Who knows when we'll meet again!'

The *ekka* man came in and said in Sethji's ear, 'Get your money out and I'll buy some snacks.'

Silently Sethji took out an eight *anna* coin and gave it to him.

Then the driver asked, 'Shall I fetch some sweets for you? We can find some here worthy of you, they'll sweeten your mouth.'

Sethji said, 'No need to get me anything. Now this four-*anna* piece is for getting something nice for the children.'

Taking out the four-*anna* coin, Sethji threw it down with as much bold assurance as if he attached no value to it, but he wanted to see the expression on the woman's face, yet he was afraid lest she think that he was giving the coin as though he were paying somebody.

The *ekka* driver picked up the coin and was already leaving when his wife said, 'Give that four-*anna* bit back to Sethji! Aren't you ashamed of snatching it up like that? Take this rupee from me and go get eight *annas* worth of sweets.'

She took out a rupee and flung it down. Sethji was embarrassed — that a poor wife of an *ekka* driver who wasn't worth a brass farthing should show so much hospitality that she would dig out a whole rupee, well, how could he stand for that? 'No, no,' he said, 'I won't permit it. Take back your rupee.' His delighted eyes gobbled her up. 'I'll give a rupee, take this and get eight *annas* worth.'

The *ekka* man went off then to see to the sweets and snacks, and his wife said to Sethji, 'It's going to take him some time —while he's gone have some *paan.*'

Sethji looked around him, for he could not take *paan* made by these people. 'But there's no *paan* shop around here,' he said.

'What,' she said, giving him a teasing glance, 'won't the *paan* I make be as good as what you get from a shop?'

Embarrassed, Sethji said, 'No, no, I didn't mean that. But aren't you Muslim?'

Playfully insistent she said, 'God's oath, for saying that, I'll feed you *paan* and then leave you.'

Then she took a betel leaf from a *paan* box and walked towards Sethji. For a moment he hemmed and hawed, then stretched out with both hands trying to push her away and shut his lips tight, but when she would in no wise accept his refusal Sethji made a mad dash to escape. He left his staff on the *charpoy.* After he'd run about twenty steps he stopped, panting, and said, 'Look, you shouldn't go against somebody's religion like that. If we people take food you've touched we're defiled.'

Then she began to chase him. He ran again. He hadn't had to run like this for fifty years. His *dhoti* came undone and started to fall off but there was no time to tie it up again. The poor fellow was veritably flying on the wings of religion. At some moment or other his moneybag slipped from the knot at his waist. When he stopped after another ten yards to pull up his *dhoti* he no longer had the purse. He turned back and looked. The *ekka* man's wife showed him the purse in her hand and beckoned to him to come back. But religion meant even more than money to Sethji. He went another few steps, but then he stopped again.

Suddenly his piety asserted itself. Could he throw religion over for a few rupees? He'd get plenty more rupees but where would he get another soul?

With these thoughts he took his way like a dog mauled in a dogfight, his tail drooping, and every so often he stopped to turn back and see whether those devils were coming after him.

# A Car-Splashing

Well, it's like this: early in the morning I finish off my bath and my prayers, paint a vermillion circle on my forehead, get into my yellow robe and wooden sandals, tuck my astrological charts under my arm, grab hold of my stick — a regular skull-cracker — and start out for a client's house. I was supposed to settle the right day for a wedding; it was going to earn me at least a rupee. Over and above the breakfast. And my breakfast is no ordinary breakfast. Common clerks don't have the courage to invite me to a meal. A whole month of breakfasts for them is just one day's meal for me. In this connection I fully appreciate rich gentlemen and bankers — how they feed you, how they feed you! So generously that you feel happy all over! After I get an idea of the generosity of the client I accept his invitation. If somebody puts on a long face when it's time to feed me I lose my appetite. How can anybody feed you if he's weeping? I can't digest a meal like that at all. I like a client who hails me with, 'Hey Shastriji, have some sweets!' whom I can answer, 'No, friend — not yet.'

It had rained a lot during the night. There were puddles everywhere on the road. I was walking along all wrapped up in my thoughts when a car came along splashing through the puddles. My face got spattered. And then what do I see but my *dhoti* looking as though somebody mixed up a mess of mud and flung it all over it. My clothes were ruined; apart from that, I was filthy, to say nothing of the money lost. If I'd caught those people in the car I'd have done a job on them they wouldn't forget. I stood there, helpless. I couldn't go to a client's house in this state and my own house was at least a full mile away. The people in the street were all clapping to ridicule me. I never was in such a mess. Well, old heart, what are you going to do now? If you go home what will the wife say?

I decided in a trice what my duty was. I got together about a dozen stones from all around and waited for the next car. I'd show them a Brahman's power.

It wasn't even ten minutes before a car came into sight. Oh no! It was the same car. He'd probably gone to get the master from the station and was returning home. As soon as it got close I let fly a rock, I shot it out with all my strength. The gentleman's cap went flying and landed on the side of the road. The car slowed down. I fired again. The window-pane smashed to pieces and one piece even landed on the fine gentleman's cheek drawing blood. The car stopped and the gentleman got out and came toward me, gave me a punch and said, 'You swine, I'll take you to the police!' I'd scarcely heard him when, throwing my books down on the ground, I grabbed him by the waist, tripped him and he fell with a smack in the mud. I jumped on top of him at once and gave him a good twenty punches one after the other until he got dizzy. In the meantime his wife got out. High-heeled shoes, silk sari, powdered cheeks, lipstick, mascara. She began to poke at me with her umbrella. I left the husband and wielding my stick said, 'Lady, don't meddle in men's business or you may get a whack and a bruise and I'd be very sorry about that.'

The gentleman found the occasion to pick himself up and give me a kick with his booted feet. I got a real knock in the knee. Losing patience, I struck out with my stick, getting him in the legs. He fell like a tree when you chop it down. Memsahib came running brandishing her umbrella. I took it away from her without any trouble and threw it away. The driver had been sitting in the car all this time. Now he got out too and came rushing at me with a cane. I brought my stick down on him too and he fell flat. A whole mob had gathered to see the fun. Still lying on the ground the sahib said, 'You rogue, we'll hand you over to the police!'

I wielded my stick again and wanted to thump him on the skull but he folded his hands and said, 'No, no, *baba*, we won't go to the police. Forgive me.'

I said, 'All right, leave the police out of it or I'll crack you over the skull. I'd get six months at the most for it but I'd break you of the habit. You drive along and splash up mud and you're blind with conceit. You don't give a damn who's in front of you or alongside of you.'

One of the onlookers said, '*Arrey*, Maharaj! These drivers know perfectly well they're splashing and when some man gets drenched they think it's great fun and laugh at him. You did well to give one of them a lesson.'

'You hear what the people are saying?' I shouted at the sahib. He gave a dirty look toward the man who'd spoken and said to him, 'You're lying, it's a complete lie.'

'You're still just as rude, are you! Shall I have another go at you with the stick?'

'No, *baba*,' he said humbly. 'It's true, it's true. Now are you satisfied?'

Another bystander said, 'He'll tell you what you want to hear now but as soon as he's back in his automobile he'll start the same old business all over again. Just put 'em in their cars and they all think they're related to the maharaja.'

'Tell him to admit he's wrong,' said another.

'No, no, make him hold on to his ears and do kneebends.'

'And what about the driver? They're all rogues. If a rich man's puffed up, that's one thing, but what are you drivers so conceited about? They take hold of the wheel and they can't see straight any more.'

I accepted the suggestion that master and driver hold on to their ears and do kneebends, the way you punish little children, while Memsahib counted. 'Listen, Memsahib,' I said, 'you've got to count a whole hundred bends, not one less but as many over as you like.'

Two men drew the master up by his hands, two others that gentleman-driver. The poor driver's leg was bruised but he began to do the knee-bends. The master was still pretty cocky; he lay down and began to spew out gibberish. I was furious and swore in my heart that I wouldn't let him go without doing a hundred knee-bends. I ordered four men to shove the car off the edge of the road.

They set to work at once. Instead of four, fifty men crowded around and began to shove the car. The road was built up very high with the land below it on either side. If the car had slid down it would have smashed to pieces. The car had already reached the edge of the road when the sahib let out a groan and stood up and said, '*Baba*, don't wreck my car, we'll do the knee-bends.'

I ordered the men to stand off. But they were all enjoying them selves and nobody paid any attention to me. But when I lifted up the stick and ran for them they all abandoned the car and the sahib, shutting his eyes, began to do the knee-bends.

After ten of them I said to the Memsahib, 'How many has he done?'

Very snooty, she said, 'I wasn't counting.'

'Then sahib's going to be groaning and moaning all day long, I

109

won't let him go. If you want to take him home in good health count the knee-bends, then I'll let him go.'

The sahib saw that without his punishment he wouldn't get away with his life, so he began the knee-bends again. One, two, three, four, five . . .

Suddenly another car came into view. Sahib saw it and said very humbly, 'Panditji, take pity on me, you are my father. Take pity on me and I won't sit in a car again.'

I felt merciful and said, 'No, I don't forbid you to sit in your car, I just want you to treat men like men when you're in it.'

The second car was speeding along. I gave a signal. All the men picked up rocks. The owner of this car was doing the driving himself. Slowing down he tried to creep through us gradually when I advanced and caught him by the ears, shook him violently and after giving him a slap on both cheeks, said, 'Don't splash with the car, understand? Move along politely.' But he began to gabble until he saw a hundred men carrying rocks, then without any more fuss he went on his way.

A minute after he left another car came along. I ordered fifty men to bar the road; the car stopped. I gave him a few slaps too but the poor fellow was a gentleman. He took them as though he enjoyed them and continued his journey.

Suddenly a man said, 'The police are coming.'

And everybody took to his heels. I too came down off the road and sidling into a little lane I disappeared.

# From Both Sides

Pandit Shyamsarup was a young lawyer of Patna. He was not like those elderly young men who often appear in polite society these days, all of whose physical and intellectual strength, understanding and sense, outer and inner resources, resides in their tongue. Not at all, our Panditji did not belong to that class of elderly young men. He was one of those joyous fellows who used the tongue less, heart and brain, hand and foot more. Once a principle had become established in his heart he followed it completely. One of his great virtues was that he did not take on many different cases all at once. Those people who surrounded him pleading, their hands stretched out, got nothing at all. If simple people hope for some practical help from a person who is the secretary of a dozen associations and the president of half a dozen societies, well let them. But nobody sensible would, for all that poor fellow's strength is dissipated via his overworked tongue. Panditji no doubt understood this subtle point.

He had established a little society for the uplift of Untouchables and devoted his leisure time and a small part of his income to this charitable enterprise. Evenings when he left the court he would have a light meal, then take his bicycle and ride to the villages close outside the city. There he would sometimes sit to chat with the tanners, sometimes among the scavengers to converse with them in their unsophisticated speech concerning morals and behaviour. He would take their children on his lap, treat them affectionately, and on Sundays, or when it was a holiday, he would go and show magic lantern shows for them. Throughout the year his company and his sympathy did much for the improvement of the Untouchables of his district. The eating of dead cattle was completely stopped. And if the consumption of liquor did not altogether cease, nevertheless Hamid Khan, the police inspector, was much displeased no doubt from the decrease in the fights and rows that liquor had formerly caused every day.

Gradually Panditji's sympathy developed a fraternal relationship with the Untouchables. In his district there were 300 villages and the number of low-caste people was no less than 6,000. Panditji had a friendly, brotherly affection for all of them. He attended their weddings and behaved with them according to their customs. If there was some altercation among them very often a petition for judgment would be brought to Panditji. It was not possible for him to hear of one of them being ill without his going to find out about the nature of the man's sickness. In Indian medicine he had acquired a little skill; he would attend the sick man and if he found him in difficult straits would help him along with money. But for the most part his love and sympathy were sufficient in themselves. For such achievements money was not so necessary as disinter-ested humanitarianism and the zeal for social service. After a whole year of his enthusiastic and unflaggingly sympathetic endeavours, a sort of revolution had been produced in this community. Their houses and huts, their eating and drinking habits, their rituals and customs, all seemed to have undergone some reform, and the most important thing was that these people had learned to respect them. Formerly two or three ignorant *zamindars* had caused them trouble but when they saw that these people had acquired a different spirit they left them alone. A few silly people wanted to institute proceedings with the police in this matter; Inspector Hamid Khan himself was also on the look-out for a little profit, but what did these scavengers and tanners possess which could make it worth his while? Panditji's ties with them went on growing even stronger, reaching such a point that at last, at the wedding of the tanner community's headman's daughter, he sat down and ate with them.

*

Pandit Shyamsarup's wife was named Kolesari Devi. Like the general run of Indian women she loved her husband with all her heart and soul. She had only a very limited knowledge of reading and writing, but through living with Panditji she had become somewhat acquainted with community and cultural problems. But —whether you call it a human weakness or a natural reaction — she could not tolerate anyone else's criticism. She herself was not sharp-tongued nor did she get involved in arguments. But any stinging word, any heart-searing taunt produced something like an ulcerous wound on her heart. She listened only to hear and had

112

never learned at all to give an answer, but in her heart she was accustomed to suffer anguish. Panditji was acquainted with this peculiarity of hers, so he never uttered a word that might wound her.

Several years ago at the time Panditji had just begun his law practice they had something of a struggle to make ends meet. On the first day of a new sign of the zodiac, Kolesari had observed the occasion with a bit of charity, distributing five rupees worth of *kichri* to the poor. Panditji returned empty-handed from court after a day of profitless labour and, finding out what she had done, became furious. He said angrily, 'I have to break my back for every pice and you waste the household money. If that's the sort of person you are you ought to have told your father to marry you to some Maharaja!' Kolesari listened with her head bowed, made no answer, neither protested nor wept, but for a full six months she suffered from fever and weakness of the liver, and Panditji learnt a lesson to last him his whole life.

Well, when Panditji returned from eating at Ramphal Chaudhri's house the news spread like wildfire throughout the city. The next day — it may have been Somvari Amavas — Kolesari went to take a ritual dip in the Ganges. Women from other wealthy families of the city had also come to bathe. When they saw Kolesari they began to whisper among themselves. One woman, who appeared to be of some aristocratic family, said to the woman next to her, 'Just look at the fine lady there — her husband goes around eating with Untouchables and she comes to bathe in the Ganges!' Kolesari heard her, as it was intended she should. In just the way the potter's thread is sucked into the tender clay the harsh remark penetrated her heart. She grew agitated, she felt as though she had been stabbed with a knife. She forgot all about bathing and hastily made her way back home. The serpent's poison had seeped into every one of her veins. She cooked the morning meal for Panditji and served it to him. He set out for court — a wealthy client was in trouble. In his good spirits about this he had not even noticed his wife's frowning countenance. When he came back elated in the afternoon he found her lying down with her face covered. Alarmed, he said, 'Kola, why are you lying down? You never do at this hour. Are you ill?' Kolesari sat up and said, 'I'm perfectly all right, I just felt like lying down.' But this answer was not sufficient to reassure Panditji. If she was feeling well, then why was there no red from

113

*paan* on her lips, why was her hair dishevelled and her face sad, and why hadn't ice been ordered for him? These were the thoughts that came rushing all together into Panditji's head. He changed clothes, had a snack, talked about this and that, even told her a few anecdotes. But the snake's poison was not drawn out by these spells. Kolesari still said nothing except an occasional 'Hm' or 'Uh.' The poison had closed up her ears.

It was now evening, time for Panditji's ride; he took out his bicycle and rode off. But the thought of Kolesari's apathy continued to trouble him. Today there was a wedding among the low-caste Pasis of Manjh village. When he arrived there the wedding procession had come from some distance away. The groom's people had insisted on liquor and the bride's had rejected the idea completely. The groom's people demanded that the women, according to a custom, should dance in the doorways. The bridal party said they no longer had any such custom. Panditji had been successful in Manjh village, but wedding parties were outside his sphere of influence. Both sides were disputing these points when Panditji arrived. He reasoned with them until they calmed down. On occasions like this he usually didn't return home until ten o'clock because his advice would produce a lot of heated discussion. But today his heart was not in his work. Kolesari's face, overcast with sadness, kept appearing before his eyes. He kept wondering if he could have said anything unpleasant to her but could not imagine that he had. Her depression, though, was not without a cause, there had to be something the matter. Troubled by these worries he returned home at seven o'clock.

*

Pandit Shyamsarup had his supper and went to bed. This time too Kolesari had eaten nothing. She still appeared downcast. Finally Panditji asked her, 'Kola, why are you sad?'

'I'm not sad,' she said.

'Aren't you feeling well?'

'Why shouldn't I be? Surely you can see I look perfectly healthy.'

'I don't agree,' said Panditji. 'There has to be some reason or other for you to be so sad. Don't you think I have the right to ask you about it?'

'You are the lord of my heart and soul. If you don't have the right, who does?'

'Then why this secrecy? I never hide my feelings from you.'

Lowering her eyes, Kolesari said, 'Am I hiding things?'

'Until now, no, but today you certainly are. Look at me, look into my eyes. People say that women can often gauge a man's love in one glance. But maybe before now you've never sounded the depths of my love. Believe me when I say that your low spirits today have really upset me. If you won't tell me even now, I'll think you have no faith in me.'

Kolesari's eyes filled with tears. She looked at Panditji and said, 'And will you pull out the thorn that's piercing my heart?'

Shyamsarup's hair stood on end. Distressed, he got up and with a trembling voice said, 'Kola! How unfair it is for you to ask me such a question. I'm ready to sacrifice myself and everything I have for you. You ought not to have such thoughts where I'm concerned.'

Kolesari had expected him to say something quite different. 'My God knows,' she said, 'that I have never doubted your love. I only asked you this question because I thought you would probably laugh at me when you heard why I was depressed. I knew that whatever I said, I shouldn't say it. I also knew that it would be painful for you to agree with me. So I wanted to hide it from you. That was all it was. It would have been forgotten in two or three months. But the way you've scolded me obliges me to tell you. The day you think I no longer have faith in you, well, you know that could only mean I'm dead. So now you're making me tell you.'

'Then tell me without being afraid, I'm on pins and needles to know.'

Said Kolesari, 'I want you to stop associating and eating with Untouchables.'

Just as the innocent prisoner sighs when he hears the sentence of punishment from the judge, so now Panditji drew a deep breath and, remaining silent for some time, went to lie down. Then he got up and said, 'Very well, I shall carry out your command. It's a violation of my feelings, quite true, but I won't object. Only tell me at least, did something happen to cause you to ask this of me or did it just occur to you for no special reason?'

'The women have been insulting me and I can't bear it. I've no right to ask them to stop talking, they're free to say whatever they want. It's from you that I can claim that right, and so I've asked you.'

115

'Very well, and so it will be.'

'Now I have yet one more request to make. Men are not worried by taunts and mockery, but women are weak, our hearts are weak,. we're easily wounded by cutting remarks. But you're not to think about that at all. You mustn't violate your own feelings to spare me some insulting remarks. I'll listen to their taunts, and if I find it too painful I'll just stop going out and having anything to do with those women.'

Shyamsarup embraced Kolesari and said, 'Kola, I'll never agree to let you suffer insults on my account. I won't let any taunting wound your tender heart. Just be happy, and sing me one of your favourite songs.'

Kolesari was content. Her face brightened. She picked up the harmonium and began to sing in sweet soft tones:

'To meet with the beloved is painful, oh mad one . . ...'

*

A week passed and Panditji did not go out to the villages. He had accepted as his life's mission the establishment of fraternal relations with his Untouchable brothers, making them able to understand themselves as human beings, drawing them out of the toils of ignorance and falsehood; and when he found an obstacle in the path of this work it is hardly surprising that he became troubled and melancholy. Man finds pleasure in life so long as he continues to believe that he is performing his duty. In the world there are numerous creatures of God who do not know what their individual or community duty is. But it's a mistake to call such people human Those people who have an irresistible urge to do evil, knowing what they do is bad, cannot desist from doing it, and if they don't find the suitable occasion to do it they will profit from occasions even less suitable. The gambler, no matter how much you explain and threaten, cannot leave off gambling. Even if you shut the alcoholic in a cage, as soon as he is free he will head straight for the tavern. Such is the intoxication of doing wrong. All day Panditji was involved with his work, but in the evening, which was the special time for his pleasant recreation, he became very restless, and to sacrifice his social commitment for a personal obligation had to go violently against his feelings. When he would sit in his garden alone and argue about this with himself at times he became irritated at his weakness and feel like going to Kolesari and saying flatly that he would not give up his duty for personal caste pride. He wanted to tell her, 'I can do anything so you'll be pleased with me, only not this one thing.' But alas, what effect could these words have on Kola? Poor dear crazy noble Kola! he thought, wouldn't her love for me suffer? No, Kola, dearer than my life, how stupid I'd be if I considered myself unlucky after finding someone as precious as you. For your happiness I could endure anything. I believe that if you knew right now how troubled I am, I'm sure you'd consider enduring insults a mere nothing, you'd be ready to be slandered by the whole world. What do I have to match your unique love? One's duty to society is no doubt a very lofty obligation. But sometimes and in particular conditions one must abandon one's civic duty for considerations of caste. King Rama's duty was to stay in Ayodhya and mete out justice and increase the prosperity of his subjects, but he regarded this patriotic duty as nothing in comparison with honoring his father's oath, which was his private and personal duty. It was King Dasharatha's patriotic duty to hand over his throne to Rama because he knew that Rama was adored by the populace of Ayodhya. But he sacrificed that responsibility so he could honor his oath, which was a private obligation.

But Panditji's mistake was to think that Kolesari did not understand his emotional turmoil. From that night when they had had that conversation not a moment passed when her heart was not stricken with the thought that she had acted very unjustly toward him. She no longer saw on his face that radiance which is the gift of a contented heart. He no longer enjoyed his meals. When he spoke it was as though his thoughts were elsewhere; if he laughed it seemed that he was merely imitating laughter. In every word one could sense his attempt to conceal his emotions. To Kolesari his feelings were as clear as though reflected in a mirror. Time and time again she reproached herself. 'How selfish I am! How mean, how petty — because I gave way before the insults of an ill-tempered woman I have been so unjust to him. For my sake he has done so much violence to himself — but I couldn't stand the hurt from an insult.' As she thought this she wanted to free him from the obligation she'd imposed on him, but Panditji would never give her the least occasion for doing so.

*

For a week Pandit Shyamsarup's Untouchable brothers were patient. They thought he might be ill or busy pleading a case or perhaps he had gone out of town. With such thoughts they consoled themselves. But after a week they could bear it no longer. A whole crowd of them, in homespun jackets, white turbans on their heads, leather shoes on their feet and wooden staves over their shoulders, came to his house to ask if he was all right. There was no way out for Panditji but to invent some pretext to explain his breach of duty, and his pretext was that his wife was ill. From evening until morning the line of people was unbroken. When people from one village left, those from another would arrive and Panditji was obliged to make the same excuse to all of them. What else was he to tell them?

A second week passed, but the illness lingered in Panditji's house. One evening he was sitting in his doorway when Ramdin the Pasi, Phallu the head man and Gobari came bringing Hakim Nadirali Khan Sahib the basketmaker with them. Hakim Sahib was the Bu Ali Sena* of his time. As Satan fled from Bu Ali Sena's incantations so did illness as soon as it spotted Hakimji, no matter how long-lasting and chronic it was, take to its heels. And generally along with the illness the sick man also passed away. As soon as Panditji saw Hakim Sahib he became flustered. My game is up, he thought, what's my next move? Where did those wretched people get the idea to bring this fellow with them to confront me? A fellow who can't be put off but will come straight to the heart of the matter. But time was urgent, there was no leisure for further reflection. At that moment in Panditji's heart, despite loving Kolesari more than a thousand lives, the thought occurred: 'Would that God could give her just a touch of fever only for a little while.' That way somehow or other he'd get out of this fix. But when does death ever come simply because you call it?

Racking his brains, coughing, shifting from side to side and bowing his head, Panditji said, 'Well, it's one of those illnesses that women have but now, thank you very much, her condition is improving. At present she's taking medicine prescribed by the English lady doctor. You know, this is the age of English civilization, people have more confidence in English remedies and the patient gets well with the help of the doctor or hakim he has confidence

---

* A renowned Persian physician and astrologer.

118

in. And that's why I didn't trouble you.'

'What you say is true,' Hakim Sahib agreed. 'Which lady doctor is treating her?' Panditji scratched his head once again and looking all about him said, 'Miss Bogan.'

At this moment Pandit Shyamsarup was obliged to call his legal skills into play. For today when he rose he surely had glimpsed the face of some inauspicious person. Circumstances, instead of improving, were steadily getting worse because while they'd been talking Kallu Chaudhri, Hardas the farmer and Jugga the washerman came into view and with them Miss Bogan herself, riding along on horseback. Panditji turned deathly pale. Silently he cursed Miss Bogan roundly — what had brought this wretched sister-in-law of Satan here at just this moment? But it was no time to fret. He immediately rose from his chair, shook hands with Miss Bogan and without giving her any chance to ask anything seized her hand, drew her into the women's drawing-room, and made her sit in a chair. Then he went at once to Kolesari and said, 'We're in a sticky situation just now. I've been telling those people you were ill as an excuse to get them off my back somehow or other, but today they've brought Hakim Nadirali Khan and Miss Bogan and got me in a corner. I've just left Miss Sahiba in the drawing-room. Tell me — what am I to do?'

Kolesari said, 'Well, I'll just get sick, that's all.'

Panditji laughed. 'I wish illness only on your enemies.'

'Their being sick won't be much use right now. Go and bring her in. I'll wrap myself up in a blanket and lie down.'

So Panditji went out to fetch Miss Bogan, Kolesari wrapped herself up from head to toe in the blanket and feigned moaning. Miss Bogan looked at her tongue, took her temperature and, looking worried, said, 'The illness is well entrenched. It's a case of hysteria. There's no superficial fever, but there's fever in her liver. You have a headache, don't you?'

'My head's splitting,' said Kolesari.

'And I don't imagine you feel hungry?'

'I don't even want to look at food.'

Miss Bogan had completed her diagnosis. She wrote a prescription and took her leave. Hakim Nadirali Khan regarded it as useless to wait any longer; in any case, he had taken a fee in advance.

Panditji came out and said to his well-wishers, 'I'm afraid you people have been put to this trouble for nothing. My wife's health is really improving now. Anyway, I'm most grateful to you.'

When the visitors had gone Panditji came inside and had a good laugh; when he'd finished laughing he began to think that today he'd had to do what he shouldn't have done. At least, would his wife relent now? But Kolesari did not laugh.

*

Pandit Shyamsarup ate his dinner and lay down to sleep, but sleep did not come to Kolesari. She tossed and turned, sometimes got up and sat or wandered around the room, sometimes opened a book and sat beside the lamp, but nothing appealed to her. In the way the moonbeams danced beneath the trees swaying in the breeze, so did her reflections go on troubling her. She thought of what a wrong she had done to her husband. 'Alas, how he must have suffered today!' she thought. 'Because of me, he who had never uttered a lie in his life, was forced to invent and weave a web of lies. If he had been disposed to tell lies, today the vast estate of Didarganj would have been under our control. I've forced this wretched predicament on a man who would be ready to die for the sake of truth. And only because I am the partner of his destiny. My job is to show him sympathy, help him in virtuous undertakings and console him. But instead of all these obligations I've forced him into a web of lies. God forgive me for my sin.'

'My duty was to share with him and help him in his charitable works. How decent, how honest, how well-intentioned, how generous these village people are! And I stopped my husband from serving these noble souls, only because a foul-mouthed woman insulted me, and not content with that I've now compelled him to tell lies as well. Despite this petty high-handedness of mine my husband, more virtuous than virtuous, nobler than noble, compassionate and pure-souled, has kept his heart exactly as before. He thinks I'm a fool, ignorant, weak, stubborn, and hide these weaknesses in the bosom of his vast love. How mean I am! I'm not worthy even to wash his feet! How he laughed today when Miss Bogan left. How pure his laughter, and only to reassure me, only to dispel my distress. My darling! I'm bad from head to toe, I'm vile. In your love for me keep thinking of me as a crazy slave-girl.'

While she reflected she looked once at Pandit Shyamsarup's face; a pleasant dream had made it bloom, a slight smile played on his lips. When she observed this Kolesari's heart seemed to mount on a wave of love. Just as the tide rises from the sea, so at times a tide of love rises in the human heart. At this moment a river of love began to flow in Kolesari's eyes. Restless with this love she snuggled close to her husband's chest, which was the shelter of her love. Just as a thief freely plunders the treasure of a sleeping householder, so did Kolesari unrestrainedly plunder the treasure of her sleeping husband's love, and just as the thief fears that the master of the house may waken, so did Kolesari's heart pound lest he might wake. A woman's love is not easily seen with the eyes; modesty and shame incline her not to lift up her eyes. She fears that this passion may be taken for show or affectation so she, as it were, puts fetters on the feet of her love. At this moment Kolesari was free of such inhibiting thoughts.

When the tide rises in the sea pieces of wreckage from sunken ships and shells are thrown up on the shore. This tide rising from Kolesari's heart drew out the thorn that had been tormenting her.

*

The next day when Panditji came home from court he said to Kolesari, 'I've been asked to go out of town for two or three days.'

'Why, where will you go?' Kolesari asked him.

'I've taken a case out in one of the country districts. I'm going to Bhagalpur.'

'Are you leaving right now?'

'It's arranged for tomorrow.'

Panditji set out for Bhagalpur on the mail coach at six that evening and was busy pleading his case for the next four days. He'd promised to be gone only three days but it took four. Finally, on the fifth day he was free. He got back to Patna at three in the afternoon and walked to his house. When he entered his quarter he met Satpat Chaudhri of Manjh village. Panditji said, 'Chaudhriji, where are you rushing off to?'

Startled, Chaudhri looked up and said, 'Your honor, you were supposed to be back yesterday. Why were you delayed?'

'I couldn't get back yesterday. Is everything all right here?'

'Everything's fine, thank you. But today there are big doings at your house.'

'At my house?' Panditji asked, surprised. 'What's going on?'

'The mistress of the house has called a meeting. All our women got an invitation.'

Panditji was delighted. As he walked on he saw a hundred friendly faces coming toward him from all directions, as if a village wedding party was marching along. He greeted everyone, and when he reached his door it looked as though a festival was in full swing. A hundred men were sitting on the carpet smoking *hookahs*. They had come with the women Kolesari had invited. Panditji went straight to his own quarters. After he'd changed his clothes he said to the servant 'Don't let them know I'm back,' and began to watch the spectacle from the window of his study.

A white carpet had been spread in the courtyard. On it were sitting three or four hundred women dressed up in their village finery. Some were laughing, others chatting, and Kolesari was carrying around a tray of *paan*. She was giving sweets and toys to the children and fondling them affectionately. When the *paan* had all been distributed the singing began. Today Kolesari was also wearing a coarse sari and had taken off her jewels. She sat down with a drum and began to sing with the women.

Sitting at the window, Panditji watched all this. His heart swelled with an excess of joy. He longed to go to Kolesari and embrace her. After the singing had ended Kolesari, in straightforward language, gave the women counsel for fifteen minutes, and then the gathering broke up. Kolesari embraced the women as she saw them off. Among them was one extremely old woman. When she stepped forward to embrace Kolesari, Kolesari bowed down, touched the woman's feet with the hem of her sari and then touched her own forehead with it. When he observed this humble courtesy, Panditji sprang up for joy and jumped three times; he could not control himself. He left his study and walked into the courtyard. He signalled to Kolesari to come inside and there he embraced her. She began to ask about how he felt and why he had been delayed. She said, 'If you hadn't come today I would have gone to you myself.' But Panditji had no time to listen to such things. He hugged her again and again, his spirit unsatisfied, and so too his love. Embarrassed, Kolesari said, 'Enough, you're going to squander all your love in one day!'

'What can I say? I can't get enough. I long to love you to the limit of my love for you. You're a goddess, really!'

If Panditji had been given — well, not a kingdom but some district — he would not have been by any means so exuberant. When he had done pouring out his love he said to the women standing in the courtyard, 'Sisters, Kolesari wasn't sick. She had forbidden me to meet you, but today she herself has invited you and established a bond of sisterhood. You can't imagine how happy I am at this moment. Because of this joy I feel, I'm going to open banking houses for lending money in ten villages with one thousand rupees each and there you people can take out loans interest free. When you borrow money from the mahajans you're forced to pay one or two *annas* on the rupee. As soon as these banks are opened you'll be free from your bondage to the money-lenders, and the banks will be under the supervision of the one who invited you here today.'

All the women lifted up their arms and began to pray for his long life and prosperity. Kolesari said, 'Hurrah! he's thrown this botheration on me!'

Panditji smiled. 'When you've stuck your foot in the water you'll learn to swim.'

'Well, I do know something about keeping books,' said Kolesari.

'And the rest will come by itself,' said Panditji. 'But when did you learn to give advice? You used to be shy of talking to women. Only two weeks ago you forbade me to meet these people, today you consider them your sisters. Then it was your turn to make a move, and now its mine.'

Kolesari laughed. 'You spread a net to trap me.'

'The net,' said Panditji, 'was cast from both sides.'

# A Moral Victory

His Excellency the Viceroy was coming to Banaras. Government officials both high and low prepared to welcome him. In the meantime, the members of the Congress Party had given notice that they would call a general strike. This produced great consternation among the officials. On the other hand, they had set flags along the streets, cleaned everything up and raised a reception dais, on the other, police and soldiers with drawn bayonets were drilling in every street and alley. The officials were desperately trying to ensure that the strike would not occur, while the Congress was determined that it should. The officials might be able to count on brute strength but the Congress had the assurance of moral power. This time let there be a test to see which one would control the field.

From morning to night the magistrate rode out to threaten the shopkeepers that he'd put them in jail, that he'd have their shops looted, that he'd do this and do that. Folding their hands the shopkeepers would say, 'Your Lordship is a king, you can do whatever you want. But what are we to do? Those Congress people won't leave us alive. They'll have a sit-down strike on our doorsteps, they'll jump into wells, they'll fast — who knows, if a few of them give up their lives we'll be disgraced forever. If your Lordship can explain it to these Congress people we'll be very much obliged. It won't be any loss to us if we don't have to close our shops. The most important men in the country will be coming and if our shops are open we'll sell the most expensive merchandise and get double the price. But what can we do? We have no control over those devils.'

Even more disturbed than the officials were Rai Haranandan Sahib, Raja Lalchand and Khan Bahadur Maulvi Mahmud Ali. They did their utmost along with the magistrate and on their own as well. They summoned the shopkeepers to their homes, cajoled and threatened them, bullied the cart and buggy drivers, flattered the labourers. But they were so scared by that handful of Congress

workers that not one of them paid any attention to these gentlemen, and it reached the point where a neighbourhood greengroc-
er's wife boldly said, 'Your Lordships, you can have us all killed but
we won't open the shops! We don't intend to get ourselves
dishonoured.'

The biggest worry was that the workmen making the dais —
carpenters, smiths and the like — might strike. If they did it would
be a calamity. Rai Sahib said: 'Gentlemen, let's invite merchants
from other cities to open a separate market here.'

Khan Sahib said, 'There's not enough time left to arrange for
another market. Let's arrest the Congress agitators and confiscate
their property — then see whether or not we control them!'

'If we start making arrests,' Raja Lalchand said, 'the towns-people
will be even more aroused. If your Lordship tells Congress that if
they call off the strike they'll all get government jobs, why — since
most of them are unemployed — as soon as they hear your offer
they'll be wild with joy.'

But the magistrate accepted none of these proposals. And so it
went on until there were only three days left before the Viceroy's
visit.

*

Finally Raja Lalchand had an inspiration: why shouldn't they too
resort to moral pressure? After all, Congress had made a great show
in the name of religion and morality. The government ought to
imitate them, beat the tiger at its own tricks. They would have to
find a man who would go on a hunger strike, even fasting unto
death, until the shops opened. Such a man would have to be a
Brahman and someone the citizens respected and would pay attention to. Raja Sahib's colleagues thought it was a fine idea, they
jumped with enthusiasm. Rai Sahib said, 'That's it, we've cracked
their front! Fine, now which Brahman shall it be —Pandit Gadadhar
Sharma?'

'Certainly not,' said Raja Lalchand. 'Who pays any attention to
him? He only writes for the newspapers. What do the people of
Banaras know about him?'

'Then would Damri Ojha be our man?' Rai Sahib suggested.

'Not at all,' Raja Sahib said. 'Who knows him except for the
College students?'

125

'How about Pandit Moteram Shastri?'

'That's it, that's it!' Raja Sahib said. 'You've hit it on the head, he's certainly the man for us! We must send for him. He's learned, he's pious and — he's shrewd. If he's willing to help then we've won our game.'

Raja Sahib immediately despatched a message to Pandit Moteram. At that moment Shastriji was at his prayers. He no sooner heard this providential summons than he cut short his morning ritual and prepared to go. If Raja Sahib had summoned him, then what a windfall it might be! To his good wife he said, 'Today the moon's auspicious! Bring my clothes and I'll find out why they've sent for me.'

'Your food's ready,' his wife said. 'Go and eat — you don't know when you'll get back.'

But Shastriji did not think it proper to keep a man waiting so long. He put on his long green broadcloth jacket with the red fringe, wound a gold-embroidered scarf around his neck, then set a Banaras gold silk turban on his head. He put on a silk *dhoti* with a wide red border and stepped into his pattens. His Brahmanic glory radiated from his countenance. From a long way off it was plain that some great holy personage was approaching. People who met him on the road bowed their heads and many shopkeepers stood up to greet him. Today the very name of Banaras, it seemed, was illustrious only because of him, there was nobody else at all worth taking note of. And what a gentle soul, pausing to say a few words to the children! It was in this style that Panditji made his way to Raja Sahib's house. The three friends rose and greeted him. Khan Sahib said, 'Tell us, Panditji, how have you been feeling? By God, you're worthy of being put on display! You must weigh a good ten *maunds.*'

Rai Sahib said, 'For one *maund* of learning you need ten *maunds* of intellect. According to this rule, for every *maund* of intellect you need ten of flesh, otherwise who could lift up the burden?'

'You people don't understand,' Raja Sahib said, 'wisdom is like a cold: if it doesn't affect the head, it goes down into the body.'

Khan Sahib, said, 'But I've heard the great ones say that a fat man's the enemy of wisdom.'

'Your reckoning was wrong,' Rai Sahib said, 'otherwise you would surely have understood that if the ratio of mind to body is one to ten then the fatter the man the bigger the intellect.'

'From which it is proven,' Raja Sahib said, 'that the fatter the man the fatter the head.'

Pandit Moteram said, 'If I've been summoned to your noble presence because of my fat head, then why should I bother to bring my sharp wits too?'

After this exchange of pleasantries, Raja Sahib explained the present problem to Panditji as well as the plan for solving it which he had conceived. He said, 'So there it is. Just understand that this time your future prosperity is in your own hands. Probably nobody has ever had so magnificent an opportunity to decide his fortune. If there's no general strike, for the rest of your life you won't have to ask for anything from anybody. So you must resolve on such a fast that the whole town is shaken. Congress has gained its power by hiding behind a screen of religious piety — so you must manage to shock the religious sensibilities of the people.'

Gravely Moteram replied, 'This is not such a difficult job. I can perform ceremonies that bring the rain down from the skies, I can calm the small pox fever, I can raise or lower the price of grain. So it's no great matter to take care of those Congress people. Great British dignitaries who can read and write think no one can do the work I do. But they have no knowledge of the occult sciences.'

'Well then, sir,' said Khan Sahib, 'one must declare you a second God! Had we known the powers you have we wouldn't have worried for such a long time.'

'Sir,' Moteram said, 'I can locate hidden treasures, summon the dead — all I need is customers to appreciate my powers. It's not virtues that are lacking in the world but connoisseurs — that is to say, virtuous people — to appreciate them. As the Bhojpuri proverb has it, "Good things galore but a dearth of good folk."'

'Fine,' Raja Lalchand said. 'Now how much will you want for this ceremony?'

'Whatever your faith in me suggests.'

'Well, can you tell us just what sort of a ceremony you're going to perform?'

'It will be a total fast, during which I'll recite spells and prayers. If I don't cause a sensation in the city my name isn't Moteram.'

'And when will you start?'

'I can start right away. But first you might give me just a few rupees to offer in my invocations to the gods . . .'

And to be sure there was no shortage of rupees. Panditji took his money and set out for home in high spirits. But when he told the news to his wife, she looked worried and said, 'It was silly to get yourself into this mess! Since when can you tolerate being hungry? You'll be the laughing stock of the whole town, they'll die laughing. Better give them back their rupees.'

Moteram reassured her. 'Who says I can't stand being hungry? I'm not such a fool as to do this on an empty stomach. First of all, prepare a meal for me. Go out and get some pastry and fudge and *rasgoolas*. I'll simply stuff myself. Then I'll eat a pound of cream with almonds. Whatever room is left I'll fill with butter curds. Then we'll see how hungry I get! For three days I won't be able to draw a breath so who's going to be hungry! Our luck is on the upswing, we'd regret it if we hesitated now. If the market doesn't close, think of how rich I'll be. If it does, well, it's no money out of my pocket. I've already got my hands on a hundred rupees.'

While she set about preparing his meal, Pandit Moteram sent out the town crier with the news that that evening Moteram Shastri was going to discuss the country's political problems in the square before the Town Hall. People surely would come. Panditji had always stayed out of political matters; if he was to speak about them today everyone would be extremely curious to hear him for he had a great reputation in the city. At the appointed time a crowd of several thousand gathered. After all the proper preparations Panditji arrived from home. His belly was so stuffed that he could scarcely walk. As soon as he reached the square the audience stood up and bowed right to the ground in greeting.

Moteram said, 'Citizens, merchants, bankers and moneylenders! I've heard that after listening to the Congress people you have decided to close your shops on the occasion of the auspicious visit of the British Viceroy. What sort of ingratitude is this? Why, if he wanted the Viceroy could have you all shot out of cannons this very minute and the whole city plowed under as well. It's no joke, this man is a king! He overlooks your mistakes and takes pity on your poverty and you're ready to go out like sheep to the slaughter. If the Viceroy wishes he can close down the railway and the post offices and shut off all your supplies. Tell me, what could you do then? If he wanted, he could put everybody in Banaras in jail — tell me, what would you do then? Can you run away from him? Is there any place where you could find shelter? Therefore, if you have to remain in this country as his subjects why do you contrive all this mischief? Remember, your lives are in his power. If you let the rabble take over the town, then the whole city will be laid low with grief. Do you think you can stop a hurricane with a broom? Beware, anybody who closes up his shop! If anybody does, I tell you, I'll fast at this very spot until I die.'

One skeptic shouted, 'Sir, it will take you at least a full month of fasting to die — what can happen in three days?'

Moteram roared back, 'The breath of life doesn't reside in the body but in the head. If I want, I can escape this life this very minute by my yogic powers. I have warned you, now you know and your way is plain. Heed my words and you will prosper. Heed them not and you will be destroyed, you'll never be able to show your faces anywhere in the world. Enough! Understand this, here I take my seat.'

*

When they heard the news the town people were stunned. This latest trick of the officials left them bewildered. The Congress leaders at once pronounced it hypocritical. The Government supporters had given the Pandit some money and got up the whole fraud. When every other means — army, police and courts — had failed, they had devised this new trick. It was nothing else than political bankruptcy. Since when had Moteram Shastri been such a patriot that, concerned about the condition of the country, he would take a fast upon himself for it? Let him die of hunger indeed — in two days he'd give up. This new stratagem had to be nipped in the bud lest it actually succeed — imagine what it would be like if the government got its hands on a new weapon like this and used it all the time. The ordinary people were not so sophisticated that they would understand these mysteries, they would let themselves be bullied.

But the city merchants and money-lenders were most of them so under the thumb of their religion that these remonstrations had not the slightest effect on them. They said, 'Gentlemen, because of you people the Government has turned against us, they're ready to take action, put us out of business. How many will go bankrupt and not even be able to show their faces to the officials? When we used to go to them before the officials would say, "Come in, Sethji" and treat us with respect, but now they shove us around in the railway carriages and no one pays any attention. Whether you have an income or not, they glance at our account books and raise the taxes. We have borne all this and will go on bearing it, but we cannot accept leadership in religious matters from you people. When a noble, learned and pious Brahman renounces food and water because of us, then how can we eat and sleep with a quiet conscience? If he should die, what answer would we have ready for the Lord?'

The upshot of the matter was that not one of them heeded the Congress. At nine o'clock a deputation of merchants set out to attend on Panditji.

Now, today Panditji had eaten as much as he could, but eating as much as he could was no uncommon occurrence for him. About twenty days of every month he managed to get himself invited out to dine, and over-eating is natural when you're invited out. Seeing one's fellow-diners one is inclined to rivalry and to demonstrating one's appreciation to the host, and above all because of the excellence of the food itself one consumes more than an ordinary amount. Panditji's appetite had never failed to meet these challenges successfully. So at this moment, at the arrival of the dinner hour, his resolution somewhat wavered. Not that he was actually beset by hunger, but at meal times if his stomach was not absolutely crammed then in his imagination he began to suffer the pangs of appetite. Such was the condition of Shastriji at this moment. He was tempted to call some street vendor and help himself to a few sweets, but the officials had posted several soldiers around for his protection. They would not hear of withdrawing. Panditji's vast wisdom was now busy with the problem of how to get rid of those kill-joys. What reason was there to post the louts there? Was he a prisoner, were they afraid he'd run away?

It was possible the authorities had put him in this situation because they feared the Congress people might try to use force to remove him. Nobody knew the tricks they might try, and of course it was the duty of the authorities to protect Panditji from any such disgraceful underhanded conduct.

Panditji was sunk in these reflections when the merchants' deputation arrived. He was reclining comfortably, propped up on his elbows. The leaders touched his feet in greeting and said, 'Maharaj, why have you brought this wrath down upon us? We shall respectfully do whatever you command. Rise up and take food and drink. We didn't know you really were going to take this vow or we would have begged you not to before you did. Be gracious to us. It's long past dinner time now. We will never disregard what you tell us.'

'These Congress people will ruin you,' Panditji said. 'They're already sinking and they'll take you with them. If the market's closed, it will be your loss alone. What does the Government care? You'll starve to death if you go on strike. Does the Government care? You'll go to jail and hard labour. The Government doesn't care! I don't know what crazy idea's got into your skulls to cut off your own noses to spite others. Don't listen to those rogues. Why do you want to shut up the shops?'

'Maharaj,' a merchant answered, 'so long as the whole city's agreed on it how can we oppose them? If the Congress gives the order to have us looted, who'll help us? Rise up and take food! Tomorrow we'll hold a meeting and let you know whatever happens.'

'So go and have your meeting and then come back,' Moteram said.

As the disappointed deputation was about to leave, Panditji said, 'Would any of you happen to have a pinch of snuff?'

One gentleman took out his snuff box and gave it to him.

When they were gone Moteram said to the policemen, 'What are you standing around here for?'

'It's the magistrate's order,' one of them answered. 'What can we do?'

'Get moving,' Panditji said.

'Can we go on your say-so? If we do we'll be dismissed tomorrow — will you feed us?'

'I'm telling you to go away. If you don't, then I will myself. Am I some kind of prisoner to have you surrounding me?'

'Just go then,' the policemen said. 'If you think you can.'

'Why shouldn't I be able to? Have I committed any crime?'

'So, go,' the policeman said, 'and then we'll see what happens.'

Panditji leapt up in all his Brahmanical splendour and slapped the policeman so hard that he fell back several steps. The others lost their nerve — they'd all assumed he was a flabby weakling, but when they saw how fierce he was they silently slipped away.

Moteram now sat gazing here and there to see if some food vendor was in sight so that he could get something from him. But then he reflected that if such a person said a word to anyone people would begin to clap their hands in derision. Decidedly, he would have to operate so deftly that not a soul would suspect a thing. These were predicaments that tested one's wits. He went on struggling for a moment with this thorny problem.

By chance at that instant a peddler appeared. Eleven o'clock had just struck, there was complete stillness on all sides. 'Peddler!' Panditji called out, 'Oh, peddler!'

The peddler said, 'Tell me — what shall I give you? You're hungry, aren't you? Giving up food and water is work for holy men, not for the likes of you and me.'

'What the devil are you talking about?' said Panditji. 'Am I less than any holy man? If I want, why I can go for months without feeling hungry or thirsty. I called you only because I want you to give me your oil lamp. I just wanted to see what was crawling around — I was afraid it was a snake.'

The peddler handed his oil lamp to Panditji, who had begun to scan the ground about him. Suddenly the lamp fell from his grasp and went out. The oil overflowed and he gave it another knock so that whatever oil was left spilled out too.

Shaking the lamp the peddler said, 'Maharaj, there's no oil left in it at all. I'd have sold another four pice worth of goods tonight if you hadn't put me out of business.'

'Brother, it's only the hand — because I dropped the lamp do you want me to cut off my hand? Take these pice and go somewhere and fill your lamp with oil.'

The peddler took the coins. 'After I've got it filled why should I come back here?'

'Just set your basket down and go and get your oil quickly. Otherwise, a snake might bite me and then my death will be on your head. There's some animal around for sure. See, it's crawling! Now it's disappeared. Run, lad, and come back with the oil, I'll look after your basket. If you're afraid, take your money with you.'

The vendor fell into a quandary. If he took his money from the basket then he feared lest Panditji think ill of him, believing that he considered the Brahman dishonourable. But if he left it who could say what Panditji intended? Nobody's intentions remained honourable all the time. Finally he decided that he would leave the basket there and let fate take its course. He set out in the direction of the market, leaving Panditji staring at the basket and feeling rather desperate. There were very few sweets left. There were some five or six bags but from each he could extract no more than two pieces. He was afraid his secret would become known. He thought, 'But what if I ate them? My hunger would only get worse, I'd be like a tiger smelling blood. There wouldn't be much fun in a sin like that.' He sat back in his place. But after a moment his hunger grew stronger. 'Still, it would be nice,' he thought. 'No matter how insignificant the amount of food, it's still food.' He got up, took out the sweets. But just as he was about to stick the very first piece of fudge into his mouth he saw the peddler hastening toward him with his lamp lit. He had to finish off the sweets before he arrived. He put two pieces together into his mouth and was still chewing them when that devil of a peddler had come another ten steps. Panditji stuffed four pieces into his mouth and swallowed them half-chewed. There were still six pieces left and by now the peddler had gone as far as the gate. Panditji thrust all that was left into his mouth. Now he could neither chew it nor spit it out. That demon was charging him like an automobile with his lamp blazing away. When he was right in front of him Panditji swiftly swallowed all the sweets. But after all he was a man and not a crocodile: his eyes filled with water, he choked, he shuddered, coughed violently. Holding out his lamp the vendor said, 'Take this and look around, though if you're ready to fast to death why are you afraid of dying from snakebite? Why worry? If you die the Government will look after your kids, won't it?'

Panditji was so angry that he determined to scold this vulgar troublemaker, but he was unable to produce a sound. He silently took the lamp and after pretending to look around handed it back.

The peddler said, 'Whatever possessed you to take the side of the Government anyway? If they're going to meet all day tomorrow they'll hardly make a decision until nightfall. By that time you'll be feeling pretty dizzy.'

With this he went away and Panditji, after coughing a little while, fell asleep.

*

The next day as soon as it was light the merchants began to discuss the problem, and there was a regular commotion among the Congress Party leaders as well. The Vigilance Committee officials also

133

pricked up their ears. They'd devised a splendid plan to intimidate those simple-minded baniyas. The Association of Brahmans held a separate meeting and decided that Pandit Moteram had no right at all to meddle in political affairs. What did Brahmans have to do with politics? In short, the whole day was passed in debating the pros and cons, and nobody paid any attention to Panditji. People said openly that he'd been given a thousand rupees by the government for taking this fast on himself. Poor Panditji had passed the night tossing about and when he rose his body felt stiff as a corpse's. When he stood up he saw stars before his eyes, his head began to spin. His stomach felt as though someone were scraping it. He kept his eyes glued on the road to see if anybody would come to conciliate him or not. He was still full of this expectation when the time of evening prayer went by. At this hour it had always been his custom to eat a snack after the ritual. Today he had not even had a sip of water. Who could say when the happy moment might arrive? Then he began to feel a great anger against his wife. She must have slept the whole night with her belly full. At this moment she would have just finished a good meal but hadn't even come here to have a look to see whether he was alive or dead. Couldn't she, under some pretext or other, bring him just a little bit of fruit pastry? But why should she care about that? She'd taken the rupees and kept them and whatever else he got she would keep as well and make a regular jackass out of him.

At any rate, Panditji waited the whole day through and no concil-iator appeared. They were reluctant to come because of the suspi-cion in their hearts that Panditji, overcome by his own selfishness, had become involved in some fraudulent bargain and was only putting on a show.

*

At nine o'clock that evening Seth Bhondumal, the leader of the merchants' association, said decisively, 'I suppose Panditji is going through this performance only for his own profit, but since he's only a mere mortal it's none the less painful for him to go without food and water. It's against religion for a Brahman to renounce food and water while we sleep peacefully with full stomachs. If he's conducted himself against religion then he will have to suffer for it. But why do we turn away from our duty?'

134

The Congress Secretary was not enthusiastic. 'I've said what I had to say. You people are the leaders of society. Whatever you decide we will accept, act and we'll move with you. I also have my share of religious feeling. But listen to one request: will you people let me go there before you? I want to talk with him alone for ten minutes. You can be waiting at the gate. When I return, then you can go to him. What objection can anybody have to this?' They granted his request.

The Secretary had spent a considerable time in the police department and knew something of the weaknesses of human character. He went straight to the market and bought four rupees' worth of sweets, taking care to select a large quantity of the most fragrant. He had them wrapped in tinfoil and went off to make his offering to the sulky Brahman. He also took a jug of cold scented water. Waves of delicious scent emanated from both the bag and the jug. The power of scent is such that it can make a man hungry even when he's not hungry — and how much more a really hungry man?

At this time Panditji was lying on the ground dozing. He'd eaten nothing during the night — for of what account were a half dozen or so pygmy-sized sweets? And he'd had nothing at noon. Now once again meal time had slipped by. He no longer felt the restlessness of the expectation of food but the very chill of desperation. All his limbs were slack, he could not even open his eyes. He tried several times but they closed automatically. His lips were dry. If he gave any sign of life it was only a very low moaning. He had never before been in such a fix. A couple of times a month he suffered from indigestion, which he would assuage with myrobolans and other medicines. But he'd never suffered indigestion so acutely that he'd given up eating. He whole-heartedly cursed the inhabitants of the city, the Vigilance Committee, the Government, God, the Congress Party and his own true wife. There was nothing to be hoped for from any of them. Now he was no longer strong enough even to stand up and go to the market. He was convinced that by tonight his spirit would have taken flight. For he knew that the thread of life is not some string that won't break no matter how much it's pulled.

'Shastriji!' the Secretary called.

Still lying down Moteram opened his eyes. They were as full of self-pity as those of a child whose candy's been snatched from his

135

hand by a crow.

The Secretary set the bag of sweets down before him and the pot of water with a cup on it. Then he said casually, 'How long are you going to go on lying here?'

The aroma put Panditji's faculties back into operation. He sat up and said, 'Until an agreement has been reached.'

'But there's not going to be any agreement. The Council met all day without settling it. Anyway, tomorrow evening the Viceroy will be here. Do you have any idea of what kind of shape you'll be in by then? Your face has already turned pale!'

'If I'm fated to die here, who can avert his fate? Are those *rasgoolas* in that bag?'

'Yes, all kinds of sweets. They were made specially to be sent to one of my relatives for a ceremony.'

'That's why they smell so good. Open up the bag a little, will you?'

Smiling, the Secretary opened the bag and Panditji began to devour the sweets with his eyes. A blind man whose sight has been restored would not gaze upon the world with greedier eyes. Moteram's mouth watered. The Secretary said, 'If you hadn't taken a vow, I'd give you a taste of them. They cost two-and-a-half rupees a pound.'

'They must be magnificent! I haven't had any *rasgoolas* for several days.'

'And you've got yourself into a pickle for nothing! If you don't survive, of what use is the money?'

'What can I do? I'm trapped!' Panditji said. 'I might have made a meal of this many sweets.' He delicately touched them. 'They must be from Bhola's shop.'

'Just try a couple of them.'

'How can I? I'd be breaking a sacred oath.'

'Come on, taste them! The pleasure they'll give you right now couldn't be bought for thousands of rupees. Who's going to know about it anyway?'

'Who am I afraid of?' Moteram said. 'Here I am dying of thirst and hunger and nobody cares in the least. So why be afraid? Bring it here, hand me the bag. Go on, tell everybody, Shastriji's broken his vow. To hell with business and the market! I don't care about anybody. When there's no religion left in the world, why should I bother to take it on myself alone?'

136

With this Panditji drew the bag toward himself and steadily applied his hand with the result that in a flash the bag was half empty.
By this time the merchants had reached the gate and were standing
there. Going to them, the Secretary said, 'Come a little closer and
see the fun. You people won't have to open your bazaar; nor will
you have to toady to anybody. I've solved the whole problem. This
is the Congress spirit!'

Moonlight filled the square. They came closer and saw Panditji
engaged in doing away with the sweets with the profound absorp-
tion of a holy man in a trance.

Bhondumal said, 'I touch Panditji's feet in reverence. We were all
coming, why didn't you wait? We had devised a plan so that you
would have accomplished your purpose without breaking your
vow.'

But Moteram said, 'I *have* accomplished my purpose. This is a
divine joy that can't be obtained for any amount of money. If you
have any respect for me, then order some more sweets exactly like
this from the same shop!'

## Man's Highest Duty

One Holi morning Pandit Moteram Shastri — that devotee of pastries and lover of sweets — sat on a broken cot in his yard, his head hanging low, the very image of care and melancholy. His faithful spouse sat nearby watching him anxiously and trying in her gentle voice to wheedle him out of his depression.

After he had remained plunged in gloomy reflections for some time Panditji said sadly, 'My good luck has gone the devil knows where. Even on Holi it deserts me.'

'Evil days have come upon us,' his wife said. 'Ever since you told me to, I pray to the Sun God twice a day, morning and evening, to get an invitation sent to you from somewhere. I've lit hundreds of lamps to Mother *Tulsi,* but the fact is, they've all deserted you. Not one of them will come to help you through these hard times.'

'The Gods and Goddesses have nothing to do with it,' said Moteram. 'When they come and help us through our difficulties then we can start talking about Gods and Goddesses but there are an awful lot of people sitting around gobbling up pancakes and *halva* without paying for them.'

'But isn't there one single gentleman left in this whole town? Have they all died?'

'They've all died — or rather, they've all gone rotten. There may be five or ten of them but in a whole year only a couple of them show their generosity even once. And when they do, they give you only five or six pounds of sweets to eat. If I had my way, I'd send the whole lot of them off to hard labour. It's all the work of those Arya Samaj religious reformers.'

'But you just sit around the house! Even these days there must be some generous person who'd invite you out. Some time or other you ought to go out and offer sermons and blessings.'

'How do you know I haven't? If any such gentlemen existed in this town, I wouldn't give him a blessing when I I went to see him. But who the devil is around to listen to me? Everybody's wrapped up in his own business.'

138

In the meantime Pandit Chintamani had put in an appearance. This was Moteram's best friend. To be sure, he was a little younger than Moteram and accordingly his paunch had not attained the splendid proportions of the latter's.

'Tell me, friend,' Moteram said, 'what news? Do you know of any good opportunities?'

'No opportunities,' Chintamani said, 'just my own luck and now even that's run out.'

'Then you must have just come from home?'

'Brother, let's become wandering *sadhus*. When there's not the slightest pleasure left in life, what's a man to do? Now tell me, if you don't get something decent to eat even on a day like this, how's a body to keep going?'

'Yes, brother, what you say is true.'

'Then you can't think of anything to do now either? Say it straight out and then we'll renounce the world.'

'No, friend, don't despair. Don't you know, without dying you can't get into heaven? For obtaining dainty morsels you have to undergo strict austerities. My opinion is that we should act, go right away to the banks of the Ganges and give a talk. Who knows, we may stir the heart of some gentle soul.'

'A fine idea,' said Chintamani. 'Let's get going.'

The two gentlemen got up and made their way toward the Ganges. It was still early morning. Hundreds of people were bathing there or reading scriptures aloud or thronging the steps and applying the auspicious vermillion to their foreheads. Some were already setting out for home, their *dhotis* still wet from the river.

As soon as the two gentlemen appeared they were greeted on all sides with the cries of 'Reverence! Blessings!' After replying to these salutations the two friends went to the edge of the river and busied themselves in the ritual of bathing. After this they climbed up the steps and began to sing a hymn. This was so remarkable an occurrence that hundreds of curious people gathered around. When the audience was several hundreds strong Pandit Moteram said with great dignity: 'Good people, you know that when Brahma created this unprofitable world he made the Brahmans from his mouth. Is there anyone who doubts this?'

'No, maharaj,' they said, 'what you say is true — who can deny it?'

'So the Brahman emerged from the mouth of the god Brahma,

this is certain. Therefore, the mouth is the most sublime part of the human body. Thus the highest duty of any living creature is to afford delight to the mouth. Is this true or isn't it? Does anyone deny it? Let him come forward! We can prove our theory by the scriptures.'

'Maharaj, you are a learned man — who would dare refute you?'

'Very well, then, now that it's been determined that to delight the mouth is man's highest duty, is it difficult to see that people who do not contribute to the mouth are creatures of sorrow — will anyone deny this?'

'Maharaj, you are blessed, a teacher of the true scriptures.'

'Now the question arises, how shall we delight the mouth? We say: according to your faith and according to your capacity. There are different ways. To sing the glories of the Gods, to offer prayers to the Lord, to converse with holy men and avoid wicked speech. From all these things the mouth will derive pleasure. But the highest, the most sublime and effective way is something different: Can any of you say what it is? Let him speak.'

'Maharaj,' they said, 'who can open his mouth in your presence? Please tell us.'

'Very well, I'll shout it out and sing it to the skies. Its greatness is as the full moon's light compared to all the other lunar phases.'

'Do not delay, tell us the way you mean.'

'Listen, then, pay attention: the way is this — to feast the mouth with the finest foods, to feed it the very best dishes. Does anyone deny this? Let him speak and we shall call scripture to witness.'

There was a sceptic among the crowd. 'I can't understand how the mouth can obtain greater pleasure in eating fine foods than in speaking truth.'

Several others agreed with him. 'We doubt it too. Maharaj, remove our doubt.'

'Does anyone else disbelieve? I shall be delighted to refute you. Good people, you ask how there can be greater pleasure in eating than in speaking truth. My answer is that the first way is visible and substantial, while the second is invisible. To illustrate, just imagine that I have committed a crime. If the judge summoned me and explained gently that what I had done was bad, unbefitting for me, such treatment would not succeed in setting me on the right path. Gentlemen, I'm not a saint. I'm a poor mortal caught in the toils of worldliness and delusion. Such a punishment would not have any

140

effect on me. As soon as I'd left the judge's presence I'd begin again on the evil path. Have you understood me? Does anyone deny it?'

'Maharaj! You are an ocean of knowledge, a pearl among the Pandits — may you prosper!'

'Now let's turn back to the illustration I gave. If the judge had summoned me, promptly thrown me in jail and there subjected me to various hardships, then when I left prison I would remember those sufferings for years, and of course I would renounce the path of evil. You will ask why this is so — since both are forms of punishment why should one have an effect and the other none! The reason is that the form of one is visible and the other's hidden. Do you understand this?'

'May you prosper for your kindness! God has bestowed great sense and wisdom on you!'

'Very well, now your question will naturally be what kind of food is best. I will explain. Just as God created different kinds of colours for the gratification of the eyes, so he created diverse flavours for the mouth. But of all these flavours which is finest? This is according to each one's taste, but according to the Vedas and Shastras the taste of sweetness is the most esteemed. The gods become intoxicated with sweetness to the point where even the omnipotent, all-encompassing supreme deity himself prefers sweet foods above all. Can anyone name a god who takes salty food? Can anybody name even one such deity? There's not one. None of the gods therefore hanker after foods that are sour, tart, acid or pungent.'

'Maharaj, your wisdom has no limits!'

'Thus I have proven that of all foods, sweet foods are the best. Now again you will ask a question: will all sweet foods afford the mouth equal pleasure? If I said yes, you would all set up a cry that Panditji has gone mad. Therefore, I will say no and say it over and over again. Not all sweets have equal savour. There's a lot of difference between refined sugar and the cane. So our first duty is to see that we eat and serve only the best of sweets. In my opinion, for a feast fit for God, you should fill a plate with Jaunpur 'nectars,' Agra 'pearl-drops,' Mathura creams, *rasgoolas* from Lucknow, rose-apple candy from Ayodhya and Delhi *halva*. The gods would go wild over such a dish. And the enterprising and noble soul who gets together such a tasty dish for the Brahmans — he will find an abode in heaven in his own corporeal form! If you have faith, then we urge

141

you emphatically to fulfill your religious obligations — for otherwise you cannot consider yourselves men.'

Pandit Moteram's speech was over. People applauded. Some gentlemen, overwhelmed by the sermon and display of knowledge, showered flowers upon him. Then Pandit Chintamani began his own flowery discourse: 'Good people, you have heard the powerful utterance of my best friend Pandit Moteram and there was no need for me to be standing by. However, although I am in agreement with him on almost every question, I hold a different doctrine on one point. In my opinion if he put only Jaunpur 'nectars' on the plate, it would be far tastier, far more delicious than five different kinds of sweets. And I can prove my point by reference to the scriptures.'

Flaring up, Moteram said, 'Your idea is utterly wrong. Jaunpur 'nectars' are not fit to be compared with 'pearl-drops' from Agra and Delhi *halva*.'

'Prove it!' Chintamani shouted.

'Visibly and substantially?'

'That shows how stupid you are!'

'All your life you've been gobbling down everything in sight,' Moteram said, 'but you don't know a thing about food.'

In reply Chintamani flung his prayer-mat at Pandit Moteram, who dodged the blow and charged Chintamani like a wild elephant. But at this moment the people gathered around and separated the two mahatmas.

# A Lesson in the Holy Life

Domestic squabbles and a dearth of invitations led Pandit Chintamani to consider renouncing the world and when he vowed to
become a wandering ascetic his best friend, Pandit Moteram Shastri, gave him this advice.

'Friend, I've been intimately acquainted with a good many first-
class mahatmas. Now, when they arrive at some well-to-do citizen's
door they don't fall in a heap and hold out their hands and call
down hypocritical blessings such as "God keep you in body and
soul, may you always be happy." Such is the way of beggars. As
soon as a holy man reaches the door he lets out his war-cry in a
regular yell so that everybody inside the house is astonished and
comes running to see what's happened. I know two or three of
these slogans — you can use any you like. Gudri *Baba* used to say,
"If anybody dies five will die!" When they heard this battle-cry
.people would fall right at his feet. Siddh Bhagat had a fine slogan:
"Eat, drink and be merry but watch out for the holy man's stick."
Nanga *Baba* would say, "Give to me, feed me, let me drink, let me
sleep." Just remember, your prestige depends a good deal on your
slogan. What else can I tell you? Don't forget, you and I have been
friends for a long time, we've enjoyed the same free dinners
hundreds of times. Whenever we were at the same banquet we
used to compete to eat up one dish more than the other. I'm going
to miss you! May God give you a happy life.'

Chintamani wasn't pleased with any of the slogans. He said,
'Think up some special cry for me.'

'All right — how's this one: "If you don't give to me I'll run you
into the ground."'

'Yes, I like that one, but if you'll allow me, I'll shorten it.'

'Go right ahead.'

'Then how about this: "Give or I'll run you into the ground."'

Moteram leaped up. 'By the Lord above, that's absolutely unique!
Devotion has illuminated you. Splendid! Now try it out just once
and we'll see how you do it.'

Chintamani stuck his fingers in his ears and yelled with all his might. 'Give or I'll run you into the ground!' The noise was so thunderous that even Moteram was startled. The bats flew out of the trees in dismay and dogs began to bark.

Moteram said, 'Friend, hearing your cry I was stirred to the depths of my heart. Such a cry has never been heard before, it was like the roar of a lion. Now your slogan has been decided, I have a few other things to tell you, so pay attention. The language of holy men is quite distinct from our ordinary way of speaking. We say "Sir," for example, to some people, and just "you" to others. But the holy man says "thou" to everybody, important or insignificant, rich or poor, old or young; however, go on treating old people with respect. Also remember never to talk plain Hindi. Otherwise the secret will be out that you're an ordinary Brahman and not a real holy man. Make your language fancy. To say, for example, "My good woman, give me something to eat" is not the style of the holy man. A genuine mahatma will say it like this: "Woman, spread a feast before me, and you will be walking in the paths of righteousness."'

'Friend,' Chintamani said, 'how can I praise you enough? You've helped me beyond measure.'

Having given this advice, Moteram took his leave. Chintamani set out and what should he see right away but a crowd of holy men sitting in front of a *bhang* and hashish shop smoking hashish. When they saw Chintamani one of the holy men pronounced his slogan:

> *'Move along, move along,*
> *Otherwise, I'll prove you wrong.'*

Another holy man proclaimed:

> *'Fee fi fo fum*
> *We holy men have finally come,*
> *From now on only fun.'*

While these syllables were still echoing in the skies a third mahatma roared out:

> *'Here and there*
> *down and up*
> *Hurry up and fill my cup.'*

Chintamani could not restrain himself. He burst out with 'Give or I'll run you into the ground!'

As soon as they heard this the holy men greeted him. The bowl of the *hookah* was refilled at once and the task of lighting it was assigned to Pandit Chintamani. He thought, if I don't accept the pipe my secret will be out. Nervously he took it. Now anyone who has never smoked hashish can try and try without being able to make the pipe draw. Closing his eyes Chintamani inhaled with all his might. The pipe fell from his hands, his eyes popped, he foamed at the mouth but not the least bit of smoke came from his lips nor was there any sign that the pipe was kindled. This lack of know-how was quite enough to ruin his standing in the society of holy men. A couple of them advanced angrily and roughly catching him by the hands, pulled him up.

'A curse on you,' one said, and another, 'Aren't you ashamed of pretending to be a mahatma?'

Humiliated, Panditji went and sat down near a sweets shop and the holy men, striking tambourines, began to sing this hymn:

*'Illusion is the world, beloved, the world is an illusion.*
*Both sin and holiness are lies — there's the philosophical*
*solution.*
*The world is all illusion.*
*A curse on those who forbid us bhang and hashish,*
*Krishna, lover, all the world's illusion.'*

# A Little Trick

Whenever Seth Chandumal took a look at his shop and warehouse crammed full with goods he would heave a long sigh. How could he sell them? The bank interest was going up, the shop rent was climbing, the clerks' wages had to come out of whatever was left. He had to provide all this money out of his own pocket. If this situation lasted a few more days there would be no alternative to bankruptcy. And still those Congress boycotters kept after him like devils.

Seth Chandumal's shop was in Chandni Chowk in Delhi and he also had some shops out in the provinces. When the city Congress Committee tried to get him to sign the pledge not to deal in English cloth he didn't so much as consider the possibility. Then several wholesale dealers in the market, following his example, refused to put their signatures to the pledge letter. Chandumal, who had never attained any eminence as a leader, won it now without even trying. He was sympathetic to the Government. At various times he would offer a little contribution to the official bigshots. He was also chummy with the police and he belonged to the municipal council as well. As an opponent of the Congress programme for action he had become the treasurer of the Peace Council, which supported cooperation with the British —this was the reward for his collaboration. The officals had purchased 24,000 rupees worth of cloth for the welcome prepared for the Prince of Wales. Why should so powerful a man fear the Congress? What was their importance anyway? The police encouraged him too: 'Never sign their pledge! Just see what those people are doing. You can blame us if we don't put every one of them in jail.' So Sethji's courage grew and he determined to do battle with the Congress. The result of this was that for three months Congress volunteers blockaded his shop from nine in the morning until dark. The police squad fired at them several times and several times beat them up, while Sethji himself often showered volleys of abuse on them. But the boycotters could not be budged; on the contrary, because of these outbreaks of violence Chandumal's business fell off still more. From the provinces his storekeepers kept on sending even more desperate news. It was a complicated problem, he saw no way out of the impasse. He had observed that the people who'd signed the pledge went right on selling foreign cloth on the sly — there were no boycott demonstrators in front of *their* shops. He was forced to bear the full brunt of the disaster alone.

He reflected, 'What advantage has my friendship with the police and judges brought me? *They* can't get rid of these demonstrators! Customers won't come at the command of soldiers. If only the boycott can be stopped somehow or other the business might still be saved.'

Meantime his chief accountant said, 'Lalaji, just look, a few traders were coming over our way. Those boycotters told them some kind of nonsense and now they've all gone away.'

'I'd be perfectly satisfied if those sinners were all shot,' Chandumal said. 'They won't give up until they destroy me.'

'If you signed the pledge — it would be a disgrace, of course — but then they'd lift the boycott and somehow or other we'd sell off everything.'

'I've considered that too,' Chandumal said. 'But think how great the loss of face would be. After putting up such a front I can't give in, I'd lose all my prestige with the judges and they'd taunt me for backing down. "Just an idiot fighting the Congress!" After a defeat like that my pride would be crushed. How would I look asking for help from the people I struck and had beaten and insulted and ridiculed? But there might be a way out. If a little trick could work then we'd be out of the soup. The thing is to kill the snake without breaking the stick! If I can just lift the boycott without toadying up to anybody . . .'

*

At nine in the morning Chandumal had come back from a ritual dip in the Jumna and reclining, propped up by his bolster, he began to read through some letters. The managers of his other shops all related the same tale of woe. With each letter he read Sethji's anger mounted. In the meantime two volunteers came with banners to stand guard outside his shop.

Sethji shouted, 'Get away from my shop, you!'

147

'Maharaj,' one of the volunteers answered, 'we're on the road —do you want us to stay out of the road too?'

'I don't want to have to look at your faces,' Sethji said.

'Then be good enough to write to the Congress Committee. We got our orders from them to come and stand guard here.'

A constable came along and said, 'What's the matter, Sethji, is this fellow talking back to you?'

Chandumal said, 'I told him to get away from in front of my shop but he says he won't leave. Just look at the way they persecute me!'

The constable said to the volunteers, 'Both of you get moving or I'll come and pin back your ears.'

'We're on the road,' the volunteer said, 'not in his shop.'

The constable was eager to show his efficiency. He also hoped for some little compensation if he did Sethji a favour. He yelled at the volunteers and when they paid no attention he struck one of them such a blow that the poor fellow fell flat on the ground. Several demonstrators came clustering from here and there, and a number of policeman gathered too. Idle onlookers enjoy nothing more than an incident like this and they flocked around as well. Someone shouted, 'Long live Mahatma Gandhi!' and everyone chimed in, and in a twinkling there was a regular mob.

One onlooker said, 'What's up, Chandumal? Can you have these poor people treated so barbarously in front of your shop without being ashamed? Have you no fear of God?'

Sethji said, 'I give you my oath I never said a word to any policeman. These people came out of nowhere after the poor fellows. You're slandering me without any cause.'

'But Lalaji,' the constable protested, 'you yourself said these two volunteers were scaring off your customers. Are you trying to slip out of that now?'

'A lie, a complete lie, a hundred percent lie!' Sethji said. 'You people started a fight with them just to show how good you are at your work. These poor fellows were standing way off from my shop, they weren't talking to anybody or causing any trouble. Then you started after them. Is my business selling or fighting with people?'

'Lalaji,' said another constable, 'Be sensible now. You got us worked up and then you kept out of it. If you hadn't told us to, why would we have hit these people? And the Inspector ordered us to pay special attention to Seth Chandumal's shop. "Don't let any volunteers gather there!" he said, So we came to protect your shop. If you hadn't made the request why should the Inspector have given us this assignment?'

'The Inspector must have wanted to show how efficient he is, I suppose,' Chandumal said. 'Why should I ask him for anything? Everybody's against Congress anyway, but the police go all to pieces just to hear them mentioned. Do you mean you do your duty only if I make a complaint?'

In the meantime somebody had informed the police station that violence had broken out between police and volunteers in front of Lala Chandumal's shop. The news got to the Congress office too. In a little while the captain of the armed police and the Inspector arrived, and a whole force of Congress officials came on the run. The crowd was enormous. Shouts of victory rang out occasionally. The police and Congress leaders began to argue. The result of it all was that the police arrested the two volunteers and marched them off toward the police station.

After the police officials had gone Sethji said to the Congress president, 'I've learned today how brutally those people treat the volunteers.'

'Then those two volunteers weren't arrested in vain,' the president said. 'You don't have any doubts about this matter now, do you? Have you really learned how violent and destructive they are?'

'Yes indeed, I really have learned.'

'But the police will surely ask you to testify.'

'Let them ask,' Chandumal said. 'I'll just tell the truth straight out, whether it ruins me or not. From now on there's not going to be any police brutality in front of my door. I hadn't understood at all.'

'The police will put a lot of pressure on you,' the Congress secretary said.

'Let them do their utmost, I'll never lie. The Government's not going to get off in the *real* courthouse,' and Chandumal looked heavenward for an instant.

'Now our honour is in your hands,' the secretary said.

'You won't find me an enemy of my country,' Chandumal said.

Afterwards when the president and other officials were about to leave the secretary said, 'The man appears truthful.'

Dubiously the president observed, 'By tomorrow we'll have the proof of it.'

*

In the evening the Police Inspector called Lala Chandumal to the station and said, 'You'll have to testify and we're counting on your collaboration.'

'I'm ready,' said Chandumal.

'Did the volunteers insult the constables?'

'I didn't hear any insults.'

'Whether you heard any or not, that's not the point. You'll have to say that they kept customers away by hitting them, that there were scuffles, that they threatened to kill — you'll have to say all this.' To the sub-inspector he said, 'Copy this description which I've taken down at Sethji's dictation.'

'You won't hear *me* lying in a packed courtroom,' Seth Chandumal said. 'There'll be thousands in court who know me. How could I show my face to anybody, where could I go?'

'These are all personal matters,' the Inspector said. 'In politics nobody worries about truth and falsehood or honour and shame.'

'But I'd be dishonoured,' Sethji said.

'In the eyes of the Government your prestige would be four times as great.'

Chandumal reflected. 'No,' he said, 'I can't testify. Get some other witness.'

'You'd better think about it, now! This could ruin you completely.'

'If it does, then so be it.'

'Your rank as treasurer of the Peace Council will be taken away from you.'

'Well,' Chandumal said, 'that's not what pays my bills.'

'You'll forfeit your license to carry a gun.'

'So I'll forfeit it — who cares?'

'And then there'll be an income tax investigation.'

'Investigate by all means — it will be to my advantage, the way business is.'

'You won't have a chair left to sit in!'

'I'm going bankrupt anyway — what good is a chair?'

'All right then. You may go now. But one of these days we'll take care of you!'

*

150

At this time the next day in the Congress office a programme was decided on for the morrow. The president said, 'Send a couple of volunteers to blockade Chandumal's shop.'

'In my opinion,' said the secretary, 'there's no need to now.'

'Why? He still hasn't signed the pledge letter, has he?'

'He didn't sign but he's certainly on our side now. He's made this plain by refusing to testify on behalf of the police. You can imagine how the officials will be after him for that. Moral courage like this can't come without a transformation of his ideas as well.'

'Yes, certainly there's been some change in his ideas.'

'No sir, it's a total revolution,' the secretary said. 'You know what it means to scorn the authorities in such matters — it's like a declaration of treason. It means just as much as a vow of renunciation for an ascetic. Now every judge in the district will be positively thirsting for his blood. It wouldn't be surprising if the governor himself was informed about this.'

'Then there's nothing else but for him to sign the pledge if only as a matter of form. Somehow or other get him over here and let's settle the matter.'

'He's very proud, he'll never come. On the contrary, if he sees that we don't trust him he's liable to try to go back over to the other side.'

'Very well then, if we're to trust him let's take the volunteers away from his shop. But still I say that you'll have to keep an eye on him by finding some pretext for going to see him.'

'You really don't have to be so suspicious,' said the secretary.

When Sethji came to his shop at nine o' clock he didn't see a single volunteer. He broke into a grin. 'We won the toss,' he said to the accountant.

'So it seems — not one of those gentlemen's put in an appearance.'

'And they're not going to. The game is in our hands now. We gambled and we got everything. Aren't you convinced? How quickly I made them my friends. Just ask me to and I'll send for 'em and make 'em lick my boots! They're not anybody's friends and nobody's enemies, they're just slaves of money. Tell the truth now, what did you think of my little trick?'

'I could go right down on my knees to you for it! The snake is dead and the stick didn't break. But those Congress fellows will be keeping an eye on you.'

'I'm ready for 'em, I can match wits with them and give them tit for tat. There are people coming, so get out a bale of the English cloth and start giving it to the traders. In a week we'll be out of the woods!'

# Penalty

Scarcely a month ever went by without Alarakkhi having some fine deducted from her pay. Once in a while she would actually get five of her six rupees; but though she put up with just about anything she had managed not to let Khan Sahib put his hands on her. Munshi Khairat Ali Khan was the Inspector of Sanitation and hundreds of sweeper women depended on him. He was good-hearted and well thought of — not the sort who cut their pay, scolded them or fined them. But he went on regularly rebuking and punishing Alarakkhi. She was not a shirker, nor saucy or slovenly; she was also not at all bad-looking. During these chilly days she would be out with her broom before it was light and go on assiduously sweeping the road until nine. But all the same, she would be penalized. Huseni, her husband, would help her with the work too when he found the chance, but it was in Alarakkhi's fate that she was going to be fined. For others pay-day was an occasion to celebrate, for Alarakkhi it was a time to weep. On that day it was as though her heart had broken. Who could tell how much would be deducted? Like students awaiting the results of their examinations, over and over again she would speculate on the amount of the deduction.

Whenever she got so tired that she'd sit down a moment to catch her breath, precisely then the Inspector would arrive riding in his *ekka*. No matter how much she'd say, 'Please, Excellency, I'll go back to work again,' he would jot her name down in his book without listening. A few days later the very same thing would happen again. If she bought a few cents worth of candy from the sweets-vendor and started to eat it, just at that moment the Inspector would drop on her from the devil knew where and once more write her name down in his book. Where could he have been hiding? The minute she began to rest the least bit he was upon her like an evil spirit. If he wrote her name down on only two days, how much would the penalty be then? God knew. More than eight *annas*? If only it weren't a whole rupee! With her head bowed she'd go to collect her pay and find even more deducted than she'd estimated. Taking her money with trembling hands she'd go home, her eyes full of tears. There was no one to turn to, no one who'd listen, where the Inspector was concerned.

Today was pay-day again. The past month her unweaned daughter had suffered from coughing and fever. The weather had been exceptionally cold. Partly because of the cold, partly because of the little girl's crying she was kept awake the whole night. Several times she'd come to work late. Khan Sahib had noted down her name, and this time she would be fined half her pay. But if it were only half it would be a blessing. It was impossible to say how much might be deducted. Early in the morning she picked up the baby, took her broom and went to the street. But the naughty creature wouldn't let herself be put down. Time after time Alarakkhi would threaten her with the arrival of the Inspector. 'He's on his way and he'll beat me and as for you, he'll cut off your nose and ears!' The child was willing to to sacrifice her nose and ears but not to be put down. At last, when Alarakkhi had failed to get rid of her with threats and coaxing alike, she set her down and left her crying and wailing while she started to sweep. But the little wretch wouldn't sit in one place to cry her heart out; she crawled after her mother time and time again, caught her sari, clung to her legs, then wallowed around on the ground and a moment later sat up to start crying again.

'Shut up!' Alarakkhi said, brandishing the broom. 'If you don't, I'll hit you with the broom and that'll be the end of you. That bastard of an Inspector's going to show up at any moment.'

She had hardly got the words out of her mouth when Inspector Khairat Ali Khan dismounted from his bicycle directly in front of her. She turned pale, her heart began to thump. 'Oh God, may my head fall off if he heard me! Right in front of me and I didn't see him. Who could tell he'd come on his bicycle today? He's always come in his *ekka*.' The blood froze in her veins, she stood holding the broom as though paralyzed.

Angrily the Inspector said, 'Why do you drag the kid after you to work? Why didn't you leave it at home?'

'She's sick, Excellency,' Alarakkhi said timidly. 'Who's at home to leave her with?'

'What's the matter with her?'

'She has a fever, *Huzoor.*'

154

'And you make her cry by leaving her? Don't you care if she lives or dies?'

'How can I do my work if I carry her?'

'Why don't you ask for leave?'

'If my pay is cut, *Huzoor*, what will we have to live on?'

'Pick her up and take her home. When Huseni comes back send him here to finish the sweeping.'

She picked up the baby and was about to go when he asked, 'Why were you abusing me?'

Alarakkhi felt all her breath knocked out of her. If you'd cut her there wouldn't have been any blood. Trembling she said, 'No, *Huzoor*, may my head fall off if I was abusing you.'

And she burst into tears.

\*

In the evening Huseni and Alarakkhi went to collect her pay. She was very downcast.

'Why so sad?' Huseni tried to console her. 'The pay's going to be cut, so let them cut it. I swear on your life from now on I won't touch another drop of booze or toddy.'

'I'm afraid I'm fired. Damn my tongue! How could I . . ..'

'If you're fired, then you're fired, but let Allah be merciful to *him*. Why go on crying about it?'

'You've made me come for nothing. Everyone of those women will laugh at me.'

'If he's fired you, won't we ask on what grounds? And who heard you abuse him? Can there be so much injustice that he can fire anyone he pleases? If I'm not heard I'll complain to the panchayat, I'll beat my head on the headman's gate —'

'If our people stuck together like that would Khan Sahib ever dare fine us so much?'

'No matter how serious the sickness there's a medicine for it, silly.'

But Alarakkhi was not set at rest. Dejection covered her face like a cloud. When the Inspector heard her abuse him why didn't he even scold her? Why didn't he fire her on the spot? She wasn't able to work it out, he actually seemed kind. She couldn't manage to understand this mystery and not understanding it she was afraid. If he meant only to fine her he would have written her name in his book. He had decided to fire her — that must have been why he was so nice. She'd heard that a man about to be hanged is given a fine last meal, they have to give him anything he wants — so surely the Inspector was going to dismiss her.

They reached the municipal office building. Thousands of sweeper women were gathered there, all made up and wearing their brightest clothes and jewelry. The *paan* and cigarette vendors had also come, along with the sweets peddlers. A swarm of Pathan money-lenders were on hand to collect money from those who owed them. Huseni and Alarakkhi went and stood with the others.

They began to distribute the pay. The sweeper women were first. Whoever's name was called would go running and taking her money call down undeserved blessings on the Inspector and go away. Alarakkhi's name was always called after Champa's. Today she was passed over. After Champa, Jahuran's name was called, and she always followed Alarakkhi.

In despair she looked at Huseni. The women were watching her and beginning to whisper. She longed just to be able to go home, she couldn't bear this derision. She wished the earth would open and swallow her up.

One after another the names were called and Alarakkhi went on looking at the trees across the way. Now she no longer cared whose name was called, who went, and who stared at her and who was laughing at her.

Suddenly startled, she heard her name. Slowly she stood up and walked ahead with the slow tread of a new bride. The paymaster put the full amount of six rupees in her hand.

She was stupefied. Surely the paymaster was mistaken! In these three years she had never once got her full pay. And now to get even half would have been a windfall. She stood there for a second in case the paymaster should ask for the money back. When he asked her, 'Why are you standing here now, why don't you move along?' she said softly, 'But it's the full amount.'

Puzzled the paymaster looked at her and said, 'What else do you want — do you want to get less?'

'There's no penalty deducted?'

'No, today there aren't any deductions.'

She came away but in her heart she was not content. She was full of remorse for having abused the Inspector.

# The Writer

Early in the morning Mr. Pravin prepared a cup of tea boiled twenty times over and drank it without sugar and milk. This was his breakfast. For months he had not had sweetened tea with milk — for him milk and sugar were not among the necessities of life. To be sure, he did go into the bedroom to wake his wife and ask for some money; but when he saw her fast asleep in the torn, soiled quilt he did not want to wake her. He thought that because of the cold the poor woman might not have fallen asleep all night and had only a moment ago managed to shut her eyes. It wasn't right to wake someone who'd just fallen asleep. Silently he came away.

After he drank his tea he arranged his pen and inkwell and became absorbed in writing that book which in his opinion would be the greatest creation of the century and which, when published, would take him out of his anonymity and launch him into the empyrean of fame and glory.

A half hour later his wife came in, rubbing her eyes, and said, 'Have you already had your tea?'

With a smile on his face Pravin said, 'Yes, already. It turned out very well.'

'But where did you get the milk and sugar?'

'I haven't had milk and sugar for a long time now. These days plain tea tastes better to me. Mixing in milk and sugar spoils the taste. The doctors also maintain that you ought to drink tea plain. In Europe, you know, the custom is not to use milk at all. It's really just the invention of our local sweet-toothed aristocrats.'

'I don't know how you can like unsweetened tea! Why didn't you wake me? There was some money set aside.'

Mr. Pravin began to write again. Right from his early years this disease had afflicted him, and he had been feeding it now for twenty years. His body had wasted away in this sickness, his health had declined, and at forty, old age had set in; but the illness was incurable. From sunrise until midnight he was immersed in the inner universe of a worshipper of literature, his face turned away from all the rest of the world while he went on offering as oblation the flower of his heart. But in India the worship of Saraswati is an offence to Lakshmi. With only one spirit how could you delight both goddesses, how could the vessel of sacrifice be made one? And this disfavour of Lakshmi's did not manifest itself only in the form of impoverishment. Her cruelest joke was that newspaper editors and book publishers did not offer any heart-felt sympathy either. Could it be that the entire world had conspired against him? It had reached the point where this constant indigence seemed to have crushed his self-confidence. Possibly he was now beginning to realize that in his works there was no substance, no genius, and the feeling tore at his heart. This human life, so difficult to attain, had been destroyed all for nothing! He did not even have the consolation that though the world had not honoured him, yet his lifetime of work was not so insignificant after all. The constant doing without basic necessities had finally surpassed the bounds of asceticism. If there was any satisfaction it was that his life's companion was two steps ahead of him in renunciation and austerity. And Sumitra was happy in this situation. Pravin might have some complaints against the world, but like an air-filled cushion Sumitra kept protecting him from the shocks of the outside world. There was no question of her bemoaning her fate, and no frown ever appeared on the brow of this goddess.

Picking up the teacup, Sumitra said, 'Then why don't you go and take a walk for an hour or two? When you know that nothing at all has come of devoting your whole life to this work why torment yourself for nothing?'

Pravin, without looking up from his paper and still moving his pen, said, 'From writing at least I have the satisfaction that I'm doing something. Going out for a walk seems to me just a waste of time.'

'Still, so many of these educated men go out to enjoy a stroll — are they just wasting their time?'

'But most of those people don't suffer any decrease in their income when they go out for a stroll, they're mostly government servants who get a monthly salary or have a profession that people respect. But I'm just a mill worker. Have you ever seen a mill worker taking a stroll? The only people who need to take walks are those who don't lack for food. Anyone too broke to get enough to eat doesn't go for walks. When people are happy and enjoying life they need health and life enhancement. But for me life is a burden, and I have no wish to keep this burden any longer on my head.'

When Sumitra heard these words so full of despair her eyes filled with tears and she went inside. Her heart told her that one day surely glory and fame would reward these sacrifices even if Lakshmi remained unfavourable. But Pravin had now reached that limit of despair from which no glimmer of any hopeful dawn could be seen rising in the hostile sky.

\*

There's a celebration at some nobleman's house, and he sends an invitation to Mr. Pravin. Today Pravin's mind is flying on the winged horse of happiness. He has been deep in dreams about it the whole day. What words will the Raja use to welcome him, what will he say to thank him, what will they converse about, and with what famous people will he become acquainted — all day Pravin has been enjoying dreaming about such things. For this occasion he has also composed a poem in which he compares life to a garden. He put aside all his own strong principles this time because he did not want to wound the feelings of the aristocrats.

By noon he had already begun his preparations. He shaved, bathed with soap, applied oil to his hair. The problem was what to wear. A long time had passed since he'd had his jacket made, and its condition had deteriorated very much like his own. Just as from the slightest chilly spell he caught cold or a headache when it turned warm, in much the same way the jacket too had suffered a decline. He took it out and brushed it.

Sumitra said, 'It was pointless for you to accept that invitation. You should have written that you weren't feeling well. To go in such rags is really bad.'

Pravin said with philosophical gravity, 'Those to whom God has given heart and discrimination don't look at people's clothes, but at their virtues and character. After all, it's something that the Raja's invited me. I don't hold any official position, I don't have any estates or property, I'm not a contractor, I'm just a simple writer. A writer's value lies in his works. Since I believe this I don't have any more cause to feel ashamed than would any other writer.'

Filled with pity for his simplicity, Sumitra said, 'By living so long in a world of dreams you've become cut off from the real world.

159

I'm telling you, at the Raja's people will be looking most of all at what everybody's wearing. It's a fine thing to be simple, certainly, but that doesn't mean one has to look down at heel.'

Pravin felt that there was some sense in this. In the way of scholarly people he had no hesitation in acknowledging his mistakes. He said, 'I understand, I'll go after the lamps are lit.'

'But I ask you, why go at all?'

'How can I explain to you now that in every being there's a hunger for honour and respect? You'll ask, why is there this hunger? Because it's a stage in our self-development. We're a minute part of that great reality which pervades the whole universe, so it's inevitable that the qualities of the whole be present in the part. Therefore, our natural inclination lies in the direction of fame and respect, self-advancement and knowledge. I don't regard this desire as wrong.'

To make an end of it, Sumitra said, 'Very well, my dear, then go. I'm not arguing with you, but do make some provision for tomorrow, for I've only one *anna* left. I've already borrowed from the people I can borrow from and I've had no opportunity to pay them back. At this point I can't think of anything at all to do.'

Pravin said after a moment, 'There's money coming to me from a few magazines for some of my articles. Maybe it will come by tomorrow. And if we have to fast tomorrow, what does it matter? Our *dharma* is to work. We work and do it with all our heart and soul. If despite all that we have to fast, it's not my fault. So — I can only die. People like us die by the hundreds of thousands every day and the world keeps going on just the way it was before. So why grieve if we die of hunger? Death is nothing to fear. I accept the practice of those followers of Kabir who carry off the bier with music and song. I'm not afraid of it. You tell me, is it beyond my powers or not to do anything more than I'm doing? The whole world can sleep peacefully but I continue to sit with my pen. People go on enjoying pleasures and amusements, but all that's forbidden to me. For months I scarcely have occasion to laugh, even on Holi I didn't take any time off. Even when I'm ill all I'm concerned with is writing. Remember, you were sick and I couldn't find time to go to the doctor. If the world doesn't appreciate it — so what? It's only the world's loss, but no loss for me. The lamp's duty is to burn away — it's not concerned with whether its light is shed or something blocks it.

160

'And do I have any friends either, any acquaintances or relations, to whom I'm not indebted? I'm ashamed now just to go out of the house. The only satisfaction is that people don't think me dishonest. They may not be able to give me any more help but they surely sympathize with me. It's enough for my happiness that today the opportunity's come for a nobleman to honour me!'

Then suddenly he became as though intoxicated. Proudly he said, 'No, I won't go at night after all. My poverty has now reached the point of being a disgrace. It's futile to conceal it. I'll go this very moment. A man invited by noblemen and rajas can't be of such little account. Those aristocrats aren't just ordinary nobles, they're among the nobles of India, not just this town. Anyone who still thinks of me as worthless is worthless himself.'

*

It was evening. Pravin put on his old thread-bare jacket, worn-out shoes and shabby hat, and left the house, looking rather like a rustic or a burglar. Had he been prepossessing in build and looks, then even dressed like this he might have created an imposing effect, since a robust physique is of itself impressive. But there is an opposition between physical well-being and literature. If some literary personage is robust and over-sized then you may assume that there's no tenderness in him, no sweetness, no heart. The lamp's business is to burn away; the lamp full to the brim is one that doesn't want to burn. Nevertheless, he marched along with confidence, his whole presence radiated pride.

Now, usually when he left the house he slipped through the back alleys to evade the shopkeepers. But today he walked right in front of them with his head high, today he was ready to give a crushing reply to their demands for payment. But it was evening, there were shoppers sitting on all the shop platforms and no one looked his way. The sums which he, in his poverty, considered shameful, in the eyes of the shopkeepers were not of such importance that they would take an acquaintance to task about them in front of everybody, particularly when today he appeared to be on his way to meet someone.

Pravin had already made the circuit of the whole market but he was not satisfied. He walked through it again, and again was unsuccessful. This time he went straight to Hafiz Samad's shop and stood there. Hafiz was a general merchant from whose shop Pravin had taken an umbrella a good while back and had not yet been able to finish paying for it. When he saw Pravin he said, 'My dear sir, you still haven't paid for the umbrella. If I had a hundred or so customers like you I'd go bankrupt! It really has been a long time.'

Pravin was delighted, his heart's desire fulfilled. 'I haven't forgotten, Hafizji,' he said, 'but these days I've had so much work that I could hardly leave the house. But, if I may say so, I've no shortage of admirers. There are quite a few people always hanging around. Right now in fact the Raja Sahib — you know, the one who lives in the mansion on the corner — I'm on my way to his place to a banquet. Something like this keeps coming up every day.'

Impressed, Hafiz Samad said, 'Excellent! You're on your way to the Raja's. Naturally, only the nobles can appreciate geniuses like you, who else can? Praise God, you're unique in this age of ours! Now, should the opportunity come about, then don't forget us poor people. If the Raja Sahib were disposed to look upon me with favour, what more could I ask? Why, he must require a whole shopful of goods. His yearly income's two hundred and fifty or three hundred thousand.'

The amount seemed trivial to Pravin. The tongue's a spend-thrift, so what harm in saying a million or two? He said, 'Two hundred and fifty or three hundred thousand! You're insulting him. His income's no less than a million. One gentleman estimates it at two million. He has estates, buildings, shops, contracts, trust funds and then, he's in the good graces of the most important people in the government.'

Hafiz said very humbly, 'Sir, this shop is yours, such is my desire! *Arrey*, Muradi!' (he called to his servant), 'just go and have two paisa's worth of the best *paan* made up and bring it for the gentleman. Come now, have a seat for a few minutes, if there's anything you'd like, let me show it to you. My business is at your disposal.'

Pravin took the *paan* and said, 'But now forgive me, I'll be late, I'll come back some other time.'

He got up and stopped in front of a cloth merchant's shop belonging to one Manohar Das. When he saw Pravin, hope revived in him. The poor fellow had been bewailing his name, thinking he might even have left town. Now he assumed he had come to pay him. He said, 'Dear Mr. Pravin, I haven't had the good fortune to see you for quite some time. I sent notes to you on several occasions, but my servant was unable to locate you.' To his accountant he said, 'Just have a look and see what the gentleman owes us.'

Pravin's spirits were suffocated by his debts; but today he stood there as though he were wearing armour which no weapon could pierce to wound him. He said, 'I'm in a hurry just now, I'll stop if I may on my way back from the Raja Sahib's and then I can sit down with you without worrying, but I'm in a hurry now.'

The Raja Sahib owed Manohar Das several thousand rupees. Still, the merchant had not given up on him, he would get back three for every one. He placed Pravin in a very high rank as one whose profession was to plunder the aristocrats. He said, 'Do come and take some *paan*, sir. The Raja Sahib's only for a day, but my dear sir, we are for all the year round. If you need some clothes, then come and take them. Holi will soon be upon us. If you find the opportunity won't you please remind the Raja's treasurer that his old account has not been paid for a very long time, so why not clear it up now! When somebody doesn't pay bills for two years at a time what kind of profit can we expect?'

Pravin said, 'Please let me pass up the *paan* for now, brother. I'm going to be late. When the Raja's so keen to meet me and does me such a great honour, then it's my obligation not to cause him any inconvenience. We writers aren't hungry for wealth you see, we want people to appreciate our quality. If anyone will do us honour, we're his slaves. If somebody is conceited about his worldly power, we don't care a straw about him.'

*

When Pravin arrived before the Raja Sahib's vast mansion the lamps had already been lit. The motorcars of the rich and noble were lined up, uniformed doormen stood at the gates. One gentleman was greeting each of the guests. When he saw Pravinji he felt rather uncertain. Then, looking him up and down, he said, 'Do you have an invitation?'

Pravin had the invitation in his pocket, but he was angered by this discrimination. Why was he being asked to show his invitation? Why aren't the others being asked? He said, 'No, I don't have the invitation. If you ask these other gentlemen for theirs I can show you one as well. But if not, I regard this singling-out as an insult. Tell the Raja Sahib Pravinji came to his door and returned home.'

'No, no, sir, come along inside. We'd never been introduced, so please forgive my rudeness. Our gatherings take their lustre only from distinguished men like yourself. God has bestowed eloquence upon you such as cannot be described!'

This personage had never seen Pravin before. But what he said he could say just as well about any literary man, and we trust that no literary man could scorn the praise.

When Pravin proceeded on he saw electric lanterns casting their glow over the spacious decorated lawn before the summer house. In the centre was a pool, with the marble figure of a nymph from whose head a fountain sprayed jets of water which appeared in the glimmer of the coloured lanterns as though a rainbow had melted and rained down on them. Tables were set up all round the pool, with bright bouquets on the white tablecloths.

As soon as he saw Pravin the Raja Sahib welcomed him: 'Come along, come along! I was thrilled when I read your piece in *Hans*.* Quite astonished, really. I had no idea that a real find like you was hidden away in this town.'

Then he began to introduce him to the gentlemen who were there. 'You surely have heard the name of Mr. Pravin. Now here he is in person! What sweetness and power, what feeling and language, what inventiveness and style, what a wonder! Bravo! My heart feels as though it's about to dance!'

One gentleman, dressed in an English suit, looked at Pravin as though he were some creature in a zoo and said, 'Have you also made a study of the English poets? Byron, Shelley, Keats, and so on?'

Pravin said curtly, 'Yes, of course, I've read a bit of them.'

'If you were to translate the works of one of these great poets you would be rendering an inestimable service to the Hindi language.'

Pravin considered himself not a whit less than Byron, Shelley and the others. They were English poets, their language, style, subjects and significance, all were according to English taste. He did not think it a matter of pride for him to translate them any more than they would have thought it a matter of pride to translate him. He said, 'We are not so lacking in intellectual worth that we have to go begging from the foreign poets. In my opinion, in this subject at

---

* An important literary magazine begun in 1930 and published from Lucknow. Premchand, its first editor, published many of his late stories in *Hans*.

least India can teach the West something.'

At this absurd statement the Anglophile gentleman decided Pravin was crazy.

The Raja Sahib looked at Pravin as though to say, Please remember where you are when you speak! He said, 'But how can we criticize English literature? In poetry no one can rival them.'

Regarding Pravin arrogantly, the Anglophile gentlemen said, 'Our poets have never yet even understood the meaning of poetry. Until the present our poetry has consisted of pathetic descriptions of separated lovers and catalogues of women's charms.'*

Pravin gave as good as he got. 'I believe you haven't studied our present-day poets, or if you have, then only superficially.'

The Raja Sahib had now decided to shut Pravin up. 'This is Mr. Paranjpe, Pravinji! His articles are printed in the English papers and he is regarded with the greatest respect.'

Which meant, Now stop talking nonsense.

Pravin understood; he was supposed to look insignificant before Paranjpe.

It was intolerable to Pravin that despite being devoted to foreign dress and customs and language and hostile to his own people, this fellow should be treated with such respect. But what could one do?

Another gentleman of the same stamp came on the scene and was cordially greeted by the Raja Sahib. 'Welcome, Dr. Chaddha, how are you?'

The doctor shook hands with the Raja and then looking with curiosity at Pravin asked, 'May I know your good name, sir?'

The Raja Sahib introduced Pravin, adding, 'A fine poet and writer in Hindi.'

The doctor said with a peculiar tone, 'I see, you're a poet!' and without asking anything walked along.

Then another gentleman of the same sort put in an appearance, a well known barrister, to whom the Raja Sahib also introduced Pravin. He said in the same peculiar manner, 'I see, you're a poet!' and walked on. The same performance was repeated several times. And each time Pravin received the identical praise: 'I see, you're a poet!'

Every time these words inflicted a new wound on Pravin's heart.

---

* The stock-in-trade of poets writing in *Braj* before Premchand's time.

165

He understood very well the sentiment behind them. The plain meaning was, 'If you want to waste your time cooking up such nonsense, go ahead. What use is it to you? But how can you be so foolhardy as to blunder into cultured society like ours?'

In his inmost heart Pravin was angry with himself. He had considered himself terribly lucky when he got the invitation but on realizing how much he had been insulted when he came here, his own contented little house was heaven. He reproached himself: This is the punishment for those greedy for prestige. But now your eyes have been opened as to just how worthy of respect you are! You're utterly useless in this selfish world. Why should attorneys and barristers honour you? You can't be one of their clients, nor can they hope to get any law-suits from you. And why should doctors honour you? They have no wish to visit your house without collecting a fee for it. You were born to write, so go and write. That's the sum, you're of no other use in the world.

Suddenly there was great excitement among the gathering: tonight's guest of honor had arrived. This gentleman had just been appointed as judge in the High Court, for which achievement the festivities had been organized. The Raja Sahib rushed to him, shook his hand, and said to Pravinji: 'I imagine you've brought your poem?'

Pravin said, 'I wrote no poem.'

'Truly? But how perfectly dreadful of you! Come, my good man, dash off something right away. Just a few lines will do, that's all. It's quite imperative for a poem to be written on such an occasion as this.'

'I can't write anything as quickly as that.'

'Have I then wasted my time introducing you to all these people?'

'You have indeed wasted your time.'

'*Arrey*, my dear fellow, then recite something by some ancient poet, who among these people would know the difference?'

'Certainly not — it you will forgive me. I'm no minstrel or street-side story-teller.'

Saying this, Pravin immediately took his departure. When he arrived home he was smiling.

Delighted, Sumitra asked, 'Why have you come home so early?'

'I wasn't needed there.'

'Come now, you're all smiles, you must have been highly

honoured.'

'Oh yes, I was honoured in a way I hadn't hoped for.'

'And you're very happy!'

'Only because tonight I learned a lesson for all time. I'm a lamp and I was created to burn. Today I forgot that principle. But the good Lord didn't let me stray for long. This wretched dwelling of mine is heaven for me. Tonight I understood the truth that the service of literature demands complete sacrifice.'

# A Coward

The boy's name was Keshav, the girl's Prema. They went to the same college, they were in the same class. Keshav believed in new ways and was opposed to the old caste customs. Prema adhered to the old order and fully accepted the traditions. But all the same there was a strong attachment between them and the whole college was aware of it. Although he was a Brahman Keshav regarded marriage with this Baniya girl as the culmination of his life. He didn't care a straw about his father and mother. Caste traditions he considered a fraud. If anything embodied the truth for him it was Prema. But for Prema it was impossible to take one step in opposition to the dictates of caste and family.

One evening the two of them met in a secluded corner of Victoria Park and sat down on the grass facing one another. The strollers had gone off one by one but these two lingered on. They had got into a discussion it was impossible to end.

Keshav said angrily, 'All it means is that you don't care about me.'

Prema tried to calm him down. 'You're being unjust to me, Keshav. It's only that I don't know how I can bring it up at home without upsetting them. They're devoted to the old traditions. If they hear anything about a matter like this from me can't you imagine how distressed they'll be?'

'And aren't you a slave of those old traditions too then?' Keshav asked her sharply.

'No, I'm not,' Prema said, her eyes tender, 'but what my mother and father want is more important to me than anything.'

'And you yourself don't count at all?'

'If that's how you want to understand it.'

'I used to think those old ways were just for silly hypocrites but now it seems that educated girls like you knuckle under to them too. Since I'm ready to give up everything for you I expect the same thing from you.'

In silence Prema wondered what authority she had over her own life. She had no right to go in any way against the mother and father who had created her from their own blood and reared her with love. To Keshav she said humbly, 'Can love be considered only in terms of husband and wife and not friendship? I think of love as an attachment of the soul.'

'You'll drive me crazy with your rationalizations,' Keshav said harshly. 'Just understand this — if I'm disappointed I can't go on living. I'm a materialist and it's not possible for me to be satisfied with some intangible happiness in the world of the imagination.'

He caught Prema's hand and tried to draw her toward him, but she broke away and said, 'I told you I'm not free. Don't ask me to do something I have no right to do.'

If she'd spoken harshly he would not have been so hurt. For an instant he restrained himself, then he stood up and said sadly, 'Just as you wish,' and slowly walked away. Prema, in tears, continued to sit there.

*

When after supper that night Prema lay down in her mother's room she could not sleep. Keshav had said things to her that shadowed her heart like reflections in unquiet waters, changing at every moment, and she could not calm them. How could she talk to her mother about such things? Embarrassment kept her silent. She thought, 'If I don't marry Keshav what's left for me in life?' While she thought about it over and over again her mind was made up about just one thing — if she did not marry Keshav she would marry no one.

Her mother said, 'Still not sleeping? I've told you so many times you ought to do a little work around the house. But you can never take any time off from your books. In a little while you'll be going to some strange house and who knows what sort of place it will be? If you don't get accustomed to doing housework, how are you going to manage?'

Naively Prema asked, 'Why will I be going to a strange house?'

Smiling, her mother said, 'For a girl it's the greatest calamity, daughter. After being sheltered at home, as soon as she's grown up off she goes to live with others. If she gets a good husband her days pass happily, otherwise she has to go through life weeping. It all depends on fate. But in our community there's no family that appeals to me. There's no proper regard for girls anywhere. But we have to stay within our caste. Who knows how long caste marriages

169

are going to go on?'

Frightened Prema said, 'But here and there they're beginning to have marriages outside the caste.' She'd said it for the sake of talking but she trembled lest her mother might guess something.

Surprised, her mother asked, 'You don't mean among Hindus?' Then she answered herself. 'If this has happened in a few places, then what's come of it?'

Prema did not reply. She was afraid her mother had understood her meaning. She saw her future in that moment before her like a great dark tunnel opening its mouth to swallow her up. It was a long time before she could fall asleep.

\*

When she got up early in the morning Prema was aware of a strange new courage. We all make important decisions on the spur of the moment as though some divine power impelled us toward them, and so it was with Prema. Until yesterday she'd considered her parents' ideas as unchallengeable, but facing the problem courage was born in her, much in the way a quiet breeze coming against a mountain sweeps over the summit in a violent gust. Prema thought, 'Agreed, this body is my mother's and father's but whatever my own self, my soul, is to get must be got in this body. To hesitate now would not only be unfitting, it would be fatal. Why sacrifice your life for false principle? If a marriage isn't founded on love then it's just a business bargain with the body. Could you give yourself without love?' And she rebelled against the idea that she could be married off to somebody she had never seen.

After breakfast she had started to read when her father called her affectionately. 'Yesterday I went to see your principal and he had a lot of praise for you.'

'You're only saying that!'

'No, it's true.' Then he opened a drawer of his desk and took out a picture set in a velvet frame. He showed it to her and said, 'This boy came out first in the Civil Service examinations. You must have heard of him.'

He had brought up the subject in such a way as not to give away his intention, but it was clear to Prema, she saw through it at once. Without looking at the picture she said, 'No, I don't know who he is.'

170

With feigned surprise her father said, 'What? You haven't even heard his name? His picture and an article about him are in today's paper.'

'Suppose they are?' Prema said. 'The examinations don't mean anything to me. I always assumed that people who took those exams must be terribly conceited. After all, what do they aim for except to lord it over their wretched, penniless brothers? — And pile up a fortune doing it. That's no great career to aspire to.'

The objection was spiteful, unjust. Her father had assumed that after his eulogy she would be interested. When he'd listened to her answer he said sharply, 'You talk as though money and power mean nothing to you.'

'That's right,' she said, 'they don't mean a thing to me. I look for self-sacrifice in a man. I know some boys who wouldn't accept that kind of position even if you tried to force it on them.'

'Well, I've learned something new today!' he said sarcastically 'And still I see people swarming around trying to get the meanest little jobs — I'd just like to see the face of one of these fellows capable of such self-sacrifice. If I did I'd get down on my knees to him.'

Perhaps if she'd heard these words on another occasion Prema might have hung her head in shame. But this time, like a soldier with a dark tunnel behind him, there was no way for her to go except forward. Scarcely controlling her anger, her eyes full of indignation, she went to her room and from among several pictures of Keshav picked out the one she considered the worst and brought it back and set it down in front of her father. He wanted to give it no more than a casual glance, but at the first glimpse he was drawn to it. Keshav was tall and even though thin one recognized a strength and discipline about him; he was not particularly handsome but his face reflected such intelligence that one felt confidence in him.

While he looked at it her father said, 'Who is he?'

Prema, bowing her head, said hesitantly, 'He's in my class.'

'Is he of our community?'

Prema's face clouded over: her destiny was to be decided on the answer. She realised that it was useless to have brought out the picture. The firmness she had had for an instant weakened before this simple question. In a low voice she said, 'No, he's not, he's a Brahman.' And even while she was saying it, agitated she left the room as though the atmosphere there were suffocating her, and on the other side of the wall she began to cry.

Her father's anger was so great at first that he wanted to call her out again and tell her plainly it was impossible. He got as far as the door, but seeing Prema crying his anger softened. He was aware of what Prema felt for this boy and he believed in education for women but he intended to maintain the family traditions. He would have sacrificed all his property for a suitable bridegroom of his own caste. But outside the limits of his community he could not conceive of any bridegroom worthy or noble enough; he could not imagine any disgrace greater than going beyond them.

'From today on you'll stop going to college,' he said with a harsh tone. 'If education teaches you to disregard our traditions, then education is wicked.'

Timidly Prema said, 'But it's almost time for the examinations.'

'Forget about them.'

Then he went into his room and pondered a long time.

*

One day six months later Prema's father came home and called Vriddha, his wife, for a private talk.

'As far as I know,' he said, 'Keshav's a well-brought-up and brilliant boy. I'm afraid that Prema's grieving to the point where she might take her life. You and I have tried to explain and so have others but nobody has had the slightest effect on her. What are we going to do about it?'

Anxiously his wife said, 'Let her, but if she has her way how can you face the dishonour? How could I ever have borne a wicked girl like that?'

He frowned and said with a tone of reproach, 'I've heard that a thousand times. But just how long can we moan about this caste tradition business? You're mistaken if you think the bird's going to stay hopping at home once it's spread its wings. I've thought about the problem objectively and I've come to the conclusion that we're obliged to face the emergency. I can't watch Prema die in the name of caste rules. Let people laugh but the time is not far off when all these old restrictions will be broken. Even today there have been hundreds of marriages outside the caste limitations. If the aim of marriage is a happy life for a man and a woman together we can't

172

oppose Prema.'

Vriddha was angry. 'If that's your intention then why ask me?' she said. 'But I say that I won't have anything to do with this marriage, and I'll never look at that girl's face again, I'll consider her as dead as our sons who died.'

'Well then, what else can you suggest?'

'What if we do let her marry this boy? He'll take his civil service examinations in two years and with what he has to offer it will be a great deal if he becomes a clerk in some office.'

'But what if Prema should kill herself?'

'Then let her — you've encouraged her, haven't you? If she doesn't care about us why should we blacken our name for her? Anyway, suicide's no game — it's only a threat. The heart's like a wild horse — until it's broken and bridled nobody can touch it. If her heart stays like that who's to say that she'll stick with Keshav for a whole life-time? The way she's in love with him today, well, she can be in love with somebody else just as much tomorrow. And because of this you're ready to be disgraced?'

Her husband gave her a questioning look. 'And if tomorrow she should go and marry Keshav, then what will you do? Then how much of your honour will be left? Out of shyness or consideration for us she may not have done anything yet, but if she decides to be stubborn there's nothing you or I can do.'

It had never occurred to Vriddha that the problem could have such a dreadful ending. His meaning struck her with the violence of a bullet. She sat silent for a moment as though the shock had scattered her wits. Then backing down, she said, 'What wild ideas you have! Until today I've never heard of a decent girl marrying according to her own wish.'

'You may not have heard of it but I have, I've seen it and it's entirely possible.'

'The day it happens will be my last!'

'But if it has to be this way isn't it preferable that we make the proper arrangements? If we're to be disgraced we may as well be efficient about it. Send for Keshav tomorrow and see what he has to say.'

*

Keshav's father lived off a government pension. By nature he was ill-tempered and miserly; he found satisfaction only in religious ostentation. He was totally without imagination and unable to respect the personal feelings of anybody else. At present he was still living in the same world in which he had passed his childhood and youth. The rising tide of progress he called ruination and hoped to save at least his own family from it by any means available to him. Therefore when one day Prema's father came to him and broached the prospect of her marrying Keshav, old Panditji could not control himself. Staring through eyes dim with anger he said, 'Are you drunk? Whatever this relationship may be it's not marriage. It appears that you too have had your head turned by the new ideas.'

'I don't like this sort of connection either,' Prema's father said gently. 'My ideas about it are just the same as yours. But the thing is that, being helpless, I had to come to see you. You're aware too of how willful today's youngsters have become. It's getting hard for us old-timers to defend our theories. I'm afraid that if these two become desperate they may take their lives.'

Old Panditji brought his foot down with a bang and shouted, 'What are you saying, Sir! Aren't you ashamed? We're Brahmans and even among Brahmans we're of high rank. No matter how low a Brahman may fall he can never be so degraded that he can countenance a marriage with a shop-keeping Baniya's daughter. The day noble Brahmans run out of daughters we can discuss the problem. I say you have a fantastic nerve even to bring this matter up with me.'

He was every bit as furious as Prema's father was humble, and the latter, unable to bear the humiliation any longer, went off cursing his luck.

Just then Keshav returned from college. Panditji sent for him at once and said severely, 'I've heard that you're betrothed to some Baniya girl. How far has this actually gone?'

Pretending ignorance, Keshav said, 'Who told you this?'

'Somebody. I'm asking you, is it true or not? If it's true and you've decided to go against your caste, then there's no more room for you in this house. You won't get one pice of my money. Whatever is in this house I've earned, and it's my right to give it to whoever I want. If you're guilty of this wicked conduct, you won't be permitted to put your foot inside my house.'

174

Keshav was familiar with his father's temper. He loved Prema and he intended to marry her in secret. His father wouldn't always be alive and he counted on his mother's affection; sustained by that love he felt that he was ready to suffer any hardship. But Keshav was like a faint-hearted soldier who loses his courage at the sight of a gun and turns back.

Like any average young fellow he would argue his theories with a passion and demonstrate his devotion with his tongue. But to suffer for them was beyond his capacity. If he persisted and his father refused to weaken he didn't know where he would turn, his life would be ruined.

In a low voice he said, 'Whoever told you that is a complete liar and nothing else. 'Staring at him, Panditji said, 'So my information is entirely wrong?'

Yes, entirely wrong.'

'Then you'll write a letter to that shopkeeper this very moment and remember that if there's any more of this gossip he can regard you as his greatest enemy. Enough, go.'

Keshav could say no more. He walked away but it seemed to him that his legs were utterly numb.

*

The next day Prema sent this letter to Keshav.

Dearest Keshav,

I was terribly upset when I heard about the rude and callous way your father treated mine. Perhaps he's threatened you too, in which case I wait anxiously to hear what your decision is. I'm ready to undergo any kind of hardship with you. I'm aware of your father's wealth but all I need is your love to content me. Come tonight and have dinner with us. My mother and father are both eager to meet you.

I'm caught up in the dream of when the two of us will be joined by that bond that cannot be broken, that remains strong no matter how great the difficulties.

Your Prema

By evening there had been no reply to this letter. Prema's mother asked over and over again, 'Isn't Keshav coming?' And her father kept his eyes glued on the door. By nine o'clock there was still no sign of Keshav nor any letter.

In Prema's mind all sorts of fears and hopes revolved. Perhaps Keshav had had no chance to write a letter, no chance to come today so that tomorrow he would surely come. She read over again the love letters he'd written her earlier. How steeped in love was every word, how much emotion, anxiety and acute desire! Then she remembered the words he'd said a hundred times and how often he'd wept before her. It was impossible to despair with so many proofs, but all the same throughout the night she was tormented by anxiety.

Early in the morning Keshav's answer came. Prema took the letter with trembling hands and read it. The letter fell from her hands. It seemed to her that her blood had ceased to flow. He had written:

I'm in a terrible quandary about how to answer you. I've been desperate trying to figure out what to do and I've come to the conclusion that for the present it would be impossible for me to go against my father's orders. Don't think I'm a coward. I'm not being selfish either. But I don't have the strength to overcome the obstacles facing me. Forget what I told you before. At that time I had no idea of how hard it was going to be.

Prema drew a long, painful breath, then she tore up the letter and threw it away. Her eyes filled with tears. She had never had the slightest expectation that the Keshav she had taken into her heart of hearts as her husband could be so cruel. It was as though until now she'd been watching a golden vision but on opening her eyes it had vanished completely. All her hope had disappeared and she was left in darkness.

'What did Keshav write?' her mother asked.

Prema looked at the floor and said, 'He's not feeling well.' What else was there to say? She could not have borne the shame of revealing Keshav's brutal disloyalty.

She spent the whole day working around the house, as though there was nothing wrong. She made dinner for everyone that evening and ate with them, then until quite late she played the harmonium and sang.

176

In the morning they found her lying dead in her room at a moment when the golden rays of dawn bestowed on her face the illusory splendour of life.

# THE WORLD

THE WORLD

## A Servant of the Nation

The servant of the nation said, 'There is only one way to redeem the country and that is to treat the low as brothers, the outcastes as equals. In the world all are brothers: no one is high, no one is low.'

The world cheered. 'How sublime a vision, how compassionate a heart!'

His beautiful daughter Indira heard and was plunged into a sea of care.

The servant of the people embraced a young man of low caste.

The world said, 'He is an angel, an apostle, the pilot of the ship of state!'

Indira watched and her eyes began to glow.

The servant of the people brought the young man of low caste inside the temple into the presence of God and said, 'Our God is in poverty, in misfortune and in degradation.'

The world said, 'How pure in heart he is! How wise!'

Indira looked and smiled.

Indira went to the servant of the people and said, 'Respected father, I wish to marry Mohan.'

The servant of the people looked at her with loving eyes and asked, 'Who is Mohan?'

Indira said joyously, 'Mohan is the honest, brave and good young man you embraced and brought into the temple.'

The servant of the people looked at her with the eyes of doom and turned away.

# The Chess Players

It was the era of Wajid Ali Shah*. Lucknow was plunged deep in luxurious living. Exalted and humble, rich and poor, all were sunk in luxury. While one might arrange parties for dancing and singing another would find enjoyment only in the drowsy ecstasy of opium. In every sphere of life pleasure and merry-making ruled supreme. Indulgence in luxury pervaded the government, the literary world, the social order, arts and crafts, industry, cuisine, absolutely everywhere. The bureaucrats were steeped in gross sensuality, poets in describing lovers and the sufferings of separation, artisans in creating intricate patterns of gold and silver thread and embroidery, merchants in selling eye-shadow, perfumes, unguents and coloring for the teeth. All eyes were dimmed with the intoxication of luxury. No one had any awareness of what was going on in the world. There were quail fights, betting on matches between fighting partridges, here the cloth for *causar*** spread out, there shouts of 'What luck, I've made an ace and twelve!' and elsewhere a fierce chess battle getting under way.

From king to beggar all were swept with the same antic spirit, to the point where when beggars were given money they spent it not on bread but on opium or *madak*****. By playing chess, cards or *ganjifa****** the wits were sharpened, the process of thought was developed, one became accustomed to solving complex problems — arguments of this sort were presented with great vehemence. (The world is not free even today of people of this persuasion!). So if Mirza Sajjad Ali and Mir Raushan Ali spent most of their time sharpening their wits, what reasonable person could object? Both of them were masters of hereditary estates and had no worry about their income, so they could lounge around at home enjoying their

---

* The last king of Oudh (Avadh); the story takes place in 1856.
** A game of dice.
*** An intoxicant prepared from opium.
**** A type of card game.

182

idleness. After all, what else was there to do? Early in the morning, after breakfast, they would sit down, set out the board, arrange the chessmen, and warlike stratagems would begin. From then on they were quite unaware of when it was noon or afternoon or evening. Time and time again word would be sent from the kitchen that dinner was ready and the answer would come back: Get on with it, we're coming, set the table. It would reach the point where the cook, desperate, would serve their meal right in their chamber and the two friends would go on with both activities, eating and playing simultaneously.

In Mirza Sajjad Ali's household there was no elder, so the games took place in his drawing room. But this is not to say that the other people of Mirza's household were happy with these goings-on. And not only the members of his household but the neighbours and even the servants were constantly making malicious comments. 'The game's ill-omened! It's destroying the family. Heaven forbid that anybody should become addicted to it, he'd be utterly useless to God or man, at home or in the world! It's a dreadful sickness, that's what.' Even Mirza's wife, the Begam Sahiba, hated it so much that she sought every possible occasion to scold him. But she hardly ever found the chance, for the game would have begun before she woke and in the evening Mirzaji would be likely to appear in the bedroom only after she had gone to sleep. But the servants of course felt the full force of her rage. 'He's asked for *paan*, has he? Well, tell him to come and get it himself! He hasn't got time for his dinner? Then go and dump it on his head, he can eat it or give it to the dogs!' But to his face she could not say anything at all. She was not so angry with him as with Mir Sahib, whom she referred to as 'Mir the Troublemaker.' Possibly it was Mirzaji who laid all the blame on Mir in order to excuse himself.

One day the Begam Sahiba had a headache. She said to the maid, 'Go and call Mirza Sahib and have him get some medicine from the doctor. Be quick about it, run!' When the maid went to him Mirzaji said, 'Get along with you, I'll come in a moment or two.' The Begam Sahiba's temper flared at this. Who could put up with a husband playing chess while she had a headache? Her face turned scarlet. She said to the maid, 'Go and tell him that if he doesn't go at once I'll go out to the doctor myself *.' Mirzaji was immersed in a very

* For an aristocatic lady in *purdab* this would be inappropriate.

183

interesting game, in two more moves he would checkmate Mir Sahib. Irritated, he said, 'She's not on her deathbed, is she? Can't she be just a little patient?'

'Come now,' said Mir, 'go and see what she has to say. Women can be touchy, you know.'

'To be sure,' said Mirza, 'why shouldn't I go? You'll be check-mated in two moves.'

'My dear fellow, better not count on it. I've thought of a move that will checkmate you with all your pieces still on the board. But go on now, listen to her, why make her feel hurt for no reason at all?'

'I'll go only after I've checkmated you.'

'Then I won't play. Do go and hear her out.'

'I'll have to go to the doctor's, old man. It's not just a mere headache, it's an excuse to bother me.'

'Whatever it is, you really must indulge her.'

'Very well, but let me make just one more move.'

'Absolutely not, until you've gone to her I won't so much as touch a piece.'

When Mirza Sahib felt compelled to go to his wife the Begam Sahiba was frowning, but she said with a moan, 'You love your wretched chess so much that even if somebody were dying you wouldn't think of leaving it! Heaven forbid there should ever be another man like you!'

Mirza said, 'What can I tell you? Mir Sahib simply wouldn't agree. I had a most difficult time of it putting him off so I could come.'

'Does he think everybody is just as worthless as himself? Doesn't he have children too or has he just let them go to the dogs?'

'He's utterly mad about chess,' said Mirza. 'Whenever he comes I'm compelled to play with him.'

'Why don't you tell him off?'

'He's my equal in age and a couple of steps above me in rank, I'm obliged to be courteous with him.'

'In that case, *I'll* tell him off! If he gets angry, let him. Is he supporting us, after all? As they say, "If the queen sulks, she'll only hurt herself." Hiriya!' she called her maid, 'Go out and take up the chessboard, and say to Mir Sahib, "The master won't play now, pray be good enough to take your leave."'

'For heaven's sake, don't do anything so outrageous!' said Mirza. 'Do you want to disgrace me? Wait, Hiriya, where are you going?'

184

'Why don't you let her go? Anybody who stops her will be simply killing me! Very well, then, stop her, but see if you can stop me.'

Saying this, the Begam Sahiba headed for the drawing room in high dudgeon. Poor Mirza turned pale. He began to implore his wife: 'For God's sake, in the name of the holy Prophet Husain! If you go to him it will be like seeing me laid out!' But the Begam did not pay the slightest attention to him. But when she reached the door of the drawing room all of a sudden, finding herself about to appear before a man not of her household, her legs felt as though paralyzed. She peeked inside, and as it happened, the room was empty. Mir Sahib had done a little shifting of the chess pieces and was now strolling outside in order to demonstrate his innocence. The next thing that happened was that the Begam went inside, knocked over the chessboard, flung some of the pieces under the sofa and others outside, then clapped the double doors shut and locked them. Mir Sahib was just outside the door. When he saw the chessmen being tossed out and the jingling of bangles reached his ears he realized that the Begam Sahiba was in a rage. Silently he took his way home.

Mirza said, 'You have committed an outrage!'

She answered, 'If Mir Sahib comes back here I'll have him kicked out straightaway. If you devoted such fervour to God you'd be a saint. You're to play chess while I slave away looking after this household? Are you going to the doctor's or are you still putting it off?'

When he came out of his house Mirza, instead of going to the doctor's, went to Mir Sahib's and told him the whole story. Mir Sahib said, 'So I guessed when I saw the chess pieces sailing outside. I took off at once. She seems to be quick to fly off the handle. But you've spoiled her too much, and that's not at all the way to do things. What concern is it of hers what you do away from her part of the house? Her work is to look after the home. What business does she have with anything else?'

'Well, tell me, where are we going to meet now?'

'No problem, we have this whole big house, so that's settled, we'll meet here.'

'But how am I going to placate the Begam Sahiba? She was furious when I sat down to play at home, so if I play here it could cost me my life.'

185

'Let her babble, in a few days she'll be all right. But of course you ought to show a little backbone yourself.'

*

For some unknown reason Mir Sahib's Begam considered it most fitting for her husband to stay far away from home. For this reason she had never before criticized his chess-playing, but on the contrary, if he was late in going she reminded him. For these reasons Mir Sahib had been deluded into thinking his wife was extremely serious and humble. But when they began to set up the chess board in the drawing room and Mir Sahib was at home all day the Begam Sahiba was very distressed. This was a hindrance to her freedom, and all day long she would yearn to be at the door looking out.

Meantime, the servants had begun to gossip. Formerly they had lain around all day in idleness, if someone came to the house, if someone left, it was no business of theirs. Now they were living in fear all twenty-four hours of the day. Orders would come for *paan*, then for sweets. And, like some lover's heart, the *hookah* had to be kept burning constantly. They would go to the mistress and say, 'The master's chess games are giving us a lot of trouble. We're getting blisters on our feet from running all day. What kind of a game is it that starts at dawn and goes on till evening? Diversion for an hour or two, that's enough for any game. Of course we're not complaining, we're your slaves, whatever you command naturally we'll do it; but this game is positively sinister! Whoever plays it never prospers, and surely some disaster will befall his home. It can reach the point where one neighbourhood after another's been known to go to rack and ruin. Everybody in this part of town is gossiping about it. We have eaten your salt, we're grieved to hear bad things about the master, but what can we do?'

Hearing this, the Begam Sahiba would say, 'I don't like it myself, but he won't listen to anybody, so what can be done?'

In their quarter there were also a few people from an earlier generation who began to imagine all sorts of disasters: 'There's no hope now. If our nobles are like this, then God help the country! This chess playing will be the ruin of the kingdom. The omens are bad.'

The entire realm was in an uproar. Subjects were robbed in broad daylight and nobody was there to hear their appeals. All the wealth of the countryside had been drawn into Lucknow to be squandered on whores, clowns and the satisfaction of every kind of vice. The debt to the East India Company kept on growing day by day, and day by day the general misery was getting harder to bear. Throughout the land, because of the wretched conditions, the yearly taxes were no longer collected. Time and again the British resident warned them, but everyone in Lucknow was so drowned in the intoxication of sensual indulgence that not a soul gave any heed.

Well then, the chess games continued in Mir Sahib's drawing room over the course of several months. Newer strategies were devised, new defences organized, and ever new battle formations planned. From time to time quarrels broke out as they played, and they even reached the point of exchanging vulgar insults; but peace was quickly restored between the two friends. At times the game would come to a halt and Mirzaji would return home in a huff and Mir Sahib would go and sit in his own chamber. But with a good night's sleep all the bad feelings would be calmed; early in the morning the two friends would arrive in the drawing room.

One day when they sat engrossed in thorny chess problems an officer of the royal army arrived on horseback and inquired for Mir Sahib. Mir Sahib panicked, wondering what disaster was about to come down on his head. Why had he been summoned? The case appeared desperate. To the servants he said, 'Tell him I'm not at home.'

'If he's not at home where is he?' the horseman demanded. The servant said he didn't know — what was this all about? 'How can I tell *you* what it's about?' said the officer. 'Maybe soldiers are being levied for the army. It's no joke, being the master of rent-free estates. When he has to go to the front lines he'll find out what it's all about.'

'Very well, go along, he'll be informed.'

'It's not just a matter of informing him. I'll come back tomorrow, I have orders to take him back with me.'

The horseman left. Mir Sahib was shaking with terror. He said to Mirzaji, 'Tell me, sir, what's going to happen now?'

'It's a great misfortune! What if I'm summoned too?'

'The bastard said he was coming back tomorrow.'

'It's a calamity, no doubt of it. If we have to go to the front we'll

187

die before our time.'

'Now listen, there's one way out: we won't meet here at the house any more. Starting tomorrow we'll have our game in some deserted place out on the banks of the Gomti. Who could find us there? When that fine fellow comes for me he'll have to go back without us.'

'By Allah, that's a splendid idea! That's certainly the best way.'

In the meantime, Mir Sahib's Begam was saying to that cavalry officer, 'You've got them out of the way very nicely,' and he answered, 'I'm used to making such jackasses dance to my tune. Chess has robbed them of all their common sense and courage. After this they won't stay at home, whatever happens.'

\*

From the next day on the two friends would set out from the house at the crack of dawn, carrying with them a rather small carpet and a box of prepared *paan,* and go to the other side of the Gomti river to an old ruined mosque which had probably been built in the time of Nawab Asafuddaula *. Along the way they would pick up tobacco, a pipe and some wine, and spread their carpet in the mosque, fill the *bookah* and sit down to play. After that they had no care for this world or the next. Apart from 'check' and 'checkmate,' not another word came out of their mouths. No *yogi* could have been more profoundly plunged in trance. At noon when they felt hungry they would go to some baker's shop and eat something, smoke a pipeful, and then return to engage once more in battle. At times they would even forget all about eating.

Meantime, the political situation in the country was becoming desperate. The East India Company's armies were advancing on Lucknow. There was commotion in the city. People were taking their children and fleeing to the countryside. But our two players were not in the least concerned about it. When they left home they took to the narrow alleyways, fearing lest some government official might catch a glimpse of them and have them forced into military service. They wanted to enjoy the thousands in income from their estates without giving anything in return.

---

*'Ruler of Oudh, 1775-97; his reign was noted both for debauchery and for the construction of many buildings, especially mosques.

One day the two friends were sitting in the ruined mosque playing chess. Mirza's game was rather weak and Mir Sahib was checking him at every move. At the same time the Company's soldiers could be seen approaching. This was an army of Europeans on their way to impose their rule on Lucknow.

Mir Sahib said, 'The British army's coming. God save us!'

Mirza said, 'Let them come, but now get out of check.'

'Maybe we ought to have a look, let's stand here where we can't be seen.'

'You can look later, what's the rush? Check again.'

'They have artillery too. There must be about five thousand men. What odd-looking soldiers! They've got red faces, just like monkeys, it's really frightening.'

'Don't try to get out of it, sir! Use these tricks on somebody else. Checkmate!'

'What a strange fellow you are! Here we have the city struck with calamity and you can only think of ways to checkmate. Do you have any idea how we're going to get home if the city's surrounded?'

'When it's time to go home we'll see about it then. This is checkmate, your king's finished now.'

The army had marched by. It was now ten in the morning. A new game was set up.

Mirza said, 'What are we going to do about food today?'

'Well, today's a fast day — are you feeling hungrier than usual?'

'Not in the least. But I wonder what's happening in the city.'

'Nothing at all's happening in the city. People are eating their dinner and settling down comfortably for an afternoon nap. The King's in his harem, no doubt.'

By the time they sat down to play again it was three. This time Mirzaji's game was weak. Four o'clock had just struck when the army was heard marching back. Nawab Wajid Ali had been taken prisoner and the army was conducting him to some unknown destination. In the city there was no commotion, no massacre, not a drop of blood was spilled. Until now no king of an independent country could ever have been overthrown so peacefully, without the least bloodshed. This was not that non-violence which delights the gods, but rather the sort of cowardice which makes even great cowards shed tears. The king of the vast country of Oudh was leaving it a captive, and Lucknow remained deep in its sensual slumber. This was the final stage of political decadence.

189

Mirzaji said, 'Those tyrants have imprisoned His Majesty.'

'I suppose so. Look here — check.'

'Just a moment, sir, I don't feel in the mood now. The poor King must be weeping tears of blood at this moment.'

'I'm sure he is — what luxuries will he enjoy as a prisoner? Checkmate!'

'Everybody has to suffer some change in his fortunes,' said Mirza. 'But what a painful situation!'

'True, that's the way things are. Look, checkmate! That does it, you can't get out of it now.'

'God's oath, you're hard-hearted. You can watch a great catastrophe like this and feel no grief. Alas, poor Wajid Ali Shah!'

'First save your own king, then you can mourn for His Majesty. It's checkmate now. Your hand on it!'

The army passed by, taking the King with them. As soon as they were gone Mirza again set up the chess pieces. The sting of defeat is bitter. Mir said, 'Come now, let us compose an elegy for His Majesty.' But Mirza's patriotism had vanished with his defeat. He was eager for vengeance.

*

It was evening. In the ruins the swallows were returning and settling in their nests, the bats began to chitter. But the players were still at it, like two blood-thirsty warriors doing battle together. Mirzaji had lost three games in a row; the outlook for this fourth game was not good either. He played each move carefully, firmly resolved to win, but one move after the other turned out to be so ill-conceived that his game kept deteriorating. For his part, Mir Sahib was singing a *gazal* and snapping his fingers from sheer high spirits, as though he had come upon some hidden treasure. Listening to him, Mirzaji was furious, but praised him in order to conceal his exasperation. But as his game worsened his patience began to slip out of control until he reached the point of getting angry at everything Mir said.

'Don't change your move, sir,' he would say. 'How can you go back on a move? Whatever move is to be made, make it just once. Why is your hand on that piece? Leave it alone! Until you figure out your move don't so much as touch your piece! You're taking half-an-hour for every move, that's against the rules. Anyone who takes more than five minutes for a move may be understood to be checkmated. You changed your move again! Just be quiet and put that piece back there.'

Mir Sahib's queen was in danger. He said, 'But when did I make my move?'

'You've already made it. Put the piece right there, in that same square.'

'Why should I put it in that square? When did I take my hand off the piece?'

'If you wait till doomsday to make your move, you'll still have to make it.'

'You're the one who's cheating! Victory and defeat depend on fate, you can't win by cheating.'

'Then it's settled, you've lost this game.'

'How have I lost it?'

'Then put the piece back in the same square where it was.'

'Why should I put it there? I won't!'

'Why should you put it there? You *have* to put it there.'

The quarrel was getting worse. Each stuck to his position, neither one would give an inch. Their words began to move to irrelevant matters. Mirza said, 'If anybody in your family had ever played chess then you might be familiar with the rules. But they were just grass-cutters. So how can you be expected to play chess? Real aristocracy is quite another thing. Nobody can become a noble just by having had some rent-free estates given to him.'

'What! Your own father must have cut grass! My people have been playing chess for generations.'

'Come off it, you spent your whole life working as a cook in Gaziuddin Haidar's house and now you're going around posing as an aristocrat.'

'Why are you defaming your own ancestors?' said Mir. 'They must, all have been cooks. My people have always dined at the King's own table.'

'You grass-cutter you! Stop your bragging.'

'You check your tongue or you'll be sorry! I won't stand for talk like that. I put out the eyes of anybody who frowns at me. Do you have the courage?'

'So you want to find out how brave I am! Come on then, let's have it out, whatever the consequences.'

Said Mir, 'And who do you think is going to let you push them around!'

The two friends drew the swords from their belts. It was a chivalric age when everybody went around carrying swords, daggers, poniards and the like. Both of them were sensualists but not cowards. They were politically debased, so why should they die for king or kingdom? But they did not lack personal courage. They challenged one another formally, the swords flashed, there was a sound of clanging. Both fell wounded, and both writhed and expired on the spot. They had not shed a single tear for their king but gave up their lives to protect a chess queen.

Darkness was coming on. The chess game had been set up. The two kings each on his throne sat there as though lamenting the death of these two heroes.

Silence spread over all. The broken archways of the ruins, the crumbling walls and dusty minarets looked down on the corpses and mourned.

# The Road to Hell

I don't know when I fell asleep last night. For a long time I was reading the 'Lives of the Holy Men.' What great souls they were, caring only for the love of God, completely intoxicated with it! Devotion like that can come only from strict spiritual discipline. Wouldn't I be capable of such discipline? What other joy is left for me in this life? There may be some who love jewels, God knows, but as for me jewels are a torment to my eyes; some might give up their life for wealth but for me just to hear it mentioned starts a fever in me. Yesterday that crazy Sushila had a wonderful time helping me to make myself beautiful — no matter how much I tried to stop her, she wouldn't listen. Then what I'd most feared finally happened. For every minute I laughed with her I was to cry all the more. Is there any other woman in the world whose husband goes into a violent rage when he sees her? Any other woman who hears her husband say, 'You're destroying my hopes for the other world and nothing else, the way you're made up makes that plain,' without wanting to take poison? Finally I went downstairs and began to read the 'Lives.' Now I shall worship only Lord Krishna in Brinda-ban, I shall show him my beauty, and when he sees it he will not grow angry for he will know what is in my heart.

*

Lord! How can I say what is in my heart? You dwell within me, you know all that is most secret in me. I wish I could tell him my desires, serve him as a wife should, move only at his bidding, I wish he might never feel the slightest pain from anything I do or anything concerning me. It's not his fault — whatever was in my stars has come to pass. But even knowing all this when I see him coming then my heart sinks, I grow deathly pale, I feel dizzy, I long not to see him, not even to have to talk to him. No one could ever feel so miserable even seeing his worst enemy. The moment I see him coming my heart starts to pound. Whenever he goes away for a day

193

or two it's as though a weight is lifted off my heart. I talk, I even laugh, a little happiness starts to come into my life, but at the first news that he's come back everything grows dark around me. I don't know why I should feel this way, but it seems to me that in an earlier birth we were enemies, and to take vengeance for this old hatred he married me — that former existence is still living in our hearts. Otherwise why would he be angry whenever he sees me and why would the sight of him disgust me? No marriage is meant to be like this! How much happier I was at home. Perhaps I might have stayed there and been happy. But because of the accursed custom it's felt to be inevitable that every unfortunate girl must be tied to the neck of some man or other. They don't know how many tender hearts shaken with longings are trampled under its foot. The sweetest imaginings — whatever is best in man, most sublime and beautiful, its living image rises up and appears before one as soon as the word is mentioned. But what is that word for me? A spear to stab the heart, a mote in the eye, an arrow of bitterness piercing the breast. I always see Sushila laughing. She never complains about being poor. She has no jewels, no clothes, she lives in a tiny rented house, she does all the housework with her own hands, but all the same I've never seen her cry. If I had my way, I'd exchange my wealth for whatever she has today. When she sees her husband coming home smiling, all the shabbiness of her life disappears, her heart is a yard wide with joy. In his embrace there's a happiness I'd sacrifice the wealth of the three worlds for.

*

Today I couldn't control myself and I asked him, 'Why did you marry me?' The question's been in my mind for months but I'd held it back. The cup spilled over today. When he heard the question he looked confused and irritated, shrugged and said, 'To look after the house, to take the job of managing it, not for anything else. Did you think it was to have a good time?' So without a housekeeper the place would have seemed like a deserted house to you? Servants would have wasted the household money, and if something fell on the floor it would have stayed there, no one would bother to pick it up. So it seemed that I was brought to this house to keep it in order! I was supposed to maintain it and be grateful to him that everything in it belonged to me. The money's the big thing and I'm just here to look after it. A house like this ought to be set on fire at once! Until now, without knowing it, I've been the chief housekeeper, not of course as good a one as he thought I should be but according to my own capacity, surely. I swear that from today on I won't touch anything under any circumstances. I know this: no man marries to get himself a housekeeper and he said what he said out of spite. But Sushila spoke true, without a wife his house would have been as empty for him as a cage without a bird. This is the fate of us women!

*

I don't know why he's so suspicious of me. From the time fate brought me to this house I've seen him glare at me suspiciously. Why? If I just put a flower in my hair he begins to scowl. I never go anywhere, never talk to anybody, and still he's suspicious! It's intolerable to be treated so shabbily. As though I didn't have any pride of my own. Why does he think I'm so vile? — isn't he ashamed of being suspicious of me? If a one-eyed man sees anybody laugh he thinks people are laughing at him. Maybe he's got the notion that I'm mocking him. Perhaps this is what happens to your mind when you try to do something beyond your powers. A beggar sitting on a king's throne can't sleep in peace; one enemy after another seems to appear on every side. I think this must be the state of any old man who marries.

Today I was going out to see the temple decorations for Krishna's birthday — Sushila had told me about it. Any man of average intelligence can understand that going out dressed like some old peasant woman is a way of making a fool of yourself, but suddenly he popped up from I don't know where and frowning at me said, 'What are you getting dressed up for?'

I told him I was just going out for a little to see the celebrations at the temple. As soon as he heard this he frowned and said, 'There's no need for you to go. For a woman who can't serve her husband properly it's not a virtue, it's a sin to go to the temple. You want to get away from me — I know women's tricks.'

I got so angry that I couldn't say a thing. I went right away to change my clothes and swore I'd never go to the temple again. Is there no limit to his distrust? I don't know what I was thinking that held me back, I ought to have answered him that I'd leave the house that instant without being afraid of anything he might do

195

about it.

He's surprised that I'm always sad and depressed, in his heart he feels I'm ungrateful. Maybe he thinks he conferred a great privilege on me by marrying me. I was supposed to be overwhelmed with joy at becoming the mistress of such vast property and wealth, I was expected to sing his praises on every mountain-top.

But I don't do anything of the sort, instead I mope around with a long face. Still, there are times when I actually feel sorry for the poor man. He doesn't understand that there's something in a woman's life which can't be lost without heaven itself turning into hell.

*

He's been sick for three days. The doctor says it's pneumonia and there's no hope of saving him. But somehow I don't feel any distress. I didn't used to be so hard-hearted, I don't know where my kindness has gone. Whenever I saw a sick person my heart used to grow faint with pity; I could never bear to hear anyone cry.

But for three days I've been listening to him groaning on his bed in the next room and I haven't gone to see him. How could I possibly even shed a tear? It seems to me as though there's no relationship between us at all. I don't care if anybody calls me a monster or a bitch, but I haven't the slightest hesitation in saying that I feel a kind of spiteful pleasure in his illness. He's kept me here in a prison — I won't give it the pure name of marriage, it's just been a prison. I'm not so big-hearted that I can revere someone who's kept me a prisoner or that I'll kiss the feet that kicked me. It occurred to me that God is punishing him for his wickedness. A woman doesn't become a man's wife just by being chained to him. For a marriage to be a marriage the heart has to be stirred at least once by love.

I can hear my husband cursing me over and over again while he lies in his room, blaming me entirely for his illness, but I don't care at all. Whoever wants his property and his money can take it, it's of no use to me.

*

I've been a widow now for three months, at least that's what people say. Anyone who wants to can say it, but I consider myself the very same as before. I didn't break my wedding bangles — why should I? Even before I didn't streak the part in my hair with cinnabar like other married women and I don't do it now. The grown-up son from the first marriage saw to the old man's funeral rites, I stayed out of it. Everyone in the house has his own way of criticizing me. If anybody sees me with a flower in my hair they screw up their faces, if they see me wearing jewellery they glare, but it doesn't bother me in the least. To irk them I wear bright saris and lots of jewels and I don't feel the slightest sorrow. I've been freed from captivity. A few days ago I went to Sushila's house. It's a tiny house, there's nothing fancy and no furniture, there are not even *charpoys*, but how happily Sushila lives in it. When I see her joy all kinds of imaginings begin to rise in my heart — why should I call them nasty when I don't really think they are? How much pleasure there is in their lives, their eyes are always smiling, tender smiles play on their lips, a stream of love seems to flow in their words. With this happiness — no matter how momentary it may be — their lives are a success, no one can mistake it, the memory of it suffices for all time, it's a plectrum to stir the heart forever with sweet music.

One day I said to Sushila, 'If your husband went somewhere far away would you just weep and die?'

Sushila answered gravely, 'No, sister, I wouldn't die. His memory would always be fresh, even if he spent years away.'

That is the love I want, my heart goes on trembling for the awakening of that music, I also want such memories as will make my heart vibrate always, an intoxication that will engulf me forever.

*

I sobbed all through the night. I don't know why my heart was so full. My life seemed to lie spread before me like a desert where there was nothing green but a few scrubby weeds. The whole house was ready to gobble me up, I was becoming so jumpy I couldn't keep still. These days I feel no impulse to look at the religious books, I have no wish to go walking anywhere. I don't know myself what I want. Yet what I don't know my body knows, I am the living embodiment of my desires, every one of my limbs cries out with the anguish inside me.

The restlessness of my mind has reached that final stage where I feel neither shame nor fear of people's contempt. For the greedy, selfish father and mother who threw me into the pit, for the heartless creature who hypocritically took the marriage vows with me, for all of them I feel an endless hatred, I want to see them shamed. I want to disgrace them by disgracing myself. By giving up my life I want to see them die. My womanliness has vanished. In my heart a wild fire has begun to blaze.

Everyone in the house was sleeping. Silently I went downstairs, opened the door and left the house, as someone overcome by the heat might go out and run toward any open place. I'd been suffocating in that house.

On the road the shops were closed, all was still. Suddenly an old woman appeared, startling me as though she'd been a ghost. She came close to me and looked me up and down and said, 'What road are you looking for?'

Bitterly I said, 'The road to death.'

The old woman said, 'In your fate it is written that your life holds many joys in store. The dark night is over, the light of dawn is in the skies.'

Laughing, I said, 'Are your eyes so sharp that even in the dark you can read the writing of the fates?'

'I don't read with my eyes, child,' the old woman said, 'I read with the mind — I haven't grown old without learning something. Your evil days are past and the good ones are coming. Don't laugh, child, I've been doing this work for a long time.

Because of this old woman many a girl who was about to throw herself into the river sleeps on a bed of flowers, and some who were ready to drink a cup of poison are drinking milk. And so I come out late of nights to see if by my help some unfortunate girl may be saved. I ask nothing in return — I have everything I need from the Lord — my desire is only to do some kindness to others in so far as I can — money for those who want money, children for those who want children, what else shall I say? I can recite the spell which will fulfill anyone's desires.'

I said, 'I want neither wealth nor children. What I want is not in your power to give.'

She laughed. 'Daughter, I know what you want, you want that thing which can make a heaven of this earth and which gives greater bliss than the blessings of the gods, the flower of heaven, the new moon, the rarest thing. But in my spells is the power to provide even this destiny. You thirst for love, and I can set you on a

198

ship to bear you over the sea of love, tossed about by the very waves of love.'

Becoming curious, I asked, 'Mother, where is your house?'

'Very close, daughter, come along and I'll bring you there —trust me.'

She seemed to me to be a goddess come down from heaven. I went along with her.

\*

Alas, that old woman I took for a goddess was a witch from hell. I looked for nectar and found poison; I longed for a chaste love and I fell into a foul, poisonous ditch. I did not find what was not to be found. I desired a bliss like Sushila's, not the sensual wallowing of a whore. But once in your life a step's been taken on the wrong road it's hard to come back on the right one.

Still, the responsibility for my ruin is not on my head but on my mother and father and that old man who wanted to be my husband. I would not write these lines except with the idea that people who read this history of my soul may have their eyes opened. I say again, for your daughters do not look for wealth, property or prestige, look only for a husband. If you can't find the right one then let your daughter remain a spinster or poison her, strangle her, but don't marry her to an ugly old man. A woman can bear the most agonizing grief, the greatest afflictions, anything, but she cannot bear the trampling down of the longings of her youth.

As for me, there is no hope left in this life. I would not exchange even this vile existence for the one I've left behind.

# Miss Padma

After she had achieved success as a lawyer Miss Padma discovered a new experience: the emptiness of life. Considering marriage an unnatural bond, she had decided that she would remain independent and enjoy life. When she had got her M. A. and Law degrees she began her practice. She was young, beautiful, soft-spoken, and also extremely intelligent. There was nothing to stand in her way. Quick as a flash she left her young male colleagues far behind as she forged ahead and by now her salary was at times more than a thousand a month. Now there was no longer much need for hard work and racking her brains; most of her cases were of a kind she was already familiar with so that there seemed to be no necessity for any kind of preparation. She had acquired considerable confidence in her powers. She had learned the formulas by which one triumphs at the bar; consequently she now found she had a great deal of leisure time, which she spent reading romances, strolling, going to the cinema and visiting friends. Holding that some minor vice was absolutely necessary to make life happy, she became addicted to gardening. She would order all sorts of seeds and enjoy watching them sprout and bloom and bear fruit. But all the same she continued to experience the emptiness of life.

It was not that she was indifferent to men; on the contrary, she had no shortage of lovers. Had she possessed nothing but youth and beauty she still would have suffered no lack of worshippers, but in her case youth and beauty were joined to wealth as well, so how could there fail to be a flock of admirers? Padma was not averse to sexual enjoyment; what she detested was dependence and making marriage the chief occupation of life. So long as she could remain free and savour sensual pleasure why shouldn't she? She saw no moral obstacle to enjoyment since she considered it merely an appetite of the body. This appetite could be appeased by any neat, clean shop, and Padma was always looking for a shop like that. The customer takes from the shop the things he likes. So also Padma. Therefore she had dozens of lovers — lawyers, professors, doctors, noblemen. But they were every one of them mere sensualists — the kind who like bees unconcernedly drank the nectar and flew away. There was not even one she felt she could rely on. This was the moment when she realized that her heart demanded not just physical enjoyment but something more as well: a total self-dedication, and this she had not found.

Among her lovers there was a certain Mr. Prasad — a handsome man, and learned. He was a professor in a local college, and also a worshipper of the ideal of free love. Padma became infatuated with him and wanted to keep him attached to her, to make him completely her own; but Prasad did not fall into her clutches.

One evening Padma was about to go out for a walk when Prasad arrived. The walk was postponed. There was far more pleasure in chatting than in strolling, and today Miss Padma was on the point of speaking of her deeper feelings to Prasad. She had, in fact, decided, after much soul-searching, to speak frankly.

With her gaze fixed on Prasad's intoxicating eyes she said, 'Why don't you come and stay here in my bungalow?'

'Oh,' said Prasad with malicious amusement, 'the result of that would only be that in two or three months we wouldn't even be talking to one another.'

'I fail to get your point,' said Padma.

'The point is simply what I'm saying.'

'But after all, why?'

'I don't want to lose my independence,' said Prasad, 'you don't want to lose yours. If your lovers come to you I'll be jealous, and vice versa. Ill feeling will spring up, then hostility and you'll kick me out of the house. The house *is* yours! If this ends up hurting me, how can our friendship continue?'

The two of them were silent for a moment. Prasad had set forth the situation in such clear, straightforward, blunt words that they could find nothing to say.

Finally, it was Prasad who thought of a new approach. He said, 'Until we take an oath that from this day forward I am yours and you are mine there's no way that we can live together.'

'Will you take such an oath?'

'First tell me that *you* will.'

'I will,' said Padma.

'Then so will I.'

'But except for this one thing I'll remain free in every other

201

matter.'

'And I except for this one thing will remain free too.'

'Agreed.'

'Agreed!'

'When do we start?'

'Whenever you say.'

'Then I say, right from tomorrow on.'

'It's a deal. But if you don't behave in accordance with the oath, then what?'

'And what about you?' said Padma.

'*You* can throw me out of the house; but how could I punish you?'

'You'd just give me up, what else could you do?'

'Not at all, that wouldn't satisfy me in the least. If it came to that, I'd want to debase you, even kill you.'

'How cruel you are, Prasad!'

'So long as we're both free, neither of us has the right to criticize the other. But once we're bound by the oath I won't be able to stand any disregard of that oath, nor will you. You have the means to punish me, but I have none to punish you. The law gives me no rights. I could enforce the oath only by my brute strength, but how could I alone do anything in front of all these servants of yours?'

'But you're looking only at the dark side of the picture. While I'm yours, then this house, these servants and property, everything is yours. We both of us know that there's no greater social sin than envy. I can't say whether you love me or not, but I'm ready to do, to bear, anything for your sake.'

'Are you really sincere, Padma?'

'With all my heart.'

'But somehow or other I can't quite believe you.'

'But I believe you completely.'

'But understand this, I'm not going to stay on in your house as a guest. I'll stay only as master.'

'You shall stay as master not only of the house but of me as well. And I shall be your mistress.'

*

Professor Prasad and Miss Padma live together and are happy. For both of them the ideal of life they had set for themselves has become true. Prasad earns a salary of only two hundred, but now it doesn't bother him to spend twice that. Formerly he drank liquor only occasionally, but now he's drunk day and night. Now he has his own private car, his own private servants, he goes on ordering every sort of expensive item and Padma happily tolerates all his extravagances. Rather, there's no question of toleration, she herself is delighted to dress him in fine suits and set him up in the most luxurious style. Now probably the grandest noblemen of the city don't have a watch to match Professor Prasad's. The more Padma gives way to him, the more he abuses her generosity. At times indeed he seems intolerable to her but for some incomprehensible reason she finds herself under his thumb. If she sees Prasad the least bit moody or worried, her heart is troubled. On top of this, he begins saying sarcastic things to her. Those who were her former lovers also try to provoke her and make her dissatisfied but as soon as she goes to Prasad she forgets everything. Prasad has acquired complete domination over her, and he's well aware of it. Prasad has read her profoundly and come to understand her perfectly.

But just as in politics authority tends to be abused, in the same way in love as well it is abused, and the one who's weaker must be made to pay. Padma, so proud of herself, was now Prasad's whore and why should Prasad fail to profit from her weakness? In analyzing her he had hit the nail on the head and gradually he was driving it in deeper every day, to the point where nights he began to come home late. He would not take Padma with him; he would make some excuse, such as a headache, not to go out with her, then when she'd left for a stroll he'd take his car out and dash off.

By now two years had passed and Padma was pregnant; she had also begun to get fat. The freshness and charm her looks had had were now no more. She was like, as it were, a once rare commodity no longer prized from over-availability.

So it was that one day when Padma returned home Prasad had disappeared. She became extremely irritated. For some time now she'd been observing Prasad's mood changing, and today she'd got up the courage to speak plainly to him. Ten o'clock struck, then eleven, then midnight, and Padma continued to sit up waiting for him. Dinner got cold, the servants went to bed. Time and time again she would get up, go to the door and scan the street. Some time between twelve and one Prasad came home.

Padma had screwed up her courage, but as soon as she stood

before Prasad she became aware of the weakness of her position. Nevertheless she asked him in a fairly firm voice, 'Where were you so late? Do you have any idea how late it is?'

At this instant she appeared to Prasad like the image of ugliness. He had gone to the cinema with a woman student from his college. He said, 'You ought to have gone to sleep. In your condition you ought to get as much rest as possible.'

Padma's courage mounted. She said, 'Answer my question even if it finishes me off.'

'Then you can finish me off too,' said Prasad.

'For some time now I've watched your feelings change.'

'Your eyesight must have gained considerably in acuteness.'

'You've been cheating on me, I can see *that* plainly enough.'

'I didn't sell myself to you. If you're really fed up with me I'm ready to leave right now.'

'How can you threaten to leave? You gave up nothing when you came here.'

'I didn't give up anything? You have the nerve to say that! I can see you're turning vicious. You think you've clipped my wings, but at this point I'm ready to shake you off. Right now!'

Padma's courage seemed to have been extinguished. Prasad was already taking out his suitcase. Humbly she said to him, 'I haven't said anything for you to get so angry. I was only asking you where you were. Don't you even want me to have *that* much right? I never do anything against your wishes and yet you scold me for anything and everything. You don't feel the slightest pity for me! I ought to get a little sympathy from you. Haven't I always been ready to do anything for you? And now, when I'm in this condition, you turn away from me . . .'

She choked up and, laying her head on the table, began to sob.

Prasad had achieved total victory.

*

Motherhood was now a very unpopular topic with Padma. One concern alone hovered over her. At times she would tremble with fear and regret. Prasad's lack of restraint got worse every day. What should she do, what should she not do? She had reached the final stage of her pregnancy and no longer went to court but sat at home alone the whole day. Prasad would come home in the evening, have his tea and then fly off again and not come back before eleven or midnight. Nor did he conceal from her where he went. It was as though he had come to hate the very sight of her. Pregnant, sallow, troubled, suspicious, depressed —nevertheless, she did not cease to try to tie Prasad to her with make-up and jewellery. But the more she tried the more Prasad was put off. In her condition, cosmetics made her seem even uglier.

The labour pains began. Prasad was not aware. A nurse and a woman doctor were standing by, but Prasad's absence made Padma's labour all the more terrible. When she saw the child beside her she felt a wave of happiness; but then, not finding Prasad with her, she turned her face away from the child, as though she'd found a worm in a sweet fruit.

When after five days she left the lying-in room, as though getting out of jail, she had turned into a naked sword. Having become a mother she experienced a strange power in herself.

She gave a check to the servant and sent him to the bank. She had to settle some bills rising from her delivery. He came back empty-handed.

'The money?' Padma asked.

He said, 'The teller told me that Prasad Babu took all the money out.'

Padma felt as though she'd been shot. She had saved up 20,000 rupees as though it had been her life's blood. For this child! Alas! On leaving the maternity room she learned that Prasad had taken a girl from the college and gone off to England to tour. Furious, she went into the house, picked up Prasad's picture, dashed it to the ground and stamped on it. Whatever he had left behind she gathered together, put a match to it and spat on his name.

A month went by. Padma was standing at the gate of her bungalow holding her child. Her rage had finally turned to grief and despair. Sometimes she felt sorry for the child, sometimes affection, sometimes hatred. On the road she saw a European woman going along with her husband pushing a perambulator with their child in it. She watched the lucky couple wistfully and her eyes filled with tears.

# My Big Brother

My big brother was five years older than me but only three grades ahead. He'd begun his studies at the same age I had but he didn't like the idea of moving hastily in an important matter like education. He wanted to lay a firm foundation for that great edifice, so he took two years to do one year's work; sometimes he even took three. If the foundations weren't well-made, how could the edifice endure?

I was the younger, he the elder — I was nine, he was fourteen. He had full right by seniority to supervise and instruct me. And I was expected to accept every order of his as law.

By nature he was very studious. He was always sitting with a book open. And perhaps to rest his brain he would sometimes draw pictures of birds, dogs and cats in the margin of his notebook. Occasionally he would write a name, a word or a sentence ten or twenty times. He might copy a couplet out several times in beautiful letters or create new words which made no rhyme or reason. Once, for example, I saw the following: Special Amina brothers and brothers, in reality brother-brother, Radheshyam, Mr Radheshyam, for one hour. Following this was the sketch of a man's face. I tried very hard to make some sense out of this rigmarole but I didn't succeed and I didn't dare ask him. He was in the ninth grade, I was in the sixth. To understand his creation was beyond my powers.

I wasn't really very keen about studying. To pick up a book and sit with it for an hour was a tremendous effort. As soon as I found a chance I'd leave the hostel and go to the field and play marbles or fly paper kites or sometimes just meet a chum — what could be more fun? Sometimes we'd climb on to the courtyard walls and jump down or straddle the gate and ride it back and forth, enjoying it as though it were an automobile. But as soon as I came back into the room and saw my brother's scowling face I was petrified. His first question would be, 'Where were you?' Always this question, always asked in the same tone and the only answer I had was silence. I don't know why I couldn't manage to say that I'd just been

206

outside playing. My silence was an acknowledgement of guilt and my brother's only remedy for this was to greet me with indignant words.

'If you study English this way you'll be studying your whole life and you won't get one word right! Studying English is no laughing matter that anyone who wants to can learn. Otherwise everybody and his cousin would be regular experts in English. You've got to wear out your eyes morning and night and use every ounce of energy, then maybe you'll master the subject. And even then it's just to say you have a smattering of it. Even great scholars can't write proper English, to say nothing of being able to speak it. And I ask you, how much of a blockhead are you that you can't learn a lesson from looking at me? You've seen with your own eyes how much I grind, and if you haven't seen it, there's something wrong with your eyes and with your wits as well. No matter how many shows and carnivals there may be have you ever seen me going to watch them? Every day there are cricket and hockey matches but I don't go near them. I keep on studying all the time, and even so it takes me two years or even three for one grade. So how do you expect to pass when you waste your time playing like this? If it takes me two or even three years, you'll fritter your whole life away studying in one grade. If you waste your time like this, it would be better if you just went home and played stick-ball to your heart's content. Why waste our dad's hard-earned money?'

Hearing a dressing-down like this I'd start to cry. What could I answer? I was guilty but who could endure a scolding like that? My brother was an expert in the art of giving advice. He'd say such sarcastic words, overwhelm me with such good counsel that my spirits would collapse, my courage disappear. I couldn't find in myself the power to toil so desperately, and in despair for a little while I'd think, 'Why *don't* I run away from school and go back home? Why should I spoil my life fiddling with work that's beyond my capacity?' I was willing to remain a fool, but I just got dizzy from so much work. But after an hour or two the cloud of despair would dissipate and I'd resolve to study with all my might. I'd draw up a schedule on the spot. How could I start work without first making an outline, working out a plan? In my timetable the heading of play was entirely absent. Get up at the crack of dawn, wash hands and face at six, eat a snack, sit down and study. From six to eight English, eight to nine arithmetic, nine to nine-thirty history, then mealtime and afterwards off to school. A half hour's rest at 3.30 when I got back from school, geography from four to five, grammar from five to six, then a half hour's walk in front of the hostel, six-thirty to seven English composition, then supper, translation from eight to nine, Hindi from nine to ten, from ten to eleven miscellaneous, then to bed.

But it's one thing to draw up a schedule, another to follow it. It began to be neglected from the very first day. The inviting green expanse of the playground, the balmy winds, the commotion on the football field, the exciting stratagems of prisoner's-base, the speed and flurries of volley ball would all draw me mysteriously and irresistibly. As soon as I was there I forgot everything: the life-destroying schedule, the books that strained your eyes — I couldn't remember them at all. And then my big brother would have an occasion for sermons and scoldings. I would stay well out of his way, try to keep out of his sight, come into the room on tiptoe so he wouldn't know. But if he spotted me I'd just about die. It seemed that a naked sword was always swinging over my head. But just as in the midst of death and catastrophe a man may remain caught in the snares of illusion, so I, though I suffered reproaches and threats, could not renounce fun and games.

*

The yearly exams came round: my brother failed, I passed and was first in my class. Only two year's difference was left between him and me. It occurred to me to taunt him. 'What was the good of all your horrible self-punishment? Look at me, I went on playing and having a good time and I'm at the head of my class.' But he was so sad and depressed that I felt genuinely sorry for him and it seemed shameful to me to pour salt on his wounds. But now I could be a little proud of myself and indeed my ego expanded. My brother's sway over me was over. I began to take part freely in the games, my spirits were running high. If he gave me another sermon, then I'd say straight out, 'With all your grinding what kind of marks did you get? Playing and having fun I ended up first in my class.' Although I didn't have the courage to say anything so outrageous it was plain from my behaviour that my brother's power over me was gone. He guessed it — his intuition was sharp and one day when I'd spent the whole morning playing stick-ball and came back exactly at meal time, he said, with all the air of pulling out a sword to rush at me:

'I see you've passed this year and you're first in your class, and you've got stuck up about it. But my dear brother, even great men live to regret their pride, and who are you compared to them? You must have read about what happened to Ravan. Didn't you learn anything from his story or did you just read it without paying any attention? Just to pass an exam isn't anything, the real thing is to develop your mind. Understand the significance of what you read. Ravan was master of the earth. Such kings are called 'Rulers of the World'. These days the extent of the British Empire is vast, but their kings can't be called 'Ruler of the World' — many countries in the world don't accept British rule, they're completely independent. But Ravan was a Ruler of the World, all the kings of the earth paid taxes to him. Great divinities were his slaves, even the gods of fire and water. But what happened to him in the end? Pride completely finished him off, destroying even his name. There wasn't anybody left to perform all his funeral rites properly. A man can commit any sin he wants but he'd better not be proud, nor give himself airs. When he turns proud he loses both this world and the next. You must have read about what happened to Satan too. He was so proud that he thought there was no truer devotee of God than himself. Finally it came about that he got shoved out of heaven into hell. Once the king of Turkey became very stuck-up too; he died begging for alms. You've just been promoted one grade and your head's turned by it — you've gone way up in the world! Understand this, you didn't pass through your own efforts but just stumbled on it by luck, like a blind man who catches hold of a quail. But you can catch a quail only once like that, no more. Sometimes in stick-ball too a lucky shot in the dark hits the goal, but nobody gets to be a good player from it, the kind who never misses a shot.

'Don't assume that because I failed I'm stupid and you're smart. When you reach my class you'll sweat right through you teeth when you have to bite into algebra and geometry and study English history — it's not easy to memorize these king's names. There were eight Henrys — do you think it's easy to remember all the things that happened in each Henry's time? If you write Henry the Eighth instead of Henry the Seventh you get a zero. A complete flunk! You won't get zero not even zero. What kind of idea do you have about it anyway? There were dozens of Jameses, dozens of Williams and scores of Charleses! You get dizzy with them, your mind's in a whirl.

Those poor fellows didn't have names enough to go around. After every name they have to put second, third, fourth and fifth. If anybody'd asked me I could have reeled off thousands of names. And as for geometry, well, God help you! If you write *a c b* instead of *a b c* your whole answer is marked wrong. Nobody ever asks those hard-hearted examiners what is the difference, after all, between *a b c* and *a c b* or why they waste their time torturing the students with it. Does it make any difference if you eat lentils, boiled rice and bread or boiled rice, lentils and bread? But what do those examiners care? They see only what they've written in their books. They expect us to learn it word for word. And this kind of parroting they call teaching! And in the long run what's the point of learning all this nonsense? If you bring this perpendicular line down on that line it will be twice the base line. I ask you, what's the point of that? If it isn't twice as long it's four times as long or half as long, what the devil do I care? But you've got to pass so you've got to memorize all this garbage.

'They say, "Write an essay on punctuality no less than four pages long." So now you open up your notebook in front of you, take your pen and curse the whole business. Who doesn't know that punctuality's a very good thing? A man's life is organized according to it, others love him for it and his business prospers from it. How can you write four pages on something so trifling? Do I need four pages for what I can describe in one sentence? So I consider it stupidity. It's not economizing time, it's wasting it to cram it with such nonsense. We want a man to say what he has to say quickly and then get moving. But no, you've got to drag it out to four pages, whatever you write, and they're foolscap pages too. If this isn't an outrage on the students, what is it? It's a contradiction for them to ask us to write concisely. Write a concise essay on punctuality in no less than four pages. All right! If four pages is concise then maybe otherwise they'd ask us to write one or two hundred pages. Run fast and walk slow at the same time. Is that all mixed up or isn't it? We students can understand that much but those teachers don't have the sense — and despite that they claim they're teachers. When you get into my class, old man, then you'll really take a beating, and then you'll find out what's what. Just because you got a first division this time you're all puffed up — so pay attention to what I say. What if I failed, I'm still older than you, I have more experience of the world. Take what I say to heart or you'll be sorry.'

210

It was almost time for school, otherwise I don't know when this medley of sermons would have ended. I didn't have much appetite that day. If I got a scolding like this when I passed, maybe if I'd failed I would have had to pay with my life. My brother's terrible description of studying in the ninth grade really scared me. I'm surprised I didn't run away from school and go home. But even a scolding like this didn't change my distaste for books a bit. I didn't miss one chance to play. I also studied, but much less. Well, anyway, just enough to complete the day's assignment and not be disgraced in class. But the confidence I'd gained in myself disappeared and then I began to lead a life like a thief's.

*

Then it was the yearly exams again and it so happened that once more I passed and my brother failed again. I hadn't done much work; but somehow or other I was in the first division. I myself was astonished. My brother had just about killed himself with work, memorizing every word in the course, studying till ten at night and starting again at four in the morning, and from six until 9.30 before going to school. He'd grown pale. But the poor fellow failed again and I felt sorry for him. When he heard the results he broke down and cried, and so did I. My pleasure in passing was cut by half. If I'd failed my brother couldn't have felt so bad. But who can escape his fate?

There was only one grade left between my brother and me. The insidious thought crossed my mind that if he failed just once more I'd be at the same level as him and then what grounds would he have for lecturing me? But I violently rejected this unworthy idea. After all, he'd scolded me only with the intention of helping me. At the time it was really obnoxious, but maybe it was only as a result of his advice that I 'd passed so easily and with such good marks.

Now my brother had become much gentler toward me. Several times when he found occasion to scold me he did it without losing his temper. Perhaps he himself was beginning to understand that he no longer had the right to tell me off or at least not so much as before. My independence grew. I began to take unfair advantage of his toleration, I half started to imagine that I'd pass next time whether I studied or not, my luck was high. As a result, the little I'd studied before because of my brother, even that ceased. I found a

211

new pleasure in flying kites and now I spent all my time at the sport. Still, I minded my manners with my brother and concealed my kite-flying from him. In preparation for the kite tournament I was secretly busy solving such problems as how best to secure the string and how to apply the paste mixed with ground glass in it to cut the other fellows' kites off their strings. I didn't want to let my brother suspect that my respect for him had in any way diminished.

One day, far from the hostel, I was running along like mad trying to grab hold of a kite. My eyes were on the heavens and that high-flying traveller in the skies that glided smoothly down like some soul emerging from paradise free of worldly attachments to be incarnated in a new life. A whole army of boys came racing out to welcome it with long, thick bamboo rods. Nobody was aware who was in front or in back of him. It was as though every one of them was flying along with that kite in the sky where everything is level, without cars or trams or trains.

Suddenly I collided with my brother, who was probably coming back from the market. He grabbed my hand and said angrily, 'Aren't you ashamed to be running with these ragamuffins after a one-paisa kite? Have you forgotten that you're not in a low grade any more? You're in the eighth now, one behind me. A man's got to have some regard for his position, after all. There was a time when by passing the eighth grade people became assistant revenue collectors. I know a whole lot of men who finished only the middle grades and today are first degree deputy magistrates or superintendents. How many eighth-grade graduates today are our leaders and newspaper editors? Great scholars work under their supervision but when you get into this same eighth grade you run around with hoodlums!

'I'm sorry to see you have so little sense. You're smart, there's no doubt of that, but what use is it if it destroys your self-respect? You must have assumed, "I'm just one grade behind my brother so now he doesn't have any right to say anything to me." But you're mistaken. I'm five years older than you and even if you come into my grade today — and the examiners being what they are there's no doubt that next year you'll be on an equal footing with me and maybe a year later you'll even get ahead of me — but that difference of five years between us not even God — to say nothing of you — can remove. I'm five years older than you and I always will be. The experience I have of life and the world you can never catch up

212

with even if you get an M.A. and a D.Litt. and even a Ph. D. Understanding doesn't come from reading books. Our mother never passed any grade and Dad probably never went beyond the fifth, but even if we studied the wisdom of the whole world mother and father would always have the right to explain to us and to correct us. Not just because they're our parents but because they'll always have more experience of the world. Maybe they don't know what kind of government they've got in America or how many constellations there are in the sky, but there are a thousand things they know more about than you or me. God forbid, but if I should fall sick today then you'd be in a pickle. You wouldn't be able to think of anything except sending a telegram to Dad. But in your place *he* wouldn't send anybody a telegram or get upset or be all flustered. First of all he'd diagnose the disease himself and try the remedy; then if it didn't work he'd call some doctor. And sickness is a serious matter. But you and I don't even know how to make our allowance last through the month. We spend what father sends us and then we're penniless again. We cut our breakfast, we have to hide from the barber and washerman. But as much as you and I spend today, Dad's maintained himself honourably and in good reputation the greater part of his life and brought up a family with seven children on half of it. Just look at our headmaster. Does he have an M.A. or doesn't he? And not from here either, but from Oxford. He gets a thousand rupees, but who runs his house? His old mother. There his degrees are useless. He used to manage the house himself, but he couldn't make both ends meet, he had to borrow. But since his mother has taken over it's as though Lakshmi had come into his house. So brother, don't be so proud of having almost caught up with me and being independent now. I'll see that you don't go off the track. If you don't mind, then' (showing me his fist) 'I can use this too. I know you don't like hearing all this.'

I was thoroughly shamed by this new approach of his. I had truly come to know my own insignificance and a new respect for my brother was born in my heart. With tears in my eyes, I said, 'No, no, what you say is completely true and you have the right to say it.'

My brother embraced me and said, 'I don't forbid you to fly kites. I'd like to too. But what can I do? If I go off the track myself then how can I watch out for you? That's my responsibility.'

Just then by chance a kite that had been cut loose passed over us with its string dangling down. A crowd of boys were chasing after it.

My brother is very tall and leaping up he caught hold of the string and ran at top speed toward the hostel and I ran close behind him.

# Intoxication

Ishwari's father was a rich landowner, mine an impecunious clerk who had no wealth beyond his working wages. There was a continual debate between us. I was forever attacking the *zamindars*, calling them jungle beasts, blood-sucking leeches, the flowering parasitic growth at the top of the trees. He took the side of the *zamindars* but of course his position was somewhat weak because he could present no real argument in their defense. It's a weak argument to say that not all men are equal, that there'd always been rich and poor and there always would be. It was difficult to prove the justness of such a system by humanitarian or moral principles. In the heat of these discussions I would often become angry and sarcastic, but even when he was defeated Ishwari would go on smiling. I never saw him lose his temper. Perhaps it was because he understood the weakness of his position. He certainly had his share of the harshness and arrogance of the rich. He never addressed a decent word to the servants. If they were the least bit late in making the bed, if the milk was by chance too hot or too cold, if his bicycle hadn't been properly cleaned, then he was beside himself. He wouldn't tolerate the least laziness or insolence. But with his friends, and particularly with me, he was always exceptionally cordial and sympathetic. Perhaps if I'd been in his place the same harshness might have sprung up in me as well, for my love of the people was not the result of conviction but rather of my personal circumstances. But perhaps if he'd been in my shoes he would have kept up the same high style, for by nature he was fond of luxury and good things.

I had decided not to go home for the coming Dassehra holidays. I didn't have the fare nor did I want to impose the burden for it on my parents — I knew that what they were giving me already was far beyond their resources. And on top of that I was concerned about exams. I had a lot left to study and who can do any studying when he goes home? But then I didn't want to stay on alone like a ghost in the hostel either, so when Ishwari invited me home with him I accepted without any urging. I could prepare for exams very well with Ishwari since he was not only rich but also bright and industrious.

When he invited me he also said, 'But pay attention to one thing, friend. If you attack the *zamindars* in my house there'll be a row and my folks won't like it. They rule over their tenants with the claim that God created those tenants just to serve them. And the tenants feel the same way — if they ever got it into their heads that there's no basic difference between *zamindars* and themselves, that would be the end of the *zamindars.*'

I said, 'Do you expect me to go there and not be myself?'

'Yes, that's just what I expect.'

'You'll be disappointed!'

Ishwari didn't answer. Perhaps he was leaving it to my discretion and he was right to. If he'd insisted then I might have been stubborn about it.

*

Second class? Why, I'd never even travelled inter-class before and now I had the good luck to be travelling in second. The train arrived at nine at night but in our eagerness we went to the station as soon as it was dark. After wandering around here and there for a while we went and had a meal in the refreshment room. After one look at my clothes and manners it didn't take the stewards long to figure out who was the master and who the hanger-on, but I don't know why I was annoyed by their impudence. The money came out of Ishwari's pocket — probably he gave them more in tips than my father earned in a month. When we left he alone tipped them — eight *annas*. Nevertheless I expected from them the same attentiveness and politeness they gave to him. Why should they all run when he gave them an order and show less alacrity when I asked for something? I didn't enjoy my supper. This discrimination completely occupied my thoughts.

The train arrived and we got in. The stewards bowed farewell to Ishwari; they didn't so much as look at me.

'How well-mannered they all are,' Ishwari said. 'Not one of our servants has such good manners.'

Sourly I observed, 'If you treated your servants to eight-*anna* tips like these you'd find them better-mannered.'

216

'Do you mean you think they're polite just because they're expecting a tip?'

'Of course not! Fine manners and etiquette are doubtless in their blood.'

The train, a mail express, started. After leaving Prayag station it stopped first at Pratapgarh. A man opened the door of our compartment. I let out a yell at once: 'This is second class!' and afterwards I shouted it in English too.

The traveller came into the compartment and looking at me with singular contempt said, 'Yes, your humble servant is perfectly aware of that,' and sat down on a lower berth. I can't describe how embarrassed I was.

By morning we reached Moradabad. At the station several people were waiting to welcome us. Two of them were gentlemen of the household, five of them servants. The latter picked up our luggage and the two gentlemen walked behind. One was a Muslim named Riyasat Ali, the other a Brahman named Ramharakh. Both of them looked at me as though I struck them as outlandish. 'You're a crow,' those looks seemed to say, 'what are you doing with the swans?'

Riyasat Ali asked Ishwari, 'Is this other young gentleman studying with you?'

'Yes,' Ishwari said, 'we study together and we live together as well. I might add that it's only because of him that I stay on in Allahabad, otherwise I would have moved on to Lucknow long ago. This time I've dragged him along with me. Several telegrams came from his home but I persuaded him to refuse them. The last telegram was marked urgent at four *annas* per word but I got him to turn that one down too.'

Both gentlemen stared at me in astonishment. They appeared to be trying to look impressed.

In a slightly suspicious tone Riyasat Ali said, 'But he seems to be very plainly dressed.'

Ishwari dispelled his doubts. 'He's a follower of Mahatma Gandhi, sir! He won't wear anything except the native homespun cotton. He's burned all his former clothes. Actually, he's practically a maharaja — he has an income of 250,000 a year, but to look at him you'd think he'd been picked up in some orphanage.'

Ramharakh said, 'One sees very few rich people with natures like that! No one would ever guess.'

'If you'd ever seen the Maharaja of Changli,' Riyasat Ali corroborated, 'you would have swallowed your teeth. He used to go wandering around the market dressed in a coarse cotton vest and wearing village-made shoes. They say that once he was snapped up to work in a labour gang — and he was the man who founded a college with a million rupees.'

I found all this very embarrassing, and I don't know why the whole lie didn't simply strike me as ridiculous. It was as though with each sentence I was coming closer and closer to this imaginary· glory.

I'm not a particularly good horseman. To be sure, when I was a child I'd several times ridden on old cart horses. I now saw that two smartly fitted out horses were standing ready for us. I was desperate. I mounted, trembling, but I managed to hide my fear. I steered the horse in back of Ishwari. It was lucky that he didn't gallop his, otherwise I might have gone back with broken arms and legs. It's possible he knew just how much of an equestrian I was.

*

Ishwari's house was a regular castle if it was anything. A gate like a mosque's, watchmen stationed at the entrance, servants beyond the counting, and an elephant tied up in the courtyard. Ishwari introduced me to his father and uncles and all the rest of his family with the same exaggerated stories. I can't tell you what a romance he invented. Not only the servants but all the people of the family as well regarded me with respect. They were landed gentry with an income of thousands, and yet the sort of people who regarded even a police constable as an officer. Several gentlemen there even called me 'Excellency'.

When we were finally alone I said to Ishwari, 'My friend, you're being a regular devil — why are you trying to get me into a jam?'

With a forced smile Ishwari said, 'The trick was necessary in front of those idiots, otherwise they wouldn't have had a decent word for you.'

In a short while the barber came to massage our feet: the young lords had just come from the station, they must be tired. Pointing to me Ishwari said, 'First massage the prince's feet.'

I was lying down on the *charpoy*. It had hardly ever happened to me in my whole life before to have someone massage my feet. I'd mocked Ishwari in the past for the follies of the rich, the fatuity of the gentry and the oppression by the big shots and I don't know what all else, and today I was caught right in the middle of it posing as a rich gentleman's offspring.

By this time it was ten o'clock. The household followed the old leisurely and courtly ways; the light of the new order had managed to reach only the highest places. The call for dinner came from the women's part of the house. We went to bathe. I had always washed out my own *dhoti*, but now I followed Ishwari's example and left it there — I would have been ashamed to wash my *dhoti* with my own hands. We went in to dine. In the hostel we sat down at the table with our shoes on but here we had to have our feet washed. A servant was standing there with water. Ishwari stretched out his foot and the servant washed it. I also stretched out my foot and the servant washed it too. I have no idea where my earlier notions had flown to.

*

I had thought that out here in the country I'd be able to concentrate on my studies in earnest. But I spent the whole day in walks and excursions. We'd drift on the river in a houseboat or fish or hunt birds or go to watch the village wrestling matches or get together for a game of chess. Ishwari would have a lot of eggs brought and make omelettes on the English stove in his room. There was always a crowd of servants gathered round. No need to stir hand or foot, you just had to stir your tongue. If you sat down to bathe they were on the spot to wash you, if you lay down there were two to keep the fan going.

Mahatma Gandhi's rich young disciple had become famous. His renown spread through the whole estate. They made sure there wasn't the slightest delay in serving his breakfast lest the 'prince' be angry, and the bed was ready right on time when he wanted to go to sleep. I was even touchier than Ishwari, or felt obliged to become so. Ishwari made his own bed but the prince, as a guest — well, how could he make his bed with his own hands? It was beneath his dignity.

One day the following incident actually took place. Ishwari was in the women's part of the house where he had probably tried to talk with his mother. Ten o'clock struck. I was so sleepy I could hardly keep my eyes open. But how could I set out the bedding?

Not a prince like me! At around 11.30 a bearer came in, a rather over-familiar fellow. In his various household chores he'd forgotten to make my bed and remembering only now he came on the run. I gave him a tongue-lashing he wasn't apt to forget.

Hearing my tirade, Ishwari came along and said, 'You've done well. All these lazy fellows deserve a scolding like that.'

It happened that one day Ishwari had gone somewhere to a party. When evening came the lamp was not lit. It was on the table and there were matches there too, but Ishwari never lit the lamp so how was the prince to light it? I was exasperated. The newspaper had been set out; I was longing to read it but the lamp wasn't lit! By chance Riyasat Ali happened to come in just then. I blew up and gave him such a scolding that the poor fellow was speechless. 'You people don't bother at all to see that the lamp is lit!' I said. 'I don't know how such lazy wretches are tolerated here. They wouldn't be kept on an hour in my house.' With trembling hands Riyasat Ali lit the lamp.

There was a Thakur who often used to come to Ishwari's house. He was a very enterprising fellow and a devoted follower of Gandhi. Believing me to be a disciple of Gandhiji he was very deferential to me. But he was hesitant about asking me for anything.

One day when he saw me alone he came to me and, folding his hands, said, 'Sir, you're a follower of Gandhi Baba, aren't you? People say that when we have Independence there won't be any more of those landowners.'

Pompously I said, 'What need will there be for the landowners? What do they do except suck the blood of the poor?'

Then the Thakur asked, 'Do you mean that the land will be taken away from all the *zamindars*?'

I said, 'But a lot of them will give it gladly. The ones who won't will have to have their land taken away from them. We people in my family are all set. The minute Independence comes we'll make over all our land and villages to the tenants.'

I was sprawled in a chair with my legs stuck out. The Thakur started to squeeze my feet and then he said, 'The landowners are very cruel these days, master! If your honour would give me just a tiny bit of land on your estate then I'd move there and work for you.'

'I have no authority over the land now, my friend, but as soon as I get control of it I'll send for you first thing. I'll have you taught how to drive a car and you can be my chauffeur.'

That day, I heard later, the Thakur drank a good deal of *bhang*, gave his wife a good beating and was all set to fight with the village moneylender.

*

So in this way the vacation drew to a close and we set out for Allahabad again. A lot of the people of the village came to see us off and the Thakur came with us to the station. I played my part to perfection too and stamped on every heart the image of my aristocratic refinement and magnanimity. I really longed to give each one of the servants a good tip but didn't have the where-withal. I already had my return ticket, I had only to get into the train. But when it came it was jam-packed with people coming home from the Durga-puja holidays. In second class there wasn't room to squeeze a stick and it was even worse in the inter. But this was the last train and we absolutely had to get on it. With the greatest difficulty we found room in third class. Our splendid get-up made a great impression there. But it really vexed me to be stuck in third. We'd come lying down the whole way in comfort and we were going back all twisted up — there wasn't even room to turn from one side to the other.

There were several educated people there too. Among themselves they were praising British rule. One gentleman remarked, 'No such justice has ever been seen in another government. Great and small, all are equal. If he wrongs anybody even the king will have to account to a court for it.'

'*Arrey*, sahib,' another man confirmed, 'you can bring a suit against the Emperor himself, the Emperor can be sentenced in court.'

There was one man going to Calcutta who had a big bundle tied to his back. He couldn't find any place to set it down. Uncomfortable with the thing on his back he frequently stood up by the door. I was sitting right next to the door so that each time he moved the bundle rubbed against my face. I didn't like it. For one thing, there was almost no air, and then this lout was just about suffocating me by crowding it into my face. I put up with it for some time, then suddenly I got mad. I caught hold of him and gave him a shove around and hit him two good slaps.

With a threatening look he said, 'Why are you hitting me, Babuji?

221

I also paid my fare.'

I stood up and hit him two or three more times.

There was an uproar in the compartment; everyone began yelling at me from all sides.

'If you're so delicate why didn't you sit in first class?'

'He's some bigshot in his own backyard, but he's not there now. If he hit *me* like that I'd show him.'

'What did the poor man do wrong? There's no room to breathe in here and he just wanted to get a breath of fresh air at the window and this fellow goes into a rage! When a man's got money does he completely lose his human-kindness?'

'This is British rule too — the very thing you were raving about.'

A villager said, 'He wouldn't try anything like that in front of those Englishmen — why's he acting so high and mighty here?'

In English Ishwari said, 'What an idiot you are!'

And it seemed to me that at this moment my intoxication began to clear a little.

# The Price of Milk

In the big cities these days you can find midwives, nurses and 'lady doctors,' as they call the female obstetricians. But in the villages it's still the untouchable sweeper women who preside over the delivery rooms, and there is little hope of any change in this situation in the near future.

Babu Maheshnath was the *zamindar* of his village, an educated man and aware of the need for reform in the way babies were delivered, but he saw no way to overcome the obstacles to such reform. No nurse would agree to go out to the villages, or if after a lot of persuasion one agreed then she'd demand such a fantastic fee that Babu Sahib could do nothing but come away with his head abjectly bowed. As for the lady doctors, he did not dare approach them; to pay one of them he might have had to sell half his property. And so when, after three daughters, his fourth child, a son, was born, once again he sent word to Gudar the sweeper and his wife. Children being apt to be born most often at night, it happened that one midnight a servant from Babu Sahib's house set up such a shout at Gudar's door that he woke up the whole neighbourhood. It was no girl this time for him to whisper the news.

For months they had been preparing in Gudar's house for this happy occasion. Their only fear was that it would once again turn out to be a girl, in which case they'd get nothing more out of it than the usual rupee and a sari. A great many times husband and wife had quarrelled and made bets about this matter. Bhungi, Gudar's wife, would say, 'If it isn't a son this time I'll hide my face in shame. That's right, I'll hide my face — but all the signs are for a son.' And Gudar would say, 'But can't you see it's going to be a girl? It's plain as day! If it's a son I'll shave off my moustache, that's right, I'll shave it off!' Gudar may have felt that if in this way he strengthened his wife's determination that it should be a son it would help to assure its actually coming about.

Bhungi said, 'You can shave it off right now, you old cheat. I said it was going to be a son but instead of listening you just went on

223

talking. I'll shave it off myself and won't leave even a bristle.'

'There's my good old woman! It'll grow again, won't it? After three days take a look, it'll be just the way it was before. And anyway, I'll claim half of whatever you get, I'm telling you now.'

Bhungi made a contemptuous gesture with her thumb. Then, handing her three-month-old son to Gudar, started out with the messenger.

'*Arí*!' Gudar called. 'Where are you running off to? I'll have to go to play the music for the celebration. Who's going to look after the baby?'

Without coming back Bhungi said, 'Get him to sleep and put him down right there on the ground, then I'll come back and nurse him.'

*

At Maheshnath's house Bhungi was warmly welcomed now. She got fruits and vegetables in the morning, *puris* and *halva* at noon, and the same things again in the afternoon and at night. And Gudar got plenty to eat as well. Since Bhungi was not able to nurse her own baby more than once or twice each day extra milk was arranged for him. It was Babu Sahib's lucky little boy who drank Bhungi's milk. And even after the twelfth-day naming ceremony* the arrangement was not stopped. The mistress of the household was a strong, healthy woman, but this time for some reason or other she had no milk. The times she'd had the three daughters she gave so much milk that they got indigestion. This time there wasn't a drop. So Bhungi was not only the midwife but the wet-nurse as well.

The mistress would say, 'Bhungi, if you take good care of my baby you'll be able to just sit around eating as long as you live. I'll see that you're given five *bighas* rent-free. You'll live at ease right down to your grandchildren's time.'

And Bhungi's darling, unable to digest the alien milk, would throw up frequently and went on getting skinnier day by day.

Bhungi would say, 'When your son has his tonsure ceremony, I'll take some bracelets, I'll insist on that.'

---

* When a child is born, the mother is considered impure until the twelfth-day naming; hence there is nothing amiss in her being attended by an untouchable woman like Bhungi.

'Of course, my dear,' the mistress would answer. 'Why that threatening tone? Which do you want, silver or gold?'

'Oh mistress! If I wore silver bracelets who could I show my face to — and who would they make fun of?'

'Very well, my dear, I promise you gold.'

'And when your son is married I'll take a necklace and, for my husband, silver wrist-bands.'

'You shall have them — God grant we see that day!'

In the household Bhungi reigned, second only to the mistress. The cook, the maids, all the various servants paid heed to her; it reached the point where even the mistress gave way to her. Once she even scolded Maheshnath himself, and he let it go with a laugh. There had been some talk about Untouchables. 'Whatever may happen in the world,' Maheshnath had said, 'sweepers will remain nothing but sweepers. It's too hard to make civilized people out of them.'

To this Bhungi had said, 'Master, it's the sweepers who make it possible for the high-caste people to be civilized. Just let somebody do the same for us!'

In any other circumstances could Bhungi have got away with this insolence without having every hair of her head yanked out? But this time Babu Sahib chuckled and said, 'Bhungi always has something wise to say.'

\*

The period of Bhungi's rule could not continue beyond a year. The Brahmans objected to the child's being nursed with an Untouchable's milk, and Moteram Shastri even enjoined a penance. So the nursing was abandoned but the matter of a penance was laughed away. To taunt the Brahman Maheshnath said, 'A penance, Shastriji? Very sensible! Until yesterday the child was nourished by the blood of this same Untouchable, so he must already be contaminated. My my, that's a great religion you've got!'

Shaking his topknot violently Shastriji said, 'In truth, the child was nourished on her blood until yesterday, and indeed on flesh as well — since she is an eater of meat. But today's business for today, let yesterday take care of itself. At the Jagannath temple at Puri Untouchables sit down to eat together with Brahmans — but they can't do it here. When we're ill we sit at our meals all dressed, we eat highly spiced stews, but Babuji, upon recovering we must once again eat according to the rules of morality. The regulations for emergencies are strange indeed!'

'So the meaning of this then is that morality changes — sometimes one thing, sometimes another?'

'What else! There's one morality for the king, another for the subject, one for the poor, another for the rich. Kings and princes can eat when they want, with whom they want, they can marry anybody they want, there are no restrictions for them! Those people have the power. Restrictions are for ordinary folk.'

So there was no penance, but Bhungi was obliged to step down from her eminence. But anyway she received so much in the way of gifts and tips that she couldn't take it away by herself, and she got the gold bracelets as well, and instead of one, two beautiful new saris, not just plain muslin like the ones when the daughters were born.

*

This same year there was a severe outbreak of the plague and Gudar was the first to fall victim. Bhungi was left alone, but she continued to live just as before. People kept an eye out to see if she'd go away now. There was talk with a certain sweeper, a certain headman paid a call, but Bhungi didn't go anywhere, she was still there five years later when her boy Mangal, despite being skinny and nearly always sick, was starting to run around. Next to Maheshnath's Suresh he looked like a dwarf.

One day Bhungi was cleaning a drain at Maheshnath's house. It was clogged with several months' accumulation of sludge so that the water had begun to form pools in the courtyard. Bhungi thrust a long stout bamboo pole into the drain and shook it vigorously. She had stuck her right arm inside the drain up to the elbow when suddenly she let out a shriek and drew her arm back out. At almost the same moment a black snake came slithering out of the drain. People came running and killed it. But they could not save Bhungi. They assumed it was a harmless water snake, so at first they took no precautions for her. It was only when the poison had spread through her body and she was seized by convulsions that they realized it was not a water snake but a venomous corn snake.

Mangal was now an orphan. He made a habit of hanging around

Maheshnath's door all through the day. There was so much leftover food in the house that they might have fed a dozen such children. There was thus no shortage of food but all the same it made him feel bad when the food was dropped down from above into his clay bowls. Everybody ate from fine plates, and clay bowls for him!

He might not have been aware at all of this discrimination but the village boys constantly shouted abuse at him. There was no one who would ask him to play with them, and even the piece of canvas he slept on was untouchable. There was a *neem* tree in front of the house. Mangal made his home directly under it with his piece of torn canvas, two clay bowls and a *dhoti* passed on from Suresh. The spot was equally comfortable in every season, winter, summer and the rains. In the scorching June winds, the freezing cold and the drenching rains lucky little Mangal stayed alive and was actually a lot healthier than he'd been before. And there was even someone he could call his own, a village dog which, fed up with being picked on by his fellows in the pack, had taken refuge with him. They both ate the same food, slept on the same canvas and even had the same temperament and understood one another's moods. There was never once a quarrel between them.

The pious people of the village were surprised at this generosity of Babu Sahib's. For Mangal to loiter and sleep right in front of his door — it couldn't have been fifty feet — seemed to them contrary to genuine religion. Disgusting! If this sort of thing continued, you could be sure that religion was finished once and for all. God created the Untouchables too, we know that, to be sure, and who isn't aware that one ought not to commit any injustice against them? — after all, God is known as the redeemer of the lowly. But the traditions of society have to be considered too! One would feel embarrassed just to approach that door. Maheshnath might be the master of the village, one would be obliged to go there, but let it be understood that it was odious.

Mangal and Tommy, the dog, had become fast friends. Mangal would say, 'Look, Tommy, move over a little and go to sleep. Where do you expect me to lie? You're spread over the whole canvas.'

Tommy would whimper, wag his tail and instead of sliding over would crowd closer and begin to lick Mangal's face.

Every evening he would go to look at his house and cry a little while. The first year the thatched roof fell in, the second one the wall collapsed and now only half the walls were standing, all jagged

227

at the top. This was the treasure of affection he had found. The memories, the yearning and the love together drew him to this ruin, and Tommy always came with him. Mangal would sit on the jagged wall and dream of his past life and the future while Tommy time and time again would try unsuccessfully to leap up into his lap.

*

One day several boys were playing and Mangal too came along, though he stood far apart. It's not certain whether Suresh took pity on him or whether the players needed someone to pair off, but in any case he decided that today Mangal should take part in the game — who was going to come along and see them here?

'Hey Mangal,' he said , 'how about playing!'

'No, brother,' Mangal said, 'What if the master should see? I'd get my hide skinned off, but as for you, you'd get away with it.'

'Who's going to see us here, you idiot? Come on, we're playing horse-and-rider. You'll be the horse and the rest of us will climb on you and ride.'

Sceptically Mangal asked, 'Will I always be the horse or will I get to be a rider, tell me that.'

This was a complicated question. Nobody had considered it. After a moment's reflection Suresh said, 'Who'd let you get on his back? Think of that! After all, are you a sweeper or not?'

But Mangal too stood his ground. 'When did I ever say I wasn't a sweeper? But it was my own mother who brought you up and fed you with her milk. So long as I'm not going to get to be a rider I won't be the horse. You people are pretty smart! You want to enjoy being riders and I'm supposed to stay just a horse.'

'You've got to be the horse!' Suresh scolded and ran to catch him. Mangal ran off with Suresh after him. Mangal quickened his step and Suresh too put on more steam. But from being so overfed he'd turned flabby and he was already panting from running.

Finally he stopped and said, 'Come and be the horse, Mangal, otherwise whenever I do get my hands on you I'll really beat you up!'

'Then you'll have to be a horse too.'

'All right, we'll be horses too.'

'You ride afterwards. Be the horse first, then I will after I've ridden.'

Suresh, in fact, wanted to play a trick. When he heard this proposal of Mangal's he said to his companions, 'Just look at the little stinker's nerve! There's a sweeper for you.'

The three of them surrounded Mangal and forced him down on all fours. Suresh jumped on his back at once and straddled him. He made a clicking sound with his tongue and said, 'Giddyup, horse, giddyup!'

Mangal moved along for a little while but he felt as though his back would break from the burden. Slowly he flattened his back and slipped out from under Suresh's thighs. Master Suresh fell with a thud and began to sound his horn.

His mother heard him crying somewhere. Wherever Suresh might be crying her sharp ears picked it up, and his crying was really quite peculiar, like the whistle on a narrow-gauge engine.

She said to the maid, 'Go look, Suresh is crying somewhere, find out if anybody's hit him.'

In the meantime Suresh himself came, rubbing his eyes. Whenever he found an opportunity to cry he was sure to come complaining to his mother and she would wipe his eyes and give him sweets and dried fruit. It's true, he was eight years old but he was a complete blockhead. Excessive affection had done to his wits what excessive eating had done to his body.

His mother asked, 'Why are you crying, Suresh? Did someone hit you?'

Still crying Suresh said, 'Mangal touched me.'

She could not believe it. Mangal was so self-effacing that she would not have credited any mischief to him. But when Suresh began to swear it was true she was obliged to believe him. She sent for Mangal and scolded him. 'What's going on, Mangal, now you're dreaming up all sorts of mischief! I told you you were never to touch Suresh. Do you remember or not? Speak up!'

In a low voice Mangal said, 'How could I forget?'

'Then why did you touch him?'

'I didn't touch him.'

'If you didn't touch him why was he crying?'

'He fell, that's why.'

'Stubborn and lying too!' Madam broke off, grinding her teeth. If she beat him she would have to take a purificatory bath that very moment. Even if she just took a cane in her hand the lightning current of contact would be conducted through the cane to course

229

through her body. And so she heaped as much abuse on him as she could and ordered him to get out at once. If he ever appeared at their door again she'd drink his blood. Though they gave him all that free food he dreamed up nasty tricks, etc. etc.

Mangal was not likely to feel humiliation, but he could feel fear. Quietly he picked up his pots, tucked the piece of canvas under his arm, put the *dhoti* over his shoulder and set out weeping. He would never come back there again. The result would be that he would die of hunger. What harm in that? What good was there in living like this? Where was there any other shelter for him in the village? Who would take in a sweeper? He went off toward the ruins of his house where memories of the happy days might dry his tears, and cried his heart out.

At that moment Tommy came looking for him, and then the two of them forgot their grief.

*

But as daylight faded Mangal's despair also began to disappear, while the hunger that had gnawed at his childhood and consumed his body had now become all the more intense. His eyes turned constantly toward his bowls. Up at the house he would be getting Suresh's left over sweets by now, but here — not a scrap to eat. He consulted with Tommy: 'What are you going to eat? I'm just going to go to bed hungry.'

Tommy whimpered as though to say, 'You just have to put up with this sort of insult throughout life. But if you lose heart, how can you keep going? Just consider my case now, sometimes somebody beats me with a stick and yells after me, then in a little while I go back to him with my tail wagging. That's the way you and I are made, my friend.'

Mangal said, 'Get along now, eat anything you find, don't worry about me.

In his dog language Tommy said, 'I won't go alone, I'll take you with me.'

'But I'm not going.'

'Then I won't go either.'

'You'll die of starvation.'

'Do you think you'll stay alive then?'

'But there's nobody around to cry over me.'

230

I'm in the same fix, friend — that bitch I was in love with last fall has been unfaithful, she's with Kallu now. Luckily she took her pups off with her, otherwise my existence would have been miserable. Who'd look after five puppies?'

After another moment hunger produced another plan.

'The mistress must be looking for us, don't you think so, Tommy?'

'What else? Babuji and Suresh must have finished eating by now. The servant must have taken out the leftovers, he's probably calling us.'

'A lot of *ghee* will be left in Babuji's and Suresh's plates and best of all, cream!'

'And every bit of it's going to be thrown into the garbage.'

'Let's see if someone's looking for us.'

'Who's going to come looking for us? Do you think they're priests who'll chant our name? They'll call "Mangal, Mangal!" just once and that's it, the food will be dumped into the drain.'

'All right then, let's get going. But I'll stay hidden if anybody calls out my name, then I'll come back — understand?'

They both started out and when they got to Maheshnath's door stayed crouching in the shadows. But how could Tommy be patient? Slowly he found his way into the house. He saw that Maheshnath and Suresh were seated at their dinner. Quietly he settled down on the verandah but all the time he was afraid somebody might come along and whack him with a stick.

The servants were chatting. One said, 'Nobody's seen hide nor hair of that Mangal today. The mistress bawled him out so maybe he's run away.'

Another answered, 'If they threw him out it's a good thing. Who wants to have to look a sweeper in the face every single morning?'

Mangal shrank back even further into the shadows. All his hopes sank deeper than the depths of the sea.

Maheshnath stood up. A servant washed his hands. Now he would smoke his *hooka* and fall asleep. Suresh would sit with his mother and listen to some story or other until he fell asleep. Who was there to worry about poor Mangal? He thought. It was so late now that there was no chance anyone would call for him, even by force of habit.

He lingered on for some time, disappointed, then, sighing, he was just on the point of going when a bearer appeared carrying a plate of leftovers.

Mangal came out from the darkness into the light. How could he resist now?

The servant said, 'Where the devil were you? We thought you must have gone off somewhere. Here, eat this — I was just about to dump it out.'

Humbly Mangal said, 'But I've been waiting here a long time.'

'Then why didn't you speak out?'

'Because . . . I was afraid.'

'Well, take this and eat it.'

He lifted up the leaf dish and dropped it into Mangal's out-stretched hands. The eyes which Mangal turned to him were full of humble gratitude.

Tommy came out from inside too. The two of them began to eat from the leaf right there under the *neem* tree.

Patting Tommy's head with one hand, Mangal said, 'Just think, we were so hungry that if we hadn't at least got this bread they've thrown away what would we have done?'

Tommy wagged his tail.

'It was my mother who nursed Suresh.'

Tommy wagged his tail again.

'They say nobody can ever really pay the price of milk, and this is the payment I'm getting.'

And once more Tommy wagged his tail.

# The Shroud

Father and son sat in silence at the door of their hut before a burnt-out fire and inside Budhiya, the son's young wife, lay fainting in the throes of child-birth. From time to time such an agonizing cry came out of her that their hearts skipped a beat. It was a winter night, all was silent, and the whole village was obliterated in the darkness.

Ghisu said, 'It looks as though she won't make it. You spent the whole day running around — just go in and have a look.'

Annoyed, Madhav said, 'If she's going to die why doesn't she get it over with? What can I do by looking?'

'You're pretty hard-hearted, aren't you? You live at your ease with somebody all year and then you don't give a damn about her.'

'But I couldn't stand looking at her writhing and thrashing.'

They were a family of Untouchable leather-workers and had a bad name throughout the whole village. If Ghisu worked one day he'd take three off. Madhav was such a loafer that whenever he worked for a half hour he'd stop and smoke his pipe for an hour. So they couldn't get work anywhere. If there was even a handful of grain in the house then the two of them swore off work. After a couple of days fasting Ghisu would climb up a tree and break off branches for firewood and Madhav would bring it to the market to sell. And so long as they had any of the money they got for it they'd both wander around in idleness. There was no shortage of heavy work in the village. It was a village of farmers and there were any number of chores for a hard-working man. But whenever you called these two you had to be satisfied with paying them both for doing one man's work between them. If the two of them had been wandering ascetics there would have been absolutely no need for them to practice. This was their nature. A strange life theirs was! They owned nothing except for some clay pots; a few torn rags was all that covered their nakedness. They were free of worldly cares! They were loaded with debts, people abused them, beat them, but they didn't suffer. People would loan them a little something even though they were so poor there was no hope of getting it back. At the time of the potato and pea harvest they would go into other people's fields and dig up potatoes and gather peas and roast them or they'd pick sugarcane to suck at night. Ghisu had reached the age of sixty living this hand-to-mouth existence, and like a good son Madhav was following in his father's footsteps in every way, and if anything he was adding lustre to his father's fame. The two of them were sitting before the fire now roasting potatoes they'd dug up in some field. Ghisu's wife had died a long time ago. Madhav had been married last year. Since his wife had come she'd established order in the family and kept those two good-for-nothings' bellies filled. And since her arrival they'd become more sluggish than ever. In fact, they'd begun to let it go to their heads. If someone sent for them to do a job, they'd bare-facedly ask for twice the wages. This same woman was dying today in child-birth and it was as though they were only waiting for her to die so they could go to sleep in peace and quiet.

Ghisu took a potato and while he peeled it said, 'Go and look, see how she is. She must be possessed by some ghost, what else? But the village exorcist wants a rupee for a visit.'

Madhav was afraid that if he went into the hut Ghisu would do away with most of the potatoes. He said, 'I'm scared to go in there.'

'What are you afraid of? I'll be right here.'

'Then why don't you go and look?'

'When my woman died I didn't stir from her side for three days. And then she'd be ashamed if I saw her bare like that when I've never even seen her face before. Won't she be worried about her modesty? If she sees me she won't feel free to thrash around.'

'I've been thinking, if there's a baby what's going to happen? There's nothing we're supposed to have in the house — ginger, sugar, oil.'

'Everything's going to be all right, God will provide. The very people who wouldn't even give us a pice before will send for us tomorrow and give us rupees. I had nine kids and there was never a thing in the house but somehow or other the Lord got us through.'

In a society where the condition of people who toiled day and night was not much better than theirs and where, on the other hand, those who knew how to profit from the weaknesses of the peasants were infinitely richer, it's no wonder they felt like this. We could even say that Ghisu was much smarter than the peasants and

234

instead of being one of the horde of empty-headed toilers he'd found a place for himself in the disreputable society of idle gossip-mongers. Only he didn't have the ability to stick to the rules and code of such idlers. So while others of his crowd had made themselves chiefs and bosses of the village, the whole community pointed at him in contempt. Nevertheless, there was the consolation that although he was miserably poor at least he didn't have to do the back-breaking labour the farmers did, and other people weren't able to take unfair advantage of his simplicity and lack of ambition.

They ate the potatoes piping hot. Since yesterday they'd eaten nothing and they didn't have the patience to let them cool. Several times they burned their tongues. When they were peeled the outside of the potatoes didn't seem very hot but as soon as they bit into them the inside burned their palates, tongues and throats. Rather than keep these burning coals in their mouths it was a lot safer to drop them down into their bellies, where there was plenty of equipment to cool them. So they swallowed them quickly, even though the attempt brought tears to their eyes.

At this moment Ghisu recalled the Thakur's wedding, which he'd attended twenty years before. The way the feast had gratified him was something to remember all his life, and the memory was still vivid today. He said, 'I won't forget that feast. Since then I've never seen food like it or filled my belly so well. The bride's people crammed everybody with *puris*, everybody! Bigshots and nobodies all ate *puris* fried in real *ghee*. Relishes and curds with spices, three kinds of dried vegetables, a tasty curry, sweets — how can I describe how delicious that food was? There was nothing to hold you back, you just asked for anything you wanted and as much as you wanted. We ate so much that nobody had any room left for water. The people serving just kept on handing out hot, round, mouth-watering savouries on leaves. And we'd say, 'Stop, you mustn't,' and put our hands over the plates to stop them but they kept right on handing it out. And when everybody had rinsed his mouth we got *paan* and cardamom too. But how could I take any *paan*? I couldn't even stand up. I just went and lay down in my blanket right away. That's how generous that Thakur was!'

Relishing the banquet in his imagination Madhav said, 'Nobody feeds us like that now.'

'Who'd feed us like that today? That was another age. Now eve-

235

rybody thinks about saving his money. Don't spend for weddings, don't spend for funerals! I ask you, if they keep on hoarding the wealth they've squeezed out of the poor, where are they going to put it? But they keep on hoarding. When it comes to spending any money they say they have to economize.'

'You must have eaten a good twenty *puris*?'

'I ate more than twenty.'

'I would have eaten fifty!'

'I couldn't have eaten any less than fifty. I was a husky lad in those days. You're not half so big.'

After finishing the potatoes they drank some water and right there in front of the fire they wrapped themselves up in their *dhotis* and pulling up their knees they fell asleep — just like two enormous coiled pythons.

And Budhiya was still moaning.

*

In the morning Madhav went inside the hut and saw that his wife had turned cold. Flies were buzzing around her mouth. Her stony eyes stared upwards. Her whole body was covered with dust. The child had died in her womb.

Madhav ran to get Ghisu. Then they both began to moan wildly and beat their chests. When they heard the wailing the neighbours came running and according to the old tradition began to console the bereaved.

But there was not much time for moaning and chest-beating. There was the worry about a shroud and wood for the pyre. The money in the house had disappeared like carrion in a kite's nest.

Father and son went weeping to the village *zamindar*. He hated the sight of the two of them and several times he'd thrashed them with his own hands for stealing or for not coming to do the work they'd promised to do. He asked, 'What is it, little Ghisu, what are you crying about? You don't show yourself much these days. It seems as though you don't want to live in this village.'

Ghisu bowed his head all the way to the ground, his eyes full of tears, and said, 'Excellency, an awful thing's happened to me. Madhav's woman passed away last night. She was in agony the whole time. The two of us never once left her side. We did whatever we could, gave her medicine — but to make a long story short, she gave us the slip. And now there's nobody left even to give us a piece of bread, master. We're ruined! My house has been destroyed! I'm your slave — except for you now who is there to see that she's given a decent funeral? Whatever we had we spent on medicine. If your excellency is merciful, then she'll have a good funeral. Whose door can we go to except yours?'

The *zamindar* was soft-hearted. But to be kind to Ghisu was like trying to dye a black blanket. He was tempted to say, 'Get out and don't come back! When we send for you, you don't show up but today when you're in a jam you come and flatter me. You're a sponging bastard!' But this was not the occasion for anger or scolding. Exasperated, he took out a couple of rupees and threw them on the ground. But he didn't utter a word of consolation. He didn't even look at Ghisu. It was as though he'd shoved a load off his head.

When the *zamindar* had given two rupees how could the shopkeepers and moneylenders of the village refuse? Ghisu knew how to trumpet the *zamindar's* name around. Somebody gave him a couple of *annas*, somebody else four. Within an hour Ghisu had harvested a tidy sum of five rupees. He got grain at one place, wood from somewhere else. And at noon Ghisu and Madhav went to the market to get a shroud. There were people already cutting the bamboo to make a litter for the corpse.

The tender-hearted women of the village came and looked at the dead woman, shed a few tears over her forlorn state and went away.

*

When they reached the market Ghisu said, 'We have enough wood to burn her up completely, haven't we, Madhav?'

'Yes, there's plenty of wood, now we need the shroud.'

'That's right, come along and we'll pick up a cheap one.'

'Of course, what else? By the time we move the corpse it will be night — who can see a shroud at night?'

'What a rotten custom it is that somebody who didn't even have rags to cover herself while she was alive has to have a new shroud when she dies!'

'The shroud just burns right up with the body.'

'And what's left? If we'd had these five rupees before then we could have got some medicine.'

237

Each of them guessed what was in the other's mind. They went on wandering through the market, stopping at one cloth-merchant's shop after another. They looked at different kinds of cloth, silk and cotton, but nothing met with their approval. This went on until evening. Then the two of them, by some divine inspiration or other, found themselves in front of a liquor shop, and as though according to a previous agreement they went inside. For a little while they stood there, hesitant. Then Ghisu went up to where the tavern-keeper sat and said, 'Sahuji, give us a bottle too.'

Then some snacks arrived, fried fish was brought and they sat on the verandah and tranquilly began to drink.

After drinking several cups in a row they began to feel tipsy. Ghisu said, 'What's the point of throwing a shroud over her? In the end it just burns up. She can't take anything with her.'

Madhav looked toward heaven and said, as though calling on the gods to witness his innocence, 'It's the way things are done in the world, otherwise why would people throw thousands of rupees away on Brahmans? Who can tell if anybody gets it in the next world or not?'

'The bigshots have lots of money to squander so let them squander it, but what have we got to squander?'

'But how will you explain it to people? Won't they ask, "Where's the shroud?"'

Ghisu laughed. 'So what? We'll say the money fell out of the knot in our *dhotis* and we looked and looked but couldn't find it. They won't believe it but they'll give the money again.'

Madhav laughed too over this unexpected stroke of luck. He said, 'She was good to us, that poor girl — even dying she got us fine things to eat and drink.'

They'd gone through more than half a bottle. Ghisu ordered four pounds of *puris*. Then relish, pickle, livers. There was a shop right across from the tavern. Madhav brought everything back in a trice on a couple of leaf-platters. He'd spent one and a half rupees; only a few pice were left.

The two of them sat eating their *puris* in the lordly manner of tigers enjoying their kill in the jungle. They felt neither fear of being called to account nor concern for a bad reputation. They had overcome those sensibilities long before.

Ghisu said philosophically, 'If our souls are content won't it be credited to her in heaven as a good deed?'

Respectfully Madhav bowed his head and confirmed, 'Absolutely will! Lord, you know all secrets. Bring her to paradise — we bless her from our hearts . . . the way we've eaten today we've never eaten before in our whole lives.'

A moment later a doubt rose in his mind. He said, 'What about us, are we going to get there some day too?'

Ghisu gave no answer to this artless question. He didn't want to dampen his pleasure by thinking about the other world.

'But if she asks us there, "Why didn't you people give me a shroud?" What will you say?'

'That's a stupid question!'

'But surely she'll ask!'

'How do you know she won't get a shroud? Do you think I'm such a jackass? Have I been wasting my time in this world for sixty years? She'll have a shroud and a good one too.'

Madhav was not convinced. He said, 'Who'll give it? You've eaten up all the money. But she'll ask me. I was the one who put the cinnabar in her hair at the wedding.'

Getting angry, Ghisu said, 'I tell you she'll have a shroud, aren't you listening?'

'But why don't.you tell me who's going to give it?'

'The same people who gave before will give the money again —well, not the money this time but the stuff we need.'

As the darkness spread and the stars began to glitter the gaiety of the tavern also increased steadily. People sang, bragged, embraced their companions, lifted the jug to the lips of friends. All was intoxication, the very air was tipsy. Anybody who came in got drunk in an instant from just a few drops, the air of the place turned their heads more than the liquor. The sufferings of their lives drew them all there and after a little while they were no longer aware if they were alive or dead, not alive or not dead.

And father and son went on slopping it up with zest. Everyone was staring at them. How lucky the two of them were, they had a whole bottle between themselves.

When he was crammed full Madhav handed the leftover *puris* on a leaf to a beggar who was standing watching them with famished eyes. And for the first time in his life he experienced the pride, the happiness and the pleasure of giving.

Ghisu said, 'Take it, eat it and say a blessing — the one who earned it is — well, she's dead. But surely your blessing will reach

239

her. Bless her from your heart, that food's the wages for very hard labour.'

Madhav looked heavenward again and said, 'She'll go to heaven, *Dada*, she'll be a queen in heaven.'

Ghisu stood up and as though bathing in waves of bliss he said, 'Yes, son, she'll go to heaven. She didn't torment anybody, she didn't oppress anybody. At the moment she died she fulfilled the deepest wish of all our lives. If she doesn't go to heaven then will those big fat people go who rob the poor with both hands and swim in the Ganges and offer holy water in the temples to wash away their sins?'

Their mood of credulity suddenly changed. Volatility is the special characteristic of drunkenness. Now was the turn for grief and despair.

'But *Dada*,' Madhav said, 'the poor girl suffered so much in this life! How much pain she had when she died.'

He put his hands over his eyes and began to cry, he burst into sobs.

Ghisu consoled him. 'Why weep, son? Be glad she's slipped out of this maze of illusion and left the whole mess behind her. She was very lucky to escape the bonds of the world's illusion so quickly.'

And the two of them stood up and began to sing.

*'Deceitful world, why do you dazzle us with your eyes?*
*Deceitful world!'*

The eyes of all the drunkards were glued on them and the two of them became inebriated in their hearts. Then they started to dance, they jumped and sprang, fell back, twisted, they gesticulated, they mimed their feelings, and finally they collapsed dead drunk right there.

# Deliverance

Dukhi the tanner was sweeping in front of his door while Jhuriya, his wife, plastered the floor with cow-dung. When they both found a moment to rest from their work Jhuriya said, 'Aren't you going to the Brahman to ask him to come? If you don't he's likely to go off somewhere.'

'Yes, I'm going,' Dukhi said, 'But we have to think about what he's going to sit on.'

'Can't we find a cot somewhere? You could borrow one from the village headman's wife.'

'Sometimes the things you say are really aggravating! The people in the headman's house give me a cot? They won't even let a coal out of their house to light your fire with, so are they going to give me a cot? Even when they're where I can go and talk to them if I ask for a pot of water I won't get it, so who'll give me a cot? A cot isn't like the things we've got — cow-dung fuel or chaff or wood that anybody who wants can pick up and carry off. You'd better wash our own cot and set it out — in this hot weather it ought to be dry by the time he comes.'

'He won't sit on our cot,' Jhuriya said. 'You know what a stickler he is about religion and doing things according to the rule.'

A little worried, Dukhi said, 'Yes, that's true. I'll break off some *mohwa* leaves and make a mat for him, that will be the thing. Great gentlemen eat off *mohwa* leaves, they're holy. Hand me my stick and I'll break some off.'

'I'll make the mat, you go to him. But we'll have to offer him some food he can take home and cook, won't we? I'll put it in my dish —'

'Don't commit any such sacrilege!' Dukhi said. 'If you do, the offering will be wasted and the dish broken. *Baba* will just pick up the dish and dump it. He flies off the handle very fast, and when he's in a rage he doesn't even spare his wife, and he beat his son so badly that even now the boy goes around with a broken hand. So we'll put the offering on a leaf too. Just don't touch it. Take Jhuri the

241

*Gond*'s daughter to the village merchant and bring back all the things we need. Let it be a complete offering — a full two pounds of flour, a half of rice, a quarter of gram, an eighth of *ghee*, salt, turmeric, and four *annas* at the edge of the leaf. If you don't find the *Gond* girl then get the woman who runs the parching oven, beg her to go if you have to. Just don't touch anything because that will be a great wrong.'

After these instructions Dukhi picked up his stick, took a big bundle of grass and went to make his request to the Pandit. He couldn't go empty-handed to ask a favour of the Pandit; he had nothing except the grass for a present. If Panditji ever saw him coming without an offering, he'd shout abuse at him from far away.

*

Pandit Ghasiram was completly devoted to God. As soon as he awoke he would busy himself with his rituals. After washing his hands and feet at eight o' clock, he would begin the real ceremony of worship, the first part of which consisted of the preparation of *bhang*. After that he would grind sandalwood paste for half-an-hour, then with a straw he would apply it to his forehead before the mirror. Between two lines of sandalwood paste he would draw a red dot. Then on his chest and arms he would draw designs of perfect circles. After this he would take out the image of the Lord, bathe it, apply the sandalwood to it, deck it with flowers, perform the ceremony of lighting the lamp before it and ringing a little bell. At ten o'clock he'd rise from his devotions and after a drink of the *bhang* go outside where a few clients would have gathered: such was the reward for his piety; this was his crop to harvest.

Today when he came from the shrine in his house he saw Dukhi the Untouchable tanner sitting there with a bundle of grass. As soon as he caught sight of him Dukhi stood up, prostrated himself on the ground, stood up again and folded his hands. Seeing the Pandit's glorious figure his heart was filled with reverence. How godly a sight! — a rather short, roly-poly fellow with a bald, shiny skull, chubby cheeks and eyes aglow with brahmanical energy. The sandalwood markings bestowed on him the aspect of the gods. At the sight of Dukhi he intoned, 'What brings you here today, little Dukhi?'

Bowing his head, Dukhi said, 'I'm arranging Bitiya's betrothal.

242

Will your worship help us to fix an auspicious date? When can you find the time?'

'I have no time today,' Panditji said. 'But still, I'll manage to come toward evening.'

'No, maharaj, please come soon. I've arranged everything for you. Where shall I set this grass down?'

'Put it down in front of the cow and if you'll just pick up that broom sweep it clean in front of the door,' Panditji said. 'Then the floor of the sitting room hasn't been plastered for several days so plaster it with cowdung. While you're doing that I'll be having my lunch, then I'll rest a bit and after that I'll come. Oh yes, you can split that wood too, and in the storeroom there's a little pile of hay — just take it out and put it into the fodder bin.'

Dukhi began at once to carry out the orders. He swept the doorstep, he plastered the floor. This took until noon. Panditji went off to have his lunch. Dukhi, who had eaten nothing since morning, was terribly hungry. But there was no way he could eat here. His house was a mile away — if he went to eat there Panditji would be angry. The poor fellow suppressed his hunger and began to split the wood. It was a fairly thick tree trunk on which a great many devotees had previously tried their strength and it was ready to match iron with iron in any fight. Dukhi, who was used to cutting grass and bringing it to the market, had no experience with cutting wood. The grass would bow its head before his sickle but now even when he bought the axe down with all his strength it didn't make a mark on the trunk. The axe just glanced off. He was drenched in sweat, panting, he sat down exhausted and got up again. He could scarcely lift his hands, his legs were unsteady, he couldn't straighten out his back. Then his vision blurred, he saw spots, he felt dizzy, but still he went on trying. He thought that if he could get a pipeful of tobacco to smoke then perhaps he might feel refreshed. This was a Brahman village, and Brahmans didn't smoke tobacco at all like the low castes and Untouchables. Suddenly he remembered that there was a *Gond* living in the village too, surely he would have a pipeful. He set off at a run for the man's house at once, and he was in luck. The *Gond* gave him both pipe and tobacco, but he had no fire to light it with. Dukhi said, 'Don't worry about the fire, brother, I'll go to Panditji's house and ask him for a light, they're still cooking there.'

With this he took the pipe and came back and stood on the

verandah of the Brahman's house, and he said, 'Master, if I could get just a little bit of light I'll smoke this pipeful.'

Panditji was eating and his wife said, 'Who's that man asking for a light?'

'It's only that damned little Dukhi the tanner. I told him to cut some wood. The fire's lit, so go give him his light.'

Frowning, the Panditayin said, 'You've become so wrapped up in your books and astrological charts that you've forgotten all about caste rules. If there's a tanner or a washerman or a birdcatcher why he can just come walking right into the house as though he owned it. You'd think it was an inn and not a decent Hindu's house. Tell that good-for-nothing to get out or I'll scorch his face with a firebrand.'

Trying to calm her down, Panditji said, 'He's come inside — so what? Nothing that belongs to you has been stolen. The floor is clean, it hasn't been desecrated. Why not just let him have his light — he's doing our work, isn't he? You'd have to pay at least four *annas* if you hired some labourer to split it.'

Losing her temper, the Panditayin said, 'What does he mean coming into this house!'

'It was the son of a bitch's bad luck, what else?' the Pandit said.

'It's all right,' she said, 'This time I'll give him his fire but if he ever comes into the house again like that I'll give him the coals in his face.'

Fragments of this conversation reached Dukhi's ears. He repented: it was a mistake to come. She was speaking the truth —how could a tanner ever come into a Brahman's house? These people were clean and holy, that was why the whole world worshipped and respected them. A mere tanner was absolutely nothing. He had lived all his life in the village without understanding this before.

Therefore when the Pandit's wife came out bringing coals it was like a miracle from heaven. Folding his hands and touching his forehead to the ground he said, 'Panditayin, Mother, it was very wrong of me to come inside your house. Tanners don't have much sense — if we weren't such fools why would we get kicked so much?'

The Panditayin had brought the coals in a pair of tongs. From a few feet away, with her veil drawn over her face, she flung the coals toward Dukhi. Big sparks fell on his head and drawing back hastily he shook them out of his hair. To himself he said, 'This is what comes of dirtying a clean Brahman's house. How quickly God pays you back for it! That's why everybody's afraid of Pandits. Everybody else gives up his money and never gets it back but who ever got any money out of a Brahman? Anybody who tried would have his whole family destroyed and his legs would turn leprous.'

He went outside and smoked his pipe, then took up the axe and started to work again.

Because the sparks had fallen on him the Pandit's wife felt some pity for him. When the Pandit got up from his meal she said to him, 'Give this tanner something to eat, the poor fellow's been working for a long time, he must be hungry.'

Panditji considered this proposal entirely outside of the behaviour expected of him. He asked, 'Is there any bread?'

'There are a couple of pieces left over.'

'What's the good of two or three pieces for a tanner? Those people need at least a good two pounds.'

His wife put her hands over her ears. 'My, my, a good two pounds! Then let's forget about it.'

Majestically Panditji said, 'If there's some bran and husks mix them in flour and make a couple of pancakes. That'll fill the bastard's belly up. You can never fill up these low-caste people with good bread. Plain millet is what they need.'

'Let's forget the whole thing,' the Panditayin said, 'I'm not going to kill myself cooking in weather like this.'

*

When he took up the axe again after smoking his pipe, Dukhi found that with his rest the strength had to some extent come back into his arms. He swung the axe for about half-an-hour, then out of breath he sat down right there with his head in his hands.

In the meantime the *Gond* came. He said, 'Why are you wearing yourself out, old friend? You can whack it all you like but you won't split this trunk. You're killing yourself for nothing.'

Wiping the sweat from his forehead Dukhi said, 'I've still got to cart off a whole wagon-load of hay, brother.'

'Have you had anything to eat? Or are they just making you work without feeding you? Why don't you ask them from something?'

'How can you expect me to digest a Brahman's food, Chikhuri?'

245

'Digesting it is no problem, you have to get it first. He sits in there and eats like a king and then has a nice little nap after he tells you you have to split his wood. The government officials may force you to work for them but they pay you something for it, no matter how little. This fellow's gone one better, calling himself a holy man.'

'Speak softly, brother, if they hear you we'll be in trouble.'

With that Dukhi went back to work and began to swing the axe. Chikhuri felt so sorry for him that he came and took the axe out of Dukhi's hands and worked with it for a good half hour. But there was not even a crack in the wood. Then he threw the axe down and said, 'Whack it all you like but you won't split it, you're just killing yourself,' and he went away.

Dukhi began to think, 'Where did the *Baba* get hold of this trunk that can't be split? There's not even a crack in it so far. How long can I keep smashing into it? I've got a hundred things to do at home by now. In a house like mine there's no end to the work, something's always left over. But he doesn't worry about that. I'll just bring him his hay and tell him, '*Baba*, the wood didn't split. I'll come and finish it tomorrow.'

He lifted up the basket and began to bring the hay. From the storeroom to the fodder bin was no less than a quarter of a mile. If he'd really filled up the basket the work would have been quickly finished, but then who could have hoisted up the basket on his head? He couldn't raise a fully loaded basket, so he took just a little each time. It was four o'clock by the time he'd finished with the hay. At this time Pandit Ghasiram woke up, washed his hands and face, took some *paan* and came outside. He saw Dukhi asleep with the basket still on his head. He shouted, '*Arrey*, Dukhiya, sleeping? The wood's lying there just the way it was. What's taken you so long? You've used up the whole day just to bring in a little fistful of hay and then gone and fallen asleep! Pick up the axe and split that wood. You haven't even made a dent in it. So if you don't find an auspicious day for your daughter's marriage, don't blame me. This is why they say that as soon as an Untouchable gets a little food in his house he can't be bothered with you any more.'

Dukhi picked up the axe again. He completely forgot what he'd been thinking about before. His stomach was pasted against his backbone — he hadn't so much as eaten breakfast that morning, there wasn't any time. Just to stand up seemed an impossible task. His spirit flagged, but only for a moment. This was the Pandit, if he

246

didn't fix an auspicious day the marriage would be a total failure. And that was why everybody respected the Pandits — everything depended on getting the right day set. He could ruin anybody he wanted to. Panditji came close to the log and standing there began to goad him. 'That's right, give it a real hard stroke, a real hard one. Come on now, really hit it! Don't you have any strength in your arm? Smash it, what's the point of standing there thinking about it? That's it, it's going to split, there's a crack in it.'

Dukhi was in a delirium some kind of hidden power seemed to have come into his hands. It was as though fatigue, hunger, weakness, all had left him. He was astonished at his own strength. The axe-strokes descended one after another like lightning. He went on driving the axe in this state of intoxication until finally the log split down the middle. And Dukhi's hands let the axe drop. At the same moment, overcome with dizziness, he fell, the hungry, thirsty, exhausted body gave up.

Panditji called, 'Get up, just two or three more strokes. I want it in small bits.' Dukhi did not get up. It didn't seem proper to Pandit Ghasiram to insist now. He went inside, drank some *bhang*, emptied his bowels, bathed and came forth attired in full Pandit regalia. Dukhi was still lying on the ground. Panditji shouted, 'Well, Dukhi, are you going to just stay lying here? Let's go, I'm on my way to your house! Everything's set, isn't it?' But still Dukhi did not get up.

A little alarmed, Panditji drew closer and saw that Dukhi was absolutely stiff. Startled half out of his wits he ran into the house and said to his wife, 'Little Dukhi looks as though he's dead.'

Thrown into confusion Panditayin said, 'But hasn't he just been chopping wood?'

'He died right while he was splitting it. What's going to happen?'

Calmer, the Panditayin said, 'What do you mean what's going to happen? Send word to the tanners settlement so they can come and take the corpse away.'

In a moment the whole village knew about it. It happened that except for the *Gond* house everyone who lived there was Brahman. People stayed off the road that went there. The only path to the well passed that way — how were they to get water? Who would come to draw water with a tanner's corpse nearby? One old woman said to Panditji, 'Why don't you have this body thrown away? Is anybody in the village going to be able to drink water or not?'

The *Gond* went from the village to the tanners' settlement and told everyone the story. 'Careful now!' he said. 'Don't go to get the body. There'll be a police investigation yet. It's no joke that some-body killed this poor fellow. The somebody may be a pandit, but just in his own house. If you move the body you'll get arrested too.'

Right after this Panditji arrived. But there was nobody in the settlement ready to carry the corpse away. To be sure, Dukhi's wife and daughter both went moaning to Panditji's door and tore their hair and wept. About a dozen other women went with them, and they wept too and they consoled them, but there was no man with them to bear up the body. Panditji threatened the tanners, he tried to wheedle them, but they were very mindful of the police and not one of them stirred. Finally Panditji went home disappointed.

*

At midnight the weeping and lamentation were still going on. It was hard for the Brahmans to fall asleep. But no tanner came to get the corpse, and how could a Brahman lift up an Untouchable's body? It was expressly forbidden in the scriptures and no one could deny it.

Angrily the Panditayin said, 'Those witches are driving me out of my mind. And they're not even hoarse yet!'

'Let the hags cry as long as they want. When he was alive nobody cared a straw about him. Now that he's dead everybody in the village is making a fuss about him.'

'The wailing of tanners is bad luck,' the Panditayin said.

'Yes, very bad luck.'

'And it's beginning to stink already.'

'Wasn't that bastard a tanner? Those people eat anything, clean or not, without worrying about it.'

'No sort of food disgusts them!'

'They're all polluted!'

Somehow or other they got through the night. But even in the morning no tanner came. They could still hear the wailing of the women. The stench was beginning to spread quite a bit.

Panditji got out a rope. He made a noose and managed to get it over the dead man's feet and drew it tight. Morning mist still clouded the air. Panditji grabbed the rope and began to drag it, and he dragged it until it was out of the village. When he got back home he bathed immediately, read out prayers to Durga for purification, and sprinkled Ganges water around the house.

Out there in the field the jackals and kites, dogs and crows were picking at Dukhi's body. This was the reward of a whole life of devotion, service and faith.

# Two Autobiographical Sketches

My life is a level plain. There are pits here and there but no cliffs, mountains, jungles, deep ravines or desert wastes. Those good people who have a taste for mountaineering will be disappointed here.

I was born in 1880. My father was a postal employee, my mother an ailing woman. I also had an older sister. At the time of my birth my father was earning about twenty rupees a month; by the time he died his salary was forty. He had been a very thoughtful man, moving through life with his eyes wide open but in his last days he had stumbled and even fallen and brought me down with him: when I was fifteen he had me married. And scarcely a year after the marriage he died. At that time I was studying in the ninth grade. In the house were my wife, my step-mother, her two children and myself, and there was not a pice of income. Whatever savings we'd had were used up in my father's six-month illness and funeral expenses. And my ambition was to get an M.A. and become a lawyer. In those days jobs were just as hard to get as now. With a great effort you might find some post with a salary of ten or twelve rupees a month. But I insisted on going on with my studies. The chains on my ankles were not just iron but of all the metals together and I wanted to walk on the mountain tops!

I had no shoes and no decent clothes, and there were the high prices — barley was half-a-rupee for ten pounds. I was studying in the High School of Queens College in Banaras, where the headmaster had waived the fees. The exams were coming up soon. When I left school at half-past three I would go to the part of town known as Bamboo Gate to teach a boy there. I'd get there at four and tutor until six, then leave for my house, which was five miles away in the country. Even walking very fast, I could not get there before eight o'clock. And I had to leave the house at eight sharp in the morning, otherwise I couldn't get to school on time. At night after supper I studied by the light of the oil lamp. I don't know when I slept. Nevertheless I was determined.

Somehow or other I passed my matriculation exams. But I made only second division and there was no hope left of being admitted to Queens College since fees could be remitted only for the first division. By chance Hindu College opened up the same year. I decided to study in this new institution. A Mr. Richardson was the principal. I went to his house and found him in full Indian dress — *kurta* and *dhoti* — sitting on the floor writing something. But it had not been so easy for him to change his personality — after listening to me only long enough for me to get half my request out he said he didn't discuss College business in his house and I should go to the College. Fine, I went to the College and he saw me there but our meeting was a disappointment. He could not remit the fees. What could I do next? If I presented suitable recommendations then perhaps he might consider my request. But who in the city would know a country boy?

Everyday, I set out from home to try to get a recommendation from somewhere, and after an arduous twelve miles return in the evening. Who was there to ask? Nobody was concerned about me.

But after several days I found someone to recommend me, Thakur Indranarayan Singh of the board of directors of Hindu College. I had gone to him and wept, and taking pity on me he'd given me a letter of recommendation. In that instant my happiness knew no bounds. Blissful, I returned home. I intended to go see the Principal the next day, but as soon as I reached home, I came down with a fever. I couldn't get rid of it for a week. I kept drinking concoctions made from *neem* leaves until I could barely stand it. One day I was sitting at the door when my old family priest came along. Seeing my state, he asked for details and then immediately went off into the fields. He dug up a root and when he brought it back washed it and ground it in with seven grains of black pepper and made me drink it. It had a magical effect. After no more than an hour the fever broke. It was as if the herb had taken it by the neck and throttled it. I asked Panditji many times for the name of the root but he wouldn't tell me. He said that if he did its effectiveness would vanish.

After a month I went again to see Mr. Richardson and showed him the letter of recommendation. Giving me a sharp look he said, 'Where were you all this time?'

'I was ill.'

'What was wrong with you?'

251

I wasn't ready for the question. If I told him it was a fever perhaps the Sahib would think I was lying. In my estimation a fever was a very light matter, insufficient to explain so long an absence. I felt I should name some disease which by its gravity would draw his sympathy. At the moment I could think of the name of none. When I'd gone to Thakur Singh he'd mentioned that he suffered from palpitations of the heart. And that was the word I thought of. I said in English, 'Palpitation of heart, sir.'

Astonished, the Principal looked at me and said, 'Are you completely well now?'

'Yes, sir.'

'Very well, fill out the entrance application form.'

I assumed that the worst was over. I took the form, filled it out and brought it back. At that moment the Principal was in one of his classes. At three o'clock I got the form back. Written on it was: 'Look into his ability.'

Here was a new problem. My heart sank. I could hope to pass no subject except English; I shivered at the thought of algebra and geometry. Whatever I'd learned I'd completely forgotten. But what else was there to do? Trusting to luck, I went to class and presented my application. The Professor, a Bengali, was teaching English; the subject was Washington Irving's *Rip van Winkle*. I took a seat in the back row. In a few minutes I saw that the professor was competent in his subject. When the hour was over he questioned me about the day's lesson and then wrote on my form 'Satisfactory.'

The next hour was algebra. The teacher here was also a Bengali; I showed him the form. Most often the students who came to a new school have not been able to find admittance elsewhere, and that was the case here; the classes were full of incompetent students. Whoever came in the first rush had been enrolled — to the hungry the meanest gruel tastes good. But now the stomach was full and students were chosen only after careful selection. This professor examined me in mathematics and I failed; in the box marked 'maths' on the form he wrote 'Unsatisfactory.'

I was so disappointed that I didn't bring the application back to the Principal. I went straight home. For me mathematics was the peak of mount Everest, I could never reach it. In Intermediate College I'd already failed it a couple of times and, discouraged, gave up taking the exam. Ten years later when it was made optional I took another subject and passed easily. Until that time who knows how many young people's aspirations have been finished off by mathematics! Anyway, I went home disappointed, but the desire for learning was still strong. What could I do sitting at home? How to improve my maths and get enrolled in college was the problem. For this I would have to live in town.

By luck I got a post tutoring a lawyer's sons with a salary of five rupees. I decided to live on two rupees and give the other three to my family. Above the advocate's stable there was a rather small, unfinished room. I got permission to stay there. A piece of canvas was spread out for my bed, I got a very small lamp from the market and began my life in town. I also brought some pots from home. Once a day I cooked *khichri* and after washing and scouring the pots I'd set out for the library —maths was the pretext, but I would read novels and the like. In those days I read Pandit Ratannath Dar's *Fasana-e-Azad* (*The Romance of Azad*) as well as *Chandra-kanta Santati* (*Chandrakanta's Children*), and I read everything of Bankim Chatterji's that I could find in Urdu translation in the library.

The brother-in-law of the advocate's sons had been a fellow student of mine for the matriculation. It was on his recommendation that I'd got this post. We were very good friends, so when I needed money I'd borrow from him and settle the account when I got my pay. Sometimes I'd have only two or three rupees left, sometimes three. On the day when I had two from my pay I'd lose all restraint — a craving for sweets would draw me towards the candy shop. I'd eat up two or three *annas* worth at once. On the same day I'd go home and give my family the two or two-and-a-half rupees. The next day I'd begin to borrow again. But there were times when I was embarrassed about borrowing and day after day I'd fast.

In this way four or five months went by. Meantime I had taken two-and-a-half rupees worth of clothes from a draper on credit. Every day I used to walk by his place — he had complete confi dence in me. When after a couple of months I hadn't been able to pay him I gave up going that way and took a detour. It was three years before I could pay off this debt. In those days a labouring man who made his home in the back of the advocate's house used to come to me to learn a little Hindi. He was always saying, 'Know this, little brother!' and we had all come to call him that by way of nickname. One day I borrowed eight *annas* from him too. Five years later he came to my house in the village and collected that half-a-rupee from me.

I still longed to study, but everyday I grew more and more despondent. I wanted to find a job somewhere but I had no idea of how and where to find one.

That winter I hadn't a pice left. I had spent a few days eating a piçe worth of the cheapest cereal each day. Either the moneylenders had refused to loan me anything or from embarrassment I couldn't ask. One evening, just at dusk, I went to a bookseller to sell a book — 'The Key to Chakravarti's Mathematics,' which I had bought two years before. I had held on to it until now with great difficulty but today in complete despair I decided to sell it. Although it had cost me two rupees I settled for one. Taking my rupee I was just about to leave the shop when a gentleman with big moustaches who had been sitting there asked me, 'Where are you studying?'

I said, 'I'm not studying anywhere but I hope to enroll somewhere.'

'Did you pass your matric exams? Then don't you want a job?'

'I can't find a job anywhere at all.'

This gentleman was the headmaster of a small school, and he needed an assistant teacher. He offered me a salary of eighteen rupees; I accepted. Eighteen rupees at that time was beyond the highest flight of my pessimistic imagination. I arranged to meet him the next day and left with my head in the clouds. I was ready to cope with any circumstances and if mathematics didn't stop me I would certainly get ahead. But the most difficult obstacle was the university's total lack of understanding, which then and for several years afterwards led it to treat everybody in the manner of that thief who made everybody, tall and short, fit one bed.

*

I began to write stories for the first time in 1907. I had read Tagore's stories in English and had Urdu translations published in the Urdu newspapers. But as early as 1901, I had begun to write novels. In 1902 one of my novels came out and a second in 1904, but until 1907 I had not written one short story. The title of my first story was 'The Most Precious Jewel in the World,' published in Zamana in 1907. After this I wrote another four or five stories. In 1909 a collection of five stories was published with the title 'Sufferings of the

254

*Motherland.*' At this time the partition of Bengal had taken place; in the Congress the radical faction had developed. In these five stories I praised devotion to the country.

At that time I was a deputy inspector in the department of education in Hamirpur district. One evening, six months after the stories had been published, while I sat in my tent I received a summons to go at once to see the District Collector, who was then on his winter tour. I harnessed the bullock-cart and travelled between thirty and forty miles through the night and reached him the next day. In front of him was placed a copy of my book. My head began to throb. At that time I was writing under the name of Navabrai. I had had some indication that the secret police were looking for the author of this book. I realized they must have traced me and that I was being called to account.

The Collector asked me, 'Did you write this book?'

I told him ¿ had. He asked for the theme of each one of the stories and finally losing his temper said, 'Your stories are full of sedition. It's fortunate for you that this is a British government. If it were the Mughal Empire, then both your hands would be cut off. Your stories are one-sided, you've insulted the British government.' The judgment was that I should give all copies of the book into the custody of the government and that I should not ever write anything else without the permission of the Collector. I felt I'd got off lightly. Of the thousand copies printed hardly three hundred had been sold. The remaining seven hundred I sent for from the *Zamana* office and had them delivered over to the Collector.

I assumed the danger was past. But the authorities could not be satisfied so easily. Afterwards I learned that the Collector had discussed the matter with the other officials of the district. The Superintendent of Police, two deputy collectors and the deputy inspector — whose subordinate I was — sat to consider what my fate should be. One of the deputy collectors, using quotations from the stories, asserted that in them there was nothing but sedition from beginning to end, and not just ordinary sedition but a contagious variety. The demi-god of the police said, 'So dangerous a man ought to be severely punished.' The deputy inspector was very fond of me. Afraid lest the affair be long drawn out he made the suggestion that in a friendly way he would sound out my political opinions and present a report to this committee. His idea was to explain to me and to write in his report that the writer was violent only with his pen and had nothing whatever to do with any political disturbance. The committee accepted his suggestion, although the police chief even at this moment was still blustering and threatening. Suddenly the Collector asked the deputy inspector, 'Do you expect that he'll tell you what he really thinks?'

'Yes, I'm intimate with him.'

'By pretending to be friendly you want to find out his secret views? But that's spying! I consider it vile.'

Losing his wits the deputy inspector stammered, 'But I . . . Your Excellency's order . . .'

'No,' the Collector interrupted, 'that's not my order. I had no intention of giving any such order. If the author's sedition can be proven from his book, then he should be put on trial in an open court, otherwise dismiss the case with a warning. I don't like the idea of a smile on the face and a knife in the hand.'

When the deputy inspector himself told me this story several days later, I asked him, 'Would you really have done this spying?'

He laughed. 'Impossible. Even if he'd given several hundred thousand rupees I wouldn't have done it. I just wanted to stop any legal proceedings, and they've been stopped. If there'd been a court case, you would definitely have been sentenced. You would have found no one to plead your cause. But the Collector is a noble gentleman.'

'Very noble indeed ,' I said.

# Notes to the Stories

## 1 The Road to Salvation

Original title: *Mukti-Marg, 'Salvation Road'*. First published in 1924. One of Premchand's finest stories of village life for its sympathy and objectivity and the mock epic humour of its battle scenes and satire.

The 'Satyanarayan' ceremony, held to honour auspicious occasions like house-warmings, consists of special prayers, the recitation of the exploits of Lord Vishnu, specially consecrated foods and banquets for the Brahmans.

The conclusion of the story makes it clear that Buddhu is of a lower social community than Jhingur. The higher caste may not eat food prepared by the lower unless, as in this case, the actual cooking is done by the higher-ranking man, since fire purifies everything it touches.

## 2 A Feast for the Holy Man

Original title: *Babaji Ka Bhog, 'The Pleasure of the Holy Man'*. Throughout the story *bhog* is used ironically in its double sense of pleasure, enjoyment, and a ritual offering of food sacrificed to the Gods. Ramdhan is described as an *Ahir*, a community associated with cow-herding — another ironic element in the story, since he has no cattle but only plough oxen. Although in his catalogue Amrit Rai gives no date for this story, it is a fine example of the compression and absence of editorial comment which characterize Premchand's last stories.

## 3 The Power of a Curse

Original title: *Garib Ki Hay, 'The Lament of the Poor'*. First published in 1911. In this quite early story there is a good deal of the moralizing that so often characterized the earlier work and considerable redundancy as well. I have cut this where it seemed in the interests of the story.

It is worth nothing that in this tale Munshi Ramsevak is ostracized not because he is a wicked man — which everyone has accepted throughout his career — but because he is technically the cause of a Brahman's death. Premchand's attitude toward the villagers is no less critical than it is toward Munshiji.

The name *'Nagin'* suggests *'nag'*, a cobra, hence the reference to her hissing, rearing up, etc.

## 4   A Catastrophe

Original title: *Vidhuvans*, *'Destruction'*. Written in the early twenties. Though usually designating a tribal community, in eastern Uttar Pradesh *Gond* indicates a person of a very low-ranking social group who are privileged, according to the complicated rules regulating the preparation of food, to handle food for high-caste groups. Cf. *'Deliverance'*.

## 5   January Night

Original title: *Pus Ki Raat*, *'A Night in the Month of Pus'*, (*Pus*, a month in the Hindu solar calendar corresponding to December-January). First published in 1930.

## 6   Neyur

Original title: *Neyur*. First published in 1933. The name Neyur is a peasant name, a dialect derivation from '*neola*,' mongoose. In the Urdu version of the story Premchand omitted the last two paragraphs, replacing them simply with his sentence: 'But he does his work exactly the way he used to and takes only a few crusts of bread for wages.'

## 7   The Story of Two Bullocks

Original title: *Do Bailon Ki Katha*, *'The Story of Two Bullocks'*. First published in 1931. The bullocks of the tale are endowed with not only a human but a specifically Hindu character, such as the belief in reincarnation and the importance of *dharma*. The political implications of this little fable today has only a slight historical interest, but the story has not lost its poignant charm, revealing Premchand's profound sympathy for abused non-human animals as well as the oppressed people of his country. The Hindi style, disarmingly simple but carefully controlled, is virtually impossible to reproduce in translation.

## 8   Ramlila

Original title: *Ramlila*. First published in 1926.

Every autumn in villages and cities throughout North India Ramlilas are performed — dramatizations with music of episodes from the epic of Rama, which may take several days to complete, culminating with Rama's return from exile with Sita, his wife, and his brother Lakshman, and triumphant coronation. Some are great spectacles, such as the famous Ramlila of Ramnagar, Varanasi; others, like the one described here, are much simpler performances with only a few characters. In this story the players are given no names beyond those of the roles they play —Rama (Ramchandra), Sita and Lakshman.

258

## 9 The Thakur's Well

Original title: *Thakur Ka Kuan, 'The Thakur's Well'*. 'Thakur' is a title of Rajputs, members of the second highest caste and thus 'twice-born,' entitled to wear the sacred thread Gangi refers to contemptuously.

'Thakur' is also used to refer to the supreme deity. Whether Premchand meant it ironically is not certain, but the idea is reinforced by the irony of the protagonist's name, Gangi, with its inevitable suggestion of Ganga, the Ganges, whose water is the holiest in the world.

This is a late story (1932) and a fine example of Premchand's later simplicity and his rejection of the editorial comment that sometimes mars earlier stories.

## 10 A Desperate Case

Original title: *Nairashya, 'Despair'* or *'Disappointment'*. First published 1924.

## 11 A Day in the Life of a Debt-Collector

Original title: *Tagada, 'Dunning'*. A story from the early thirties.

## 12 A Car-Splashing

Original title: *Motor Ke Chinte, 'Splashing from a Car'*. A late story. Though Indian commentators have paid little attention to this story, it is interesting for a number of reasons: the title is not an abstraction (such are comparatively rare), the villain is allowed to talk for himself — unlike the other heavy-eating pandits of the stories — and it pictures sudden, irrational violence erupting, in this case provoked by hostility to the westernized rich.

## 13 From Both Sides

Original title: *Donon Taraf Se*. First published in 1911 in Urdu, this story was not reprinted until 1983 in Sripat Rai's collection *Solah Aprapya Kahaniyan* in the original Urdu but in Devanagari script. Premchand apparently never prepared a Hindi version.

## 14 A Moral Victory

Original title: *Satyagrah*, the Gandhian term for an act of civil disobedience. First published in 1923.

This is one of the more elaborate episodes in the cycle of Moteram Shastri stories. Premchand obviously enjoyed the fat rogue's shrewdness, cheek, garbled eloquence and unabashed wickedness, and most of the stories about him share a vitality of narration that is not matched by structure and direction.

### 15 Man's Highest Duty

Original title: *Manusya Ka Param Dharm*, *'Man's Supreme Religious Obligation'*. First published in 1920.

### 16 A Lesson in The Holy Life

Original title: *Guru-Mantra*, *The Precepts of the Teacher'*. Written in the twenties. In this sketch, which is a part of the satirical saga of Moteram Shastri, the slogans are half nonsensical and the concluding hymn highly ironical. The hashish is *ganja* commonly smoked by *sadhus*, particularly in Banaras.

### 17 A Little Trick

Original title: *Chakma*, *'A Trick'*. First published in 1922. This is one of about a dozen stories by Premchand that dealt with the boycott of British cloth as a part of the Congress drive for independence.

### 18 Penalty

Original title: *Jurmana*, *'Penalty'*. A late story. The story hinges on a point that may be obscure — the fact that the Inspector is persecuting Alarakkhi because she has rejected his advances. The Inspector's return to decency is a favourite theme of Premchand's and, in view of what we know of the character, not so surprising as it may at first appear. His one conversation with Alarakkhi is a kind of precis of the dialectics of poverty, developed in similar though much longer dialogues in the novels and other stories. Premchand's affinity with the Russian novelists is clear here in the affecting way he brings out the simplicity and humility of the poor.

### 19 The Writer

Original Title: *Lekhak*, *'The Writer'*. First published in 1931. Though the story is uneven it provides an interesting satirical glimpse of provincial urban society (probably Allahabad, because of the mention of the High Court) where Premchand spent much of his professional life, and sharply defines, with some hyperbole, the author's quarrel with the philistines who dominated that society. Typical of many stories is his pairing of the avaricious Muslim merchant with an equally avaricious Hindu shopkeeper, with which he no doubt intended to emphasize his anti-communalism.

### 20 A Coward

Original title: *Kayar*, *'Coward'* or *'Cowards'* — ironic and ambiguous in either case. First published in 1933.

## 21 A Servant of the Nation

Original title: 'Rastra Ka Sevak'.

## 22 The Chess Players

Original title: *Satranj Ke Khilari*, The Chess Players. Perhaps Premchand's best-known story, though not his best; like *Sadgati* (Deliverance), it has been made into a film by Satyajit Ray. As with a great many of Premchand's stories, there are versions in both Hindi and Urdu. The Chess Players was first published in 1924, in Hindi; the Urdu version, *Satranj Ki Bazi* (The Chess Game) appeared some time before 1928. Earlier publication does not always establish the priority of a version, though in this case, in view of the priority in publication, the Hindi may be the original one. In the preparation of the alternate version of his stories Premchand sometimes employed collaborators, so the question of the author's language is thorny and requires detailed investigation. The Hindi *Satranj Ke Khilari* is spare and abstract in its delineation of Lucknow society, while the Urdu *Satranj Ki Bazi* is more detailed and moralized explicitly at the conclusion. In making this translation I have followed the Hindi version throughout.

## 23 The Road to Hell

Original title: 'Narak Ka Marg, 'The Path of Hell'. First published in 1925.

## 24 Miss Padma

Original title: *Miss Padma.* Amrit Rai, Premchand's son, does not include this in his list of his father's short stories; it appears to be a late work, probably from the early thirties.

## 25 My Big Brother

Original title: *Bare Bhai Sahab.* First published 1934.

## 26 Intoxication

Original title: *Nasa, 'Intoxication'.* First published in 1934.

## 27 The Price of Milk

Original title: *Dudh Ka Dam, 'The Price of Milk'.* A late story, first published in 1934. This is representative of Premchand's best work, objective, compassionate and free of editorializing, the scene of Mangal's departure from his home under the *neem* tree is one of the finest in all Premchand.. Lest it be considered in the least sentimental, it should be pointed out that, sentimentality being an expression of emotion in excess of what is warranted by the situation, the emotion of the story is, on the contrary, beautifully banked. Nowhere else has Premchand so well dramatized the plight of the sweeper (i.e. untouchable). In his biographical study of his father Amrit Rai justly observes that in these late stories the anger of the earlier works has given way to anguish. It seems scarcely possible to do justice to Premchand's style in translation, for obviously no exact equivalent can be found for Bhungi's earthy conversation, Moteram's inflated rhetoric (complicated humorously by provincial pronunciation) or the idiomatic ellipses of Mangal's speech. In this dark story the ironic significance of Mangal's name — auspicious, fortunate — should be kept in mind.

## 28  The Shroud

Original title: *Kafan, 'The Shroud'.* First published in 1936.

## 29  Deliverance

Original title: *Sadgati 'Deliverance'*, implying a death in a state of bliss or grace. First published 1931.

Dukhi is a *Chamar*, an untouchable who works with skins and hides and hence particularly objectionable to a Brahman 'Dukhi' means sorrowful — such names are common in villages and are usually bestowed to discourage or avert the envy of the gods; in this case, of course, it is ironic. The *Gonds* are a community of low standing but considerably above the *Chamars.* Cf. 'A Catastrophe.'

## 30  Two Autobiographical Sketches

Original title: *Jivan-Sar, 'The Substance of Life'.* In the original there is a third sketch which deals mainly with Premchand's deteriorating health. His father's 'stumbling' and 'fall,' refer apparently to the father's second marriage late in life and his early marrying of his son.

In the second sketch, the sentence Premchand would most probably have received if his case had been brought into court, was banishment to Burma. The final line is ambiguous: Indian interpreters feel that Premchand is being ironic, and irony is certainly there, but for all that he represented British oppression the Collector's sense of fairness doubtless was respected by Premchand, who makes a point of similar anomalies elsewhere in his work.